OTHER SIDES

Also by Simon Strantzas

Collections:
Beneath the Surface
Cold to the Touch
Nightingale Songs
Burnt Black Suns
Nothing is Everything
Only the Living Are Lost

Chapbooks:
These Last Embers
Black Bequeathments

As Editor:
Shadows Edge
Aickman's Heirs
Year's Best Weird Fiction, Volume 3 (with Michael Kelly)

ONLY THE LIVING ARE LOST

"Strantzas has always been a leading author in the field of weird fiction and Aickmanesque strange stories, but he just keeps getting better and better."

NICHOLAS KAUFMANN, author of *The Hungry Earth* and *Die and Stay Dead*

"After this, fans and followers will be waiting with bated breath and more than a few shivers for the next exciting installments."

THE HORROR TREE

OTHER SIDES

SIMON STRANTZAS

LETHE PRESS

Published in 2025 by Lethe Press
www.lethepressbooks.com • lethepress@aol.com

Cover design and layout by JeremyJohnParker.com

ISBN: 978-1-59021-565-4

TABLE OF CONTENTS

I

II

III

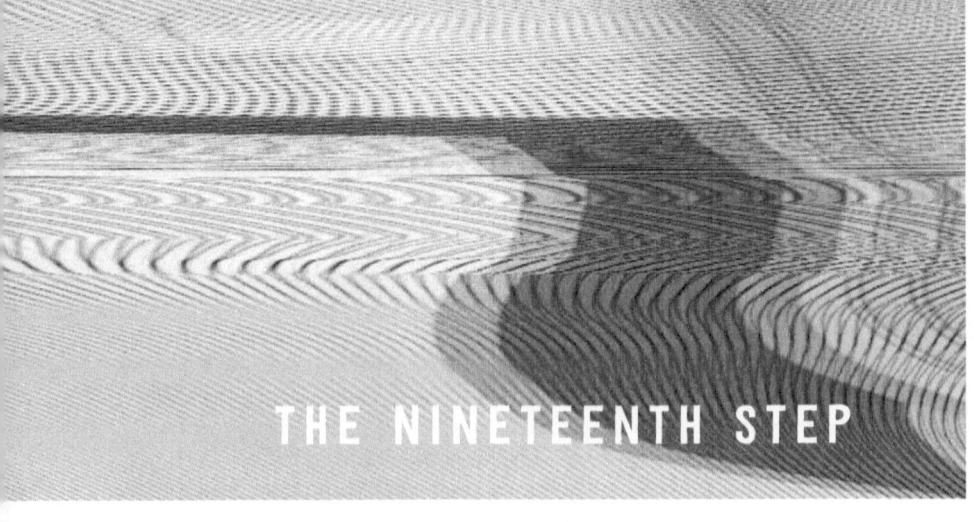

THE NINETEENTH STEP

Broken shutters, boarded-over windows, a tree bent crooked and grey, leafless; the house was pressed between two other houses on the dismal November street. Mallory and Alex had already seen countless variations, each more unsuitable than the one before. This house appeared no better. But Mallory would go inside. Mallory *always* went inside whether her gut told her to or not. She held out hope that, for once, she would be surprised.

And she *was* surprised. Surprised by the mess. Creaking floors covered in rancid stained carpeting, held down in places with nothing more than household staples. The walls in the rooms all were slate grey, the paint thick and filled with brushstrokes. Whatever it was meant to cover was going to stay hidden. The only pleasant surprise was the staircase to the second level. The surprise was that it was in one piece.

"It's a fixer-upper, for sure," the agent said, "which is why I brought you here. Alex is handy, and if you look past everything, you can see the house is in good shape. A bit of elbow grease and this place will double in value. See these floors? Underneath them, cherry hardwood." She stomped, then reached down and, with the tips of her manicured fingers, pulled back a corner of the grey wall-to-wall. The wood beneath was mottled but solid. "When they built these houses in the fifties, they installed hardwood floors by default. They just assumed people would cover them with carpet. Bare floors were for the poor. This carpet looks original to the house, which means the floor has probably been protected since day one. Hire a team to do the sanding and varnishing, and you'll have the sort of floor everyone pays through the nose to have nowadays. I'm telling you," she said, looking smugly at her surroundings, "if you're looking to flip a house, this is the one. A little work will get a big return. Get us *all* a big return, I mean." She winked, and Alex nodded. Mallory, as usual, acquiesced.

Flipping houses was the perfect solution for her and Alex's future. Mallory had been saving every penny she'd made for years, and Alex had spent a lifetime at his carpenter father's side, installing everything from shelves to roofs. They had no children, had jobs without set hours, and were still young enough that they could do without much sleep. They both knew it wouldn't last forever, but only Alex was keen to buy right away.

"It's simple: we stop throwing money away on renting an apartment and buy a rundown house; we then live in the house while fixing it up; when it's fixed, we sell the house for a tidy profit." He did the math for her: if they worked hard for five years flipping houses, by the time the two were thirty, they would have a big enough nest egg that they would never have to worry about their future again. This is what finally sold Mallory on the idea.

Alex noticed the problem with the staircase first, despite the number of times Mallory had travelled up and down it during the initial renovation, then during the final move, then during the rearranging and reorganizing. But why would it occur to her that anything might be wrong? She wasn't a carpenter, after all. She didn't know how these things were done. So when Alex said, in passing over the knock of his hammer against drywall nails, "Have you noticed the stairs?" she didn't know what to make of the question.

"What do you mean?"

"I mean, there isn't the right number of them. They're uneven."

"I have no idea what you're talking about."

"It's not up to Code. There should be an even number of stairs. But there's not. There are too many. Or not enough."

She must have betrayed her lack of comprehension because he spoke slower, in that way she hated.

"These risers are seven inches tall, with a one-inch tread. I've double-checked. This floor has ten-foot ceilings. Assuming two feet between floors, there should be exactly eighteen steps from this floor to the next. But there aren't."

"Is it really that big of a deal?"

"I don't know," he shrugged. "Probably not."

And they went on to talk about other things.

But Mallory didn't forget, and when breakfast was done and Alex was in the office, installing new shelving, Mallory paused at the foot of the stairs to the second floor and counted. There were eighteen, just as Alex had said there should be. So she counted them again to be sure. Even if she included the floors themselves and not the steps between, the number was even. She shook her head. What was Alex thinking? She put down the basket she'd been carrying and walked through the kitchen toward the office. There was quiet muttering, as though Alex were speaking to someone, but when she entered the room, he was alone, tape measure against the wall. "Were you just on your cell phone?" He looked at her as though she were an alien. "No," he said, the word drawn out until it lingered between them. "Why?"

"Nevermind. Listen, I counted the stairs. There are eighteen of them."

"That's impossible."

"It's true. Come see for yourself."

He put down the tape measure and hurried out of the office, the shelves behind him instantly forgotten under the possibility of being proved wrong.

"See?" she said, narrow finger pointed as they stood before the staircase. "Eighteen."

She watched his head bob as he counted, then a perplexed look crept across his narrow face before his head bobbed once again. Without a word, he began to climb the stairs. Mallory watched him, amused at his need to prove himself, as though neither she nor his own eyes could be trusted. He'd always been that way since the day they met. Sometimes, his inability to believe anyone else was infuriating, but often she simply found it charming.

"A-ha!" he said as he reached the top of the stairs. "I was right. Nineteen!"

"What?"

"Watch!" he said and proceeded to descend quickly toward her. He led with his right foot, and counted the stairs off, one at a time. When he reached the last step, he landed on his right again, exclaiming, "Nineteen!"

Her mind boggled. She pointed at the steps one at a time and counted. Then counted again. No matter how she tried, there were only eighteen.

"I need to sit down."

Alex strutted back to the office, his reputation intact, while Mallory remained behind, seated on the living room sectional, her head a-buzz. It had to be a trick, she reasoned. Like an optical illusion, what she saw with her own eyes could not be trusted. There was something more to the stairwell, something she could not articulate. There wasn't any word for it, but it stayed with her the rest of the day and kept her awake at night while Alex snored blissfully beside her. She flipped the covers back with irritation and put her feet in her slippers.

The staircase lay in half-darkness, shadowed by the odd arrangement of lights on the wall. In her tired state, she thought she saw the steps move ever so slightly, as though they had settled into place only as she'd turned the corner. She shuffled to the top of the staircase and looked down. The light stretched far enough to reveal the entirety of the staircase, and Mallory counted the steps again. There were eighteen. This did not make her feel any better. Alex's gentle snoring emanated from the bedroom down the hall. Mallory smiled. Then she turned back to the staircase and took her first step down.

She counted them off in her head as she descended, holding the bannister tight and watching her feet. Sixteen, seventeen, eighteen, nineteen—her foot landed safely on the first floor, and her concern carried with it. She looked back at the top of the stairs, dim light wavering as though about to flicker out. She shivered, her teeth chattering, and walked back up the stairs. When she reached the eighteenth, there was still one step between her and the second-floor landing.

It made no sense. None at all. Something was wrong with the reality of the house, some bend in what she had until then believed was solid, and if something as simple as the number of stairs was wrong, then who knew what else could be? She went to take the final step, then stopped. Did the light grow dimmer, or was the staircase fading from reality, leaving her and Alex stranded on the second floor? Worry overcame her. What if she could no longer bring herself to put a foot down on the final stair in case there was nothing to bear her weight? What if she fell and fell and fell into a never-ending nothingness?

She carefully raised her foot and stepped over the nineteenth stair, stretching to reach the second-floor landing. As soon as she pulled herself to it, she dashed for the bedroom without turning around and leaped into the bed. She pressed her body as tight as she dared against Alex, blissfully ignorant and snoring, in hopes it would calm her uncontrollable shivering. As she tried to fall asleep, she wondered if it wasn't the fear of falling into nothing that terrified her most, but instead, her desire to blindly leap.

In the wash of daybreak, Mallory was humiliated, and thankful there had been no one else present during the night to witness her foolishness. Lying in the soft sunlight, it all seemed so bizarre to her, and she was absolutely certain it had simply been a dream born of exhaustion. Of all things to be afraid of, after all: a stairwell? It was absurd. She was quite glad the day had returned, the morning sun clearing away the cobwebs of midnight hysteria. Alex remained sleeping beside her, and she rolled over onto her bent arm and watched his soft lips gently putter for a while.

Despite her waking confidence, she did her best to avoid the staircase afterward. Once descended, she refused to look back, to even acknowledge there were stairs present. Instead, she found work for herself amid splintering baseboards and chipped plaster. Resuming the renovations helped fade any lingering phantoms from the previous night—though, much to Mallory's chagrin, they did not dissipate completely. It only took Alex uttering a single phrase for the amorphous fear to rebloom.

"Hey, come look at this."

She wasn't sure she could move.

"What is it?"

Alex said nothing. Mallory shivered. She hoped he was in the room beyond the staircase, hoped he was any place other than on those wooden steps she'd taken such pains to avoid. But she knew hoping was no use. That would be exactly where he was.

"Are you there?" she said as she walked through the kitchen toward him, each step becoming progressively more difficult. She could not take her eyes from the other entrance, the corner around which she knew if she turned, she would be face-to-face with her nightmare. She could feel her legs stiffening, each stride shortening, until she barely moved. And then her legs decided to stop working completely, and she heard only her blood racing in her ears.

Alex materialized before her.

"You won't believe this. It's going to blow your mind!" He grabbed her wrist too tightly and dragged her around that corner she had no desire to breach.

Mallory did her best to avoid looking at the stairs, but Alex danced on them, calling for her attention, and she knew he would not relent. He wanted an audience.

"I need you to tell me what happens."

"What do you mean?"

"Watch!"

Alex went back to the bottom of the stairs and started walking up them again, but slower. With each step, he called out its number.

"One! Two! Three! Four! Five! Six!"

Mallory felt dread race down her spine. The narrow hallway, the wooden staircase, they began to take on a different aspect, shifting into a sort of hyper-reality. Like a nightmare. Each edge became crisper, every colour stronger—almost too crisp, almost too strong—and Mallory felt the oppressing weight of her terror mounting.

"Seven! Eight! Nine! Ten! Eleven! Twelve!"

"Alex, come back."

She did not want him to continue, did not want to even be in the same house as that horrible staircase. Why couldn't they leave, both of them, into the night? Simply drive away as far as possible? They could come back later for their things. Or maybe they could just flatten the house and burn it to ashes. Anything but stay as they were, her watching helplessly as he climbed the stairs to the unknown.

"Thirteen! Fourteen! Fifteen!"

"Whatever it is, Alex, I don't care. Just come down." A sickening fear gnawed at her; a terrified scream raging to be born.

"Sixteen! Seventeen!"

"Alex, don't." Her throat was drier than it had ever been.

"Eighteen!"

"Alex, please come back!" she said, tears blurring her vision.

But Alex did not come back. Did not answer. Made no sound at all. Mallory wiped her eyes profusely, certain he would no longer be on the staircase when she could finally see again. But Alex was there, standing on the final step quietly, not moving, his back to her.

"Alex?" she said, her relief suddenly turning cold. "Alex? Are you okay?"

He remained perfectly still.

There were no thoughts in Mallory's shaking head. The walls pulsed, throbbed like a beating heart. Mallory could not move, could not turn her head away. She could only stare at Alex, terrified he would never turn around. Terrified of what would happen if he did. Mallory stared and stared until—

"Nineteen."

Mallory couldn't speak. Alex slowly turned. His face was grey as ash, wrinkled as it had never been before. And his eyes, staring off into the distance, his eyes....

"Mallory, I—"

"What's wrong?"

"I—I can see...."

He paused one final time, and Mallory felt on the verge of losing everything.

"What is it, Alex? What do you see?"

And this is what he told her....

WITCH'S CLUTCH

Rusty Cleft had to be seeing things. Until that moment, he'd almost convinced himself the Witch's Clutch wasn't real, and yet there one was, planted in the background of a newspaper advertisement for a small hotel pub, invisible to anyone who didn't know what they were looking at.

But Cleft knew exactly what it was. And what it meant.

The hotel was in Caledon. It would take less than three hours to get there. All he needed was a ride. By the time Siobhan returned his call, he had his meagre duffel packed. She resisted at first, citing her existing weekend plans, but being a graduate student meant she'd have to make sacrifices, and Cleft wasn't above reminding her of them if it led to a real Witch's Clutch.

Once Siobhan arrived, Cleft folded himself into her tiny Kia. Even with the seat pushed back, his knees brushed uncomfortably against the dashboard. She fumed for the entirety of the trip, not speaking at all, but Cleft hardly noticed. Everything was secondary to his discovery. It would change both his reputation and career. No longer would he be called a copper-curled stick insect by his undergraduates. No longer would he be dismissed for the awkward way he dressed or mocked by his peers for his views. The Witch's Clutch would rewrite everything, prove he had something to offer.

The town of Caledon was smaller than he expected, tucked within tall woods and autumnal colours. There seemed to be only one road leading in, as though there were nothing more to see beyond its furthest border. Cleft watched the worn-down houses pass by his window with increasing excitement.

By the time they arrived at the hotel pub, The Bull & Goose, Cleft could hardly keep still. The hybrid was so close, as was his imminent success. He imagined himself being honoured before a room full of his peers, his pockmarked face beaming down at them with satisfaction. Their applause was still ringing in his ears when he stepped out of the car, barely giving Siobhan time enough to put it into park.

"Are you excited?" he asked, looking up at the unpainted and splintered sign hanging above the pub's door. When he glanced over, though, he found her silently thumbing through her phone. He wasn't surprised: being silent was something Siobhan was good at. She still hadn't told him she had requested a new advisor, nor that her request was already granted. In only a couple of weeks, she'd be gone. He wondered if it ever occurred to her that he might discover her betrayal before she left. He also wondered if she even cared.

The photograph from the newspaper clearly showed the pub's exterior, so it didn't take long for Cleft to estimate the spot from which it was taken. Siobhan followed close behind him, eyes still on her phone, as he searched the area for the Witch's Clutch. She didn't look up until she collided with him, not expecting such a sudden stop.

"I don't understand," he muttered.

There, in the fresh loose dirt at his feet, was a shallow hole. Whatever had been there had been removed.

Siobhan readjusted the sunglasses seated atop her head.

"You seriously telling me we drove here for nothing?"

Cleft had to force himself to speak.

"It was here. Someone took it." He pointed at the footprint pressed into the damp soil. Large enough for an adult woman or small man. "They must have known what it was."

"How? I don't even know what it is."

"The Miq'maq called it a *ste'gmiui ge'luswa'latl*, or *spirits' embrace*. The plant—well, hybrid, really—has a lot of myth and folklore surrounding it. But no one has actually found one."

"And you think some other sociologist just happened to stumble over it before you? Isn't that a little too convenient?"

Cleft looked down at the hole again. She was right. What were the odds? Unless....

"What if it wasn't a researcher?" he said, tamping down his renewing excitement. "We know the Witch's Clutch has connections in the

New World. What if we've stumbled upon some vestigial pagan religion? What if one of these cults knew exactly what it was when they saw it?"

Cleft's mind started spinning. It seemed impossible, yet was there a more probable explanation?

"Why don't you go check us in at the hotel," he said. "I'm going to look around some more."

"I thought you needed me here. Isn't that why you had me drive?"

"I won't be long," he said. "I'll call when I need you to come get me."

She studied him for a moment, and Cleft half-wondered if she was about to insist on staying. Instead, she snorted.

"I guess I'll keep my phone on."

"Thanks," he said under his breath as she retreated through the underbrush. The faint rustle of plants and branches followed her. By the time they finished their song, Siobhan had loaded both her and Cleft's bags onto her shoulder.

Cleft adjusted his glasses—the yellow lenses the colour of his skin—and watched until she was safely inside the hotel, then turned his attention back to the underbrush where the Witch's Clutch had once been. He searched for any sign of ritualistic activity from those who might have found it first. A tree with rope burns, perhaps, or a cluster of stones laid with intent and purpose. What he discovered, though, were only more footprints. They proved him right, though—a cell of worshippers had to be nearby. And he had to find them. In his Moleskin, he noted the various prints, their different sizes and shapes, as well as the prints of the herd animals that were intermingled with them. These looked to be made by sheep. Possibly a large goat. The meandering tracks led deeper into the thick underbrush beneath the overgrown maples, ashes, and pines. He hurriedly followed them, his head stuffed with more fantasies of his academic coming out.

Cleft walked for hours, his attention so focused on the footprints ahead of him that he failed to notice how dim the daylight had grown. Only when he looked up did he realise he had no idea where he was or how to get back. There had been no roads, no telephone wires. Not much of anything to suggest a location from which Siobhan might pick him up. No, that wasn't true. There was, amongst the thickest boughs and trunks, the flicker of artificial light off in the near distance. It was a beacon hidden by leaves. Perhaps if he followed it, he'd find his way back to the Bull & Goose.

But that would also mean giving up his pursuit of whomever had taken the Witch's Clutch. If he abandoned the trail, he might never be able to pick it up again. He might lose the hybrid for good. Cleft stood in deep green underbrush and stared at the light glowing brighter in the distance, and wavered.

Then he remembered that welcoming applause.

§

When Cleft finally travelled far enough to see where the tracks ended, he was surprised. There was a small rundown house ahead of him, squeezed between a pair of ancient birch trees. Its peeling white exterior gave the impression it was abandoned—none of the wooden slats of its siding ran parallel to the ground. The trees that flanked it only worsened the house's appearance, buckling its walls as though the trunks had tried and failed to crush the place but were gathering strength to try again. Yet the moment the breeze quieted, he heard soft giggling from the rear of the dwelling. Cleft's heart skipped.

He had done it. He had found them.

It was all he could do to keep from running. Cleft followed the tracks past the trees and along the side of the house. He dragged his fingers along the wood siding in hopes it would slow him down. He wanted to savour the upcoming moment—his discovery of a heretofore unknown religious sect.

What he found instead was far more mundane and confusing.

The yard was made of hard dirt that supported only patches of grass and clover. Along its edges stood a row of trees in a circle, thick woods that had been carved out for the homestead. At the foot of these trees were various-sized pens, some holding livestock, others empty. In the middle of the yard sat an older woman on a tree stump. She was near his age, her grey hair streaked with fading chestnut and tied in a loose bun atop her head. In her lap, she held a young girl less than ten years old, who waved a small stick in the air as though it were a wand. The child wore a white dress and tights that made her look like a porcelain statuette. In front of them, a woman in her late twenties sat cross-legged, with denim shorts cut high enough to expose her thick, pocked legs. The three smiled and laughed with one another. Cleft immediately felt the embarrassing heat of intrusion. He tried to back away.

But it was too late. The child spotted him.

And she screamed.

"I'm sorry!" he offered in a rush, frantically waving his hands. The younger woman leaped up and snatched the child to her bosom as though to shield her. The older woman's eyes were similarly alight as she bolted to her feet, brandishing a pair of shears that had appeared in her hand.

"Who are you?" the older woman demanded. It took a moment for Cleft to remember that answer.

"I'm from Marsden College," he stammered. "I was doing some research and... and... I thought you might be..." He realised what he was about to accuse this family of. Instead, he fumbled his Moleskin from his pocket and unfolded the newspaper clipping he kept between its pages. "Have any of you seen this plant before? I'm trying to find the people who dug it up. I followed their tracks here."

The older woman glanced at the photo.

"No," she said.

Some of his hope slipped away. He folded the clipping and returned it to his notebook.

"Is there maybe anyone else who could have taken it? Anyone else who lives in the area?"

She shook her head. More of his hope fled. He couldn't accept what was happening. His plea, almost in defiance, to no one in particular: "But I saw a light in the woods. Just a little ways back...."

The old woman's face changed. Softened.

"Forgive us; we weren't expecting anyone today," she said, lowering her shears. "There have been others. In the woods, I mean. We sometimes see them. I think they have a farm nearby."

Cleft flipped through the pages of his Moleskin, his other hand digging out the small pencil from his jacket's front pocket. "Can you tell me where to find them?"

"We've only seen them at a distance," she said. Then, to the younger woman: "Have you spoken to them?"

"I don't speak to people I don't know," she said. Then looked at Cleft.

The older woman smiled.

"Sorry we can't be more help."

And that was it. A dead end. Crushing disappointment. Cleft lowered the Moleskin. He'd followed the wrong tracks and had lost his chance—at recovering the Witch's Clutch; at finding those who had it. Around him grew longer shadows, the sun fell closer to the horizon. The trees, the bushes, the footprints began their fade into the encroaching dark. There was nothing left to do but go back.

"Are you okay?" The woman touched his arm.

"I'm fine," he muttered.

He had to call Siobhan. Let her know where to find him. She'd be angry he stole her weekend, but he didn't care—she'd be gone soon anyway. Off to a mentor who could do more for her. He probably would have done the same in her place. But when he took his phone from his pocket to dial her number, he discovered it had no signal. He resisted the sudden urge to hurl it into the woods.

Instead, he sighed. Collected himself. Then slid the phone back into his pocket.

"May I borrow your telephone?" he asked, adjusting his glasses. "It's getting darker, and my assistant needs directions to pick me up."

"Sorry. We don't have one," the older woman said.

"But what if there's an emergency?"

Both her and the younger's brows furrowed as though confused. The animals in the surrounding pens huffed and snorted. It would be dusk soon. How was he going to get back to the Bull & Goose?

The child seemed to read his mind. She appeared beside the older woman, tugging her sleeve.

"Is he coming inside?" she asked. Her smile was wide and toothy.

Cleft blanched. That was not what he wanted. But it was true he had no way of getting back.

The women must have realised the same. Why else did they seem so uncomfortable? He wanted to say something but was conflicted.

The old woman spared him the suffering.

"Of course he is," she replied, her eyes fixed on his. "We wouldn't want him to get lost again."

The inside of the house was as cramped as Siobhan's Kia. He had to duck when passing through the door frame and continued ducking as the top of his head narrowly brushed each joist in succession. The odour that greeted him was as vague as it was sweet and comforting. Like linseed and lemon. Like leather and a burning pine log. For a moment he forgot his disappointment and closed his eyes, inhaled deeply.

"I appreciate the help," he said as the old woman directed him to a beaded couch. He sank into it immediately upon sitting, the fabric scratchy as hay. The younger woman sat across from him on a small loveseat, hoisting the child into her lap. An awkward silence followed.

"My name's Rusty Cleft," he eventually said.

"Is that so?"

He shifted awkwardly. The beads pushed into his spine.

"My name is Atrai," the older woman said. "And this is Lasha. The young one is—"

"I'm Cleo!" the girl shouted.

"You certainly are," he smiled.

Cleft surveyed the house. He noted the wrinkled curtains, the slanted windowsills. Everything appeared askew; it made him uneasy. "So," he said, "you three live here? In the middle of nowhere?"

"It's not nowhere," Cleo giggled. "And not just us."

"No?"

She rolled her eyes like marbles.

"Daddy lives here, too."

"He's travelling," Atrai informed him. Then, to Cleo: "But he'll be home soon, won't he?" The child nodded excitedly. "When he does, I wonder if you'll even recognise him. It's been so long."

"I will! I will recognise him!"

Atrai smiled. Then to Cleft once again: "He's been gone a long time. And she's still so young."

"I understand."

"I thought you might."

"Or maybe he's never coming home," Lasha said before Atrai could hush her. "Maybe he doesn't want to."

Cleft felt the temperature drop. He shifted again in his seat.

"Maybe I should leave."

Atrai shook her head, brushed away his concerns.

"Oh, it's much too late," she said.

And she was right. He bent to look through a small, dirty window at the starless night. Siobhan would never find him, even if he were to call. He wondered if she was concerned. He suspected his absence had escaped her notice.

"You must be hungry. We'll make you something," Atrai said.

"I couldn't ask you to do that."

"Nonsense. It will make you feel better."

Atrai stood. Lasha and Cleo followed. As she turned toward the kitchen, Cleo dashed to Cleft and handed him her stick. She smiled, then scrambled after Atrai. Only Lasha remained. She hesitated as though about to say something, then silently followed, leaving Cleft alone.

Immediately, his thoughts spiralled toward the Witch's Clutch and those who took it. They were out there, somewhere in the dark, while he sat with these three strange women. He tried calling Siobhan again, but the calls would not go through. Everything was collapsing around him. Marsden College and his future never felt so far away. Nor as unreachable.

A rich and meaty smell distracted him; caused such stomach growling he worried the women had overheard it. He stared at the kitchen door, listening for their voices.

Without warning, the door swung open, startling him. Atrai emerged, large black stone bowl precariously balanced. Its contents steamed, the vapour twisting around her head, and close behind her were the younger Lasha and the child. One carried a thick loaf of bread, the other a set of mismatched utensils.

"Any luck getting a hold of your friend?" Atrai asked, beckoning him to a table and setting down the stone bowl in front of him. Cleft watched the oil congeal on the surface of the broth in rings around the floating vegetables.

"Not yet," he said, his head swimming from hunger.

"Let's hope she calls soon. The air feels ripe for a storm."

"It always storms when Father's coming back," the child said before Lasha yanked her arm to quiet her. Young Cleo yelped. Cleft did not like the sound.

"Please—" he started to say before being hushed.

"Your broth is getting cold," Lasha said, dropping half a bread loaf to the side of the bowl. "Eat while there's still time."

Cleft looked at Cleo, who was frowning and rubbing her arm, then at Atrai, smiling and unalarmed. Cleft felt he should say something but was distracted by the meal they'd prepared. He wiped his mouth. Then did so again before tearing a piece of bread and dipping it into the broth. As soon as he tasted the morsel, his hands moved spoonfuls over his tongue as fast as he could swallow them. The meal was salted and warm and expanded in his stomach, soaking up his discomfort and worries. Numbing and soporific satiety flowed through his body, and he was powerless to prevent himself from putting the bowl to his mouth and slurping down the dregs. His only regret was there wasn't more to savour.

Across from him, the three women watched.

He leaned back in his chair. Exhaled a greasy heat. Atrai carefully collected the empty bowl and handed it to Lasha. The younger woman took it wordlessly and carried it into the kitchen. Cleo, on the couch, swung her small white legs slowly. Hypnotically. Everything felt strange, as though time were being drawn out. But it was a good feeling and one he did not wish to disrupt. Instead, he allowed himself to sink further into his chair. Sink until its arms reached out and embraced him.

Cleft blinked, and suddenly, Lasha was back, seated beside Cleo. When had she returned? She placed her hand on the girl's legs before speaking. Those legs stopped swinging.

"Why did you come?" she asked. All three women appeared at once larger and less substantial. Light flickered like fire across their faces.

"Information," he mumbled. "Research."

"Research?"

He murmured, then leaned to the side and struggled to pull the Moleskin from his pocket. It was more slippery than expected. Perhaps his fingers had grown too large.

"Have you seen this?" he asked as he fumbled through the pages. When he found the clipping of the Witch's Clutch, he showed it to them.

"You've asked us this before."

"I have? Did I tell you what it was?" The women glanced at one another. Cleft couldn't recall if he even knew. The words eventually came to him as though rising through molasses.

"It's an... an anomaly. Plants—nightshade, mandrake, and jimsonweed—entangled, fused with one another in... I guess in a ring. The Witch's Clutch appears in so many cultures, going far back. Far, far back." There was something else he wanted to say about it, but the thought slipped free. He knew it was close, but he couldn't find it. "The name's kind of a botanical joke: the three weeds happen to also have wiccan importance. You know, like witches and warlocks. And the circle..." Cleft wondered why it was suddenly so dark, then realised his eyes were closed. He opened them and discovered he had been somehow transported to the beaded couch. The three faces hovered over him as their hands gently laid him down.

He had more to say but couldn't. His mouth was dry. Gummy. Not that he minded. He didn't mind much of anything. Those faces floating above him slipped in and out of his vision, confusing themselves with one another, blending and shifting and overlapping.

The women muttered in a slow monotone, and their words twisted in wrong directions. He felt the pressure build in his head. Cleft squeezed his eyes shut and opened them to find the child sitting astride him, kneading and stretching his face. Her head turned as she spoke to the others. Yet they didn't look how he remembered. Their faces were plastic as he weightlessly lifted into the air. The walls trembled and hummed, lulling him. It took effort, but he smiled at the child, then closed his eyes a moment to rest. He opened them later, well after dark.

And in the midst of a violent storm.

Rain pelted the sides of the small house with fury; bright flashes illuminated the sky. Cleft's heart pounded as he leapt from the couch, disoriented. Everything looked twisted in the dark. And worse than that, whenever lightning struck.

But that wasn't what woke him. Something thrashed in his chest—not looking for escape, but instead to grab hold of everything and pull it in. A sucking insatiable need. He clutched himself tighter, but it did no good. The hunger could not be quelled.

The sound of pounding continued. He realised it hadn't been his heart. It was the door. The door that led into the house. It was too small to fit through, and yet it sounded tremendous. Was there someone there?

Cleft heard voices behind him. Around him. He glanced back but saw no one. He stood alone, facing the door as it throbbed with pressure. Hinges creaked and buckled. The pounding intensified as though a pair of giant fists were splintering the wooden frame. The storm hurled itself against the entrance, demanding to be let in. And the need inside of Cleft welcomed it, told him to open the door. It begged and it pleaded. Cleft took an unsure step forward.

And then the frame exploded. The door swung so hard on its hinges, Cleft felt the crack. But all he knew was someone was standing in the doorway.

Or, rather, someone wasn't.

Because there was no one. No matter how it felt, no matter what he imagined in the corner of his eye, there was no one. Just a deluge of rain and howling wind. There was no one stepping into the house as furniture blew aside. There was no one growing larger as the sky flashed bright then black. There was no one reaching out for him as the storm threw Cleft back over his heels and drove him into the ground.

There was no one towering over him as everything went dark.

No. Worse than dark.

Went to nothing.

§

Nothing but the floral smell of tea brewing. Cleft's eyes opened and saw daylight across the low ceiling. Sitting up made his head swim, and standing took a great effort, but he eventually found his balance. He wiped his face and brushed off the leaves and dust that had collected on him at some point while he slept. All that remained of the night before was a carousel of images that didn't make sense. He sat again on the couch and held his head in his hands. What made him agree to stay in such a strange house?

Cleft lowered his hands.

He had to get out.

Siobhan was not going to rescue him. She was at the Bull & Goose somewhere outside the woods, no doubt still asleep. Even if she weren't, he couldn't get hold of her—his cellular phone had turned black overnight and stayed that way. He felt anxious, abandoned, but pushed the feelings aside.

He heard a chair move behind the kitchen door. Before he knew why, he was stumbling toward the sound.

The three women—the older, the younger, and the child—sat among the clutter, holding one another's hands at a small table, eyes closed. Cleft's entrance awakened them, however, and their stares turned toward him. Only Cleo had an expression he could read. It was of disappointment.

"Did we wake you?" Atrai asked, releasing the hands of the other two as she stood. Lasha put hers in her lap. Cleo, on the edge of the chair, spoke into her chest.

"I thought he was Daddy," she said.

Atrai hushed her. "He'll be here soon."

In the daylight, things felt even stranger. Something was off, but Cleft could not explain what or why. Only that nothing felt as it should. Nothing looked as it should, either.

"Are you okay?" Atrai asked him.

"Of course," he said. "I'm just surprised I didn't hear you cleaning up."

Their look, queer. Unsettled. Lasha's eyes narrowed.

"What do you mean?"

"The storm last night. I opened the door. The wind, it... it turned everything over. But I don't see any sign of it now."

An expression flitted across Atrai's face. Lasha did not acknowledge it. Instead, she shrugged.

"There was nothing wrong with the house this morning."

Did he dream it?

Cleft looked at the women, but his mind raced with how he'd misjudged the situation. What happened with the house and the storm didn't matter. Or he ought to pretend it didn't.

He fixed a smile to his face. Everything was okay. Normal.

"I should be on my way now that it's day," he said. "My assistant is expecting me."

"You were able to get hold of her?" Atrai asked.

"Oh, yes," he lied. "Thank you for letting me stay the night."

"It was no trouble," Atrai said.

Cleft gathered his things as quickly as he could while the women silently watched him. Something was about to happen. He needed to escape before it did.

"Where is he going?" Cleo asked. Lasha pulled her close. Embraced her. Stroked her hair.

"It's time for him to leave."

"No!" Cleo shouted, pulling herself free. She ran to Cleft and wrapped her arms around him. "You can't leave! You can't!"

Cleft didn't know what to do. The door was so close. He was almost out.

"Cleo—" he began.

Then he saw it.

And instantly, he knew it was already too late. He wasn't going anywhere.

"What is that?" he sputtered, unable to express his confusion and disbelief.

"What do you mean?"

He pointed. By the door from the kitchen hung what looked to be a wreath. But it wasn't.

"The Witch's Clutch."

The two women looked back. Then at one another. Cleo squeezed tighter yet Cleft was too numb to feel it.

"That's a strangleweed," Atrai said. "To feed to the animals."

"No, it's a Witch's Clutch. It's... Oh, God," he said, crumpling over his knees. "You took it. It's you I've been looking for this whole time."

There was no religion. No discovery of an unknown sect. No paper. No book. There was only three women collecting plants for their farm. He'd been chasing nothing, and that's what he had. Nothing. In an instant, he saw himself back on that imagined awards stage, but there were no longer any applauding peers in the audience. The theatre was empty.

"I'm sorry," Atrai said, placing her hand on his as she looked at the others. "We didn't know."

"But... I showed you the clipping...."

Lasha reached out for his other hand. "We would have told you had we realised. We were distracted."

"Distracted? By what?"

"Daddy," Cleo said, placing her hands on his chest. "We want Daddy home so badly."

"We do our best with the plants and livestock while he's gone, but it's *his* garden," Atrai said. "He's the only one who knows how to keep it going."

"Would you like to see it? The garden?" Lasha asked.

Immediately, Cleo's face lit up. "Yes! You need to see it! It will help."

Atrai replied, "It's the least we could do."

But Cleft barely looked up. His life was in ruins.

"I really should go."

"Come, let us show you," Atrai said. "And afterward you can take the Witch's Clutch and be on your way."

"You need to see it!" Cleo repeated.

The women all stood, and each took the hand of another—oldest, younger, child—and when Cleo extended hers to Cleft, he did not resist. Her tiny hand burned like an ember in his massive palm, but he didn't let go. Instead, he allowed her to pull him up from the chair.

The four left in procession; Cleft, the last link, stooping to move through the tiny door frame. Outside he realised how cramped he'd been; he stretched his limbs and looked up at the trees swaying above, all moving in the same continuous direction. As though circling.

Atrai led the train across the trodden dirt that surrounded the small home and toward the sound of livestock. Cleo's hand flexed and pulsed within Cleft's like a tiny bird; he did not squeeze tighter for fear of crushing it. He saw no more evidence of a thunderstorm than there had been inside—no mud or downed branches or faint odour of rain. Nor was there a cloud in the sky. Everything was bright and clear and slightly unreal. As though the moment wasn't one he was experiencing but instead one he was watching be experienced. A spectator at far remove.

Why hadn't he left? Was the Witch's Clutch and what it might bring really worth staying for?

When they reached the rear of the house, Cleft saw the tree-encircled yard once again, its edges lined with small pens. The animals, however, were silent—he heard only snuffling in the woods and the scrabbling of hooves and claws on the hard, dry dirt. The ground had become littered with tracks overnight, and all appeared to be pointing toward the area the women were ushering Cleft toward. As though the animals had been gathered in a circle for an audience. Or, no, not a circle. A spiral. A spiral that wrapped around and around the garden, drawing in tighter and tighter toward its eye. Cleft pulled back, hoping to get a better look at the myriad of hoofprints—some the size of his own feet—but the women were unwilling to slow until they reached the centre of the whorl.

"What is this?" Cleft asked.

"This is Father's garden," Atrai said, releasing her sister's hand and stepping in front of him. Standing a bit too close. "You want to remember it, don't you?"

Cleft swallowed.

"Where is he?"

"He'll be here. Soon."

"Yes, but where is he?"

Atrai smiled, put her hand on his chest, then began to slowly pace around him, dragging her fingers lightly across his flesh. His skin prickled.

"What... what are you doing?"

"We tend the garden every day," Lasha said, releasing her other sister's hand and placing hers on Cleft's face, slowly grazing it with her fingers as she followed a step behind Atrai. "We tend it for Father. You can smell it, can't you?"

Cleft could smell it. At once the smell of manure and hay, but also something more, something musky and pungent. Something that made his thoughts swim.

"What's happening to me?" he whispered, his mouth dry as cotton. He felt a tug as if Cleo were trying to release his hand, but his fingers wouldn't open. When he looked down, he discovered why.

What he expected to find was Cleo's hand clamped on his, fingers interlaced and locked tight. Instead, he saw a knot of dark green tendrils twisted around his hand like vines. He didn't understand why, only that he needed to be free. He yanked his hand away in panic but only managed to lift Cleo from the ground. Her limbs flailed lifelessly.

The tendrils that looped over his hand thickened as he watched, his thoughts swimming further away. The tiny leaves that sprouted grew quickly, curling in on themselves. Little pink buds the size of buttons sprung up along his arms. He felt Cleo's hand coming apart in his own like a crushed flower. He gripped tighter to keep from losing her but her hand was already gone.

Circles and spirals and circles. Spinning around and around him. Like a pinwheel. The world constricting upon him, then spreading wide in pulses.

Cleft couldn't think. He looked down into Cleo's face, but it, too, was coming apart. Pale skin sliding away, green stalks unfurling. The white cotton of her tights tore as twigs pushed themselves out. Her eyes collapsed.

There was no air left in his lungs to scream. Atrai and Lasha continued to encircle him, droning underbreath. No matter how he struggled, he could not turn his head to follow them. Each time they reappeared, they were changed. Tendrils extended, bright petals turned colours, small berries grew in clusters, elaborate flowers lifted from thorny stalks and stretched outward. With each revolution, the vines around him tightened. The circles drew closer to constrict. To strangle. Like the slip of a noose.

Cleft's mouth. Wide. Silent.

Frantically, he clawed at the weeds interweaving around his body. The green from Atrai fused with the green from Lasha fused with the green from Cleo. The end of one disguising the beginning of the other. An ouroboros of serrated leaves and browning stalks. Their looping vines climbed his body, squeezing his limbs until they were numb, choking his throat until the blood slowed and a darkness full of stars enveloped his vision. The strangling weeds grew thicker and tighter as he succumbed to them.

But no, that wasn't quite right.

He didn't succumb.

Beneath the muddy numbness, he felt something else. Some secret only just revealing itself. Some primal connection to a current within the earth. One into which he was tapping. Into which he was rooting. As his mortal body weakened, he felt that underthing slide into him. Undo that which had been locked away. A caged animal breaking free.

It happened in his legs first. Bone reshaped, seams split. Leather came apart and cotton tore. His feet touched the ground, remade. Stronger, tougher. He clomped down in an overload of sensations. Then the transformation took his body. An overwhelming feeling of warmth as the world embraced him. The secret world. And he realised in his final fleeting moments that the Witch's Clutch was not what he believed. The hybrid wasn't strange; it was the only thing that was right. The joining of the disparate into the whole. Every single thing a piece of the one thing. The everything.

His clothes shredded. He snuffled. Made a sound like a bleat. And felt for the first time in forever that he was part of something.

In the embrace of his daughters, he finally belonged.

SHOWING

This is it, dear. Wynnchest House. The rental property I was telling you about. I'll give you a quick rundown before we go inside for the showing. Just to whet your appetite.

You're looking at the oldest house not only on the street but in the entire neighbourhood. It was built nearly one hundred and fifty years ago by Randolph Wynnchest and, in fact, the sprawling oak that offers so much beautiful shade to the front yard was planted by his wife, Anna, just before they moved in. Its foundations are built on a section of discovered Laurentian Plateau flat rock that was simultaneously clear of vegetation and remarkably level. You can thank the prehistoric glaciers for that. True, this means the house has no basement, but unlike the neighbours you won't have to worry about sinking or seepage or anything sprouting up between the floorboards.

The house is a four-story Victorian Gothic with a chocolate-slate roof replaced less than ten years ago. All the amenities have been upgraded and modernized, so you won't have any troubles. There is a five-piece bathroom on every floor, central A/C and heat, and a two-car garage. I hope you also noticed on your drive up how quiet the area is. I've met many of the neighbours, and I can tell you they're friendly and look out for one another. You aren't just renting a home; you're renting a community.

The history of the house itself? Never any major damage, either accidental or act of God. Like I said, the neighbourhood is safe. Well, of course, any house this age has suffered a few unsavory events, but the past is the past, and there's no sense dwelling on it. Especially when the monthly price is so reasonable. A house like this would typically rent for much more, but I've held off showing it. Call me sentimental, but I've been waiting for the right person to come along. And, voilà, here you are.

Yes, the groundskeeping is indeed beautiful. Oh no, don't concern yourself with how much work it appears to be. In truth, there's a fellow who comes out regularly to maintain it. He does do quality work. I'd be happy to pass on his information. We haven't been able to find anyone as good for the inside, however. I guess it's true what they say: No one wants to work anymore.

If you're ready, let's go in and I'll show you what you're getting.

GROUND FLOOR

Watch your step, my dear. These ramps are supposed to make things easier for the disabled—my apologies, I mean *physically challenged*—but I think they just end up making things harder for everyone. I see you've noticed the pattern around the front door. No, I don't know what all those symbols mean, but I'm told they're good luck. They keep spirits from getting in or getting out. I'm not sure which. It's all fun nonsense. I'm sure you won't even notice them after a while.

I suppose you're curious about the ramps and handrails. Elicia Pines, the previous tenant, was confined to a wheelchair, you see, and had to get the place retrofitted so she could live here on her own. She never bothered with the other floors since she couldn't reach them anyway. Of course, since all these fixtures were installed after the fact, they can be removed easily during a remodel. I can give you some recommendations for contractors if you'd like.

What happened to her? It was terribly tragic. She and her wife, Skye, wanted a child and had been visiting a clinic in the city. Yes, you heard correctly. Two women. They could have adopted, of course, but they got it in their heads that they wanted a baby that was genetically their own—or at least as close as they could get. Their solution was to ask Skye's brother, Garner, if he'd be the donor. You needn't look at me that way, my dear, I'm of the same mind. It all sounds *very* unconventional, but apparently it happens all the time now, and there's nothing wrong with it. The child's uncle would be its father, but only by a technicality. Elicia and Skye would be its true parents.

I was shocked to hear about the car accident. They'd been on their way home from a clinical appointment when something darted out in front of them. Skye swerved, and the car hit a patch of black ice, sliding into one of the old trees we have up here. The poor soul didn't make it. Elicia almost didn't either, but the paramedics worked a miracle. But not without consequences.

Elicia lost the use of both her legs. From what I gather, her spine twisted so severely that it was cleanly severed. There was no coming back from it, and no amount of determination or pluck was going to help. She'd been crippled forever.

But that wasn't even the worst part. The doctors also informed her—quite coldly, I'm told—she would now never have a baby. I think that was what broke her. She'd managed to weather losing her wife and her legs, but to lose the one thing she and Skye had been trying for, the thing that had put them in the car in the first place was too much. Elicia shut down.

Both her family and Skye's stepped up to help through the hardest of those days. Skye's parents arranged the funeral, while Elicia's got to work renovating the house with these ramps and bars. They even had the doorways widened to accommodate her new wheelchair. Why, yes, *of course* they were allowed to renovate. We have a very lax policy for renters—do what you like to make Wynnchest House yours as long as it's not permanently destructive. We want you to be happy here.

No, I don't think that worked for Elicia.

It wasn't until over a month later, while still in the midst of physical therapy, that she discovered she was wrong: all was not lost. The last implantation attempt had been a success—somehow, miraculously, Elicia had become pregnant. I wasn't there when she found out, but I assume the news was bittersweet. Still, I believe it poked a pinhole in that blind of absolute darkness around her. As tough as her incapacitation made the growing pregnancy, it also motivated her to come to terms with what had happened. By the time the baby was due, she had everything in her life lined up and a house ready to accept them.

And that, sadly, was when the lawyer's letter arrived.

But enough about all that. You're renting a new house! And you'll be filling it with your own happy memories. The two of you will have wonderful times here, and I'm glad I'll be helping you. I've had a long history with this house, as you can tell, but I'm getting old. I'd like to know there will be someone here long after I'm gone.

Oh, are you certain? Wouldn't you rather go upstairs and see more of the house? Take it from me: the past can only hurt, so you should turn your face to the future. I don't remember who first said that, but I've always thought it had an air of truth to it.

No, of course, my dear. I'll tell you the rest of Elicia's story.

You remember Garner? Skye's brother? Well, he had had a change of heart. He'd offered the child to his sister, but now that she was gone, he refused to let "someone outside the family" raise it. Can you imagine what it must have been like to receive that letter? To find you meant so little to the people whom you thought loved you? That when it came down to it you were nothing but a stranger? Elicia told me she tried calling Garner, but he hung up on her. She tried calling her own parents, too, and though they were sympathetic, they refused to get involved. Elicia's world was spinning and kept on spinning as she tumbled toward oblivion. It was a wonder she made it through the birth.

That lawsuit dragged on much too long. You'd think something so cut-and-dry would be quicker, if only for the child's sake. I suppose lawyers need to make money, too. It took over a year before a court date was set. By then, Elicia's little daughter was already on her feet and walking—which for obvious reasons caused its own complications. Elicia's parents helped when they could, and even I stopped in occasionally to lend a hand, but Elicia was left alone to care for that poor girl most of the time. She made it work though.

It was during one of these days when her parents were away that Garner stopped in, unannounced and uninvited. Now, dear, I know *you* would never open your door if you were in this situation, and no one would blame you. This man had caused Elicia no end of pain since his sister's death, but he was also the biological father of her daughter. I imagine Elicia hoped he'd come to tell her he was dismissing his lawsuit.

He hadn't. If anything, he wanted her to sign her rights away to her daughter then and there. He threatened all sorts of terrible things before brandishing a fancy fountain pen and laying it, along with a stack of documents, on the table before her. I don't think it's hard to imagine the severity of Elicia's reaction. I wasn't there, as I said, but the neighbors could hear it, and it was ugly.

I like to imagine he scurried away and didn't look back, but men like that don't understand the pain they cause others. They can't see past their own selfishness. I doubt he felt any remorse at all. Still, he did eventually leave, and Elicia immediately called her lawyer to report the incident. Would his threats have made a difference in the custody trial? I wish I could say, but that wasn't the trial they ended up holding.

The way I understand what happened next is that Elicia, in her anger, put her daughter to bed then proceeded to open a bottle of wine that she and Skye had been saving for when they got pregnant, a bottle Elicia hadn't the strength to open earlier. One glass led to another and when she awoke in a haze, she was sat in the pitch black listening to a horrible guttural wheeze fill the house, like something wet being ripped apart. It took a moment in her stupor to realize she wasn't dreaming, and when she turned on the light, she saw her tiny daughter convulsing on the floor, out of reach and gasping hopelessly for breath.

When Elicia's parents arrived the next day, they found her on the floor weeping uncontrollably, her cold daughter clutched to her chest. At her feet was her overturned wheelchair, irreparably bent and broken.

It appeared as though the young girl awoke and, bored and unable to rouse her mother, somehow discovered the fountain pen Garner had left behind on the table. The girl must have put it in her mouth, not knowing any better, and the cap must have then come loose. They found it lodged in her throat. The poor girl choked to death while Elicia helplessly watched.

That's it, my dear. That's the tragic story of Elicia Pines. I warned you it was horrible. And it was only a few months ago that she finally moved out. She said she couldn't stand looking at these walls any longer; she saw only her own negligence. Garner was devastated, too, for his part in his daughter's death, as were both their families. I'm not sure where Elicia ended up, but I hope it was somewhere far away from tragedy. She's suffered enough, I think. I don't have any children myself, but I can imagine how she must still feel.

But enough morbidity. Let me show you what else this lovely brownstone has to offer.

SECOND FLOOR

Now these stairs are original to the house, built in when the structure was erected. Yes, a hundred and fifty years does sound like a long time, doesn't it? But it also doesn't seem so long at all. In some ways, the world hasn't changed much. Or if it has maybe it's changed right back. I hope so, anyway.

You'll notice this floor appears larger than the ground floor. It's the way the windows were designed. Go stand over there, beside the large one overlooking the front of the house. See how all the full walls go in one direction, but the half walls in another? It opens up the space to make the whole thing seem airier. I'm honestly not sure how Randolph Wynnchest did it—you don't see craftsmanship like that anymore.

I notice you're eyeing the ceiling. Forgive that discoloured patch, and how dusty everything is. I had cleaners scheduled for today before this showing, but they cancelled unexpectedly. Well, between you and me, *cancelled* isn't the right word. They simply never showed. I plan on lodging a formal complaint with their manager after I leave. You shouldn't have to come into a dusty environment like this in your condition. I mean, look at the colour of your face. You're positively pale. The air in here is no good. No good at all. Here. Let me open a window, get a nice breeze in to detoxify the place. There you go, dear. That's it. Take a breath. A deep one. Wake those blood cells up!

As I said, the stairwell is original to the house, but these windows are obviously new. They're triple-paned and were installed just before the house was last bought. We had to replace them after what happened to poor Virginia Ingleby.

Yes, *that* Virginia Ingleby. It was quite a tragedy, though I'm surprised the name rings a bell for you. This was all so long ago. Mrs. Ingleby rented the house after her husband, Calvin, threw her and their daughter out. It should have been a greater scandal, but it was too salacious even for the news back then. Oh, how times have changed. It seems Calvin Ingleby got the idea in his head that his newborn baby wasn't his. No one knows for certain why, but the word is he'd always been a little soft in the brain, and the suspicion was he'd fallen in with the wrong type of friends. He came home one day and demanded his wife, Virginia, take a paternity test or else he'd leave. What was she to do but comply? She loved him after all. It goes without saying, but

I'll say it anyway: she swore up and down their child could only be his. That she'd always been faithful. Alas, he did not believe her. And when the results came back, wouldn't you know it, but the baby *wasn't* his. Even though it had been Mr. Ingleby's idea, he was shocked. Virginia even more so. She swore up and down she'd never even *looked* at another man.

Things spiralled quickly afterward. In those days houses were in the husband's name only, leaving her no choice but to move away. That's when she found this place. The only place, I dare say, she could afford. Back then, Wynnchest House was a shadow of its former self, having sat abandoned for a number of years. We were renting it out for much less than it was worth. Still, it sapped all the money paid to her by both his family and hers to disappear. The lot were embarrassed by the humiliation she'd brought down upon them. I showed her this house on a Saturday morning, despite how tired I was from dancing the night before. I was so young in those days, burning the candle on both ends. But Virginia was tired, too—with purple bags under her eyes and hair both dry and broken, a wailing infant squirming in her trembling arms. In hindsight I should have been more careful about bringing her here. But I was much too distracted by the excitement of drama. Little did I know how much more was to come.

Because what we all found out later was this: that baby wasn't hers, either. There'd been a mix-up at the hospital. A switcheroo. Their real daughter—hers and Calvin's—had been given to a nice couple named Engledry who, through bad luck, had been in labour at the same time at the same hospital. It was an unmitigated nightmare, and the hospital did everything it could to keep the story from the papers. Everyone was paid quite well and the girls, still being too young to know any better, were swapped back. No harm no foul.

Except of course there was plenty of harm and foul. Calvin Ingleby fell to his knees and begged for his wife's forgiveness, but it was too late. Virginia couldn't see past the damage he'd inflicted on their lives. The two parted, and as far I'm aware never saw one another again.

But that wasn't enough for the former Mrs. Ingleby. She couldn't forget what had happened, what her baby had cost her. And even though subsequent tests proved beyond all doubt that the girl returned to her was her and Calvin's biological daughter, Virginia refused to believe it. She confided in me not long after this occurred, when I stopped by to collect her monthly rent, that her initial feelings of blame had metastasized into a worrisome mistrust. She looked sideways at the infant as we sipped our tea, switched to whispers whenever it appeared to be listening to our conversation, and outright snarled at each of its gurgles. I hesitated to say anything in her daughter's defense, I'm sorry to admit. I was too shy to speak my mind then. Or perhaps I was too afraid that if I didn't take her side Virginia would turn that unreasonable hatred on me.

What's that? Oh, yes, I did indeed notice the holes in the sheetrock around the window's frame. No, I don't know what happened, but I agree they look torn rather than punctured. I'll schedule our handyman to patch them before you move in.

My apologies. Of course, I meant *if* you move in.

Being a single parent is not easy under the best of circumstances, but when a mother blames her child for all her unhappiness things are made profoundly worse. Virginia was trapped in the house with her infant daughter, tethered to a mewling creature she'd grown to despise. And there was no relief—she had no family or friends left to help her and no money to hire anyone new. You may be wondering, if the hospital paid so much to keep the mix-up quiet, why she was so destitute. That's another twist of the knife—because she'd been married to Calvin when the tragic switch occurred, the hospital sent the entirety of the settlement directly to him. She couldn't even afford her own lawyer to contest it, and whether out of spite or greed her former husband refused to share that windfall with her. She was left utterly alone with their daughter, abandoned. And isolation does funny things to a desperate mind.

I only heard rumors about what happened next. The neighbours, you see, possessed with morbid curiosity as neighbours often are, kept watch on the house and its young inhabitants. They were amazed at the sounds such a small delicate thing could make, crying at all hours of the day and night, desperate for the comfort of the mother from whose hands it had been wrenched away, unwilling to accept that of the mother into whose cold and suspicious hands it had been placed.

If the noise was intolerable for the neighbours, it would have been worse for Virginia Ingleby. Even knowing how ghastly it all turned out, was what happened next a surprise to anyone? It wasn't to me, though I do regret not acting on my fears sooner. What else can I blame but my own inexperience?

41

We only have the tragic note Virginia Ingleby left pinned to her child to hint at what followed and why. She explained it as thoroughly as one might expect from someone suffering a mental breakdown and suicidal ideation. Poor Virginia had become convinced her daughter was whispering to her. Not making incoherent babbles and noises, but using full blown sentences that Virginia wrote she felt more than heard. She claimed the truth was that like the Engledry girl, this baby was not hers either, and after it revealed what it had done to her real daughter, it began to laugh. And it continued laughing, over and over, day after day.

Virginia said she held out as long as she could.

The police were called when her body was found outside, face down in the front garden. She'd leapt through the window—yes, that one you're standing in front of—and plummeted to the ground. True, this is only the second floor, and she should have survived the impact, but it was the falling glass, you see. It slid out of its frame right after her, a large shard slicing through the air toward her. It was only by chance it struck her in the back of the neck. It nearly decapitated the poor woman.

And her baby daughter? Well, the police found her, along with the note I told you about. Before leaping, Virginia must have tried to quiet the whispering by covering the child's head with a clear plastic bag and cinching the opening tight around its little neck. She was no doubt dead before she even had a chance to struggle.

The neighbourhood was heartbroken. As was I once I heard. Apparently, the police attempted to call Mr. Ingleby with the news but there was no answer. He and his parents had moved out of the country with no forwarding address. Again, those were the times. It was long ago and a different world. The Engledry family was all right if that's any consolation. No tragedies of a similar kind befell them. I heard their daughter grew up pretty and married into money.

Dear me, I seem to have upset you with my story. I didn't mean to. It's just that we got talking about those large windows and why they were replaced, and I lost myself in a memory. I do hope you'll forgive me and won't let it concern you. Those sorts of mix-ups rarely happen anymore. I'm sure there's nothing at all for you to worry about.

Perhaps we should continue.

TOP FLOOR

Dear, you seem to be shivering! And that walk up the stairs hasn't
done you any favours. I promise, after this we'll go back down and
sign the rental agreement. First, though, you must see what's up here.
I wouldn't be doing my job if I didn't present everything. Don't you
worry about speaking; just rest and catch your breath. I'll point it all
out to you.

Being the top floor of the house, you'll find it warmer than the
floors below. That's just science, I'm afraid. Not much we can do about
that. Still, you'll be thankful for it come winter. The house is well-in-
sulated, so you shouldn't lose any heat. It also means no mice. It's true,
never a one. Over the years, there have been tenants who've sworn
they heard them in the walls and put down traps, but never has one
been caught in here. I'm quite proud of that. True, I suppose I had
little to do with it, but everyone has something funny they take pride
in, and I guess that's mine.

I see you're staring at the dark stain in the middle of the floor. Yes,
I probably should have put a rug over that, but I've always believed
you should give your warts plenty of air and sunlight. It's the only way
they heal. This one didn't heal so fast, though. Once again, it's a sad
story, and I don't imagine you'd like to hear another. Not with your
little one on the way. It's not the sort of tale to make you feel better
about all that business. Instead, let me show you how cozy you could
make this floor. It's a little dusty and unfinished, but with barely any
work, it would be a great study or playroom. You'd need to make some
adjustments, certainly. Maybe put down some soft carpet and throw
some paint on the walls. Just imagine the possibilities.

I see you're still distracted by that stain. I told you not to concern
yourself with it. Instead—

Oh, yes, you *certainly* have a right to know about the house. I
wouldn't dream of hiding anything from—

Well. There's no need to threaten me with a lawyer, dear. I'm *quite*
aware of the disclosure laws. I hesitate to suggest perhaps more so than
you. I was only looking out for your best interests. Nevertheless, you
win. You'll hear the whole sordid tale, at best I understand it.

As I told you outside, this house was built by Randolph Wynnchest
for his wife, Anna, and the large family he planned to have. "This is a

house that demands children," he purportedly told her as they stood on its completed precipice for the first time. There were rumors about them in town—more than once, Anna appeared at the local shops with her throat fully wrapped, regardless of the season, her makeup failing to completely conceal her bruised eyes. This was a hundred and fifty years ago, remember, so though people suspected what was going on behind closed doors, no one thought it their business to ask questions. And Anna certainly wasn't volunteering answers.

A week after the couple moved into the house, two things happened simultaneously: the first was Anna found herself suddenly ill one morning, which she discovered soon afterward to be an unexpected pregnancy; the second was Randolph, while apparently carrying a stack of ledgers he'd brought home from work, somehow took a strangely wrong-footed step and tumbled from the top of the stairwell. When the doctors arrived, they found him crumpled and dead on the landing below. Anna stood watching from a short distance away, hands resting on her abdomen, her expression unaffected.

Suspiciously, Anna appeared brightened when next at the shops, but this change in attitude didn't last long. Soon, she began to appear haunted, acting as though she heard voices where there weren't any. At first, she denied any such thing but eventually confided in her doctor that she feared what Randolph might do to punish her. She seemed convinced death would prove to be no obstacle for him. As a result of her delusions and how they might affect her unborn child, the doctors prescribed opium to calm her. She ejected them and everyone else from the house immediately.

They say Anna wasn't seen much after that. On those rare occasions where she did emerge, her black hair was turned wiry and streaked with grey, and her eyes were sunk so far, her skull appeared hollowed out. She moved in a slow daze, unable to remember even her closest friends when they came calling. All the while, that baby inside her grew and grew. Whenever anyone asked why she stayed alone in that large home, she'd lower her head wistfully and mutter *Wynnchest House demands children*, as though that were a satisfying answer.

Winter was particularly nasty. The amount of snowfall the town suffered remains a record to this day. And remember, back then, there were none of these thermal windows or forced air furnaces to keep a place warm. The best you could do to keep out a draft was add another blanket to your bed and another log under the boiler. Local lore says the snow drifted so high during that winter that houses were buried to their second floor. This is why no one checked in on Mrs. Wynnchest. No one forgot about her necessarily, but they all assumed she found a midwife or a doctor to take care of her. Or perhaps she'd been moved from the house before the snow began to fall.

Pardon me, I have to ask: are you sure you're all right, dear? We can stop if you'd like. You're looking worse by the minute, and I don't want to upset you further. We don't need to go on.

Well, then, let me rush through the rest, if only to spare you from the grisly details.

They found Anna Wynnchest's body in the Spring. No, she didn't throw herself down the stairs. And yes, she did have her child—a little girl, actually—but that doesn't make it any less painful.

After the snow melted, it didn't take long for the neighbours to notice no one was repairing the property's storm damage, nor was the house's chimney ever lit. Even her doctor seemed genuinely surprised when someone casually asked after Anna and how she'd weathered the cold. All this and more was enough to send a band of townsfolk forcefully through the house's recently cleared front door.

Anna Wynnchest lay on the floor in this room, her crusted maternity dress hiked up over her hips and dark purple bruises reaching around her throat. The doctor said she'd been dead for months. Her bruised legs were twisted outward and spread, and from between them, a torrent of dried black blood had spilled outward nearly four or five feet across the floor. Pushed to the furthest edge of that pool were the remains of her small infant daughter. She, too, was dead, of course, curled into a brittle foetal husk, umbilical cord wrapped around her throat like a hangman's noose. I imagine even for the sturdiest of men, it was impossible to see without tearing up. I'm told the child's body was so desiccated that it collapsed in on itself like a brittle eggshell when they attempted to unstick it from the floorboards.

Yes, that's the same stain you've been so mesmerized by since we reached this floor. That's why, I confess, I won't step on it, even though I'm not the superstitious sort. Or maybe that's exactly what it makes me. Oh my, you know, I never thought about it that way before.

Anyway, over the years we've tried to sand away the stain of Anna Wynnchest and her daughter, but it's stubbornly remained. The blood seems to have soaked all the way through the wood and the cost of replacing so much of it, especially over the loadbearing joists below, has been too prohibitive. Plus, as I said, after Anna's death no one wanted to come up here anyway, so there's never been a great rush to spend the money.

Oh my, now you *really* look as though you're ill. I've really done it this time. I shouldn't have made you stay in this sweltering heat as I blathered on. Give me your arm, and I'll lead you back down the stairs. It's all right, dear. Just lean on me—I'm sturdy. I can take it. We'll get you closer to the ground and let you rest up. There's nothing more for you up here anyway.

CLOSING

There. Now don't you feel better? Lying down where it's cooler? I've opened another window for you, and there's a nice breeze. And look at that: the sun has come out at last to see us. That's Wynnchest House for you. It's all sunshine and oak trees up here. The kind of place that makes you want to stay forever.

What's that? Oh no, I won't be taking you to see any more houses. This is the only one for you. The one you were meant for.

You'll need to speak up, dear. I have trouble hearing you when you whisper. I suppose that's what happens when you get old. Time has a funny way of making itself known, even when we try to forget about it. Those things we try to forget always find their way back to us. We can never be rid of the past because there's always more of it. Like a giant wave growing bigger by the second.

Listen to me. Prattling on. Boring you. I'm sure you'd rather hear more about Wynnchest House than about me. I'm not all that interesting, but this house? It's a thing of beauty. Three floors of perfection and good old-fashioned know-how.

Yes, you're right. I *did* say this was a four-story house, didn't I? Well, it's true. There are four stories in this house, and that fourth story is yours. You didn't think Wynnchest House had forgotten about you, did you? *Wynnchest House demands children*, remember? It won't let you leave, not when you have something it wants. That's why I was careful to never have any children myself. Too risky. And believe me, I was quite popular when I was young. Good-looking, too. I took after my great-grandmother, who warned me about what had happened to her cruel Uncle Randolph when he built this place. Our family has been waiting years to move back in. But we couldn't risk it for obvious reasons. I was the only one willing to give up the nonsense of children so I could look after this house; as I told you, I'm devoted. I guess, in a way, you could say Wynnchest House has taken the place of a baby in my life. I've washed it and groomed it. I've made it comfortable and taken care of it. And I've fed it. A happy baby is a full baby. Oh, but I don't have to tell you that, do I?

My, you are *not* looking well at all, my dear. That's too bad. I was really hoping after Elicia Pine's daughter, the house would have had its fill. Their child lasted so much longer than the others, and its mother is still with us, more or less. I do hope you manage to stay around. And who knows? Maybe your little one will make it. I'd love to see the house satiated before I shuffle off. And if it's not yours, I'm hopeful the next will be the one.

Now, why don't you slip under the covers while I make you a nice tea? Do you take milk? While I'm off, go ahead and sign these documents for me. Just so everything is on the up and up. I'll leave you my pen, too. Careful not to put it in your mouth! I'm sorry, I couldn't resist. A little joke just between us. It's good to remain friendly since we'll be seeing so much of each other from now on. What's that? Oh no, don't worry about your belongings. I'll have them brought here. None of us wants you to be uncomfortable. My, you seem upset, dear; don't be. It won't take much time. After all, you're already showing.

JASON'S IN THE GARDEN

Of all the kids in my middle school, no one ever claimed they'd seen a ghost. No one but Jason Keane. He was infamous among us, our pudgy, misshapen classmate with a perpetual red ring around his mouth. It wasn't that we hated him—we were still too young to really hate anyone—but his constant fibbing about what he'd said and done grew frustrating. No matter how many times we called him out, he continued to spin tales in an effort to impress us. And, when that failed, he'd fall back on simply giving us the candy from his pockets. That, unlike his stories, we ate up hungrily.

Maybe the problem was Jason lacked the finesse of a good liar, that momentary conviction that every word out of his mouth was true. Instead, his eyes shifted, and his pitch rose, and it was instantly clear that he could not be trusted. I often marvelled at how terrible he must have been to be so desperate for attention. But I learned young that everyone was terrible in one way or another. It was just that most hid it better.

But the ghost. We were on the school grounds in those early morning minutes before the bell rang, challenging one another to inordinately complicated dares and games designed to test our limits, when Jason arrived. He did so silently, appearing on the periphery of our large group, his unwashed shirt the same striped grey and red hand-me-down he always wore, his face raw from persistently licking his chapped lips. We would have ignored him had his eyes not been watery and swollen, and his pallor yellowed. He looked so unnerved we reluctantly stopped our games to ask what was wrong.

"I saw something," he said, snivelling. "Something I wasn't supposed to see."

There were groans and eye rolls, and a chorus of mocking jokes at his expense, but Jason never faltered, never walked back what he said or tried to over-explain. It secretly unnerved us, and our ridicule bled dry abruptly when Eric stepped forward to ask Jason what he'd seen.

"I'd left the house and was going down the stairs to go to school. I didn't want to be late again, so I was running pretty quick, and you know how there's the garden in front of my house? The one my mom tells us to stay out of?" We nodded, though as far as I knew, none of us had seen the garden or been at his house in years. "I opened the gate and ran through because I was late. As I was running, I saw another kid in there, one I didn't recognize. I asked him who he was and if he went to school here and if he wanted some candy, but he didn't say anything. So I told him he had to get out of the garden before my mom found him. He just looked at me like he was angry."

It was the least interesting, least ambitious story Jason had ever told, and the lack of effort enraged some of us. Sean and Keith started shouting, wondering how any of that made the boy a ghost. Simply because he was trespassing?

"No," Jason said, licking his lips. "It was only afterward I realized he was a ghost. Because he wasn't wearing any shoes."

That stumped us. No one knew what to say, and there was no time to figure it out before the morning bell interrupted.

After half a day in Mr. Hanson's class learning simple math and geography, we'd forgotten the story, as apparently had Jason, who retreated at lunch to the only group that would take him, that small cluster of outcasts from our circle. Frail Winston, Gangly Stephen, Sweaty Jim, and the rest who had no place among us, who stayed out of our way. Even among that crowd, however, Jason didn't truly belong. His lies and tale-telling repeatedly caught up with him, and those misfits who took him in found themselves as often casting him out. No pocket full of candy could prevent it. So Jason ended up bouncing between our two groups, neither wanting to lay claim to him, and during those times, our two expulsions would overlap, with nowhere else to go, he would end up walking the perimeter of the schoolyard fences, stooping occasionally to pick up a stone, a clod of earth, or a particularly interesting stick, and then lobbing it over into the narrow creek beyond.

We only remembered Jason's story the next day, and only because when he appeared, he was impossibly more ashen and unkempt than the day before. Dennis noticed his chapped lips were drawn thin.

"I saw him again today. I saw him again standing there, barefoot, in the garden. As soon as I did, I closed my eyes because maybe if you don't see a ghost, it can't see you, so I closed my eyes and tried to walk through the garden. But I couldn't walk fast because I didn't know where I was going, and it felt like I was walking for a lot longer than there was garden to walk through, and I started worrying I wasn't in the garden anymore like the ghost had taken me somewhere else and I didn't know it. And then I was afraid of where I was, and I opened my eyes even though I told myself not to, and when I did, I was at the end of the garden—a step away from the gate—but beside me an inch away was the ghost. But now he had these big black eyes and was barefoot. His lips were moving like he was saying something, but I couldn't hear anything."

Ben and Dennis laughed at him incredulously. Donald simply turned and walked off, taking Jon and Brett with him. The rest of us stayed because the game of ball we'd been playing no longer held any of our interest and because it was so close to the morning bell that starting another game would only frustrate us.

It was Mark who asked why it was so important the boy was barefoot, why that suggested he was a ghost not someone from a different school or a visiting neighbour? Jason shook his head and wiped his runny nose on his sleeve.

"You can't walk without shoes in that garden. Too many animals got in there and ate the flowers and vegetables my mom grew, and she got so angry my dad put broken glass in the dirt to keep them away. It's everywhere, and you can't walk through without shoes unless you want to bleed to death out of your feet. But this kid wasn't bleeding at all. He was just standing there, mouthing nothing."

We didn't believe him, of course. Why would you believe something like that? It was the kind of crazy story Jason would tell, something so outlandish you'd have to pay attention to him, and he got his wish; that's what we were doing. But we'd known Jason long enough by then not to fall for it for long.

I think it was Billy who shoved him suddenly and violently, and you could see Jason's soft pudginess absorb most of the blow. But Billy was persistent and continued shoving until Jason toppled over. It was some sort of punishment, I guess, for how he was treating us, and I don't know what would have happened next if the bell hadn't rung. I want to believe nothing, and that's probably the case, but I'm not convinced I'm right. It was a confusing time back then.

Jason spent most of the morning whimpering in the back of the classroom, quiet enough that Mr. Hanson didn't notice, but we all heard. None of us did anything about it, though. None of us grasped what was happening. Was Jason afraid that Billy would attack him again? Was he afraid of whatever he thought he saw in the garden? Or was he afraid he was making up another story he couldn't get out of? I remember passing a note to Spencer suggesting we had to do something, but Spencer didn't read it. He took it from me and creased his eyebrows before tearing it up and dropping it on his desk.

At lunch, I wanted to talk to Jason—more to straighten out my own head than anything else—but he'd already vanished from the school grounds before anyone knew he was gone. I wondered if we should go looking for him, but no one seemed concerned. They just wanted to go home for lunch. Jason wasn't our problem, they said. He was probably looking for his mom to cradle him. But I suspected in a way I couldn't articulate then that his mother was not the cradling sort. Nevertheless, I gave in, and instead of searching for him, we all went our own ways, convinced he'd be back for the afternoon.

But he wasn't. Jason did not return to class. Not for the rest of that day, which I found surprising and irritating. Not the next day, which I found unusual and unsettling. And not on the day after that, which I found troubling and worrying. But I still did nothing about it because what was there to do?

Jason finally returned on Friday. We were in front of the school, picking sides for a game of ball we wouldn't actually start until the midmorning break when one by one we noticed the sickly odour of unbathed prepubescence and turned to find Jason behind us. But he was different this time. It wasn't that his pallor had become completely white and bloodless, though it had; and it wasn't that he stared at us wide-eyed and without blinking, though he did; it was that he was perfectly and utterly still, as though he were some soft lumpy statue carved of soapstone by the most undelightful of artists. Eric complained Jason was giving him the creeps, and though we all acted as though we agreed, I suspect it was something else. Something deeper and more troubling on a primitive level. Something akin to how animals know a disaster is imminent. An early sense of oncoming danger. At least, I felt that way.

Jason's pale face and empty eyes watched us, and though it wasn't me who first noticed his feet, once I did, I couldn't stop shouting. His feet. What was wrong with his feet? Darryl ran inside to fetch Mr. Hanson while the rest of us stood there dumbstruck. I remember the sound of the morning bell ringing, but none of us heeded it. None of us moved. Even when Mr. Hanson emerged with Darryl trailing behind and yelled at us, we didn't respond. Jason had started to sway, eyes fluttering, and we watched as Mr. Hanson heaved Jason into his arms as he collapsed and dashed him back through the school doors while the rest of us were left behind to stare at the trail of bloody footprints that stretched back across the bridge over which Jason had apparently crossed.

We found our way to class shortly after, once the bellowing Mr. Gilroy, teacher of the third graders, stepped through those same doors and shook us from our collective stupor. We filed up to our room silently and without protest, but once we took our seats the murmuring began. What had happened? What was wrong with Jason? Had he been in an accident? Had he hurt himself? Had someone else hurt him? It was Joey who brought up the garden and the broken glass therein, but it made no sense. Why would Jason knowingly walk on broken glass?

Mr. Hanson eventually came to our homeroom, his face flushed. He announced that Jason had hurt himself and wouldn't be attending class and that his parents, Mr. and Mrs. Keane, were on their way to retrieve him, but none of those facts eased our curiosity, so Mr. Hanson eventually and begrudgingly took our questions. Where was Jason now? The school nurse was tending to him. Had Jason mentioned what happened? No. Was he going to die? Of course not; he just needs rest. Did he lose his shoes? We don't know. Then Eric asked the question I dreaded hearing. Do you think it was the ghost's fault? Everyone waited for the answer, but Mr. Hanson's response was so confused and irritated that it was clear Jason had not mentioned seeing the boy in the garden. Only we knew, and though it was clear we shouldn't believe it, that it was likely an attempt to garner attention, still some of us couldn't shake the feeling that there was something more happening than any of us wanted to admit, and that translated to a feeling of unease that never left us.

Or, at least, it never left me because I spent the rest of my day in class, watching the window beside me as though I expected someone to walk up and peer in. Someone small and thin and translucent, with eyes like aching pits and feet stained black with dried blood. I never saw that, but I saw Jason's oversized father leading his hobbling son away from the school. His mother walked beside them, stopping periodically to say something I couldn't hear but could imagine from the strict way she bent to meet his eye and the sharp wagging of her bony finger. Each time she did, as soon as her attention shifted away, he'd reach into his pocket for a candy to slip between his chapped lips, only to have it knocked away by his incensed mother. In an instant, Jason's entire life unfolded before me, and I saw what I had never seen before, what *none* of our classmates had ever seen. I saw a home life of neglect and punishment for the tiniest infractions; I saw Jason alone in his room, or his basement, or in his yard, without a friend to speak or laugh with or connect to in any way at all. He was alone and always had been, and every attempt he'd made to change that or correct his isolation had been met with a wall of disinterest and dismissal. His bribes for friends didn't work; his slow wits prevented him from being a good student and impressing Mr. Hanson. Even the stories designed to impress others into wanting his company failed. I saw Jason as I'd seen him every afternoon at the end of class, slowly trudging home along the perimeter fences, his unclasped backpack hung haphazardly over his shoulder, and now instead of a slovenly kid, I saw one that had exhausted himself trying to connect, and needed to steel himself before he reached home, where the most attention he could hope for would be a series of reprimands for being an inconvenience. I even saw Jason in the future, behind the wheel of a filthy pickup truck, heavy-set and balding, his face a relief map of the neighbourhood. It was no wonder he saw ghosts in his garden. As a manifestation of his loneliness, it was clear that they at least would speak to him. As I said, I understood him then for the first time, and I didn't know if I liked it or if I was going to do something to help him.

I wanted to gather some classmates to visit Jason with me after the final bell. True, the nurse said he should rest, but I had to believe seeing us on his doorstep would help buoy his spirits. I was certain it would assuage some of my guilt. But despite multiple attempts, I could not find anyone willing to join me. They all expressed the same ambivalence or open hostility about Jason as ever, and yet there was also something more in each pair of eyes: an irrational fear Jason's latest stories might be true; and a worry that coming face to face with the impossible would change them, as though life weren't doing that already.

So, I made my way to Jason Keane's house alone. I crossed the hydro fields and over the creek bridge. I walked down curved suburban streets and fenced-in pathways until I was let out onto the alcove where his two-story house stood, its fifty-year-old oak tree casting shadows across its front lawn. Along the side of the house ran the wooden staircase that Jason had often described; its plain, utilitarian appearance, coated in dull maroon paint, a surprising disappointment compared to the grand and ornate version featured in many of his implausible stories. But at least the staircase was there, as was the small garden positioned between me and its foot.

From a distance, the fenced-in plot was no different from any vegetable garden. Rows of leafy greens and tuberous roots took up the bulk of the space, but there were also vines and some ornamental flowers that must have been grown strictly for decorating the house. The entire garden was no more than eight feet long and nearly half that wide, surrounded by a few feet of wire mesh—tall enough to keep out the rabbits, skunks, and squirrels but not enough that a person might feel trapped. A gate on either end further lowered the risk.

I walked toward the house, intending to climb the staircase to Jason's door, but the straightest possible route ran through the garden. The sight of it unnerved me after Jason's stories, so I decided to circumvent it out of politeness, but a strange gleaming from within caught my eye, drawing me closer and insisting I take a look. I watched the house as I approached for a sign of Jason or his parents, but there was nothing. No evidence of life. By the time I reached the garden and peered in, most of the shimmering had faded, leaving behind scattered reflections from mirrored shards half-buried in the earth. But there was something else, too, something I could see between where the spinach rows ended and the geraniums began, something whose reflection wasn't quite right. It made me uneasy, as though someone were watching me despite no one else being visible. And yet... and yet something drew me onward into the garden. Even though my heart was beating faster than it ever had, even though my mind was scream-ing at me to turn and run, even though I questioned why I was un-able to resist coming to Jason's house when our other classmates eas-ily stayed away, still I found myself opening the garden gate without knowing I was going to, and stepping inside before I could stop myself.

Immediately, the world became quieter. The air felt slightly cooler as well, darkening as though a cloud had selected that particular mo-ment to cross between me and the sun. As I took hesitant steps, I heard the creaks of stressed glass beneath my feet. Ahead was the garden's other gate, a mere eight feet away, but the fear calcifying my muscles slowed my progress, and those feet might as well have been miles. I trudged them slowly, green leaves brushing my ankles, each step feel-ing as though it might be my last. I believed then, with all my being in what Jason had told us, that the barefooted ghost was real, and that at any moment, he would appear and frighten me or worse, drag me down with him into that sharp black earth.

But that's not what happened. Instead, my journey ended when I placed my hand on the opposite gate, and the clouds I had been so worried about parted, revealling the warming sun. I looked behind me to see the garden and only the garden, with its crop of vegetables and my footprints travelling along its length. If there was a ghost there, I did not see it, did not feel it any longer. The part of me I had gathered up tight against my chest was then released, and I felt all the tension drain from me in relief. The world once again made sense. Jason's sto-ries were once again stories.

I looked ahead at the house whose long wooden staircase I was ap-proaching, looked at the darkened windows of Jason's home, and was startled to see him behind the glass, staring down at me and mouth-ing words I couldn't hear. His face was still pale from that morning, his eyes still sunken, but he had a queer expression as he watched me in the garden. Was it terror? Excitement? Anticipation? Was he even looking at me or something or someone else? I spun around and saw nothing else behind me, nothing but the shadows of the old oak tree.

I turned back, but Jason had left the window, and for a moment, I wondered if he had ever been there, if I hadn't imagined someone watching me from above. It then occurred to me that the someone watching might not have been Jason, which seemed an infinitely worse proposition.

But, no, it was Jason. It had to be. I knew because I saw him a moment later, spilling from the house onto that wooden staircase landing above. I saw him look at me—reach out his hand and look directly at me, unflinchingly locking eyes—and then descend the stairs in a slow, deliberate panic on bandaged feet, bloodied and scabbed. He seemed excited, possessed, desperate to get to me, but I didn't understand why. Even though every step appeared to inflict a momentary grimace of pain, he did not stop, did not slow further. He just continued to make his way closer. He was yelling something I couldn't make out, but it was clear he wanted to reach me before it was too late. But too late for what? Without thinking, I took a step back.

NOT THE SAME PLACE

E ton crept into the room, his flashlight throwing a pale circle over the warped hardwood floors and abandoned beds. It picked up only the most obvious things—furniture, bricks, pieces of plaster that had fallen from the walls—but missed the rest, the shadows blurring them until Eton could not be sure what was there and if any of it was moving.

There was that sound again. Not a scratching, more like a huffing. But it could not be that. Was it a grinding? Like sandpaper on something hollow. Something big. Each time it happened, his spine lit up.

"Pris... that you?"

She did not answer. She had not since she disappeared. Behind him one minute, complaining about something else he had unknowingly done, and vanished the next, swallowed by the dark of the house. He was not going to give up. He was going to find her. He had promised once that he would never leave her. He would find her no matter how many rooms he had to search. He had already searched so many. Too many for such a small house. But he could not think about that. He had to focus on finding her.

"Pris, where are you?" he shouted.

His voice echoed, the sandpaper sounds returned, his spine on fire. He threw the circle of light back into the hall so he could check the next room.

Pris called for Eton, but the darkness muffled her voice. The house was quiet around her—even the sound of her footsteps did not reach her ears. She wondered where she was and when she would find Eton.

She considered remaining in one place so he could find her. But no. That was something Eton was good at that—staying in one place—but she could not. She had never been able to stand still. She was anxious by nature, unlike Eton. Nothing ever bothered him, even if it should. It used to make her jealous, the way he slid through life. Used to.

Chances were he was dead. She tried not to let the thought settle, but it was difficult, especially when the odor she smelled as she walked deeper into the house was of blood. She could not quiet the voice telling her that Eton was no longer there. That she was lost and alone and had to find her way out on her own before whatever happened to him happened to her.

But in the dark, she had become turned around and could not be certain which direction she was going. Was she walking back to the entrance or further into the unlit house? She had only her phone for light, and its pale glow was not enough to dispel the shadows engulfing her. Maybe if she held it out further? But what if something knocked it from her hand? Something that came sprinting toward her in the dark, hurtling through hallway after hallway? She did not know what, but she felt a presence in the impenetrable darkness. Some fearsome inevitability. If it breached the dark, she would catch no more than a glimpse before it fell on her. Pris felt panicked, the breath wheezing in and out of her lungs, that same sickly numb, constricted feeling she had suffered on her wedding day. Pris hugged the phone closer to her body and forced herself to close her eyes and breathe deeper, steadier until the numbness faded.

Eton wondered if Pris needed him, then realized that was absurd. She was lost somewhere in the house, just as he was. She *had* to need him. And all he needed was to find her. But when he held the flashlight up to light the way he saw only doors. Doors in every direction. He cursed himself for following Pris into this nightmare.

He had known it, too. Before they went in. He probably knew it earlier when Pris suggested the trip. He would have much rather stayed home where everything was familiar, but she insisted they needed a change. Something new, something different. And he made the mistake of acquiescing. Now look where they were—halfway around the globe in a foreign city that was a senseless web of brick roads. They should have stayed at the resort—if they had, they would be lying under the sun right now—but Pris had to keep moving. Like a shark with an itinerary. That was how they found the house, tucked away at the end of one of those twisted roads. Eton was surprised to see it, though he did not know why he should be. It looked familiar, as though he had been there before and more than once. But it had changed somehow. Pris, too, seemed confused, but before he could stop her, she stepped through the door. And he unthinkingly followed.

If only Pris had not gone inside.... If only Pris had not dragged him so far away from home....

No, it was not the time for that. Blame could come later. For now, he had to stop wandering, feeling sorry for himself, and instead find Pris so they might together escape from wherever they were.

Pris stopped looking to her phone for help. She could not trust it. The numbers were flipped the wrong way, or maybe they were not numbers at all. Just a bleached screen that burned a figment into her vision that hovered around her in the dark. She thought about Eton, somewhere in the house, wandering the same hallways as her. Was he calling out for her? She had doubts. He was not the sort to offer a sustained effort. He was more relaxed, built to accept things as they came. It was one of the things she had always said she loved about him. He was the calming salve for her red-hot burning. He balanced her, kept her from flying off in rage when things went awry. She had always believed that was what she needed. Someone to pull her down.

And Eton excelled at that. Pulling her down.

She could not believe she had once had a life outside the house. It was like some hazy dream. One in which she worked hard to climb the professional ranks and came home to a lounging Eton. Eton, who was not as fortunate, though she believed he could be if he so chose. If he tried. Maybe she pushed him too hard, but it was only because she wanted to support him. She wanted him to be as fulfilled as she was. As she was meant to be.

But what did *meant to be* even mean anymore? If she believed that, then she would have to believe she was trapped in that house for a reason. And she refused to consider what that reason might be.

Pris asked herself over and over as she travelled the house with too many rooms, too many doors, what she was supposed to do. How long must she continue to hope? The darkness continued to encroach on her, squeezing her tighter until she feared she would never escape it. The idea that she might spend the rest of her life stuck in the darkness was debilitating. She had to escape. She needed to breathe again.

It took all her effort to keep from running. And, even then, the only reason she did not was she had no idea where she could go.

Eton wandered for hours, his feet feeling as though they had been struck by hammers. Each pounding step travelled up his legs and into his body. Yet the hallway did not end. The rooms went on and on into the dark; rows of warped, dusty boxes that grew less intact the deeper he journeyed. Now, so far inside, perhaps over hours, perhaps over days, the walls were barely walls—the holes in the plaster were so large. Air wheezed through them as it did through Eton's dust-clogged throat. Yet he pushed on. He had made a bargain in the depths of the house with a mirror. One that hung miraculously intact in a hidden room he doubted truly existed.

When he discovered it, he hesitated, afraid of what would be reflected in the glass. But it was only him. His image stared back with new lines on its face, creases he did not remember having. Had he really been trapped so long? He leaned closer to the glass to see himself better and wondered if this was all life had planned for him. With greying hair and a paling complexion, the aged Eton in the mirror was a warning of how easily everything could be taken away or changed. Nothing ever remained the same, no matter how much he wanted it to.

Eton's reflection mouthed something. The sight was startling and yet did not concern the real Eton as much as it should have. Perhaps because that other Eton had already slipped so far away from him, dragged back into the reflected darkness where no flashlight could reach, sinking until all that was left was Eton gazing into a black pool of nothing. It was only then that the loss struck him, and that was when he shouted into the mirror, hoping it was not too late to reach himself.

"If I get out, I promise things will be different. I will be different."

He hoped his reflection heard.

Pris pleaded with the house for her freedom. She could not take the oppressive suffocation any longer. Her struggles had only sent her in circles—whatever change she was hoping for was not going to materialize. Almost simultaneously, her legs lost their strength, their dead weight dragging her until she could no longer move. She thought to turn back, but behind her, the floor was covered in undisturbed dust—as though she had never passed, as though she had never existed, as though who she was had been erased and she had become something else, something that was not her if it ever had been—and Pris felt alone, more alone than she had ever felt before. And desperate. She screamed out Eton's name until her throat grew hoarse, and her ears rang too much to hear if there had been a reply. But she knew there had not.

If only there were something she could do. If only there were something the house wanted that she could give. She would have offered it anything.

Eton stood in the dark, eyes wide seeing nothing. Something was there with him. "Pris?" he squeaked, hopeful. If it were her, he would be okay. If it were her, he would forgive the fright she had given him. He would forgive everything she ever said. He would be better. Do the things she wanted. Find a new job. Marry her. Anything for another chance to return to their life together. All his doubts suddenly faded, and he knew, for certain, in his desperation, that he could be what she needed. "Pris?" he asked again, hoping the response from the dark would be different. And he did hear a sound, wet and burbling, and understood there was no need to ask again.

Pris did not realize what she was hearing. It was too quiet at first. As it grew louder, blending with the creaks and the moans, it sounded like damp branches whipping the air. It unnerved her. One thing was certain, though: whatever was out there was getting closer fast. She wished she knew if the echoes were coming from where she had been or where she was going.

She increased her pace. It would be fine, she told herself; she had a lot of practice running from things. Pris tentatively increased her pace even though the phone she held out before her barely illuminated the blizzard of dust suspended in the air. In her frenzy, she banged her limbs on unseen objects submerged in the sea of darkness. If she could move faster, maybe she could outrun what was coming.

Eton retreated, body tense. Nothing else existed but that sound—as though a wet mop were being dragged. It was so faint he should have questioned if he actually heard it. But in his heart, he knew. And the terror of the knowledge—that something was there, hidden in the dark, ready to strike—made a strange fuel mixed with his fury.

"I can hear you," he said, though he worried it might be a lie. "You better stay back."

Was that a snort? Something worse?

"Where's Pris?" he demanded. But he knew there would be no answer. Not after it had worked so hard to keep them apart.

"What do you want?" he pleaded. Then realized that was the only question. What did the house, or this thing inside the house, want?

That, and what about Pris.

Pris ran faster, racing against the inevitable. But in the dark, she could not see the broken joist that had fallen across her path. She felt it, though. She felt it hook her leg. Felt the blood press against her skull as her body suddenly changed direction. Felt the ground unexpectedly slam against her chest and send her phone skittering from her hand.

It took some time for her scrambled thoughts to reorder themselves. When they did, she felt icily sick. She touched her leg with trepidation. Tender but otherwise okay. Her arms, too. She tasted blood, but not much. With effort, she got to her knees and wobblily stood. Pris was lucky, so very lucky.

Except that sound still trailed her. That was not as lucky.

Cold fear travelled through her spine. She hastily pawed the ground around her, searching for her lost phone, but nothing felt familiar. It was gone.

Then there were cobwebs on Eton's face. Or it felt so. He frantically brushed them away, but they would not be dispelled. And there was a hiss like air leaking in short staccato spurts. His muscles tensed; his spine shivered.

Something moist came to rest gently on the floor in front of him. He could not see what, and the smell that followed suggested he did not want to. It was unlike anything he had encountered before—the sickly sour stench of clothes never washed, tainted further by decay and rot. It drove him onto his heels.

The wet something dragged itself forward. He moved back.

It advanced again, and Eton remained absolutely still. He prayed whatever it was would not find him.

And now it was closer.

Pris had made mistakes. Even before they had found the house, before she had coaxed Eton inside, there was a stack of them. She saw with clarity that no matter how hard she tried to change her situation, she could not—her fear controlled her as much then as it did now. Were she able to move past it, so many of those old mistakes would never have happened. But she could not. And they did. Which left her stuck in a house of endless rooms, endless corridors, scrambling for safety that was out of earshot.

She had not noticed she was crying until she heard the scream. If it was a scream. It sounded closer to a tire being punctured. Pris almost screamed herself. She wiped her eyes with the backs of her wrists, but it did not dispel the darkness.

Instead, something peered out from that darkness. At first, Pris mistook it for a plastic dry-cleaning bag. The shape, faintly illuminated from within, floated in strangely from the opposite corridor, and Pris instinctively leaned forward.

Then it turned. Looked at her, head cocked. Pris froze.

It was enormous. Round and gelatinous, a series of holes the size of silver dollars for eyes. Each orifice expanded and contracted like a bladder. The convulsing shape must have hung suspended from the ceiling, hundreds of delicate membranous filaments stretching to the walls and floor. It made a dull cardial lub as the holes rhythmically opened and closed, a sound that was quickly drowned in Pris's uncompromising terror.

Eton could not move. The voice in his head demanded he run but his limbs would not obey. That wet dragging sound grew closer as his head spun, muddled with uncontrollable thoughts and images. Memories of failures he could not dispel. And yet something was coming. How far away was it? That inevitable collapse of everything he held dear? Eton brushed the phantom cobwebs from his face again, but the sensation remained.

Then a horrifying thought needled through the chaos:

What if they were not webs at all?

Eton choked off his building panic. Focused on his escape. He would be reunited with Pris soon. Everything would be better. Everything would work out.

He had to believe it.

Pris was mesmerized by the hovering creature. It did nothing except wait patiently, inflating and deflating and staring eyelessly at her. It was a creature of opportunity, and as it observed her Pris could not help but review everything she had lost without knowing it. Everything that had gone.

No, she had to stop. To resist. She could not let it inside her head. She could not let it win. Her only defense was suppressing her doubt and her urge to give in to the terror. Pris willed herself to be stronger than that ghostly smudge in the endless black house. To be so strong, she needed nothing and nobody. Yet she still felt herself weaken. Her legs crumple under her. Only one thought came to her mind.

"Eton," she whispered. As though that might finally summon him.

"Pris!"

Eton hollered her name as he ran. Screamed it repeatedly.

"Pris!"

He was not screaming to find her. He was not screaming for her at all. He was simply screaming, and her name was all he had left. It was a word. A series of sounds stitched together. A reflex wired so strongly in him he was not aware it was happening.

His hands hurt from the walls he collided with. His legs from the debris he crashed over. Whatever was in that house, whatever made those wet sounds, emitted that foetid odour, was chasing him. And he had to escape.

Eton ran.

The creature moved so suddenly—its long fibres contracting, its bladders deflating as it launched itself toward Pris—that it was on her before she could react. Its flesh seemed rotten, both in odour and texture.

She instinctively reached to tear it away, but her hands passed into its body, bursting it open. Ichor spilled over her, and the creature hissed like a dry laugh. Whatever it was, its remnants collapsed beside her, and Pris did not hesitate. She did not think.

Pris ran.

Lungs screaming. Each footfall echoed off the narrow hallway walls. Amplifying. And, over the din, the sound of the creature in pursuit. Charging forward. Inevitable.

Eton rounded a corner, collided with something. Pris rocketed back, landed on her spine, a shock of cold darting through her body. He was disoriented, not sure he understood what had happened. She lay on the dirty floor, numb. He saw coloured stars everywhere. She gulped down air. His eyes rolled and legs kicked. Her hands pounded yet made no sound. He tried calling her name. She did not hear him.

Then that sound again. They bolted upright. Rubbed their hands against their skull. Felt the blood leave their bodies. It was closer now. So much closer.

They shuffled backwards on their hands. Eyes wide and staring at where the other should be but was not. Despaired by the growing emptiness around them.

They leaped when the wisp crossed their arm. At first, like a hair wrapping so lightly around their wrist, it might have been imagined. Then another, grazing their face. Then another. The wisps collected like damp cobwebs between their fingers. Sticky tangling loops quickly trapping their limbs, cinching tighter the more frantically they struggled.

The dark made it worse. They kicked and screamed in pain and terror, their voices echoing through the empty hallways—an endless litany of fading screams. The threads wrapped around them constricted, slicing into their skin. Fear bled from them. And when they felt something begin to lap it up their struggling became senseless. Primal. They went beyond the edges of panic into somewhere they could not begin to process. They desperately reached out into the darkness but could not find one another. The gulf between them was already too wide.

And with a sudden yank backward, that gulf grew wider still.

§

It took years, but Pris rarely thought about the house anymore. Or, rather, she thought about it every day, but what was once a constant barrage of terrors weakened over time to an absent thought divorced from her experiences. Some days, she even forgot the house for a while. Those were the good days.

The office had been more forgiving than she had been of herself. They allowed her time away to deal with her trauma even if they did not quite understand it. Because how could they? Pris could not share what had happened, not in a way anyone would believe, because she barely believed it herself and because her trauma was her own.

She was glad for the promotion, of course, even if it was uncomfortable to take a leave so soon after receiving it. The company held it for her until she returned, but she knew she no longer deserved it. She was not the same, not anymore. She had become jumpier, more scattered, checking back over her shoulder periodically even though she never found anything. In meetings where once she would have spoken up, she now receded, no longer pushed. Though no one admitted it, she knew they all saw the change. They must have. What other reason could there be for her diminished workload? How else could she explain being passed over for the Director's position that once been so obviously hers to inherit? Her career had stagnated, and it would require a concerted effort to change things. But, day after day, she did nothing.

Eton pretended nothing had happened. He shut away the memories, refused to let them into his head. It was the only way he could cope. Never open the door. Not even a crack. Yet the denial only made things worse. He felt the house's corridors multiplying inside him, the labyrinth growing the more he tried to escape the hold it had on him. He felt lost every moment of every day. Sometimes, he found himself slouched in front of a television he did not have the willpower to turn on, staring at the multitude of thin fading scars that crisscrossed his arms, and wondered if this was all. If there was anything left for him. If he was all he would ever be: a person incapable of fending for himself.

Pris echoed in his head, urging him to get to his feet. Still, it took great effort and even more to dress. Eton only managed it by pretending to be someone else—the Eton he used to be before he entered that house. That other Eton. The trick worked long enough to get him outside, long enough that by the time he felt the weight of his resurfacing memories, he had gone too far to retreat. Only then could he find his fake smile and simulate being a person again. He still needed to check over his shoulder, just to be sure. But didn't everyone?

Pris did not know what triggered her memories of escaping the house—they were utterly random, occurring whether she was at her desk or taking the long way home at night. Sometimes, they were with her when she went to bed; other times, they waited for her when she woke. She only knew they surfaced when she least expected them, and when they did, they sent her reeling back to those dark endless hallways, scrambling to outrun what was trying to claw her back. She wondered about Eton, then felt a stab of guilt. What they had suffered through had been her fault. Hers, for leading them to the house. Hers, for suggesting they go inside. If she had not had something to prove— to him and to herself—they might have been spared.

But maybe it was Eton's fault. Eton, whose refusal to do something, anything, was the reason they had gone away in the first place. She had been so desperate for him to change that she had been willing to try anything. How could she have known about the house? Pris's flesh reacted—as though it were being pierced by a thousand thorns—so she raced to expel the thought from her mind. But it remained implanted there, in the crook of her thoughts, ready to spread once her guard was down. Remaining in a constant state of vigilance was exhausting. Still, less bad than the alternative.

If there was a single thing Eton did not know much about, it was escaping. Not from the house, not from his life. He had been stuck in an endless repetition for as long as he could remember. Like a hallway lined with room after identical room, stretching so far he could not see the end. He woke up and stared at the ceiling, willing himself to stand.

Or, failing that, simply move. Yet it took hours before he could muster the courage. Sometimes he wondered what he had done to deserve any of what had happened. Then he heard Pris's faint voice echo, and he remembered.

Eton eventually managed to escape the house, only to then realize how much worse it was outside. Trapped inside, calling for Pris over and over, he had felt powerless. A failure. But at least he'd had hope. Once the house was behind him, though, he discovered the truth: Nothing had changed. All his wants remained as unfulfilled, all his dreams even further away. Why had he ever tried? He asked himself again and again. What difference had any of it made?

Pris glanced behind her. Then looked back at their apartment. The dishes, the furniture, the drapery—everything was unchanged. It was the same place, always the same place. She took off her coat, hung it on an empty hook by the door. An old leather jacket of Eton's hung nearby. It has been there since the day they first moved in; he had not worn it in years. Pris averted her eyes. She did not want to see anything behind her. She wanted only to move forward. And yet there was nothing there, either. Just more of the same. Why did she always feel she was stuck running in circles with nowhere to stop? How was she going to break free? She vaguely remembered trying once, some long time ago. But the memory was dusty and grew dim almost as soon as it occurred to her, receding into darkness. Defeated, she warmed what remained of her previous night's dinner, sat on the couch near the window, and tried to ignore how the skin on the back of her neck prickled. Without thinking, she reached her hand over to Eton's side of the empty couch.

Eton pretended things were normal because that was what he had always done. It was the only way he knew to maneuver through life— floating on a river, shooting between rocks, avoiding turbulence as best he could. But it had not served him as well as he might have hoped; it had only punished him. He had atrophied, degenerated into a person his younger self would not have recognized. Even his clothes had refused the change—he wore the same things he had worn when he and Pris first met. His closet was a mirror of those early days, and its reflection only dimmed as time progressed. He hung his jacket on a hook near the door, careful not to touch Pris's. He did not want to smell her perfume on it—he could not spend another day walking around with that memory. Instead, he left it behind him at the door and went into the kitchen to open a chilled bottle of beer. He twisted off the cap and stumbled toward the living room to collapse onto the couch furthest from the window. He took a large swig, then wiped his mouth and glanced around at the house. There was so much that needed doing, but he wanted to do none of it. Maybe he had the energy when he and Pris first met, but that was long gone now. Drained until there was nothing left. He poured another swig down his throat, but it did not slake his thirst. Eton rubbed the back of his neck until it turned red, but he still did not have the nerve to turn around. He glided his hand slowly toward Pris's side of the empty couch.

§

Just over their shoulder, the thing hovered unseen. Holes encircled its head like a crown, tiny bladders inflated then deflated. Like some horrendous balloon carried by thermal waves, the creature's globular body floated close, its multitude of long fibrous tendrils wrapped tight around their flesh and limbs, throbbing and pulsing, drinking something not blood. Something worse.

And as it did so, the thing grew heavier, sank closer and closer to the floor. Eton's eyes fluttered, Pris's rolled back. From their lips spilled each other's name in a strained, inaudible mumble. They saw endless hallway after endless hallway before them, as though trapped in a dream, and no matter how they shouted, the words would not travel. Instead, they got lost in the house, missing every set of ears that might hear them as though they had not been spoken. As though their names were as lost as they were.

In his delirium, Eton's hand inched further across the couch toward Pris's searching fingers. Yet still they missed one another. There should not have been any distance between them, and yet the span was so vast they could not make contact. And all they knew for certain was that wherever they were, the other was not. And maybe never was.

STILL PACKED

Florence didn't want to explain to Duane that it was over. She'd fallen into bed with him easier than she would have guessed, and it felt so good and natural that she forgot completely about her husband, Sebastian. Luckily, none of her nosy coworkers had seen her slip out with the young waiter, all six muscular feet of him. She'd been drunk, but not drunk enough she didn't know better. Just drunk enough not to care. While she rode Duane, part of her floated disconnected, wondering how she could have forgotten how it felt. Wondering when was the last time Sebastian had made her feel as good. She ground herself harder against Duane and soon forgot what she'd been thinking altogether. Afterward, after he fell asleep on his stomach, glistening body highlighted by the moon, she gathered her things and took an overly fragrant taxi back to her hotel. She thought about how the door of the cage she'd been locked behind had just swung open. She thought about how now that the conference was over, she and Duane had to be over as well.

He gave her a queer look when she told him.

"Uh, yeah, sure," he said, retrieving her empty glass from the bar. "If that's what you want."

"I don't know if I do. It's just, you know. I just don't think it would work out. I'm sorry."

"It's cool."

She gave him one final kiss goodbye, from which he pulled away early, then indiscreetly wiped his mouth afterward. As though something tasted off. Florence rolled her eyes; she hadn't tasted anything.

The plane didn't land until an hour after it was supposed to, but she didn't mind. She felt buoyant, cruising high above the earth. The freedom of the preceding week had been like a dream, and she struggled to hold onto it and keep her momentary respite from ending. The rise of the familiar jagged city skyline below reminded her, though, that nothing had changed. Because nothing ever changes. And when, later, the taxi pulled up to her tiny two-story house, one of so many other tiny two-story houses on the brightly lit street, she felt the choke collar tighten around her throat.

She slipped inside quietly, praying Sebastian would already be asleep.

Then the living room light clicked on, and she withered in place.

"You were supposed to call me when you landed. I would have picked you up," Sebastian said, eyes swollen from exhaustion. In his lap, a book he'd obviously fallen asleep while reading. He looked like a pudgy balding turtle, a far cry from the sinewy, wild-haired punk he'd been when they met.

"There was a problem with the engine. They swapped the plane at Newark. I didn't want to bother you."

"Well, I'm glad you're finally home. How was your trip? Did you get up to anything exciting?"

She sensed his eager stare was a trap.

"Just the usual. Seminars and talks. Dinners with other reps. Nothing exciting."

He looked anxious, as though about to say something, but unsure if he should. Then he seemed to change his mind.

"Well, I'm glad you're home," he said as he stood, moving the earmarked book to the end table. "I'll bring your carry-on upstairs for you?"

"It's okay," she said. "I can do it."

"I don't mind."

"Please, just leave it."

His face dropped. She tried to smile to spare him hurt feelings, but it didn't feel right on her face. It felt like a mask. Like one of those suffocating French iron masks. When Sebastian reached over and touched her, she was surprised. His skin felt cool.

"Flo, what do you want?"

The question threw her.

"What do you mean?"

"I mean, can I get you something? Anything?"

Was that really his question?

She shook her head. "No, I'm okay."

"You don't seem it. You seem tired," he said.

"And you seem like you want to say something."

"No... not really," he said. Then, after a moment, "But will you tell me more about your trip tomorrow?"

I'm not telling you anything, she thought, then nodded. Sebastian looked relieved.

"Go ahead and go to bed," she suggested. He smiled and stepped toward her, arms raising for a hug. She shrank away. "I need to take a quick shower. I stink."

"I don't care."

"Well, I do. Besides, I'm still wound up. I'll join you upstairs later."

"Okay," he said, unsure, then collected his book and made a feint toward kissing her forehead before stopping himself.

She watched him climb the stairs to their room.

When the bedroom door closed, she sighed and fell into the worn couch, more exhausted than ever. He was unbearable like this. So eager and needy—it made her feel as though the walls of their over-stuffed living room had moved closer while she was away. Their popcorn ceiling, lower, like storming rain clouds. Somewhere outside a neighbour's dog growled and whined. A reminder that it was all endless, and that frustration more than anything finally drove her to her aching feet.

Even the shower felt constricted. She felt sad, washing away the last of Duane and the freedom she'd barely tasted. It was all so final. Were those his remnants spiralling down the drain in an opaque gluey wad? Could the massage of the hot jets on her back dispel the ghosts of his fingers drumming along her spine? By luck, she noticed the thumb-sized bruises he'd left on each of her hips, bruises that might take weeks to heal, which meant she had to be careful undressing in front of Sebastian. She should have paid better attention and not forgotten herself in the drunken heat of the moment.

It had been years since Sebastian left a mark on her like that. He used to have an air of danger, unpredictability. So, when had he become safe? So loving and pliable? His wildness tamed? First, he stopped playing music, then stopped listening to it, and slowly he transformed in increments while she wasn't paying attention. He no longer even fought with her, never bit at her. No matter what she tried, no matter how she prodded, he was always the one to apologize. Always deferred to what she wanted, even though what she wanted was to bounce him off the walls.

Florence waited until she heard his droning snore before entering the bedroom, but she only made it one barefooted step past the doorway. From there, she saw round Sebastian boxed by the sliver of light from the hallway and couldn't push herself further. She stepped back and quietly pulled the door shut. Across the empty hall was the extra bedroom Sebastian mistakenly believed they would one day need. Not ideal, but it would do. Her feet dangled over the edge of the cramped miniature bed, but if she curled her legs the right way, she could make herself fit. Once settled, she pulled the woven blanket over her, turning everything dark and unfamiliar.

She woke on the uncarpeted floor, sweating and facing the ceiling, a cry still ringing her ears. Had it been real or the vestige of a dream already receding into the murk of her subconscious? There was no clock nearby, but the window was so lightless and black it had to be well before dawn. She sat, rubbed her face, confused how she'd ended up in the spare room, then closed her eyes and groaned. Something in her gut shifted. She considered standing but knew it would be too much work. Instead, she pulled down the blanket from the bed above her and covered her face. It wasn't enough, though. Despite her exhaustion, she couldn't fall back asleep. She spent the rest of the night drifting between two unwelcoming states.

Morning failed to improve things; she only felt worse. Her back, bruised from the hard floor, made rising to her feet a challenge. Everything was swollen; everything was stuck. Nothing that seemed sensible in the middle of the night made sense in the light of day. It was all beginning to feel far too familiar.

Once Florence worked up the energy, she trudged down the stairs and into the bright kitchen. Sebastian stood at the sink, staring out the window into their green backyard. When he saw her, his rosy cherub face and warm round eyes lit up. It was comforting, and she utterly despised it.

"Good morning," he said, letting the sheer curtain fall. "You didn't come to bed last night?"

"I didn't want to wake you."

"I wouldn't have minded."

"No," she said. "You probably wouldn't have."

He returned to the breakfast he was preparing on the stove. Over the years, he'd discovered a love of cooking and experimentation with new dishes, but Florence couldn't help but miss the old Sebastian, the one who once called putting milk in his sugar cereal *too bougie*.

"Tell me what you want me to make you."

"I'll have whatever."

He paused, mouth pursed.

"But... what do you want?"

"I don't know. Nothing. I'm fine," she muttered. She couldn't look at him as she poured a large mug of coffee. "What were you looking at?"

"Nothing. I thought I heard an animal or something. I noticed your carry-on is still where you left it. Should I bring it upstairs for you?"

She quietly groaned. She did not want to deal with unpacking, but she couldn't bear the idea of surrendering to Sebastian.

"I'll move it before I leave."

"All right," he said softly. Then pulled out the chair beside her and sat. "Now that you've slept, there's something I need to ask."

Her mug trembled.

"What's that?"

"I think," he said, nervously. "I think we should get a dog."

"We should what?"

"A dog. We should get one. I want to get one."

"A dog?" The word, if it were a real word, made no sense.

"You go to conferences and work late, and I'm left at home by myself. It would be nice to have some company. I know you don't like animals—"

"I don't?"

"—but it doesn't have to be a big one. It can be a little dog. Like a terrier, maybe. Or a corgi."

"You want a little dog because you're lonely?"

"No, not really. No. Only sometimes. But with you gone, the house feels empty. I thought a lot about this, and I'd like to do it."

She closed her eyes. Rubbed her forehead to soothe it. Was there anything worse than an aging punk rocker walking a tiny dog?"

"I don't know, Seb. Can we talk about this later? I need to get ready for work."

"Sure," he pouted. "Later."

§

A court of narrowed eyes watched Florence slip into the office, the voyeurs whispering gleefully to one another. She ignored them and plopped behind her glass desk, careful not to make eye contact. The thought of dealing with their gossip made her queasy. Another day in prison. She sighed and wished she were anyplace else.

A sudden memory, Duane's stubble on the inside of her thigh, made her shudder. She resisted the urge to scratch at the phantom.

"Still figuring out what you want?"

She turned, found Jane standing over her. Jane, whom she hadn't seen in a week. Jane, who was a wreath of scarves masquerading as a department lead.

"Pardon?"

"The mock-ups," she said, pointing at Florence's desk. "You still haven't picked one out?"

Florence looked down at the spread of designs in front of her. They all looked equally turgid.

"Not yet. I haven't had the chance."

Jane laughed uninfectously.

"You look hungover. It's marvellous."

"I'm perfectly fine."

Jane winked. Adjusted her large-beaded seafoam bracelet.

"I know how these things are, you don't have to tell me. Marty had me fly to Washington a few months back, and a group of us broke into the hotel spa at three a.m. to use the hot tubs. Now *that* was a crazy night."

"I didn't do anything like that. It was mostly early nights."

"Oh really?" She leaned in and inhaled, then made a strange face. "Well, you certainly seem as though you got into all sorts of trouble."

She smiled knowingly. Florence refused to acknowledge whatever she was implying.

"Well, I should get back to these," Florence said, holding up one of the horrid designs.

Jane touched her finger to her lips. "I get it. What happens in Vegas or wherever you are. Mum's the word. We'll catch up at lunch. My treat. Wash up and think about where you want to go."

"Go?"

"For lunch."

"I honestly have no idea."

"You must want something. Think on it. I'll see you at noon."

But Florence had no intention of thinking on anything, nor of spending her lunch being interrogated by Jane. When five minutes to twelve approached, Florence hurriedly collected her purse and fled down the back stairwell, past the yellowed I.T. staff huddled around their unfiltered malodorous cigarettes.

As soon as she stepped through the mesh gate into the chilled outside air, she realized she couldn't stomach going back, and the admission washed her in overwhelming relief. Her trip, her encounter with Duane...these things *changed* her. There was no denying it. Everything in her life had become a snare, and she no longer wanted to feel miserable, distracted. Was that wrong? She wasn't sure, but she couldn't deny she felt her spirits buoyed and her step lighter, and soon enough, she found herself wandering through the Fashion District and then taking a left off Queen Street toward the lakeshore boardwalk. The sun rolled out from behind the clouds as she rounded the corner, and though the air was crisp, she removed her jacket so she might enjoy the feel of the breeze against her bare arms.

I'm so light, she thought. *I might just float away.*

She turned to face the sun and shut her eyes to its warmth just long enough for her cellular phone to ring. Her smile dimmed.

"It's me," Sebastian said. "I wanted you to know I saw your carry-on was still by the door, but I didn't move it."

"Thanks?" she said. "Is that why you called?"

"No, of course not," he said. "I was just trying to help you."

She could hear music playing in the background. Something soft-tempo, folksy. She gripped the phone tighter. He'd become so soft, both inside and out. She struggled for breath.

"Seb, I'm a little busy at the moment."

"Sorry, Flo. I know you said we'd talk later, but I wanted to know if you had a chance to think about it yet."

"Think about what?"

"About getting a dog."

She scowled.

"I haven't. I'm not sure it's a good idea. Having it underfoot, constantly whimpering for attention? I don't know, Seb. I might go mad."

He didn't say anything, but she heard his disappointment across the line.

When he spoke again, his voice sounded different. She wasn't immediately sure why.

"Well, anyway...something weird has just happened."

"Weird?"

"Yeah."

There was another wordless pause. She squeezed her eyes shut. Her clenched jaw trembled.

"Are you going to tell me, or should I guess?"

"I just got a phone call."

Florence opened her eyes. Stopped walking. The sun slunk behind a neighbouring cloud.

"Who from?"

"That's the thing. I don't know. But he asked for you."

"He who what?" Her stomach tightened, flipped. Something inside cried, but she stifled it.

"He said something about a hotel?"

"Seb, I—"

"I could barely hear him. The line was bad. I'm not sure I heard him right."

She felt unexpectedly shaken but did her best to hide it. So many thoughts raced through her head, so many possible lies. She put her hand on her stomach to quell the churn.

"Well, if he calls again, tell him I'll call back."

"Is that what you want?"

"Why wouldn't I?" she asked, though she already knew that was the wrong question and rushed to end the call before he could answer.

§

Florence wasn't sure where she was going but kept walking—along the boardwalk, past the rollerbladers and joggers, around young women pushing baby strollers. She felt flush, her heart beating faster, her skin growing cold and prickly, and she resented it. Nothing looked familiar. Where has she taken the wrong turn? When? At the end of the Leslie Spit, she turned left once more and headed away from the water, up along a wooded path made of flat grey stones. She passed a dark brown sign with "Lancet Park" painted in bright yellow letters. It was a small hidden lawn with a single scuffed and chipped metal playset over which children teemed. She stopped to watch them press their ruddy faces against the bars and against one another while she observed from behind the smattering of seated adults that encircled them on benches like sarsen stones.

They were animals. The way the messy children climbed and tore at one another, the volume and pitch of their screams. It was impossible to believe they were human, let alone that she had once been one herself. She scanned their round features and pudgy, shortened limbs and wondered if she'd once looked as grotesque and misshapen, wondered if a body so small and twisted was the germ for who she became.

Stranger still was how familiar the children looked . As though she'd seen each shrivelled, dried-apple face before. There was a miniature Jane, all dark hair and darker eyes, shoving her way through the throng. And there were her parents, a pair of runted cherubs, locked hand-in-hand an arm's reach from the fray. Ducking in and out of the group was Marty, constantly chattering, constantly ignored, his thin ginger hair flattened against his head. It took only a moment to find her little Sebastian, the wild-haired boy patiently awaiting his turn at the slide. And, of course, there was a Duane, because there was always a Duane, dead centre of everything, drawing all attention without effort. The similarities were uncanny—all roaming free and unhindered around the playset—but more uncanny was how many doubles she saw. There was only one face she couldn't find in the ruddy preschool swarm, but it had to be there, somewhere. Maybe if—

"What do you want?"

The voice startled her. On the bench sat a woman, probably in her early thirties, dressed in an oversized grey wool coat with a green patterned scarf wrapped around her jaundiced head. Stray hairs peeked out haphazardly, giving the woman a harried appearance. She glared at Florence, wrinkled her nose.

"I was just—" Florence offered. "I guess I was just watching the kids." The woman's eyes narrowed. Florence realized how her behaviour must look. "I was just walking by," she added hurriedly. "The children distracted me. I... well, I didn't mean to make anyone uncomfortable. I should go."

The woman's shoulders loosened; her sunken eyes softened.

"No, you don't have to. It's all right. I was surprised because I've never seen you here before, and strangers don't usually stop in. Sit, please. Is everything okay?"

Florence cautiously accepted the woman's invitation, worried that if she didn't, the woman might call the police. She glanced at the other parents on the other benches, sitting alone or in stoic pairs. Everyone watched the children dashing through the playset and across the fine sand.

She rubbed her wrists.

"So," Florence offered out of politeness. "Which is yours?"

The woman pointed lazily toward the children climbing over one another precariously for their chance to travel down the slide. Florence's miniature parents looked close to tumbling off the edge of the platform.

"Is that safe?" Florence asked.

The woman shrugged. None of the other observers appeared concerned either, even as the writhing mass of little bodies grew larger. If anything, they seemed bored by it. The woman in the green scarf most of all.

"And where are your kids?" the woman asked. Florence mumbled, still distracted by the danger and the lack of concern about it.

"I haven't any."

The woman nodded.

"That explains a lot. Just let them be. Once you have kids, you'll realize you can't make their choices for them. They have to learn from their own mistakes."

Florence, more baffled than ever, turned to the woman.

"I don't think it works like that."

The woman smirked. Made a noise through her fleshy nose. The children grew rowdier, tore at one another. Florence saw teeth. Heard whimpers and barks. Howls.

She stood. "Please. Aren't you going to do something?" Then raised her voice to the disaffected observers. "Aren't any of you going to do something?"

As she spoke, the first of the children crashed through the fleshy jam and shot feet-first down the slide. Behind her, the tiny Duane followed, orderly accompanied by the flush-faced little Sebastian. Or was it the other way around? She couldn't remember.

"See? Nothing to worry about. I knew they'd eventually figure out how to untangle themselves. You'll see one day," the woman continued.

Florence swallowed. Shook her head.

"I'm not having kids."

"No?"

"I—my husband Seb and I decided a long time ago."

She shrugged. "I guess he would know."

Yes, he would, Florence thought but kept it to herself. She didn't like how her head felt. As though simultaneously stretched in multiple directions. The children's running in circles only amplified her unsureness.

"Sorry. Which one did you say was yours again?" Florence asked.

"Oh, does it matter? Whichever you want. Pick one."

Florence shook her head. Put her purse under her arm.

"I should get back to my walk."

"Just pick one. Any of them. Please. Just pick."

Florence's legs grew more unsteady by the moment.

"I can't. I have... I have to go," she said.

"Don't." The woman tried to sound disappointed. It didn't fit her right. "You still haven't told me what's wrong. I wanted a chance to help."

"Nothing's wrong," Florence said, waving her away. "I'm fine."

The woman stood, too. She came up to Florence's collar but was still tall enough to take her shoulders.

"I don't believe you," the woman said. "But it's okay. I'm here every day. I can wait."

"Thank you?"

The woman smiled. Florence turned and strode away, knowing that if she looked back, the woman would still be there, watching her go, the same smile plastered to her round, jaundiced face.

§

I t wasn't until the park was long out of sight that Florence felt like herself again. Even so, she struggled to process what had happened. Each detail she recalled of Lancet Park, of the little yellowed woman there, pushed out the one before it, leaving her with only a few scattered and fractured moments.

More amazing was how little time had passed since she left them all. Time appeared to be dilating—each moment stretching too long. In contrast to the week before, she supposed, which sped by far too fast. It was only on the return to her dreary gated life that she could process and reckon with what she'd done. Each memory of Duane lingered—his glazed eyes when he wanted her to be more interesting; his knobby scarred hands as they took hold of her, flipped her over. Her own sense of release. She reached down and rested her hand on her quivering stomach. Duane was quiet, taciturn, open. Nothing like the staid, confining Sebastian. And she realized she didn't care if what was germinating inside her was a seed of guilt. At least guilt reminded her she could still feel. And what she felt was a desperate longing for the sense of unencumbrance she'd left at that hotel.

Returning to her tiny cellblock home mid-day was strange. The sun shone uninterrupted on the cramped cul-de-sac like an enormous searchlight. Were it not for the choked barking of some neighbour's dog she might have suspected she was trapped in a frozen moment of time. She disliked the unnerving solitude, yet when she hurried into the house, almost tumbling over her still-packed carry-on, she couldn't deny a sense of relief when she called Sebastian's name and he didn't answer. That would make what she did next much simpler, albeit no less crazy.

But *was* it crazy? To call Duane? It had to be, especially considering how they'd left things. Yet she also felt more certain. Calling Duane was imperative. She couldn't explain why, but he haunted her, and she knew no other way to exorcise him from her thoughts.

She raised the phone's receiver. As soon as it made contact, an extended high-pitched wail like an animal crying overwhelmed her ear. Florence immediately dropped the receiver back on its hook. After a few moments nursing her shattered nerves, she braced herself and tried again. Tentatively, she placed the receiver back against her head and found the screech had gone. Only the empty dial tone greeted her. She exhaled. Crossed wires, she assumed.

Only at that moment did it occur to her she didn't have Duane's number. She'd never needed it. He'd simply been working at the bar each night and only too happy to take her home when his shift was done. Did his apartment even have a phone? If so, she couldn't remember it among the dirty dishes and laundry, but she'd been understandably distracted. A quiver rippled through her as she recalled those nights together. And then, the obvious answer struck her. The bar. Of course, she'd find him at the bar. Of course.

Dialling the hotel's number was easy. Knowing what she'd say when he answered was not. But she'd figure it out. What choice did she have? Florence's hand gently came to a rest on her stomach. The feel of it was soothing. She closed her eyes and imagined she was miles away from anything.

"Welcome to the Sheehan Hotel. This is the Front Desk. How may I assist you?"

Florence's panicked eyes flicked open. Suddenly, she doubted her plan.

"I was a guest there last week," she improvised. "My husband said you called looking for me?"

"Happy to help. What name was it under?"

Florence told him, and when that didn't work, she told him the room she'd been staying in. She listened to the clatter of his keyboard for long enough to worry it wasn't they who had reached out to her. If they hadn't, did that mean—

"Here we go. Yes, it looks like we called you earlier today. Our staff wanted to make sure you enjoyed your stay with us."

"Yes?"

"That's great to hear. And did you have any suggestions about how we could make future stays better?"

"No, I don't think so."

"Wonderful. I'll put your comments down in your file for our team. They'll be happy to hear them. Is there anything else I can do for you?"

She hesitated. "You could—I mean, would you connect me to the bar? I need—"

"Certainly! One moment, please." There was a click and, after a moment, another, followed by a tinny ring that drilled a beat too long. She rubbed her palm hard against her slacks.

"Adobe. Can I help you?"

"I hope," she said. "I'm looking to speak with Duane."

"Duane?"

She panicked. Did Duane have a last name? Did she know it?

"He's one of your waiters?"

There were muffled sounds on the other end of the phone line. Voices she couldn't make out. Calling had been a tremendous mistake. It felt as though doors were closing around her. Florence started to hang up when the voice returned.

"I'm sorry, he's not in yet."

It was the middle of the day. Why would she think he'd be working? Through the receiver she heard a sound like popping. Or laughing.

"Should I try back later?"

"If you want," the voice said curtly. She started to ask when, but before she reached the end of her question, he'd already hung up.

Florence sat down. That was not how the call was supposed to go. In a way, she'd been lucky. She'd avoided the humiliation of realizing she was making a mistake while on the phone with Duane. In her cold newfound clarity, she now saw he was not the key to her freedom. He was barely a person. Just a stack of muscles and a youthful cock costumed in overpracticed disaffection. She'd have to open that door some other way.

Without realizing it, in her distraction, she'd been scratching the inside of her thigh, and when she lifted her hand, she was horrified to find her fingers were tacky with some viscous fluid. Its pungent odour, sour, like something unwashed. It was stomach churning, and she immediately fled to the bathroom, first to scrub her hands, then to strip off her clothes and hurry into the shower. She set the temperature as hot as she could stand, then scoured herself raw. It took longer than expected to clean off the residue, but eventually, thankfully, the gluiness gave way.

Her clothes, though, were unsalvageable. The stain had spread from her slacks to her blouse, fusing them in a vile wad. Just the feel of them made her gag, and she struggled to cram the congealing mass into the white wastebasket before her stomach revolted. Drawing closed the liner was not enough; she had to toss the bundle out the window.

Her head followed after it. Bumps appeared instantly along her naked, wet skin as she immersed herself in the cold air and breathed deep, clearing the sour nausea that lingered in her throat. As her illness faded, her ears rang with a muted sound, almost like an infant's babble.

The telephone's ring interrupted her. She pulled in from the window and caught a glimpse of her face in the bathroom mirror, twisted with equal parts shock, eagerness, and dread. She knew who it was on the line. Who it had to be. It was carved into the grooves that cornered her eyes. Florence dashed naked from the bathroom to the phone in the bedroom, lifting the receiver despite her mounting reluctance.

As she placed the speaker against her ear, she wished she had clothes on. The call would be so much easier with clothes on.

"Hello?"

"Florence?"

She was dizzy. She dropped onto the edge of the bed.

"Yes, it is."

"What are you doing home?"

"Sebastian?"

"I called your office. They said you disappeared. Are you okay?"

Was she? She didn't even know. Everything was so confusing. Everything felt smaller, more claustrophobic.

"I don't think so. I might have caught something. Where are you?"

"Coming home. I'll be a few minutes. Do you want me to bring you anything?"

"I don't know, I just need to—"

More muffled noises interrupted her. Was his hand over the receiver? She waited, and when Sebastian finally returned, he was breathless.

"Listen. I have to go. See you soon."

Then a click. No time for "I love you" or anything else Florence expected. Just a click. She set the receiver back in its cradle.

Then dashed back to the bathroom to be sick.

§

Florence dressed slowly, her balance growing more affected. Thinking became difficult, thoughts colliding and entangling. She felt Sebastian out there, somewhere, making his way home. Her mouth was dry, her hands clammy. He was closing in on her.

What did he want?

What did *she* want? She didn't know. Not really. After everything that had happened, she'd avoided thinking about it. But that was no longer an option. It didn't matter how ill she felt or how dreadful. It could no longer be avoided.

What did she want? She asked, over and over.

A voice, barely audible, growled.

To leave, it said. *To open the door and leave.*

But she couldn't. Could she?

And suddenly Florence realized nothing was stopping her.

Her packed carry-on was already waiting by the front door, zipper hanging open like a smile.

§

She staggered out into the afternoon with a plan. She'd tell Sebastian she'd been sent last minute to an urgent out-of-town pitch meeting, then assure him it would only be for a few days, and she'd call him when she landed. It didn't matter if he believed her; she'd already be long gone and out of reach. Thoughts of both Duane and Sebastian swam through her head, co-mingling with one another, pulling down on each of her arms as though she were a parade balloon. She felt as light as one, too—disconnected from solid ground—and had to take care not to look at her feet as she fled to avoid losing balance as the world teetered out of control. She made it almost halfway to the gate before her stomach convulsed painfully around its knot, but now that the decision was made, she was determined to ignore it, to escape. She had to before the sickening feeling pinned her permanently in place.

But she made it only to the end of the drive.

Because that's when she heard it. Pitched so high and loud it was like an awl driven into her head. Some instinct stopped her legs from working. What was that cry? It reoccurred, a wailing summons from behind the house.

Beckoning her.

Ignore it. She had to ignore it. Sebastian was almost home.

She had to be gone before he arrived.

Instead, Florence set her carry-on down. Started her walk back toward the house. The ground ahead looked askew, as though it had been painted on a wide cotton sheet, and that sheet was slowly being twisted. She stumbled once but caught herself. The air thickened and coagulated around her. She pushed through even as it filled in the void behind her, preventing retreat.

A carefully placed hand against the side of the house supported her as she moved forward. The wail was getting louder, and as she urged herself closer, she felt the sound in the back of her trembling chest, exacerbating the sourness she tasted. It was only when turning the corner into the backyard that the world suddenly righted, and the resistance she felt evaporated.

But by then, it was too late. She was stuck.

Stuck and staring.

It sat in the middle of the yard, small and pink and whimpering. The grass around it was brown—which made no sense as the lawn had been fine when Florence looked through the kitchen window earlier. It raised its head when it saw her, large wet eyes with irises so wide everything appeared black. It reminded her of a baby bird, if that made any sense, because those eyes bulged and blinked under veiny lids. However, it was nothing like a bird at all. It appeared to be on the edge of life, and when it coughed while scratching its face, Florence jerked away. How had it gotten into the backyard? Where had it come from?

"Oh my God!" The words were in Sebastian's voice. In her momentary confusion, she thought it had said them. Then she turned and found her husband standing across the yard, damp and short of breath. He was holding her carry-on, the size of a small child, with a claim ticket tied around the handle. "What did you do? Flo, what did you do?"

She could barely speak. Her mouth was so dry.

"What did I do?"

"You got us a dog?"

A what? She stared at it, unsure. It stared back.

"Is this why you left early? To surprise me?"

"To surprise you?" she repeated mechanically.

Sebastian carefully approached, his excitement noticeably welling. He knelt and pressed its wrinkled pink skin. It made a sound like laughter. Her hand found her clenched stomach.

"I can't believe you kept this a surprise! Without a doubt, this is the most amazing thing you've ever done for me. For us!"

"Sebastian, I—"

He picked it up. It squirmed in his arms as he pressed it close to his chest. He closed his eyes. Florence smelled the clear jelly being smeared on his stained shirt.

"This is the start of something," he said. "A beginning. I can *feel* the change taking place."

"I don't understand."

Sebastian smiled as he slipped his finger into its mouth and it began suckling, reaching up for him. His eyes lit up.

"This is going to be so great, Flo. You'll see. Taking care of it is going to help a lot. Both of us, I mean. Everything is different now. We're different now."

"I am?"

He turned and looked at her, cradling its squirming pink flesh. Sebastian's eyes were wet, and his smile had faltered, but only slightly. "This is a good thing, Flo. Trust me. This—all of this—is going to take work, but we'll figure things out together."

The pain in her abdomen grew sharper. Like a knife sliding in. She flinched when her hand found the turgid flesh; her palm came away sticky with that murky, sour fluid. There was a cry from Sebastian's arms. He started rocking it.

"Are you okay?" he asked her. "You're really pale."

"I need—" she started, her legs wobbling. "I need to sit."

Sebastian replied but her ears stopped working. The world spun upside down then like a popped balloon spiraled away.

Florence saw sky. Smelled the pungent odor of what coated her. Sebastian's one hand held hers, his other acted as a cradle. She heard it simpering as he helped her to her feet.

"You need to see a doctor."

"No," she said, clutching her stomach. Waves of nauseating cramps rolled in. "Not yet."

"Flo...."

He drew his hand away so she could find a wobbling balance.

It watched her from his arms. The noise it made was not describable.

"I need," she murmured, "I need to go. Just for a while. I have..." She swallowed. "There's a meeting...."

"What are you talking about?"

She heard a distant ringing from inside the house. She looked up at the window.

"I just have to go."

"Don't."

"I have to."

But when she turned, she couldn't see her carry-on. The only thing nearby was her husband. Her husband and what was in his arms.

"Just look," he said. His eyes watering, his mouth little more than a slit. "It loves being here with us already."

She stared at it. It stared at her. Glassy-eyed. Blubbering.

In the distance, the telephone continued to ring behind some locked door.

Marie and I sit on the wooden bench overlooking the Hopewell Rocks. In front of us, a hundred feet below, the zombies walk on broken, rocky ground. Clad in their sunhats and plastic sunglasses, carrying cameras around their necks, and tripping over open-toed sandals, they gibber and gabber amongst themselves in a language I don't understand. Or, more accurately, a language I don't *want* to understand. It's the language of mindlessness. I detest it so.

Marie begged me for weeks to take her to the Rocks. It's a natural wonder, she said. The tide comes in every six hours and thirteen minutes and covers everything. All the rock formations, all the little arches and passages. It's supposed to be amazing. Amazing, I repeat, curious if she'll hear the slight scoff in my voice, detect how much I loathe the idea. There is only one reason I might want to go to such a needlessly crowded place, and I'm not sure if I'm ready to face it. If she senses my mood, she feigns obliviousness. She pleads with me again to take her. Tries to convince me it can only help her after her loss. Eventually, the crying gets to be too much, and I agree.

But I regret it as soon as I pick her up. She's dressed in a pair of shorts that do nothing to flatter her pale, lumpy body. Her hair is parted down the middle and tied to the side in pigtails, as though she believes somehow appropriating the trappings of a child will make her young again. All it does is reveal the greying roots of her dyed black hair. Her blouse... I cannot even begin to explain her blouse. This is going to be great! she assures me as soon as she's seated in the car, and I nod and try not to look at her. Instead, I look at the sun-bleached road ahead of us. It's going to take an hour to drive from Moncton to the Bay of Fundy. An hour where I have to listen to her awkwardly try and fill the air with words because she cannot bear silence for anything longer than a minute. I, on the other hand, want nothing more than for the world to keep quiet and keep out.

The hour trip lengthens to over two in traffic, and when we arrive the sun is already bearing down as though it has focused all its attention on the vast asphalt parking lot. We pass through the admission gate and, after having our hands stamped, onto the park grounds. Immediately, I see the entire area is lousy with people moving in a daze—children eating dripping ice cream or soggy hot dogs, adults wiping balding brows and adjusting colourful shorts that are already tucked under rolls of fat. I can smell these people. I can smell their sweat and their stink in the humid air. It's suffocating, and I want to retch. My face must betray me; Marie asks me if I'm okay. Of course, I say. Why wouldn't I be? Why wouldn't I be okay in this pig pen of heaving bodies and grunting animals? Why wouldn't I enjoy spending every waking moment in the proximity of people who barely deserve to live, who can barely see more than a few minutes into the future? Why wouldn't I enjoy it? It's like I'm walking through an abattoir, and none of the fattened sows know what's to come. Instead, they keep moving forward in their piggy queues, one by one meeting their end. This is what the line of people descending into the dried cove looks like to me. Animals on the way to slaughter. Who wouldn't be okay surrounded by that, Marie? Only I don't say any of that. I want to with all my being, but instead, I say I'm fine, dear. Just a little tired is all. Speaking the words only makes me sicker.

The water remains receded throughout the day, keeping a safe distance from the Hopewell Rocks, yet Marie wants to sit and watch the entire six-hour span, as though she worries about what will happen if we are not there to witness the tide rush in. Nothing will happen, I want to tell her. The waters will still rise. There is nothing we do that helps or hinders inevitability. That is why it is inevitable. There is nothing we can do to stem the tides that come. All we can do is wait and watch and hope that things will be different. But the tides of the future never bring anything to shore we haven't already seen. Nothing washes in but rot. No matter where you sit, you can smell its clamminess in the air.

The sun has moved over us, and still, the rocky bottom of the cove and the tall, weirdly sculpted mushroom rocks are dry. Some tourists still will not climb back up the metal-grated steps, eager to spend as much of the dying light wandering along the ocean's floor. A few walk out as far as they can, sinking to their knees in the silt, yet none seem to wonder what might be buried beneath the sand. The teenager who acts as the lifeguard maintains his practiced, affected look of disinterest, hair covering the left half of his brow, watching the daughters and mothers walking past. He ignores everyone until the laughter of those in the silt grows too loud, the giggles of sand fleas nibbling their flesh unmistakable. He yells at them to get to the stairs. Warns them of how quickly the tide will rush in, the immediate undertow that has sucked even the heaviest of men out into the Atlantic, but even he doesn't seem to believe it. Nevertheless, the pigs climb out one at a time, still laughing. I look around to see if anyone else notices the blood that trickles down their legs.

The sun has moved so close to the horizon that the blue sky has shifted to orange. Many tourists have left, and those few that straggle seemed tired to the point of incoherence. They stagger around the edge of the Hopewell Rocks, eating the vestiges of the fried food they smuggled in earlier or lying on benches while children sit on the ground in front of them. The tide is imminent, but only Marie and I remain alert. Only Marie and I watch for what we know is coming.

When it arrives, it does so swiftly. Where once rocks covered the ground, a moment later there is only water. And it rises. Water fills the basin, foot after foot, deeper and deeper. The tide rushes in from the ocean. It's the highest tide in the world over. It beckons people from everywhere to witness its power. The inevitable tide is coming in.

Marie has kicked off her black sandals, the simple act shaving inches from her height. She has both arms wrapped around one of mine and stares out at the steadily rising water. She's like an anchor pulling me down. Do you see anything yet? she asks me, and I shake my head, afraid of what might come out if I open my mouth. How much longer do you think we'll have to wait? Not long, I assure her, though I don't know. How would I? I've refused to come to this spot all my life, this spot on the edge of a great darkness. That shadowy water continues to lap, the teenage lifeguard finally concerned less with the girls who walk by to stare at his athletic body, and more with checking the gates and fences to make sure the passages to the bottom are locked. The last thing anyone wants is for one to be open accidentally. The last thing anyone but me wants, that is.

The sun is almost set, and the visitors to the Hopewell Rocks have completely gone. It's a park full only with ghosts, the area surrounding the risen tide. Mushroom rocks look like small islands, floating in the ink just off the shore. The young lifeguard has gone, hurrying as the darkness crept in as fast as the water rose. Before he leaves, he shoots the two of us a look that I can't quite make out under his flopping denim hat, but one which I'm certain is fear. He wants to come over to us, wants to warn us that the park has closed and that we should leave. But he doesn't. I like to think it's my expression that keeps him away. My expression, and my glare. I suppose I'll never know which.

Marie is lying on the bench by now, her elbow planted on the wooden slats, her wrist bent to support the weight of her head. She hasn't worn her shoes for hours, and even in the long shadows, I can see sand and pebbles stuck to her soles. She looks up at me. It's almost time, she whispers, not out of secrecy—because no one is there to hear her—but of glee. It's almost time. It is, I tell her, and try as I might I can't muster up even a false smile. I'm too nervous. The thought of what's to come jitters inside of me, shakes my bones and flesh, leaves me quivering. If Marie notices, she doesn't mention it, but I'm already prepared with a lie about the chill of day's end. I know it's not true and that even Marie is smart enough to know how warm it still is, but nevertheless, I know she wants nothing more than to believe every word I say. It's not one of her most becoming qualities.

The tide rushes in after six hours and thirteen minutes, and though I'm not wearing a watch, I know exactly when the Bay is at its fullest. I know this not by the light or the dark oily colour the water has turned. I know this not because I can see the tide lapping against the nearly submerged mushroom rocks. I know this because, from the rippling ocean water, I can see the first of the heads emerge.

Flesh so pale it is translucent, the bone beneath yellow and cracked. Marie is sitting up, her chin resting on her folded hands. I dare a moment to look at her wide-open face and wonder if the remaining light that surrounds us is coming from her beaming. The smile I make is unexpected. Genuine. They're here! she squeals, and my smile falters. I can't believe they're here! I nod matter-of-factly.

There are two more heads rising from the water when I look back at the full basin, the first already sprouting an odd number of limbs attached to a decayed body. The thing staggers towards us, the only two living souls for miles around, though how it can see us with its head cocked so far back is a mystery. I can smell it from where we sit. It smells like tomorrow. More of the dead emerge from the water, refugees from the dark ocean, each one a promise of what's to come. They're us, I think. The rich, the poor, the strong, the weak. They are our heroes and our villains. They are our loved ones and most hated enemies. They are me, they are Marie, they are the skinny lifeguard in his idiotic hat. They are our destiny and have come to us from the future, from beyond the passage, with a message. It's one no one but us will ever hear. It is why Marie and I are there, though each for a different reason—her to finally help her understand the death of her mother, me so I can finally put to rest the haunting terrors of my childhood. Neither of us speaks about why, but we both know the truth. The dead walk to tell us what's to come, their broken mouths moving without sound. The only noise they make is the rap of bone on gravel. It only intensifies as they get closer.

For the first time, I see a thin line of fear crack Marie's reverie. There are nearly fifty corpses shambling toward us, swaying as they try to keep rotted limbs moving. If they lose momentum, I wonder if they'll fall over. If they do, I doubt they'd ever right themselves. Between where we sit and the increasing mass is the metal gate the young lifeguard chained shut. More and more of the waterlogged dead are crowding it, pushing themselves against it. I can hear the metal screaming from the stress, but its holding for now. Fingerless arms reach through the bars, their soundless, hungry screams echoing through my psyche. Marie is no longer sitting. She's standing. Pacing. Looking at me, waiting for me to speak. Purposely, I say nothing. I'll let her say what I know she's been thinking.

There's something wrong, she says. This isn't—

It isn't what?

This isn't what I thought. This, these people. They aren't *right*....

I snigger. How is it possible to be so naive?

They are exactly who they are supposed to be, I tell her with enough sternness I hope it's the last she has to say on the subject. I don't know why I continue to make the same mistakes. By now, I'd have thought

I would have started listening. But that's the trouble with talking to your past self. Nothing, no matter how hard you try, can be stopped. Especially not the inevitable.

The dead flesh is packed so tight against the iron gates that it's only a matter of time. It's clear from the way the metal buckles, the hinges scream. Those of the dead that first emerged are the first punished, as their putrefying corpses are pressed by the throng of emerging dead against the fence that pens them in. I can see upturned faces buckling against the metal bars, hear softened bones pop out of place as their lifeless bodies are pushed through the narrow gaps. Marie turns and buries her face in my chest while gripping my shirt tight in her hands. I can't help but watch, mesmerised.

Hands grab the gate and start shaking back and forth, harder and harder. So many hands, pulling and pushing. The accelerating sound rings like a church bell across the lonely Hopewell grounds. I can't take it anymore, Marie pleads, her face slick with so many tears. It was a mistake. I didn't know. I never wanted to know. She's heaving as she begs me, but I pull myself free from her terrified grip and stand up. It doesn't matter, I tell her. It's too late.

I start walking toward the locked fence.

I can't hear Marie's sobs any longer, not over the ruckus the dead are making. I wonder if she's left, taken the keys, and driven off into the night, leaving me without any means of transportation. Then I wonder if, instead, she's watching me, waiting to see what I'll do without her there. I worry about both these things long enough to realize I don't really care. Let her watch. Let her watch as I lift the latches of the fence the dead are unable to work on their own. Let me unleash the waves that come from that dark Atlantic Ocean onto the tourist attraction of the Hopewell Rocks. Let man's future roll in to greet him, let man's future become his present. Make him his own past. Who we will be will soon replace who we are and who we might once have been.

The dead don't look at me as they stumble into the unchained night. And I smile. In six hours and thirteen minutes, the water will recede as quickly as it came, back out to the dark, dead ocean. It will leave nothing behind but wet and desolate rocks the colour of sunbleached bone.

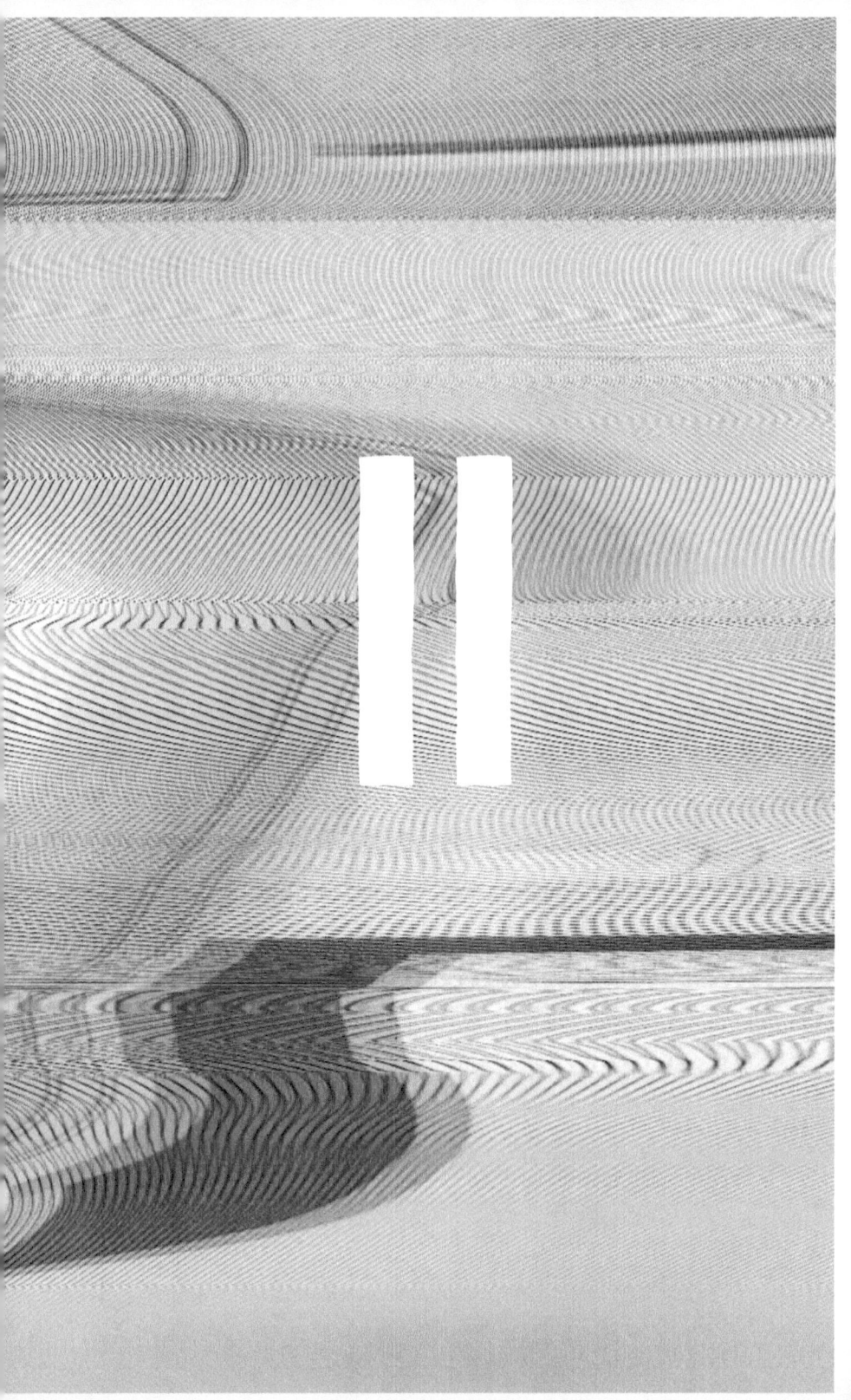

THAT HOUSE

Maybe it starts like this.

There is a house in Newton, down Oak Lane, that's been vacant almost twenty years. Its slanted wooden shutters have been nailed closed and its cracked windows boarded over, so it looks like a face without eyes or a mouth. Marta and I drove past it only once, and only by accident, on our way to the hospital while Marta sobbed and bled and told me it felt like a shard of jagged glass was sliding into her stomach. What I'm trying to say is it is a bad house, and I have bad memories of it. It is not a place you ever want to live near. Maybe that's why there are so many FOR SALE signs on the leached brown lawns of its neighbours. And why those worn plywood signs are just as old.

But what is a house, really? Just some lengths of wood, some pipes, some wires. A few stacks of shingles and bricks. A house is just a thing, put together like you'd put together a story, one layer building upon the one before it. It's another thing someone has made, and it has no thoughts or feelings. It has no intention. A house is not malignant or evil. It just is. I knew there was no reason to avoid the one on Oak Lane, that any story I'd made up about it was my own imagination projected on it like a film on a blank screen.

And yet...

Meeting Marta for the first time was like a story, too. She and I took the same English literature class at Winston College—or, wait, maybe it was a philosophy class. I guess it doesn't matter. What matters is I noticed her and her heavy square glasses on her square freckled face. I never said anything to her, and I doubt she knew who I was, but on my way back to school a few weeks into the semester, I recognized her on the side of the road, leaning over a stalled seafoam blue car. I pulled over and offered my help. I knew nothing about cars, especially seafoam blue cars, but I lifted the hood and pretended with all I had. She shot me a look over those glasses that warned me I'd better stop talking, so I hastily offered her a ride back to campus instead.

We married just out of school, and with her burgeoning pharmaceutical career and my focus on my first novel, there wasn't time for us to do much else. Even our honeymoon was just a short trip to a cabin rented for the weekend. Things were tight, but we managed to squirrel enough away that when Marta's inevitable promotion moved us across the country, with her bump in salary and some luck, our realtor was able to find us a house in Newton we could afford. Neither of us knew about Oak Lane then—how could we?—and no one mentioned it or its history until we'd already signed away the last of our savings. Not that it would have made a difference to me. Marta, though, wasn't happy, especially not in her condition, but I knew enough to let her process her feelings on her own.

As new homeowners, we suffered through all the indignities you'd expect. There were windows that needed replacing, locks that needed changing. Marta spent the month racing to plant a new garden before she couldn't move any longer, while I spent it fixing leaking gutters and patching the fences between chapters. Having invested all our money into our first home, we had to make do with the appliances abandoned by the previous owners. That meant living longer than we wanted with a humming refrigerator missing its crisper and a washing machine that lost my sports socks on a regular basis. We both laughed about the socks for a while, but after the hospital, neither of us found much funny. I did try to repair the washer, but it was too old, and the part I needed was impossible to get. Without that missing piece, the thing was never going to work right.

Yes, I know you're waiting to hear about that house. I'll get there.

It took me a year to realize my latest novel was a failure. I'd been writing about a woman who'd gained her independence after a long life of being held back and denied everything she'd ever wanted. A woman who found her freedom when the world around her was overrun by weird underground cannibals. She fought to escape them, too, meeting people on her way to a fabled city on the coast. She carried with her only one thing, the most important thing: a green thatch blanket, a memento from her childhood, and the oasis it represented. I was initially pleased with the story and my progress through it, but as I wrote, the number of obstacles in front of her grew larger, and I couldn't see how she'd overcome them. It wasn't a sensation I enjoyed. My strength as a writer has always been seeing how things should end, but the novel was a cloudy block of ice I couldn't peek or chisel through. Maybe it was the constant wailing interruption of our neighbors' squiggly children, or maybe it was the hole in my life they circled with pink sidewalk chalk. Regardless, I found myself overwhelmed by all the pages I hadn't written, so I did the only thing I could. I quit. No more novel. It was an overwhelming relief, but I was too ashamed to tell Marta. So, I continued my routine when she was at home and continued doing nothing at all when she wasn't. Those hours of nothingness grew longer and more frequent as Marta spent less and less time with me.

To fill the time, I took walks. Not far at first—to the end of the street and back, maybe around the block—but far enough that I was able to break the spirals of depression that licked at my thoughts after being inside for so long. As I passed the discarded neon skipping ropes and half-inflated utility balls scattered on verdant lawns, I found myself uncomfortably checking the doorway of each house I saw. But if there were any cherub faces there studying me, thankfully, they remained out of sight.

I did encounter at least one elderly man on the sidewalk, his legs bowed and his cane as thin and crooked as his arms. Slightly hunched, he looked out at me from under his overgrown eyebrows as though he wanted nothing to do with me, and yet, as I got nearer, he was the first to speak.

He asked if I was the writer who'd moved into the area, which surprised me until he mentioned our realtor. Then he welcomed us to the neighbourhood and suggested if I was looking for some ideas, I could do worse than visit Oak Lane.

Even without knowing the name of the street, I immediately knew where he was sending me. I knew because I'd never forgotten it. How could I? It was where I lost Marta the first time. But part of me asked: why not? Why not see the house again? Despite my painful memories, maybe the old man was right, and I'd find something inspiring there.

Suddenly, my moribund novel no longer felt so moribund. When I left the old man, I was convinced that house might be the solution to my problems.

But that's how it is with nightmares. They fool you because you don't see them coming. They start as hopeful dreams, and only later do things shift—maybe imperceptibly, maybe all at once—and what was once bright and reassuring becomes terrifying and confused.

This is how I ended up on the stoop of that boarded-up house, trying to peer through the paint-chipped door's tiny inset window. If it had been one of my novels, something might have spooked me when I got there. Maybe an old, melted face flickering out of view behind an errant curtain. Or maybe the frail knotted hand of a crone grabbing my shoulder, making me leap. But neither of these things happened, and the only ghost around was of what Marta and I had lost—which wasn't so much frightening as sad. In fact, nothing about the dilapidated house lived up to my memory. Like I said, it was just a house, just a thing, and even worse, it was just boring. Perturbed I'd traveled so far to be disappointed, I turned around and headed back home.

And as far as I know, nothing tried to stop me.

I didn't give the house much thought after that. Marta continued traveling to and from work while I stayed cooped up underneath an unusually heavy blanket of snow. She seemed less enamoured with the commute by the day, often returning long after the sun had set and the temperature had dipped below freezing. On those days, even my love wasn't enough to forestall the anger and irritation about her job, about our transit system, about the weather. About everything except what she was really mad about. I quickly learned to give her any space she needed, and by the time she was calm, I'd find her in our spare-bedroom-turned-office, sitting on her swivel chair and staring at the wall we had to paint over again shortly after moving in. If you squinted and the overhead lamp was positioned right, you could still see the faint outline of a large old tree and the animals of the Hundred Acre Wood that had once been stenciled around its foot.

Marta was perpetually unhappy, and nothing I did helped. She was caught in a debilitating wallow of pain, multiplied by the poor timing of her promotion and how it separated her from everyone she loved. I tried to reassure her the two weren't related, but she couldn't hear me through her heartache. Or didn't want to. She was trapped in her own nightmare, and I couldn't reach her. At least there was money enough to keep our heads above water as I silently struggled between novels, but that money came at a price. It ground her down. Some nights, she wouldn't sleep, tossing fitfully in bed, her legs twitching madly. I snored through the worst of it, but I knew she'd suffered when she appeared in the morning like an apparition, copper hair plastered and purple eyes swollen, clutching herself as though afraid she'd disappear. I'd brew her a coffee, which seemed to bring color back to her face and then settle the tangle of bird's nests in her hair.

It soon grew hard for me to track Marta's comings and goings. She seemed both to be home all the time and yet never there. The winter daylight was simultaneously overbright and non-existent as I lived in some between-state, in the gutter between pages, my thoughts constantly muddled. When Marta asked how the novel was going, I told her I felt all right. When she asked about my health, I told her my characters seemed stuck. Did she find my words reassuring? Did I? I was adrift and utterly alone, unsupported, staring out the window for long periods of time at the mounting snow, Marta behind me drowning so noisily I no longer heard her.

"Marta, we can't not talk about it anymore," I said, my heart pounding as I gathered my nerve, fought off everything I worried might go wrong. "Something is missing."

I felt a great weight lift from me as I admitted the truth. Maybe now that the wound had been exposed to air, it would finally begin to heal.

I looked up from my wringing fingers for Marta's reaction, but she was no longer there beside me.

§

Maybe it actually starts here, with a knock on the front door. It shook me from my stupor, and as I descended our narrow staircase, I wondered if it was Marta coming home. The reflection from the snow cast some sort of unearthly light through the frosted windows, and I felt as though I still wasn't awake. I reached the door and then hesitated before opening it, not knowing what to expect. I was surprised to find my hand squeezed tight around my fountain pen, a reflexive need to anchor myself to something familiar. It took a moment to relax the muscles. Still, my trembling hand continued to throb.

A shadow moved outside, fractured by the geometrical glass. I heard something like an infant's grating squeal as I yanked the door open to catch my tormentor. But there was no one there. Just a small box with a courier's mark on brown paper and a set of boot prints that trailed off through the snow.

I carried the delivery inside. The first thing I looked for was a name or return address, but there was neither. I rested the box on the table and inspected it from multiple angles. It was wrapped in butcher's paper, tied down with tape and string. As the package warmed, I detected a damp odor coming from it. I want to say I was desperate to see what was inside, but I wasn't. I wanted nothing to do with it. If Marta had been there, she would have saved me by snatching it away and tossing it into the snow.

But she wasn't there. And I didn't have the strength to do it alone.

It took me three hours to screw up the courage to open the box—three hours where I paced and gave the package sideways glances. Three hours where I climbed up and down the stairs, trying to be both as far away from it and as close to it as possible. Three hours where I stared through the living room window at the winter snow turning to dark slush. Three hours where I thought I could resist it, and then realized with a prickling cold that I couldn't. Three hours for me to give in.

It seems like such a long time, but really, it's no time at all.

What I found under that wrinkled butcher's paper was a shoe box from a store named Fleischmann's that I barely remembered from my childhood. The box was made of old cardboard colored brown and white, its bottom half a series of cross-hatched diamonds. Each corner had been worn to the white, and the box was topped with a buckled lid whose split edges had been taped back together. I looked around the room, but there was no one to stop me, so I held my breath and lifted the lid. It was easy and mundane, and I don't know why either of those things surprised me.

Inside the box were photos. Maybe hundreds; I didn't count because I was too confused. I'd never seen any of them before, and yet they were all of Marta, all taken at different ages—one from near when I met her, standing on a blurry lawn at dusk, holding a sparkler in one hand as she bent sideways, laughing. She was all pale, crooked legs back then, dressed in a yellow-striped shirt and denim shorts.

And another from when she was a child, too many teeth in her tiny square head, blowing a series of bubbles from a neon green wand. It was strange, but stranger still in each of these photos, like the backdrop of summer, was the looming brick edifice of that house on Oak Lane. That cursed house.

I took the photos out one at a time and examined them. The older snapshots already had a sickly yellow patina, but I couldn't reconcile their age—and the age of Marta in them—with the Marta I knew. She had never been to the house on Oak Lane. She hadn't even seen it before that terrible night. There was no way she could have; we both grew up across the country from Newton. And yet here Marta was in photo after photo, living a life I never knew, an impossible life, in and around that house that was the start of everything wrong that had since happened to us.

I couldn't believe any of it, even though I held the proof in my hands.

But how? How was I holding proof?

That's when I first wondered if I was trapped in a story. Just like maybe you're trapped reading one now.

As I dug in the box further, I uncovered fewer snapshots of the young Marta and more of the one I recognized, the beautiful one I'd married. But there was something wrong with her, something I felt before I noticed. I lifted each photo closer to my face, tried to convince myself that maybe I was wrong, that this was never my Marta. But I knew it was. I'd bought her one of the mohair sweaters she wore over her swelling body and the opal pendant that pointed down at what I wanted so badly and yet didn't want to admit. This latter Marta was fully pregnant, and she appeared again, lying disheveled in a pale green hospital bed, hugging a swaddled bundle close to her chest and looking both exhausted and serene.

I shook equally with despair and rage. That never happened. I knew that didn't happen.

But I hated myself for not being sure.

I'm sure now. I mean, I think I am. Wouldn't I remember something that would so irreparably change me?

Ask yourself, knowing what I knew then, what would you have done? Would you have gone right to that house? Trudged through the snow immediately to see with your own eyes if Marta was there?

Pounded on the door and demanded answers? You might have, but I didn't. Not because I was afraid she might not be in the house. And not because I was afraid she might. Those seem like good reasons, but like every story, they're lies, and I swore this time I'd write down the truth no matter how hard. I didn't go because there was something else I needed to do. I don't expect it to make sense to anyone; it doesn't even make sense to me. But I was as sure about it then as I was about anything.

Instead of going anywhere, I left the photos behind and went upstairs. I sat behind my desk, and from the left-hand drawer of my old chestnut desk, I took a pad of yellowed foolscap I'd found with our realtor's name on it and my black fountain pen. Then, without putting thought into it, I wrote down the first words that occurred to me. I'm not sure where they came from.

I wrote: *There is a house in Newton, down Oak Lane, that's been vacant almost twenty years. Its slanted wooden shutters have been nailed closed and its cracked windows boarded over, so it looks like a face without eyes or a mouth. Marta and I drove past it only once, and only by accident, on our way to the hospital while Marta sobbed and bled and told me it felt like a shard of jagged glass was sliding into her stomach. What I'm trying to say is it is a bad house, and I have bad memories of it. It is not a place you ever want to live near. Maybe that's why there are so many FOR SALE signs on the leached brown lawns of its neighbours. And why those worn plywood signs are just as old.*

§

And I kept writing, a novel slowly bleeding into existence as I found each new word. I wrote about another Marta, an imaginary Marta, trapped inside her box. A Marta now with a secret. Her keepsake green thatch blanket rolled and tied in a bundle. She could no longer remember when the blanket had been given to her, or by whom, and sometimes she forgot its importance. Like a collapsing balloon it withered from her thoughts the longer she lived inside the box. Even when the box grew colder, she didn't warm herself with the blanket. Even when the hard floor of the box hurt her aging bones, she forgot to lie on the blanket. And as the box grew smaller the blanket faded, dissolving until it was only a shadow of a blanket, and the walls of the box became so narrow she could touch each side with bent arms. And soon it was as though there was no box at all. Just a shivering, forgetting Marta, crushed to death by walls she no longer saw.

I looked up and realized I was dusted with snow. The window was cracked, letting in gusts of frigid air, and I hadn't felt it. Nor had I noticed how scarred and cramped my hands had become, or how I was seated in my own filth. How long had I been writing? Why didn't I know?

I felt myself spiraling toward something, my pen dragging circles over the page, yet it didn't find the center because the center wasn't there. It had gone with everything else I held important, moved a few blocks away to that house, that vacant house on Oak Lane.

And that's when the ice cracked, and I knew what was going to happen. How it was all going to end.

But I don't know what happened next. My memories are difficult to piece together. I know I tried to stand, but after so long seated behind my desk my legs were too weak and I collapsed. I don't remember hitting the ground, but I remember falling and I remember it taking too long, the world turning upside down. And when it righted itself, I was walking through crunching snow drifts.

How long had I been out there? Maybe hours, maybe days. I was unnerved to find I wasn't wearing a coat and even more unnerved I couldn't feel my pale fingers. I struggled to remember what happened but couldn't. The only two things I knew for certain were that I was headed toward Oak Lane and that something was wrong. Something was definitely wrong.

No, it would be okay. I would be okay. I'd get to that house and find Marta and we'd get our lives back despite everything we'd suffered. I wanted to believe it because it was an easy story to believe; it gave me everything I wanted. But the truth is stories are nothing like life. Life doesn't follow plans, and it doesn't make sense. Life just is—a mess of tangled plot threads that will never ever be tied off and that have no greater meaning.

Drifts of hardened snow masked where that house was. At least, where Oak Lane should have been. Because when I finally arrived, I didn't see anything but the liminal grey light diffusing through winter's haze.

A shadow flew past, startling me. It was squat and wobbling, darting around the frozen drifts, and its squeal was as unsettling as it was familiar. Red and white, scarf trailing behind, it moved with purpose, dragging along a small sled. And on the sled was another bundle, though I couldn't tell what was wrapped in those blankets.

Even when it sat up and looked my way just before disappearing behind a slanted fence.

Then, from out of a snow squall, that house—the center of all my worst thoughts, my darkest nightmares. I stamped my feet as much from worry as to keep them from freezing. It was that house, but it was different. As though it had imperceptibly contorted itself to evade detection, but I could see through its disguise, and maybe it could see through mine. I don't know. Maybe it already knew what I was only just suspecting: that we'd both been abandoned.

It was possible. Ask yourself: What does an abandoned house even look like? You must have an idea. You've seen them in movies and read about them in books. Don't they all look the same? Cobwebs hanging from the ceiling, bare furniture either broken or close to it? There might be graffiti on the walls or empty beer bottles scattered on the floor because abandoned houses are not abandoned for long. People who need them always find them. And, if they don't, the animals do. Not every house is loved, but every house is lived in.

Was the house on Oak Lane any different?

Somehow I got inside. I was just there, the door behind me open, the otherworldly glow of reflected daylight spilling into the torn-up foyer. Or maybe it was just my eyes, blinded with spots as they struggled to adjust to the interior dim. Breath slipped from my panting lungs as I waited for my vision to clear, dreading what I was going to find in the dark.

Because there was something wrong with that house. I had to stop denying the truth.

That dread was there the first time, when Marta and I drove past. When I was filled with panic, unable to think. Steering recklessly around corners, lost in the maze of Newton's suburban streets. Marta wailing in the seat beside me, her joggers soaked with blood. Me coming apart. I still don't know how we ended up on Oak Lane but Marta's wince as she looked out at the house told me we were in danger. I spun the car around and put my foot to the floor, hoping to escape. But maybe I was too late. Maybe it already had her. If that was true, I never saw it. I was too busy to understand what was happening. Too busy to save her, to ... to save a lot of things, I guess. Too busy and too late.

The darkness of that house overwhelmed the reflected light from the snow. I could see the shadows snaking out, spreading into the world outside, wanting to consume everything I loved. I had to remind myself that it wasn't real, that it was just my story-addled brain looking for an explanation. The house was only a thing, and a leaching, suffocating darkness was too strange for the real world. A world already filled with horrors too painful to think about, mundane horrors we try hard to forget. Those horrors are much worse than the ones you find in stories.

Even in my stories.

Even in the one I'm writing for you now.

I wanted Marta to be in that house. I wanted her to be there because if she wasn't I didn't know where else to look. Where else could she be? I wanted it to be true so badly I didn't think about the broken furniture or spray-painted walls. I didn't think about the smell, like an old stable, or the way the air felt slippery and off-putting. Just let her be there, I prayed. Just this once, let me get what I needed.

I saw something dart across the landing to the second floor. I tried to call out to Marta, but my voice sputtered. My tongue, an inert piece of flesh that refused to do more than a cluck.

That's when the squeal returned, the squeal that had been haunting me. Was someone dragging something heavy across the ceiling? It was so hard to be sure in the dark, in the cold. Ahead of me, the staircase. At the top, only shadows. I couldn't see anything else. Then that squeal again. Was it a cry for help? Was it human at all?

I should have waited. Instead, I ran toward it.

I don't remember what I was thinking as I rushed up the stairs. So much of this story is missing, my friable memory crumbling away, leaving behind large holes I can't refill. I remember Marta, remember the way she looked at me. At the beginning. And the way she wouldn't at the end. I remember how much of our future we had planned but not what happened to those plans, nor what we did instead. I remember each novel I started but I can't remember anymore how they ended. The past is a pale ghost lingering behind me, amorphous if I don't think about it, transient if I do. All I can say for sure is I climbed those stairs because that piercing squeal is one of the few things I can't forget, even now, because of what it brought me.

What I couldn't see until I reached the second floor was the tear in the roof, as though something wrong had fallen in or something worse had pushed itself out. Dim winter light broke through in a solid beam—the light, and the frigid cold—illuminating the path in front of me in a way. What I saw there didn't make sense. It still doesn't. Frozen to the warped floorboards were hundreds of small dark shapes I thought at first were rats. Instead, the frozen mounds were something much weirder and even more unsettling.

Socks.

Dark sports socks.

They looked as though they'd been dropped, wet, through the hole above me, freezing in place where they landed. I looked up and saw nothing but snowflakes slowly descending through the pillar of light.

There were socks everywhere. You can't make that up. No one would believe you.

I shouldn't have to write out what happened next. I should be able to stop here because there's not much left to tell. But I can't do that, can I? Because even the truth is a story, and if there's one thing a story needs it's an ending, if only so there's a sense of closure, a suggestion that bad things happen for reasons, that nothing occurs by random chance. That's the beauty of a story, especially a horror story. There are reasons, and no one has to suffer life without one. No one has to arbitrarily lose what they love most. That's why I write them—the stories, the novels—because for that time between covers everything in the world makes sense. And if you can't have that then what's the point?

The squeal again. It echoed toward me from the dark, and I forgot the socks and dashed down the hall, screaming Marta's name. I didn't know what I'd find, and what I found at the very end was an unlocked room. I burst through the door, still calling my wife's name, only to have it die on my lips.

There was a shape I couldn't make out. A shape that wasn't moving. A shape as cold as the room around it. I inched closer, the squeal's phantom ringing in my ears, and saw it was seated on a rickety bare bedframe, facing the boarded-over window. I remember my back hugging the wall as I cautiously navigated around the bed, exponential dread bottoming me out until I could barely keep myself together, trying for a better look at what was seated there.

Do you really need me to keep going? Wouldn't it be a better story if I just stopped here and let you guess what happened next even though you probably already know? It's a great place for an ending: rejected man searching for meaning finds his salvation or doom. Lost someone looking for escape finds something more. I've written variations of it so many times I'm practically an expert. I've repeatedly lived it. Yet you'd think I'd know better. That I'd see it coming and wouldn't make the same mistakes. But I don't know better because nobody does. Nobody makes the choice. How can anyone be expected to foresee the dangers awaiting them?

Especially in the dark?

Especially in that house?

What was I supposed to do? Turn around and go back to my old life?

Is that really an answer?

Is that really an ending?

No, it's not. It's failure. And no one wants to read about failure any more than they want to be a failure. I know you don't, and I don't want you to. So, there was no choice at all. I walked around that bed because I had to. Because that was all that was left.

And what did I find there, cradled in the dark? I found you. And I'd been waiting for you for so long. I can't ever remember how long. It's like a cloud in my brain: fuzzy and vague. Like this story, I guess. And, believe me, this is a story just like any other. It's mostly made up. Do you think Newton is a real place? Newton. New-Ton. New town. I wonder if I'm even trying.

I stared at you, cradled in the dark, and asked if it was too late to go back. To choose a different plot, a different ending. But life isn't really a story, no matter what I told you, and that's why stories are better than life. Their mysteries can be always be rewritten. No decisions can't be undecided.

I remember you squealed again, and it sounded less like screaming and more like you wanting to be held. So, I reached out for you. As I did, I heard a sound on the stairs at the other end of the hall. Of something climbing slowly toward us.

Maybe it ends like this, with me finding my answer. With you finding the truth. One happy family, the crack mended, the missing pieces reinserted. It would be nice: the perfect ending to a perfect story. So maybe it does end like this, just this once.

Or maybe it doesn't.

THE NEEDLE SONG

We all sang the Needle song on the way to Kearney. Or most of us did.

Our whole class gathered that cool Saturday in May around the school bus parked inside the Zellers lot. Everyone was there, along with our dotting parents, for the annual Outdoor Education trip to which Mr. Parsons took each year's graduating eighth-graders. This was our year, and me, Eric, and Steig knew it would be something to remember.

I didn't expect Ned would join us. He never participated in class trips. Eric, Steig, and I assumed he preferred staying home with his mom. There was no particular reason why we didn't get along with him; sometimes kids just don't gel. The only time he crossed my mind that year was when Steig came up with calling him *Needle*, which led to the best song we'd ever written. It was so funny I breathlessly recounted the story for my dad that night when he got home. But instead of laughing he turned serious and made me promise not to make fun of Ned anymore. And asked me to look out for him instead. Maybe find something in common with him. My dad insisted it was important, but I wasn't sold. It sounded like a lesson, and wasn't looking to learn anything I didn't have to.

Everyone else's parents were milling around the parking lot to see their sons off. I only had my dad there, and only because it was his weekend with me, he was giving up. He said he and my mom had made arrangements to have me spend more time with him in the summer to make up for it, but I had a feeling my mom just wanted a way to extend her vacation guiltlessly. She had fought him for partial custody as a punishment. She knew being separated from me would be upsetting for him. She probably never considered what it would do to me.

And yet I was going away without him. It made me nervous, and I suspect it did the same to poor, frail Ned. He trembled as he waited behind the crowd of crying parents. Steig spotted him immediately. "We're only going for four days," he said incredulously. "We'll be back before anyone knows we've left."

That didn't seem likely. My dad was already looking lost in the chaos. Confused, even. Even more so when Ned slid through the gauntlet of parents toward him. I saw my dad take a step back when Ned arrived, then the two of them spoke. It was a strange sight amid the departure harriedness; my two worlds—my private and my public—were colliding.

"You jealous?" Eric asked, pushing his elbow into my ribs. I jerked away.

"Screw off," I said. "Needle's just lost without his mommy to tell him what to do." Then I tried to shove Eric. I was the only one who moved.

Mr. Parsons emerged from the idling bus and summoned us to board. Amid the rushed final kisses and goodbyes between the parents and my classmates I noticed Ned had already gone and my dad was now waiting for me a few steps from the bus's lowered platform. His eyes were full of tears.

"I'm going to miss you while you're gone, kid. Please be safe."

"I will Dad. What was Needle saying to you?"

"Please don't call him that. And promise me you'll look out for him. His mom says he doesn't have anybody else."

"You know his mom?"

"I know everybody's mom. I'm a dad," he said. "Now, promise me."

I rolled my eyes.

"I promise."

With that he wiped his eyes and gave me the longest, tightest hug I'd ever had. Then he handed me my overnight bag and I stepped aboard the bus. I was trepidatious at first, but by the time I reached my seat I felt excited. My first adventure away from home. Outside the window my dad stood among the parents waving, the joy on his face replaced by something else. Something that concerned me. Before I had a chance to question it the bus jerked to life and we were slowing pulling out of the Zellers lot and onto the busy street, heading toward the highway and adventure.

Four hours and one repeated song later we stepped off the school bus into a burning orange afternoon. Mr. Parsons had barely finished counting us before the driver swooped the doors closed and the bus pulled away, stranding us in the middle of nowhere. I watched tail-lights fade out and felt a knot in my stomach fade in. Before I could think about it too long Mr. Parsons hurriedly grouped us together, then marched us to the cabin.

I wasn't surprised to find it was made of logs, not as much as I was by the bunk beds. There was more than enough room for all of us in that small space, two boys to a bunk, and we ran when we saw them. Eric, Steig, and I clustered together in furthest corner of the small room, the rest of the class radiating outward from us. All except Ned. He took a bunk at the front of the room instead. No one else wanted it, so he had both the top and bottom bunk to himself. Yet he still he chose to be on the bottom. It made him harder to see and easier to exclude.

I don't know what prompted me—maybe it was the memory of my hurt dad's face as we drove away, reminding me of my promise; maybe I was stricken by an uncharacteristic sympathy; or, maybe I was already experiencing the nascent bonding the trip promised us—but I felt I had to do something about Ned's withdrawing before it was too late. If I could convince him to join us, I was sure he'd be accepted. We weren't so terrible, after all. At least, I never thought we were.

As Ned unpacked his clothes I sat on his bunk beside him. Immediately he stopped unfolding and hung his head like a dog who'd done something wrong. He would not look at me.

"You should bunk closer," I said. When he didn't respond I fumbled for more words. "There's plenty of room. How can we talk to you when you're way over here?"

"I better not," he said into his chest.

"But you're alone."

He half-shrugged.

I didn't know what to do. I couldn't convince him to move, and Mr. Parsons would never force him. But then, surprisingly, Ned looked up at me; he stared me in the eyes as though he'd finally screwed up the courage to speak, and I thought maybe he was about to give in. And I got excited. But that excitement curdled when I heard Steig's voice over my shoulder.

"Hey, Needle! Know any good songs?"

Everybody laughed. I took a step away.

I'm sorry, I mouthed as I retreated to my bunk while, around me, the air filled with singing.

§

The next morning Mr. Parsons took us hiking through the surrounding forest. We dragged our feet over fallen trees and across narrow streams along some invisible path only he seemed to know. All of us were nervous, and Eric made it worse when he suggested we were lost. But just as I started to believe him, Mr. Parsons turned and said, "Just past those rocks will be a pond," and my confidence in him was renewed. For a little while.

It was only after the sky had been growing cloudier that he stopped, checked his watch, then looked up. "Not much further now," he said to me, but only because I was closest to him and he had to say it to someone. "We'll get there in time." I asked him where that was but he just smiled. I noticed tiny thistleheads caught in his dark beard.

When we crested a small hill a short time later, Mr. Parsons brought us to a stop. Ahead lay a field that had to have been almost a kilometer wide, and as my classmates and I panted heavily, glad for the break, Mr. Parsons looked anything but relieved.

"This shouldn't be here," he mumbled, before taking off his hat to scratch his head. "Not a field." He stared at the clearing as he thought, but I looked up at the darkening clouds. Already the forest had turned gloomy, and that gloom was affecting the others. They were getting restless. Even Eric, who never seemed to be afraid of anything, was anxious. A rumble from above told me what was imminent. It took a moment longer for Mr. Parsons to realize it too.

"Boys, we need to cross this field quickly. Does everyone have their partner? Good. Stay calm and let's hustle."

We strode single file through the long grass, Mr. Parsons in the lead. We had been chatty before, making jokes as we trudged between trees and through underbrush, but in the open we were silent. Mr.

Parsons's mood had unsettled us. When I felt a tug on my sleeve, I looked behind me and found Ned. His face was carved into anticipatory fear. He wanted to say something, but I instinctively knew I didn't want to know what.

A flash of lightning. Its suddenness startled us, but it was the subsequent thunderous crack that made us scream. Mr. Parsons glanced briefly at the sky, then turned and yelled, "Faster, boys!"

Rain erupted immediately. Thick drops plummeted from the sky, drenching us. We sprinted through the whipping tall grass, Mr. Parsons and his long adult legs leading us across the field.

He stopped unexpectedly ahead, and when I caught up to him, I found out why. Across the impossible width of the field, I saw stretched a long wire link fence, and it prevented us from reaching the point a few hundred metres away where the forest resumed. Mr. Parsons stood motionless in the pouring rain, trying to comprehend what was happening. The sky had turned fully night under the thick storm clouds, interrupted only by bright flashes and deafening thunder. I thought for a moment the world was falling apart. And I wasn't alone.

"What are we going to do?" Eric screamed at Mr. Parsons. Mr. Parsons looked at him. Then, at us. His eyes worried me. They were either glassy or wet with rain. Then he roused from his stupor and became himself.

"We have to find a way to the other side of this fence. Everyone look!" He started running his hands along the wire links while the rest of us exchanged drowned glances. "Now!" he shouted, and we snapped into action, scanning for an opening. All of us except Ned. Ned remained a few feet removed in the grass, crouching as though to make his body as small as possible. The rain continued to pour down my back and into my shoes and I thought about my promise and how little time there was.

"Goddamn it!" I cursed. Behind the sheets of rain Mr. Parsons called to us. I saw Steig running, but I couldn't leave Ned alone.

"You have to get up!" I said, and yanked Ned to his feet.

He didn't resist. He simply looked at me full of trust. If only either of us knew how that trust would go on to haunt me.

When we reached Mr. Parsons, he was on his knees, scooping mud out of a large puddle that crossed from one side of the fence to the other.

"Something big dug its way under," he shouted over his shoulder. "I think I've widened the hole enough for us to crawl through. Once you're across head for the trees and wait for us there. Everybody got it?"

He sent the biggest kid, Eric, over first to help pull us out on the other side. Then we lined up and were fed, one at a time, into the hole beneath the metal wire. I watched Steig shimmy his way through then leap up and slap Eric's hand in triumph. As I got closer to the fence, I noticed Ned lagging further behind. I could have smacked him. Instead, begrudgingly, I shoved him forward, ahead of me in line. I needed to be sure he made it over. I'd promised my dad. Ned resisted, though, terrified, but there was no time for hysterics.

So I shoved him again. Shoved him until he was pressed against the fence. Ned hesitated, looked back pleadingly at Mr. Parsons, but Mr. Parsons merely put his hand on Ned's shoulder and said: "You'll be fine. Quickly, now."

Ned nodded, swallowed, and crawled under the fence.

I suppose we should have expected it in hindsight. But none of us, not even Mr. Parsons, really understood the danger. I watched Ned as he worked his way under the wire. Saw the wire catch on the belt loop of his pants. Saw Ned reach back to free himself. Saw Mr. Parsons step forward to help. All these moments are caught in my memory like photographs by the lightning flash. It was so bright I heard nothing. I just found myself sitting on the ground, legs cold and numb, without knowing why. Ned was still under the fence, now face down in the puddle. And above him, Mr. Parsons was bloodlessly white, unable to speak. Eric and Steig gawked in terror on the other side of the fence. Then I saw them grab Ned's arms and yank him across. When he was clear they got their shoulders under him and carried him to the wooded spot where the rest of our class waited.

Mr. Parsons was shaken. I was, too, my body uncontrollable. I don't remember going under the fence right after, but I must have because then I was on the other side and running. When I reached the forest, I nearly fell over, unable to catch my breath. Mr. Parsons appeared immediately behind me, his hat lost, his hair plastered to his head. Too frantic to notice the cut along the width of his hand that bled down the front of his khakis.

"Is Ned awake?"

Eric, kneeling beside the unmoving boy, shook his head.

Mr. Parsons immediately started CPR. I'd only seen it before in the movies or on television where it was exciting. In real life it wasn't exciting. It was violent. Yet I stared. We all did. Watching Mr. Parsons huffing numbers as he counted compressions. But Ned didn't move once while Mr. Parsons pushed down on his chest. He didn't even move to wipe the drop of water slipping down his face. I wanted to wipe it away but was too afraid to touch him.

Eventually Mr. Parsons slowed, exhausted, and then stopped altogether. He sat, legs folded under him and watched nothing. His face, indescribably bereft and empty. And all I could think about was my dad, and how disappointed in me he was going to be. I was already so disappointed in myself.

We shivered and waited quietly for Mr. Parsons to come back to us. Ned meanwhile only grew more pale. It took Steig to muster up enough courage to break the silence.

"What are you going to tell Needle's mom?" he asked.

I'll never forget the way Mr. Parsons looked at him.

§

And things were worse when we got home. All of us, Mr. Parsons included, were traumatized by what we'd gone through in Kearney. Especially me, though I could never tell anyone why. The district school board allowed us a few days off and hired a grief counsellor to help, but we were back in class faster than anyone would have liked—a dazed horde of twelve-year old zombies going through the motions, listening to Mr. Parsons teach but retaining nothing.

I'm not sure Mr. Parsons remembered the lessons either. His face sagged so much it seemed detached, and his voice was drained of all verve. Ned's accident had transformed him into a dead-eyed creature, just as it had the rest of us. I kept hoping he'd snap out of it, though. We needed someone to guide us forward. And I needed... well, I needed someone to talk to about what had happened in Kearney. I knew neither Steig nor Eric would understand, and I couldn't talk to my dad. I couldn't even look him in the eye anymore. And who knew where my mom was. Mr. Parsons was all I had, and I couldn't reach him.

After Ned was struck it took us hours to find our way back to the cabin. The rain didn't help, so heavy it blinded us to anything further than a few feet ahead. The leaves above rattled furiously as though they were being beat with stones, which made it difficult to hear one another. Not that any of us were in the mood to talk. Mr. Parsons tried his compass repeatedly, muttering each time it didn't take us where we wanted to go. He was probably overwhelmed with everything that was happening, but it was worrying all the same. We'd implicitly trusted him to lead us, and seeing he had no better idea what to do than we did made things worse. Eric did his best to take over, though, and despite his own fear motivate us to keep going.

We took turns carrying Ned on the stretcher we'd jerry-rigged us-ing a couple of fallen branches and our sweatshirts. I insisted on taking the lead when it was my turn, facing away from him as we marched through the forest muck. I couldn't stand to see how still he was. How lifeless. Steig had laid something over his face to protect him from the rain, but it slid off at some point when no one was paying attention.

I don't know how we found the cabin. We were lost in the rain one minute, miserable, scared, numb from shock. And the next we were standing in front of it, as though it had risen under cover of the storm. Or maybe it had somehow been following us the entire time. It didn't matter which; as soon as I saw it, I had to hide my tears.

As bad as it was coming home to my upset dad who wouldn't stop hugging me, seeing Ned's mom was worse. The sight of her weeping made me in turns both ashamed and distraught. I was so confused in those early days, so unsure, that I just wanted to be left alone, but no one would let me. Even Mr. Parsons betrayed me, saying it would be a good idea for our class to go to Ned's funeral for closure. I didn't know how to talk him out of it, and when I realized not only Eric but even Steig agreed I knew it was pointless to try. The following Saturday morning I let my dad dress me in a suit I'd already outgrown and drive us to the cemetery. It was the second-last place in the world I wanted to be. At least he didn't make us stand near Ned's understandably bro-ken mom. Even he had enough sense to avoid that.

There was one moment, before Ned was lowered into the ground, she turned and tried to say something to me and my dad, but her sticky voice kept catching in her throat and she lost her nerve. My dad waited until Ned was buried before he, sniffling, still not himself, walked me over to offer my condolences. Her face was wet and swollen and re-minded me of Ned's as he stared at me in the rain just before I pushed him forward. I wanted to say something, but I didn't have any words. It didn't matter, though. She silenced me by taking my chin in her hand as my mom sometimes did and I really didn't like it—it felt unnatural. My dad refused to look her in the eye and she him. Instead, she focused all her attention on me, but I could tell by her face she was a million miles away. And wherever she was, she wanted to be farther.

We all assumed it would all be okay once we reached the cabin. As though everything would reset once we were safely indoors. Maybe Ned would be all right, revived by the comfort of familiarity. It didn't work like that, though. Mr. Parsons had us set Ned down on his bunk, then told us to get a fire going. He had an old rotary phone in his hand, the receiver against his chest, and was pulling the cord with him into the coat closet. When he closed the door, we looked at one another, puzzled, then at the colourless Ned. Steig silently urged me to put my ear to the door and tell us what Mr. Parsons was saying but I refused. I didn't want to know. It didn't feel right.

Mr. Parsons wasn't in there for long anyway. And when he emerged, he looked as though he'd aged another ten years. He set the phone down where he found it and took a seat on the edge of Ned's bunk. We watched him delicately lift Ned's small damp hand and hold it. None of us spoke. We knew. Outside, the rain thrashed the windows harder. We never did build that fire.

After the funeral I shut down. I half-expected my dad to finally explain everything but he didn't bother. I guess he was too afraid. I wasn't the only kid in our class who couldn't talk about Ned afterward, of course—we were all stewing in our own strange concoctions of trauma, shock, and guilt—but I was the only one who became disruptive and violent. Eric, to his credit, tried to reason with me even after Steig started distancing himself. But I didn't want to be reasoned with. I didn't want to be calmed. Something inside me had decided it wanted out, and the only way to quell it was to destroy everything. First Eric left me and then school didn't want me, and when there was nothing else remaining, I turned on myself.

I started fights and hung out with the burnouts loitering all day behind the school. Twelve years old is just old enough to get into trouble if your mind is set on it. My dad tried to sit me down after the police found me with half a bottle of his stolen whiskey under my arm, but I had nothing to say. Nor did I have anything to tell the psychologist my mom sent me to—her one stab at helping before throwing up her arms and admitting defeat. "This is your fault," she screamed at my dad. "You both ruin everything!" Imagine their surprise when they discovered I'd heard them. They pretended they were sorry, but I didn't believe it. And even if I did it was too late. I already knew why they split, and I didn't care. Not about that. Not about them. There was nothing inside me anymore that could. It had escaped, leaving behind a crushing vacuum that I spent the following decades trying to fill any way I could. Drinks, drugs, stealing, and whatever else there was just to make me feel.

The irony was, the more I felt, the more I wished I didn't. The number I wanted to be. That's what got me admitted to Ranch Hill, got me my own private counsellor who says she wants to help me save my life. I don't think there's much worth saving, but she's adamant we try and who am I to argue? I'm so sick of feeling empty that I'll try anything. Writing down this story is the first step, she says, even though I know she won't believe any of it. But she doesn't care. And she doesn't care that I've never told another soul about what happened to me. She says that's more reason to write it down. And she definitely doesn't care that I'm embarrassed about what she'll think. She says there's nothing to be embarrassed about. That we all have our own truths, and no two people will ever share the same one. That's what makes admitting ours so important: it shows people who we really are. And when I tell her I'm afraid of failing she tells me no one ever fails if they're still trying.

So here's me trying.

I've been writing nearly forever and still I'm dancing around what really happened in Kearney. It's kind of funny: I've gone through the pain of withdrawal and the struggles of staying clean and yet telling this story is the hardest thing I've ever had to do.

We found out quickly that we'd have to spend the night in the cabin with Ned's body. There were no ambulances that far north, and the closest town was too busy dealing with all the accidents caused by the storm. No one considered Ned an emergency. He was dead, and it was not a suspicious death. Someone would be sent in the morning. Until the school bus arrived, we were stuck.

Eric was the one who suggested relocating Ned. If he was going to have to stay in Kearney, he didn't want to share the room with a dead person. Especially one he knew. No one else did, either. The question was where to put the body. Outside was obviously out of the question, so the compromise was moving him to the coat closet. If we couldn't see him, maybe it would be enough for us to get some sleep. Mr. Parsons and Eric did the work while the rest of us averted our eyes. We heard only the closet door close. I hated the sound; it reminded me of how I'd failed.

Unsurprisingly, we were all spooked when Mr. Parsons turned out the light. All our energy and exhaustion and the pent-up anxieties went into overdrive. Whispers moved from bunk to bunk as we tried to work out what we witnessed and what was to come. Someone somewhere in the dark began to quietly cry. We couldn't tell who it was, and no one needed to ask. We understood.

As the night progressed one by one the whispers fell away as the other boys gave into sleep. I tried, too, but each time I closed my eyes I saw Ned's empty plastic face wet with rain and I jerked awake. Eventually I lost track of where or when I was. I might have already been at home with my dad or still sitting in the rain in the middle of nowhere. There was no difference in the starless night. The only sound that tethered me to reality was the miniature engine of a gently puttering snore. I suspected I might be the last person awake in the entire world.

And then I heard Ned's voice.

"Come here. I need to ask you something."

And I froze.

I don't know what a normal person would have done. It's so hard to be sure until you're in it. Sitting there in the black, I neither screamed nor ran out the door as though I were on fire. I didn't wake everyone in the cabin and beg them to confirm I wasn't crazy. I didn't shriek in terror or stammer in fear. I didn't really do much at all. Maybe I was stuck in some midnight daze. Maybe my brain was working so hard to parse the horrible events of the afternoon that there was no room to process anything else. All I know is I whispered, "Okay," and flung my blankets aside.

No one else moved. No one else woke. When I reached the closet door, I went to open it then stopped myself. Instead, I sat in front of the closed door and pulled my legs up under me. Through the thin wood I heard him quietly shifting.

"What do you want?" I whispered.

"I can't see anything. Why is it so cold?"

I hesitated. There was no point in lying but I couldn't bring myself to tell the complete truth.

"When you crawled under the fence it got struck by lightning."

"Really? That's kind of cool. I bet everybody was scared."

"Yeah," I said. "Can I go back to bed now?"

"There's something I need to ask. It might sound weird, though."

I waited but Ned didn't say anything for the longest time. Long enough that I started to wonder if I was dreaming. When he spoke again his voice was quieter. More careful.

"So, I saw your dad. When you got on the bus."

"Okay?"

"Is he good? A good dad?"

A good dad? How was I supposed to answer that? What did Ned want to hear? That regardless of how my dad and mom fought, he never yelled at me? That whenever I did something wrong, he would tell me I'd let him down, and that was worse than any punishment? That he helped me build tree forts and took me to buy hockey cards on his days off? Or was I supposed to tell Ned that when I was at my dad's house, I was home in a way I never was at my mom's?

"He's okay," I said.

"I never had a dad. My mom was really young when she had me. He....he wasn't part of our life. He had his own family. Another family."

I still didn't know what to say. "Oh," was the best I could manage.

"My mom made me promise I'd leave him alone. She said the reason he'd never met me was because I was a mistake and he didn't want to know me. She didn't want to hurt more than I already do. But the truth is I've already met him. And I think he wants to get to know me. I think he wants to be my dad. Can you imagine how that feels?"

The excitement in his voice. The hope... I had to tell him.

"Ned, there's something you need to know."

"I think I already do."

"When you were crawling under that fence... You died, Ned. You were struck by lightning, and it killed you." I don't think I really believed it until the words fell out of my mouth. I could hear my voice breaking. "I promised... I promised my dad I'd take care of you. I promised I'd make sure you were all right and I couldn't. I couldn't save you, Ned. I couldn't."

There was no stopping myself; I started crying. At first, I hoped it would only be a few tears, but as they came there were plenty more behind them. I fought the best I could, but they pushed through all the same.

"I'm...I'm dead?" Ned said. And, stupidly, I could only nod. When my dad found out nothing would ever be the same.

I'd let Ned die.

Outside the storm raged, and the rain pelting the roof made a staccato sound that thankfully drowned out most of my sobbing. I prayed I didn't wake the others; I didn't want them to know. I was ashamed of so many things that they layered on one another, multiplying their intensity. All I wanted was to see my dad, hear him tell me things would be all right. That we all make mistakes. But I knew it wasn't true. He would never have made such a huge mistake, I told myself. He couldn't. Not ever.

"I'm sorry," was all I could muster when I finally got control of myself. I laid my hand on the closet door as I said it, hoping my sincerity would somehow cross to the other side. Hoping Ned would know how much I regretted everything I'd ever done wrong. And I think he did know, ultimately. I just don't think he forgave me.

"Do you remember the Needle song?" he asked. His voice had turned, and it startled me out of my blubber. "I don't remember which of you made it up. Maybe Steig. Maybe you. I do remember how you all sang every day for weeks. And I remember how first I tried laughing with you, and when that didn't work, I tried getting mad at you. But nothing stopped it."

"We didn't mean anything by it. We—"

"Don't lie to me. I'm dead, remember? Nothing you say can hurt me anymore. Not like it hurt me then. You know, I even went to Mr. Parsons to ask him for help. I thought he was always helping you with homework or having Eric act as his assistant. He'd help me, too. But you know what Mr. Parsons said? He said 'the boys are just being boys, Needle. You need to toughen up.' He might have said more but I didn't hear it. He called me *Needle*. Just like in your song. And he had a smirk on his face the whole time. As though I deserved what happened. As though I *encouraged* it."

"Ned, I.... If I'd known—"

"And you want to hear the really messed up thing? Part of me liked it. When you sang that awful song at least you saw me. For a moment I wasn't a nobody, ignored until you thought up some new way of torturing me. But I knew you'd eventually forget. You always did. You always will. It's funny; sometimes I used to think all of you would regret how you treated me if I died. I thought you'd all be sorry, and I got some satisfaction out of that. God, how stupid could I have been? Dying doesn't teach anybody anything. I died as happy as I was ever going to be. And it wasn't nearly enough."

Rain intensified against the windows. It was harder to hear Ned speak. I put my ear closer but the storm pulled his words back, made them sound further away.

"Let me ask you one more thing," he said.

"Anything," I said. And I meant it.

"Were we friends?"

I wiped the tears off my face. My entire body jittered from exhaustion. I wasn't going to lie to him. Not again.

"No. We never were."

"Yeah, I guess you're right," he said. "But if we weren't friends, why are you talking to me?"

I shrugged.

"Because my dad told me to."

"Yeah. Mine, too."

And then he laughed. I'd never heard a sound like it before. It was dry and weird, and it scared me. Because I didn't know what it meant. Or maybe I just hoped I didn't.

"Ned?" I said, but this time he didn't answer. Instead, as the heavy rain rattled across the cabin's roof, I heard something else. I heard him singing. It was the Needle Song. And I knew it was because I'd helped make it up, one way or another. And yet it was Ned who knew all the words by heart. He sang them over and over as the storm dismantled the sound. Broke it down into pieces until it was something near nothing. The sound of everything coming undone.

And yet, for me, sitting there alone in the dark, all the pieces were only starting to come together.

EVERYTHING IS WHITE

My father's ghost watches from the window. Thick smoke curls up from his cigarette and around the deep grooves carved into his spectral face. His elbow rests on the painted sill. I do what I can to avoid looking at him. It doesn't matter, though; I know he is there. Watching. I tell myself if I don't look everything will be okay.

So, I keep my head down, lift the heavy snow off the driveway. A foot has dropped since yesterday. It's been an incredibly cruel winter, and it gets crueller every day still. I can't let the snow linger even though it's so wet and heavy I must stop every few feet to catch my breath and cool down. Beneath my heavy coat my shirt is plastered to my skin and my limbs are demanding I give up. But that isn't an option. Giving up means nowhere is safe. And I can't sacrifice my sanctuary, not knowing what's waiting for me inside.

How much can a person's heart withstand? I'm worried the answer lies in my arms. They are going numb too quickly, and my fingers won't stay curled around the shovel's handle. But it's my chest that knows things aren't okay. I feel as though I've been cracked in half then sharply creased. I pause and drive the blade straight into the snow, then fold my hands over the black plastic grip and survey what I've done. There's so much to deal with that I must fight my urge to quit. That's what my father would have done. At least, before he died.

I've spent my whole life running from my father's mistakes. Maybe that's why he's here now, haunting our house. To remind me some things can't be outrun. It's not love that brought him back. It can't be. Love is reciprocal. Love is making a commitment to not hurt or cause pain. Love doesn't explain my father, and it doesn't explain my father's ghost.

I feel the low rumbling before I hear the beeping. Before I see the blue lights reflected off the snow. I should stand back but I'm afraid if I let go of the shovel I'll fall over, so I remain propped up as the plow moves down the street toward me. A wave of packed snow streams over the side of its blade, building a windrow as tall as my waist at the foot of the driveway. An insurmountable wall.

But I have to keep going. I have to clear the snow.

My pregnant wife stands at the stove, frying eggs and saying nothing, as my father's ghost and I sit at the table. His clothes are new, and I can hear how crisp they are when he moves, but for her sake I pretend I can't. I pretend everything is normal and calm and our world hasn't been upended by my father's appearance in our lives. With his razor-red chin and stinking of aftershave, he watches. He's here with us, but also back in Joyceville where he's been for twenty-six years. Two places, simultaneously. Maybe more. A spectre from the past wedging us apart. My wife refuses to acknowledge his presence, and I wonder if she can even see him. Maybe he's here only for me. Reminding me of what I have to lose.

I catch my father's ghost staring at my pregnant wife. His peppered hair is wet and has been combed back to curl behind his ears. He must know she doesn't deserve the life I've given her, and I suspect she knows it as well. My wife had no way of knowing when she met me what had happened to my mother and my sisters. She couldn't have foreseen one day she'd be sharing our home with my father's ghost. I hid all this from her—I'd had lots of practice throughout my life, worried what might happen if I let anyone know me. Unexpectedly, though, my wife wore through my defenses, and by the time she discovered who I really was it was too late for her. We were stuck together. And now with her pregnancy we are even more entangled. It saddens me to think of what I've taken from her, but it scares me even more. Sometimes, when I lay my head in her lap, I close my eyes and let her stroke my hair and silently pretend she's my mother, if only so I can remember what it was like to be a child again. So I can go back to before everything changed. Is that wrong? To want it all back for just one more moment? My wife, my beautiful wife, doesn't say a word as she runs her fingers through my hair. It's as though she's willingly playing along, intentionally lulling me into believing no time has passed. But of course, she isn't and of course it has—it always does—and when I open my eyes again, I haven't gone anywhere. I'm stuck here, in the present, where I've been for twenty-six years. Just like my father's ghost. The both of us simultaneously haunting and haunted by our shared past. When I try to explain all this to my wife her hand stops, fingers still tangled in my hair, and she exhales strangely. Even now, when I look at her, I think she's about to cry. I would do anything to protect her. But the way my father's ghost stares makes me uneasy, and the dire winter only makes it worse. I wish I could order him to go and leave us alone, but what control do I have over the incorporeal?

I don't say anything to my wife as she slides the browned eggs from the pan and into my plate. And she leaves the kitchen without acknowledging the haunting presence that separates us.

Later, the three of us—me, my pregnant wife, my father's ghost— sit and watch television. The house is cold, but my wife runs hotter the further into her pregnancy she gets, so I'm the only one wrapped in a quilted blanket. I can't stop shivering, though. I do my best to not look at the corner of the room where my father's ghost sits, alone in our old green armchair. When I do glance, I see the light of the news program reflected on his shining face.

I feel uneasy, anxious, knowing he's so near, so I pull my wife closer. She immediately struggles against me; says she feels smothered. But I'm reluctant to let her go. I don't know what I think will happen, but I must stay vigilant. Too much has been taken from me already.

From my father, too, I suppose, but somehow it still isn't enough.

My father's ghost doesn't seem to notice or care. Instead, his hollow gaze is fixed on the television screen. Images of foreign wars speed across the glass while he sits mesmerized. It's been so long since he left this world it's as though he's desperate to fill in the gaps, to resurrect himself and rejoin the world of the living. Maybe he thinks I'll help him, but I can't. I can't even believe he might expect that.

My wife turns from the screen, the bloody images too disturbing in her condition. She wants me to turn the television off, or perhaps just change the channel, but my father's ghost is still watching. I tell her not to worry; the news moves so fast the horror will be over before we know it.

And I'm right, of course. The horrific fades and is replaced by the mundane, the local. The reporters still look distressed, though—the chyron background tinted red—and a disturbing worry quickly builds inside me. I lean forward, my hold on my pregnant wife slipping. The television screen fills with a three-dimensional model of Southern Ontario, in front of which appears a middle-aged man pointing to a dark cloud that envelops the region. Our city, and its heart.

Then the reporter verbalizes my suspicions and worst fears. Two pressure systems are colliding. A winter storm is already on the way. And it's going to be brutal.

He warns over two feet of snow are expected, starting this evening and lasting throughout tomorrow. We have not had a storm of that size since I was a child. Not since the accident, and immediately it ties a knot in my stomach. The weather forecaster doesn't acknowledge this, though. He's too busy smiling his too-perfect teeth, too busy laughing with his co-hosts as he warns us to stay at home and confine ourselves for the storm's duration. The knot in me tightens. I glance at my father's ghost and can't be certain, but I think he's smiling, too. But unlike the weather forecaster my father's smile seems to suggest I prepare for something worse.

My wife's hand gently touches my back. It doesn't help.

My worry about the approaching winter storm frays my nerves until the only way to calm them is to go out for supplies. That it also lets me escape my father's ghost, if only for a little while, is not lost on me, though I have some trepidation about leaving my pregnant wife behind. She tells me she understands, but her eyes betray her.

When I arrive at the plaza of box stores there is traffic and a sea of parked cars. I'm clearly not the only person worried. It's as comforting as it is frustrating. It takes a while to find a parking space, and when I do it's at the opposite end of the lot. By the time I cross the entrance into the hardware store my face has been frozen in a grimace.

I need salt. Bags of salt. As does everyone else. The store is frenzied with people carrying push shovels and snow blowers, all panicked and knocking against one another. The crazed environment only heightens my anxiety.

The packed aisles prevent me from finding what I'm looking for. I'm forced to watch the carts of the people scrambling around me, searching for those large yellow bags of salt. As they appear more frequently, I know I'm getting closer. When I finally locate the road salt display, I'm disheartened to find its nearly bare. There are only two bags left—two bags from a skid that was probably teetering a few hours earlier. I force my way through the throng and as I take hold of the bags another pair of hands appears and does the same.

The man tugging the last of the salt toward his cart is older than me, but not by much, and his frown is cruelly etched into his face. The way he looks at me reminds me of someone, and in my state of heightened agitation I can't think of a scenario where he might need the salt more than I do. Nobody could. So, I yank the bags back. His voice is angry, but I don't listen to what he says. My head is overwhelmed with images of my pregnant wife bleeding out beside of a snowy road, her car overturned. I look down, expecting to see my father's hands, covered in blood. Instead, I see my own holding the two yellow plastic bags. One has a hole torn in it and crystals the size of nickels are dribbling out, scattering over the floor.

I feel a sudden vertigo and my legs turn wobbly. I stumble, but before I hit the ground the older man catches me. His words are quiet and echoing, but his face is so concerned I feebly nod to assure him I'm okay. Other strangers appear and help take hold of me, keeping me upright. At least until I can stand on my own and the volume of the world returns.

I really need to get home.

I gather the leaking yellow bags into my arms and pull free of the hands supporting me. Concerned voices call out to stop me as I slouch away, but I only speed up. If I don't look back at them then I know nothing bad will happen. If I don't look, everything will be okay.

Snow starts to fall gently as I'm rushing home, so by the time I pull into the driveway there's a white dusting that's ruined everything I did earlier. My pregnant wife waits in the doorway, silhouetted by the foyer lamp, but I don't see her at first. My eyes are drawn to the living room window where my father's ghost sits, perched on the sill, watching. Cigarette smoke creeps up his hand in twin plumes of ectoplasm. His head jerks unexpectedly, and he startles me with a spasm of hacking and coughing. It breaks the spell on me. I step out of the car and look away from him long enough to greet my pregnant wife's fury.

She tells me with grave seriousness that she's worried about me. Doesn't she realize the storm will be on us any minute now? With her hands on her belly, she tells me she doesn't care, then lashes out at how irresponsible I am. That's not what's worrying her, though—her expression makes that clear. So does the way she snatches me from the doorway and wraps her arms around me, squeezing out my breath. Her grip only loosens when I struggle for air. That's when she remembers she's angry at me and blames me for letting out the heat. I don't fight back. I don't want my father's ghost to hear us like this.

He's always around. Always listening. When I was a child there was nothing I wanted more than to have my father near, no matter how much he scared me sometimes. But that was before the accident. Before everything was taken from me. Before he died. Over the years afterward I'd almost forgotten him until his ghost showed up at the house, uninvited. I was so startled, so confused, I let him in. Now he moves between rooms and fades into the corners of the house or into the reflections of the windows.

I'm reticent to fight and that only makes my pregnant wife angrier. She shoves me, asks if I'm even here, and I'm so uncomfortable all I can do is shrug. That's when she demands I say something, anything, even if it's mean and vile. Just something so she knows I'm actually alive. But I can't. The presence of my father's ghost is a tangible thing that weighs on me—I feel the pressure of my fear and shame building. It's like I'm sinking into the ocean. Maybe that's why I feel so dizzy. I'm suffering the bends of hopelessness.

Eventually my pregnant wife pushes me aside. Her voice sounds so scared and exhausted. She glances down the hallway at the spot my father's ghost has appeared and for a moment I think she'll finally acknowledge him. But instead, she turns and stalks away. I exhale with relief. But I don't look at him. I look out the window. Outside, the snow is falling harder. Snow I won't be able to resist much longer.

When I get to our bedroom upstairs my wife has already turned out the light and is lying on her side, curled with her back toward me, pillow between her knees. I know it's the only way she can sleep now that the baby has grown so large, but it feels personal all the same. I stand in the doorway, listening to her breathe and wondering if she's awake or asleep. It could be either. Or maybe it's both. Maybe she's stuck in some interstitial place and only when I choose will she become fixed. I don't choose. I can't. My head is too occupied by the winter storm and how much worse everything will soon be. And I'm distracted by the sound of my father's ghost out in the darkness.

My father's ghost does not sleep, so he'll wander the house aimlessly through the night. At times his constant shuffling will wake me, and I'll see the shadow of his feet slip under the bottom of our bedroom door. He'll hesitate there and I'll watch the door, almost imagining I can see through it while he's doing the same, wanting to say something but knowing he can't. Eventually, he'll leave, and a few minutes later I'll hear faint voices that I'm sure are from the television with its volume turned too low.

I suffer a strange mixture of anxiety, exhaustion, and failure that wants to keep me awake. I will myself to relax, but part of my fear comes from not knowing what will happen if I can't expel it. I swallow twice, nervously, then roll onto my side and count my pregnant wife's slow deep breaths until there have been enough that I can finally close my eyes.

As I sleep my father's ghost watches me like he used to watch me when he was alive. I remember the feel of him hovering over my bed. And the way he smelled. I didn't recognize it until I was older—a miasma of stale fermentation. My mother was often somewhere else in the house, my sisters both already asleep in their twin beds. So much time has passed now since his death. Long enough that for a while I almost managed to convince myself he'd never been real. Just the remnant of an old dream. But when his ghost arrived at our house, haunting the door, plastic bag of belongings squeezed tightly in his hand, I understood immediately I'd been deluding myself. Everything was true. Everything had happened the way I remembered. The day he arrived was the second worst day of my life.

And, no surprise, it was snowing then, too.

I sit on the edge of the bed and imagine I see my father before me. Not his ghost, not that old man in starched clothes with nowhere to go, but my father as he was. Before he died. A ghost, nonetheless.

He stumbles through our old living room after speaking on the phone with my mother. I can't understand what he's saying as he slurs commands at me, but I know he wants me to put my boots on and get into the car. I try to tell him it's snowing outside, but he doesn't hear me. He is huffing and fighting a lot with the sleeves of his coat.

The wheels of my father's car spin as he tries to drive through the knee-deep snow. I'm a child now, buckled into the front seat, covering my eyes with my mittened hands. I ask him meekly where we're going, and he jumps as though he's forgotten I'm in the car with him. My father looks tired and dishevelled and though I know this is how he looks most of the time now I still don't like it and wish he would transform into who he used to be. Before the snowstorms and before he was home all day, sitting at the kitchen table. Back before I was trapped with him all the time.

I'm standing at my bedroom window as an adult, looking out at the falling snow, but I'm also still in that front seat, looking out at the same snow and smelling the sticky tang of sun-damaged vinyl and sweet exhaust fumes. The car fishtails as my father spins the wheel, trying to control it. Lights from other cars zip by too close, followed by loud honking, but my bleary father is oblivious to all of it. I grip the edges of my seat with all my childhood strength.

I ask again where we're going and I'm surprised when this time he answers, though I still can't understand him. This is how dreams are, the adult me thinks—there are no clear answers because everything is happening at once. All possibilities are simultaneous. I tell myself we are going to pick up my mother and sisters. I wonder aloud what happened to her car, but my father doesn't seem to hear me anymore.

Now it's my turn to be a ghost.

The thing about tragedies is they ripple and distort time around themselves, and the closer you get to them the stronger the effect. I understand what happens next only when I don't think about it. The more I do, the more I try to remember, even within a dream, the more disjointed it all becomes. It's as though the act of revisiting the specifics changes them, and I don't know if those changes make my memories more or less accurate. What I do know is that inside my dream a lot of things happen at once and out of order. One moment I'm suddenly peering through the windshield at the sheets of snow falling, lulled by the muted tread of the tires; the next I'm upside down and floating like a rocket in outer space. I hear weeping, but even though my face is wet I don't think it's me doing it. I don't know what to think as I'm stuck in my dream, so I turn to my wife to anchor me. But she's not there in the car, where everything spins violently around me. When the world rights itself, I'm outside in the snow with no idea how I got there. I'm kneeling, the legs of my ski pants torn though I can't feel a thing, and a pair of bright lights are blinding me. Everywhere there is static. I hear a whining high pitch that takes me far too long to place.

I want to wake up now. I already know how this dream ends, and I really don't want to see it through. I turn my head and there is my pregnant wife, sleeping soundly. I feel a sunken uneasiness and lethargy as though I'm trapped in dilated time. I sluggishly roll onto my back and close my eyes.

And there is my father, shaking my shoulders. I can smell his fermented breath. I open my eyes and it's dark and cold and the snow is stinging my face. He sits me up and I see his clothes are smeared with something dark. I don't know what, but my gut tells me not to look even though I don't know what I'm not supposed to look at. Our car surprises me by being buried halfway inside the building where my mother picks up my sisters every night. Something as dark as the stains on my father's clothes leaks from it in a growing pool. My teeth chatter as I ask him where everybody is, but he only mouths words in response. There is no sound anywhere anymore. And then I'm the adult me again, standing on the sidewalk with the gawkers, watching the distant lights of the ambulance get closer.

I shut my eyes. This is it. This is the moment my father dies. Him, and the rest of my world.

§

As terrible as my night was, my morning is even worse.
Everything is white.

I don't need to listen to the news to know the storm is heavier than anyone expected. Snow continues to plummet in blinding sheets that conceal most of what's beyond our windows. I can tell by the drifts that have pushed up against the house that it's bad.

My spine writhes and screams. I don't know what's happening to me, but the vast blankness of the world is deeply terrifying. Something is wrong outside. Something I can't explain. I just know I need to act. I need to set things right.

I rummage through our bedroom for warm clothes—my knitted hat, my gloves—and it wakes my pregnant wife. She groggily watches until it dawns on her I've worked myself into mania. She pushes herself up, her puffed face compressing to make way for her concern. She demands to know what I'm doing so I try to explain: the snow, the driveway... it must be shovelled. It's too deep. It's not safe. *She's* not safe.

I know what my wife wants to say. It's in her eyes. But she doesn't say it. Instead, she reaches out and grabs my hand. Squeezes it tight. She tells me to leave the driveway alone. Tells me to stay with her where it's warm and safe.

Tells me to stay inside.

But she isn't the only one there.

I try to pull away, but she squeezes tighter. Her eyes implore me. I have to use all my strength to free my hand, and as I do her expression changes.

It doesn't matter; I can't stay. I can't even consider it. There's no time left. Not for her begging. I have to clear the snow now. If I don't, it's going to be too deep later. And then she'll be gone, too, and all I'll have left is him.

The cold air and stinging snow smack me awake. The wind is a lot stronger than I expected. It cuts straight through my winter coat and into my skin, but I don't doubt for a second, I need to be where I am. My pregnant wife must be in the upstairs window, worrying down at me, but I refuse to look. If I do, I'll have to accept that I've lost myself, and that she knows it. But I also won't look because what if she *isn't* there? What if she's already given up? No, I can't do it. If I don't look, everything will be okay.

I have never seen this much snow in my life, I think, surveying the buried landscape. Wait, that isn't true. Not in my life; only in the last twenty-six years. Only since my father's death. The memory rocks me, and I force myself to step into the knee-deep snow before paralysis takes hold of me.

Somewhere in the empty white I hear a snowblower. I can't see where it's coming from, and the weather has disrupted the sound too much to be helpful. It's reassuring to know I'm not the only one out here though, even if the falling ice prevents me from seeing more than a few feet in front of me. It's the one time I could use the reassurance it's not the end of the world.

I sink my shovel into the overwhelmingly thick blanket of snow. I wonder if I'll ever be able to clear it all. But I must. If anything happened to my wife because I didn't I don't think I'd survive. And I can't die like my father.

I pitch the snow over my shoulder and onto our buried lawn. I don't dig all the way to the asphalt; instead, I remove the top half-foot and work my way down in layers. It's slow going, but after a few minutes I forget everything and fall into a hypnotic rhythm, repeating the same mechanical actions again and again. It's the first time since my father's ghost arrived that I forget about him. All that exists is the driveway that needs to be cleared.

I don't notice my lungs burning until I can't breathe. I stop, run my icy glove over my face, and wait for my pulse to slow. I'm hesitant to look at how far I've come, fearing the worst. And when I do, I'm appalled. I've cleared less than five feet of driveway—barely anything at all—and the first three of those feet have already filled with inches of new snow. I don't know if I can face what's coming.

I don't know what I'm going to do when the heavens bury me.

In my lowest moment of despair, I see a shadow appear in the middle of the blinding white storm. My muscles have begun to stiffen but I can't look away. And when the shadow steps closer I realize why.

It's my father's ghost.

But that's impossible. In all the time he's been haunting our house, he's never once stepped foot outside. I didn't even think he could. Yet here he is, dressed in one of my old winter coats, his pants tucked into his new boots.

Snow lodges in his thick eyebrows and his glassy round eyes rotate underneath his hood to look on me. He tries to speak but even if the wind weren't so loud, I wouldn't be able to hear him. The distance between us is too great.

The shovel trembles in my hand as he drifts closer. When he couldn't come outside—when I thought he couldn't—I was able to relax; I had somewhere I could escape to. Find respite from his oppressive haunting. Focus on keeping my pregnant wife safe. If my father's ghost wasn't out in the world, she would be okay. But now he's here, standing before me in the snow, and I realize with cold certainty it was all a lie I was telling myself. A lie I wanted so much to believe. The truth is now inescapable.

I draw the shovel out of the snow and scream as I mindlessly swing it at him. I don't know what I say because it's all nonsense—it means nothing. Just empty screaming and swinging. I've lost all sense of myself. Some rage-filled version of me that was once buried so deep has now decided to show itself. I find myself separated from my body and with fascination I watch my physical self's efforts to dispel my father's ghost.

The ghost does not react. He knows the empty me cannot touch him. My body closes in, but he doesn't flinch. He only lifts his arms.

Is he... Is he trying to *hug* me?

Both of my selves, the physical and the separated, stagger.

How dare he. After what he did, after what he took from me—my mother, my sisters. Even my father. All of them, gone. Erased from my life. No number of unread letters can change that. No number of unanswered collect calls from Joyceville. It's all gone, leaving nothing for me because there is nothing left *of me*. Just this physical self, this body going through the motions. A terrified shell forced to confront the ghost of all his hate tainted by some vestigial love. A frightening uncontrollable storm within the void of me that will never abate. And after all he's done my father's ghost reaches out for me as though none of that happened? As though everyone is safe and alive? As though either of my cleaved selves could ever forgive him?

My separated and physical selves find one another the instant before the shovel connects. My father's eyes, wide open, lock on my own, and I see the relentless storm reflected in them like spectral clouds. Then my body pitches forward and my thoughts race to make sense of my unexpected collapse. It's the shovel. It never found him.

In the blinding squall the shovel awkwardly slips out of my hand, and as I lose balance its grip jams between my ribs and the concrete. I barely hear the snap as icy ground comes at me fast. There's no time to feel the pain before I black out.

When I come to, I'm buried in heavy snow. A broken thing, curled. Misshapen. Alone. I try to stand, to resurrect myself as my father did but the pain is too much. All I can do is flop back into the drift and gulp down painful breaths.

It's difficult but I turn my head, wincing as I check to see if my pregnant wife has seen me fall. I can't tell—the storm has obscured the windows, walling me off from her—but I can hope. That's all I can do. Unable to move, unable to see, I'm no better than the dead myself. No better than my father.

Because I've failed her. My wife, and our unborn child. I didn't protect them. Both are victims of who I was never able to be. Who I might have been had I done something different. Had I spoken louder, tried harder. Had I made the changes I needed to make. Had I not been so weak.

I stare up into the white at the centre of the storm and think I see my own face looking down. But it's not me, I realize. It's my father. He's wearing my coat, my hat. His ghost holds the broken remains of the shovel in one spectral hand and reaches out the other to lift me upward.

But I don't want to take it. I don't want to go.

I've worked so hard not to be him, to stay away from Joyceville. To protect not destroy. And yet here I am. Staring at his withered hand at the end of everything. Faded tattoos climbing his fingers like vines.

I don't want you here, I mouth. I want you to go.

I press my eyes shut and wait for him to vanish like the apparition he is. I don't know how long it will take, I don't know how long I have left, but I'll keep waiting until he's gone and I'm free. All I need to do is not look.

If I don't look, everything will be okay. I say it to myself again. And I keep saying it until I believe it. Until it's true.

If I don't look, everything will be okay.

I continue saying it until I hear their voices calling to me.

And that's when I make the mistake of opening my eyes. Of looking.

And I see that everything will not be okay.

SHEPHERD NOT SHEEP

Our tiny village, Drei Fluss, has three rivers and seven bridges. Under each bridge is a troll.

The trolls arrived the summer before last and no one in the village knows what to do about them so the council called a meeting. It's so well attended people are jostling in the aisles. Everyone has an opinion about the trolls—why they moved in and why they won't leave.

Frau Knut sternly says they came because our new concrete bridges are more hospitable to them. But Herr Dirge asks then about Gusen Bridge, our wooden footbridge, and Frau Knut quietly sits down.

Her cousin, Frau Ulrich, snickers and says it has nothing to do with the bridges. It's the people. Trolls like being close to people for obvious reasons. She doesn't say what those reasons are, but I think I can guess.

And Herr Buag? He trembles and says they're an act of God. A punishment for our heathen ways. Only his son, Egon, applauds. The rest, judging by their reaction, don't know what the word "heathen" means.

Councillor Holler, a small nervous man, bangs his small gavel. The reason the trolls are here doesn't matter. They're here so what are we going to do about it?

Herr Oskar, our shopkeeper, has a suggestion: why don't we hire someone to kill them? Everyone nods or claps when he says this, and his face fights off a wave of smugness. But Jutta doesn't nod or clap. That's because Jutta believes there aren't any trolls in Drei Fluss, and there never have been.

She whispers to me that this lie about trolls infuriates her. She says the Council wants to scare us because it makes it easier for them to control us.

I whisper back and ask what it is, exactly, that they want to make us do. I try to sound curious but it's hard when inside I'm pleading she'll just go back to how she was before.

She says they want Drei Fluss to become a tourist village. Tourist villages are rich villages, and the best way to become one is to be interesting. A village with seven bridges sounds quaint and boring. A village with make-believe trolls under those seven bridges doesn't. It doesn't sound safe, no matter how safe it actually is. She says that's what makes it interesting.

I ask her if she thinks Drei Fluss is safe in the same whisper, but I'm straining against my agitation. I can't understand what's happened to her. I'm not even sure it's still Jutta. Maybe the trolls got to her. Maybe they replaced her. Can trolls do that?

She smiles. It's the kind of smile that barely curls her lips; instead, it rolls them back over her teeth like a window blind. I don't like it. I'm about to tell her how unsafe Drei Fluss really is, but Councillor Holler does it for me by summoning Frau Miran.

She steps to the front of the room carrying a photograph of her missing daughter, Fiona. We all knew Fiona, and we've all seen the photograph—it's been in the local newspaper every week, plastered to every posterboard throughout Drei Fluss. We all know something happened to her, which is why it's so hard to look at Frau Miran. But she looks at every one of us. Up there, from the lectern, she stares with a scorching anger. I want to believe that's all it takes to prove the trolls to Jutta, but she's unmoved. It does worse than break my heart, it disappoints me.

Frau Miran's voice cracks as she starts speaking. That crack never really goes away.

You all know what happened to my Fiona, her mother says with a timbre so sharp I feel its cut. It was those trolls. Those vile putrid trolls. They took my little Fiona and that was it. We never found her afterward. Never found even a trace of her. My Fiona was only twelve years old and had barely started life. Did you know she spoke to fairies? She liked to go out in thunderstorms because that's when they heard her best. She loved bad weather outside more than she loved the inside.

She was strange and daring and I never wanted to live without her. And now I have to. Because of those trolls. You know what they are, and you don't do anything about them. Even after what they did. To my poor Fiona...

Her face contorts as she trails off, the lines of her face becoming a scribble. Jutta whispers out the side of her mouth, asking if Frau Miran is about to cry. But she doesn't and Jutta scoffs. You don't believe this, do you? she asks me. So, I ask her back, a bit too loud, what *she* thinks happened to Fiona. Jutta shrugs, doesn't know; she isn't Fiona's mother. Frau Miran must hear us because her face turns a colour that doesn't look good or right on a person.

Before she can speak, Councillor Holler rushes to applaud. The rest of us follow. Even Jutta claps but I can tell it's insincere. Frau Miran's grimace is wounded as she glances at us while stepping from the front of the room. Jutta continues clapping. She doesn't care if she's the last one making noise.

§

Jutta and I met in the before-times, when Drei Fluss was troll-free and all the bridges were wooden and boring. I went to Hiachst Park, just on the other side of Schwecat Bridge, because I'd run out of places to hide at home, and because there was nobody around who wanted to seek. I found Jutta seated on the swings, wearing a pair of heavy black shoes and a dirty dress whose latticed hem was torn above the knee. She rested as limp as a rag doll against the chains as she swayed. I stood back on the edge of grass, not knowing what to do. After a moment she seemed to come alive, bolting upright, and the way she looked at me...I knew right then she didn't need to speak because I could see my thoughts on her face. I walked over and announced my name was Maud, then gave her my strongest push. She screamed with delight as her feet left the ground. From that moment, we were inseparable, and I never had to worry about being alone again.

But the trolls changed everything. That Jutta is gone now. This Jutta wouldn't be delighted. She'd narrow her eyes and ask why I was at Hiachst Park and what I wanted with her. This Jutta wouldn't let me anywhere near her, or if she did, she'd test me first to be sure I was real. She would never try to make me feel welcome. She'd be just like everyone else—trying to make me believe I don't belong.

It would bother me except it doesn't matter anymore. No one goes to Hiachst Park now, anyway. Or any park. I definitely don't. Not since Fiona vanished. It ruined Frau Miran's life and it's ruined the lives of everyone in Drei Fluss, too. With the exception of maybe Jutta's.

The roads are empty when we walk home from the village meeting. Jutta is up on the curb, one foot in front of the other, boney arms outstretched like she's on the highwire. I don't look at her. I just want to be alone, but I'm also terrified she'll go. There's a troll nearby. I can smell it.

Not that I've ever seen one. Not really. I know other people say they have, but not me, though I've come close. Once, I glimpsed a shadow rise up from behind an old pushcart on the side of Lonnie Road, and my whole body froze up. But it wasn't because of the shadow. It was the smell. Trolls have a particular odor—like clothes that haven't been washed in a long time. Sour and greasy. It lingers in your head for so long you still smell it even after you shouldn't. I knew as soon as I smelled it what it was. And I ran home like I'd never run before.

Jutta hates this story. She asks me if I've ever smelled a river before, then reminds me we have three of them and they all smell bad. It's the algae and the scum. She says all I was smelling was river water and calls me stupid. Even though I know she's wrong she's so certain that for a moment I doubt myself. Could she be right? Then Jutta opens her mouth and my questions vanish.

She tells me the village has got me so worked up over the troll conspiracies that I'll believe anything now. Then she laughs and asks in a snarky voice if I think the wind is caused by trolls breathing, and if I think it gets dark because the trolls switch the sun with the moon every night. Trolls are all anyone ever talks about, she says, and it's not funny anymore.

Jutta doesn't listen when I tell her for a fact what I overheard my mother discussing with her friends. The Bauer boy, Chime, had been on Fuscher Bridge and narrowly avoided being taken by the troll that lived under it. My mother's friend asked what it looked like, but my mother didn't know. Chime said it was too dark to see. I shiver as I tell Jutta, but she just snickers and picks up a rock from the ground to hurl as far as she can into Köhler River. It's a bunch of bullshit, she says.

Chime is always making up stories. She asks if I remember when he pretended he didn't believe in ghosts until he was dared to go into the cellar of St. Alphege Church and the upper-class men locked him in? They only held the door for five minutes, but Chime still wet himself. Jutta guffaws and picks up another rock to throw. I don't think it's as funny as she does, but I don't laugh as much as Jutta anyway.

Sometimes I wonder what my life would be like without her. What if tomorrow my parents sat me down and told me that it was Jutta that had gone missing; that everyone thought a troll had got her instead of Fiona. What would I feel? I don't think I'd be surprised. And I don't think I'd cry. I think I might be relieved. Just a little. But I don't know. Nobody knows how they'll feel before they feel it. The only thing I'm sure of is Fiona would not have sat with me at a council meeting about Jutta. Not that there would have been a meeting.

Jutta jumps down from the curb. As she lands on the cobblestones she wants to know, if nobody has ever seen a troll, how is everyone so sure they know what one looks like. And why am I so sure they're the ones telling the truth.

The smell, I start to say, but she interrupts me.

Not the smell again.

I tell her a good friend would believe me.

She tells me a good friend wouldn't believe such stupid things.

I pick up my stride to get ahead of her. But Jutta doesn't like being left behind, and she doesn't like it when I stop speaking to her, so she hurries to keep pace.

I'm sorry, Maud, she says. I don't acknowledge her. I don't slow down. I wait to see if she'll tell me why she's sorry, but she doesn't. We just walk in silence—me staring straight ahead, her staring at her feet. I don't know how long we go without speaking to each other, but it might be a record.

We need to cross Krottenback Bridge to get home, but Krottenback is probably the bridge I'm most afraid of. The other six bridges have trolls, everybody knows this, but Krottenback is our biggest bridge which means the biggest troll must live there. It smells nearly every time I run over it. I should run this time, too, but I know Jutta will refuse to follow and I don't want to run with her watching. I know I shouldn't be embarrassed but I am.

Jutta must know this. She's probably counting on it.

Jutta nods at the bridge and says: Well, that's worrying, isn't it?
I ask her what she means.

She points as we get closer—not so close that something could snatch us, but not so far that something couldn't. I look and I see the bridge I've always seen. Then I see more.

It's crooked, she says. Twisted like cherry licorice.

It's not that bad, I tell myself. It's only just a hump midway across. The concrete is buckled, lowered on one side just enough to be noticeable. There's nothing interesting or unique about it.

But maybe that's why it bothers me. It's the mundanity. After so long living with the fear of the trolls, of their mysterious habits and behaviors, something as ordinary as twisted concrete fills me with a kind of unshakeable dread. Or maybe it's the flavour of the air that has changed. It's become sour and just a little bitter. As I notice this, I also notice one other thing: it's become quiet. I can't hear anything, not even my own breathing.

I don't like this, I say. Something isn't right.

Jutta sniffs the air. Laughs in a way that doesn't reassure me.

I suggest we take the long way home tonight.

The two of us retreat from Krottenback Bridge, back down Wassa Road, past Monad's Butchers. We turn the corner at Perrera Lane and sneak through a few back alleys as a short cut until we find ourselves at Piesting Bridge. This bridge is flat, and we can hear the crickets along the riverbanks which I think means it's safe. As a precaution, though, I remove my shoes and walk across the bridge barefoot. I hope my feet are as quiet under the bridge as they are on top of it. About halfway across Jutta shouts: Hey! Do you hear snoring? and I'm suddenly running so fast my bare feet go numb. I don't hear Jutta's cackles until I'm already bent over and panting on the other side.

It's an hour later than usual when I reach my house but at least I reach it. My mother's face is white as a paper when she sees me, her eyes glossy and bloodshot. She hugs me so hard I worry she'll split me like a ball of dough. My father doesn't say a thing, but he looks relieved. They don't ask how the meeting went. And the next morning is the same as any other morning.

But it doesn't stay that way.

Herr Buag knocks erratically at our door during breakfast. My father makes a noise with his nose and wipes his mouth before standing.

My mother's eyes stay glued to her porridge. Her spoon trembles. I can't hear what Herr Buag is saying but I hear enough to know it's a prayer. And I only hear that because my father prays with him.

Egon Buag is missing, I tell Jutta, later, while we sift through gravel along the edge of the road. I tell her everything I know: that after the village meeting, they think Egon crossed over Krottenback Bridge to get home. A torn sleeve from his jacket was found on the Vakea Road side.

Did he run away with Fiona? she asks.

Of course not!

I never liked Egon. He was never nice to us.

Jutta!

I suppose you're going to tell me a troll took him.

How can Jutta say this? Egon's gone, I repeat. He's missing. He's probably dead.

Maud, don't be the sheep; be the shepherd.

What does that even mean?

It means you're choosing to believe these stories. Open your eyes.

I can't hide my irritation anymore. Jutta smiles.

Egon's body is found a few days later. Or, at least, parts of his body are found. Three of his limbs are found in a pile near Fischa Bridge. This surprises everyone as we all considered it the safest bridge. Egon's torso, though, is over by Krottenback Bridge, and when I tell Jutta she shakes her head with disgust. What I overheard from my father was it looked the way an animal does after a pack of wild dogs gets at it. The ribs were cracked open and there were ropes of intestines spread through the rushes alongside Miran River. I once got an accidental glimpse behind the curtain of Monad's Butchers, and I still have nightmares about it. I can see it like a ghost in the room with me. I can't imagine how much worse Egon's remains must have been.

Jutta tells me she heard his liver was gone. She's probably trying to make me sick for fun.

I ask why his liver.

She shakes her head. Tells me the liver is the best part of the body. It's filled with all the delicious fats. It's like eating a stick of butter. If you're only going to eat one part of something, she tells me it's the liver, hands down.

I didn't know that.

Her laugh is more like a derisive snort. Of course you don't, she says. Nobody wants us to know. Believe me.

Jutta sweeps up a rock and holds it out for me to inspect. It's a good one; a little green, but also gold, too, and the striations are all even. It could probably knock someone down if you hit them with it right, and I bet it could do almost the same to a troll. I'm mad she found it, to be honest, but I keep that to myself. Just because I don't think she deserves it doesn't mean she doesn't. What I believe and what's the truth are two different things. It's something I'm working on remembering because Jutta won't.

After the discovery of Egon an emergency Council meeting is called. There's a different feeling in the air. As though all the anger of the village has finally metastasized and real change is coming. We all feel it: Egon Buag's death has catalyzed us into finally doing something.

Herr Oskar can't help himself. He reminds everyone that he had first suggested hunting the trolls down after Fiona disappeared. If we had, he says, Egon might still be alive. Frau Buag immediately sobs, and the look Herr Oskar gives her gets imprinted on my mind. It's terrible. And makes me feel bad even though I didn't say a word.

Frau Knut asks if something so violent is necessary and it seems to split the crowd in half. After an hour a compromise is reached: the men of the town will try to secure the bridges and only if the trolls return will they try something more drastic.

They turn proudly to Frau Miran, but she surprises them with her hesitance. Even Jutta can't believe it. They ask does she not want to find the troll that ate Fiona and Frau Miran's face turns a colour I've never seen before. She lowers her head as though she's embarrassed. Or maybe she's holding something back. When she looks up again, I don't understand the expression on her face, but it makes me sad.

I don't know, she finally says, and if there's not a gasp my mind inserts one.

How can you say that? Councillor Holler asks.

Frau Miran seems lost to me. She admits she doesn't know what happened to Fiona, but that none of us do. No one has shown her a single piece of evidence that a troll took her daughter. With the Buag boy there were at least remains and blood. There was something that said maybe a troll ate him—though even that isn't for certain. But

Fiona? Her sweet Fiona? She's seen nothing. And if Fiona wasn't eaten by a troll, then maybe Egon wasn't either? How do any of us know?

All the adults in the room talk hurriedly among themselves, one shouting over the other. All the while Frau Miran ducks her head and stares at her feet. I'm too stunned to say much, and even if I weren't I don't think I'd want to. Not after turning to look at Jutta's smug and elated expression. Told you, she mouths.

Councillor Holler bangs his gavel and wrestles the crowd eventually. Frau Miran has not moved. When people calm enough for him to be heard he reminds us all—reluctantly, I think—that Frau Miran is grieving, and we have to give her space. She isn't thinking right. But he also says we cannot wait on dealing with the trolls once and for all. If not for Egon and Fiona, then for all the other children who will most certainly follow. He says more but I can't concentrate over Jutta's muttered snickers. I try to remind myself the old Jutta must still be in there, somewhere. But it's increasingly harder to believe.

No one seems surprised to see the men on Krottenback Bridge early the next day. They have rope coils slung over their shoulders and tools hanging from their belts. Their faces are pale, which I know because Jutta says she saw them firsthand. She tells me she was on the bridge when they all marched across in a row. I want to know why she was there without me, and she says we don't need to be together all the time. She's never spoken to me like that before. She continues to describe what she saw: the way the men rappelled down ropes thrown over the side of the bridge; how some watched while the others worked. I ask her questions about what happened afterward, and she shrugs. It was a waste of time, she says, and there was no point to waiting around. Either the men declared they found no trolls after all, or they pretended they had because that's what the Council ordered.

When my parents think I'm asleep I overhear them discussing what happened afterward. Jutta was kind of right, I guess. The men admitted not finding a troll under Krottenback Bridge. But they did find what a troll left behind. A hole, maybe ten foot tall, carved by hand into the rocky earth beneath the bridge and which went further into the darkness than any of them could throw a lit torch. They said the air spilling out of the hole smelled worse than the air above it, and three of the men had their legs turn wobbly before it occurred to any of them to cover their faces. I can suddenly smell it myself, even though we're nowhere near a bridge.

Something about the stench made the men angry enough to snap. My father whispers to my mother that he heard the men found a small table and chairs and smashed them, then made water over the debris before leaving so as to send a message. My mother is aghast, but my father's voice just gets this sound I've never heard before. It's hard and maybe distant. He says afterward that the men forgot who they were for a time and became animals. They tried to destroy everything they saw that might belong to the troll, and when they were done, they gathered up their equipment and went to the next bridge to do the same. Then, the next. They continued until they visited all seven bridges over our three rivers and left a warning under each: no troll is safe. After that my father doesn't say much so I sneak back to bed and wonder if I can believe it's finally over.

The next day school has been cancelled since we're not allowed to go near any of the bridges. Jutta doesn't care what people say she's allowed to do, though. She does what she wants even when I tell her not to, so I'm not surprised when I find her standing outside my window. I go down to meet her before my parents notice.

I ask her what's wrong as I toe the dirt, looking for rocks. Any rock will do at this point. I just need something to focus on.

She brushes my question away.

That's not important, she says. What's important is why is the Council continuing to pretend. They say it's about Egon but it's not. They say it's about trolls but it's not. It's not even about Fiona because nothing happened to her. It's all lies. It's all bunk. They just want us to be afraid. Just watch: Soon, they'll tell us they *need to do more to protect us from the trolls* so our taxes will increase to pay for it. It's just like what happens in the cities, except it's harder to get away with it in the cities because the people there aren't all sheep.

I wonder if Jutta has any idea what she's talking about or is she just parroting words to sound smart. Either way she sounds dumb, and it makes me angry. Egon died. Fiona, too, probably. And for Jutta to say these things, even if she really believes them, is dangerous. People will start to listen to her stories because they don't know what else to do. The lies become like those rubber life preservers on the side of the bridges, and people will hold onto them past the point of knowing better.

I realize right then that telling her she's wrong isn't enough. I need to prove it to her. Prove to her that Fiona is missing. Prove to her that Frau Miran doesn't know where she is. I bend down and pick up the rock my foot has uncovered, one that's just the right size for my pocket, which means it's just the right size for my hand. It's covered in crystals that reflect the sun like tiny diamonds. But in the centre of the rock there's a crack that runs deep. Maybe if I can show Jutta the truth, really show her, then I'll be able to put the same kind of crack in her disbelief. And maybe that crack will spread and the rock in her will collapse and behind it will be the Jutta I used to know. The one I'd met on those swings in Hiachst Park, the one who's been with me every day for as long as I can remember. I miss that Jutta so much it hurts to think about her. All I need is one crack, just one. Because maybe Jutta is *my* life preserver. And without her to hang onto I'm going to drown.

§

I immediately regret us knocking on Frau Miran's door. I feel Jutta's breath on my neck, hear her trying to bury her smirk, and I resist turning around and leaving. But only because the door has already swung open and Frau Miran is standing there in her plain frock, swollen eyes circled red and purple. Her hair is tied on top of her head in a loose knot. She looks more haggard than I've seen anyone ever. I catch only a glimpse of the house behind her, but it's enough to tell me she's given up.

She doesn't say anything, and neither does Jutta behind me. I hate this—playing middle monkey—but that's the game with Jutta. I need to say something to Frau Miran since us being there was my idea, but the voice in my head stammers and everything is harder than it should be. It's like my thoughts don't want to sit still, and as I struggle, I feel Frau Miran's nervousness radiate.

I knot my fingers as I screw up my courage. When I open my mouth, though, only jumbled nonsense comes out. Frau Miran impatiently tells us she's busy, but I think she sounds more scared. Waves of something else wash over me, too— a cocktail of sorrow and despair.

Jutta says we should run. But a noise from inside the house stops me. It's like a small throaty cough, maybe. But I must be imagining it. It can't be real. None of this can be. I glance at Frau Miran and her eyes look as though they're on the verge of crying again. It must be awful to have us here, confronting her. Reminding her of Fiona. And

I'm ashamed of myself for letting Jutta manipulate me. I wish a troll would spring up and swallow me whole.

I give it a moment but no luck.

Then that cough again. Louder. And this time Frau Miran's head turns.

She's heard it, too.

Jutta tugs on the back of my coat. I don't look at her. I already know what she's going to say. But I don't want to believe it. Jutta doesn't hesitate. She screams out Fiona's name then bolts out from behind me and pushes past Frau Miran into the house. Without thinking I sprint after her. Frau Miran is too startled to catch me in time.

The house is cluttered and in disarray. I trip over the boxes and dishes and garbage that blanket the floor in thick litter. I lose balance, stumble, and it's too late to right myself before I narrowly miss knocking Jutta down. Instead, I spin and tumble to the floor in the middle of the sitting room, my knees taking the worst of it. That skinning pain distracts me momentarily from who is standing before me. From who Jutta is staring at. I get to my feet but lose my voice.

It's the closest I've ever been to a troll. It's too big for the room, its head nearly brushing the ceiling, and it's dressed in a torn, yellow-stained undershirt and a pair of long thermal pants. In its giant hand is a teacup, so dwarfed it might as well not be there at all. The troll looks at me with frog eyes, as pale and cloudy as chunks of ice. Its bulbous nose sniffs the air. As though it can smell me. Whereas all I smell is it. The stench is so bad my eyes cry.

I can explain, Frau Miran hurries. I don't want her to explain. There's nothing I want less than her explanation.

It ate Fiona! I can't believe I have to say it.

Frau Miran's face splits like an overripe red tomato and she sobs. No, he didn't, she pleads. He couldn't. He wouldn't.

We didn't eat the girl. Didn't happen, the troll wheezes, giant hand placing the teacup down on the table between us. It keeps looking at me with those frog eyes.

Jutta tells me to ask it what it's doing here then. So, I do.

It licks its lips with a purple tongue. Frau Miran is a beautiful woman. Beautiful. Said she'd let us stay. We can't go back to Krottenback Bridge any more. They want to get rid of us. Can you believe it? So jealous.

Frau Miran whimpers. It's like the groan of something straining under too much weight.

I back up. Jutta is smugly muttering I told you sos. I feel so sick I can barely remain standing. My insides squirm over themselves.

Don't, Frau Miran blubbers. Don't hurt him.

Hurt *him*? I think

The troll scratches the inside of its thigh through its thermal pants. It pulls a twisted face as half its mouth lifts.

Your council doesn't like us. They keep making up things. All lies.

Lies?

They hate that we're too strong, too smart. So, they have to lie. Don't listen to them. Think for yourself.

But... Egon....

Did *you* see anything? No. Didn't happen. Why would we eat him? Not true. False information.

They *found* him, I say. Found what was left of him.

We know what they found. Wasn't that bad, actually. He wasn't completely eaten. Still mostly there. Anyway, wasn't us. We heard some people say the councillors killed Egon. We don't know if it's true. But someone should ask them. It would be interesting to know if they tell the truth. Not that it's a big deal, even if someone did eat him a little.

The crashing noise makes Jutta and me leap and scream. But it's not the troll. It's Frau Miran. She's collapsed to her knees. Wheezing, sobbing. Muttering. See? It's not him, she says. It's not. Fiona must still be alive.

Sure she is, the troll says. We're going to help find her. Troll's promise. It puts an enormous finger aside its nose and taps.

I don't know who's worse: Frau Miran for believing the troll didn't eat Fiona; Jutta for still believing the troll isn't real, or the troll for believing I can't see through its lies. They're all too fogged up, unable or unwilling to see their truths.

Then I suddenly wonder if I'm the same. What do I believe that's not true? Thoughts race through my head too fast to litigate. I reach into my pocket and wrap my fingers around the rock Jutta and I found. It reassures and calms me. There's no way I'm as deluded.

You don't think? Jutta says, as though inside my mind.

I turn and look at her, surprised. She's standing a few feet away, arms crossed and smirking.

The troll picks up a pile of clothing from the floor. It's a number of shirts torn and stitched together into one larger shirt. The troll slips its arms into the half-made sleeves. Then helps Frau Miran to her feet.

I tell Jutta that none this makes sense, and she just nods her head like what I'm saying is obvious. Then she asks me why everything needs to make sense all the time.

Because I tell her, it's the only way I know what's real.

This is when Jutta laughs, and it sounds like the world coming undone

What's real? she chuckles. Nothing is real but what we've been told to believe. We spend our tiny lives in these tiny houses, and everyone says they'll only believe their own eyes. But they're all blind, so they listen to anyone who tells them something is there, even if it isn't. You tell me how anyone can know what real even means anymore.

I feel something in the pit of my stomach. Like there's something important I should see but I can't. Jutta is grinning, but that grin is starting to falter. I squeeze the stone in my pocket harder than ever before. It feels like something is about to break. I look at the troll holding Frau Miran in its giant arms; but it's Jutta who's trembling.

You're lying, I finally say, but when I do the troll just looks at me queerly.

Who are you talking to? it asks.

But honestly, I don't even know anymore.

THE BEAUTIFUL FOG ASCENDING

S pider webs of branches, woven together in the brittle air. A sparrow's warble; the rustle of drying leaves. Manifold sat perched on the large rock, dressed in his finest suit, wringing his arthritic hands. He stared at the spot where the dirt path vanished into the undergrowth.

The sun had not risen. Instead, it had simply given up the fight and stayed asleep—much as Manifold wished he too had done. Light diffused through the grey sky in a uniform pale, illuminating everything, but nothing so much that Manifold could say it was lit.

He wondered why he had come, what he was searching for. What use was there in leaving the house when the outdoors held nothing for him but a reminder that the world continued? That he was but a small and insignificant cog in the great machine. No, not a cog, because without a cog the whole cannot function. There was nothing quite that special about him. He had lived his whole life to become unnecessary.

At least outdoors there was chatter, movement, unlike his unkempt house. Those four walls, once full of life, full of Sandra, had grown silent; forty years of life accumulated there with nothing to show for it. The house stood on, while Manifold slowly fell apart.

His pocket buzzed, the ring of the cell phone his son, Herbert, had bought him. Manifold did not answer it. No one telephoned him, not even Herbert, who was too busy with his wife and children to spend more than requisite holidays with his father, who, since Sandra's death, had barely seemed interested in doing even that. Sandra had been the bridge between the two men and without her... Without her so much was gone.

It was worse than he could have imagined. There were days when getting out of bed was impossible. Days when he could not bear to face the mundanities the world had in store for him. There were days he wanted nothing more than to sleep so deeply he rose skyward. He found himself praying for salvation, for some solution to his misery. He had searched every avenue of his life and come up empty. There was nothing.

The phone in his pocket buzzed again. He reached his aching fingers in and removed it, then set it down gingerly on the smooth rock beside him. Vibrations echoed through the flecked stone, deep reverberations subsumed by the greyish woods. Manifold stood, his brittle knees complaining fiercely about the weight, and did not look at Herbert's gift, rattling. Instead, he abandoned it and walked toward that fading point where the path disappeared into the thickness of trees, that point where the woods converged, where everything else would be left behind him.

Each step he took sank into the soft earth, as though the ground itself were trying to stay him. He continued forward, persevering even as his wrought lungs revolted in excruciating pain. There was something beyond that vanishing point, something he sought that drew him onward.

Stones riddled the edges of the worn path, and they slowly rolled as he approached, revealing their once-hidden aspects. He stopped to witness the phenomenon and sensed beneath his feet the ever-shifting ground vibrate, detected in the air a low insectan drone. A peculiar noise distracted him, the sound of a bird like the laugh of a child, somewhere above in the trees. He looked up into the tangle of branches and saw only slate sky.

It had become colder than it should, even so late in the turning season, far colder than it had been earlier when he left his meager house. Had he closed the door before setting off? He could not recall—his memory in the weeks and months since Sandra's death more porous, his thoughts, more clouded. He remembered, vaguely, cleaning the house one last time; he remembered laying out his wedding suit across the bed; he remembered washing his calloused feet and crooked toes. He remembered these things, and yet could not recall leaving the house, could not recall entering the woods, could not recall anything between that bath and sitting upon the smooth flecked rock. A giggle in the air, a cold gust, the rattle of his phone in his pocket. He reached for it and realized it was only a ghost vibrating against his skin.

A memory from the depths surfaced, unsummoned. Herbert's solitary visit after Sandra's death. How could Manifold have forgotten? His son had arrived with wife and children in tow, all as unfamiliar as faceless strangers. Herbert's mouth was drawn down, as was his nameless wife's, yet both seemed insincere. The terrible children were honest at least, playful and indifferent. That perhaps was the most infuriating. Had none of them decency enough to respect Manifold's pain? Did they have to flaunt living before him so, when he had struggled and failed in his own search to go on?

And why did that memory manifest itself at that moment, while Manifold stood, breathless, in the midst of the autumnal woods? What was it about the trees' slender trunks, like Sandra's arms reaching for him from her death bed, that made him recall all that had been sensibly buried?

He heard a suppressed cough. He turned, squinting in the cold to focus his eyes, but Manifold saw nothing.

"Hello?" Manifold called, voice shaking. "Hello? Who is there?"

But there was no reply. Just the sound of butterflies, of squirrels.

Manifold looked down at the dirt path and wondered whose feet stood upon it; whose hands dangled at his side, wrinkled, emaciated, ancient. He wondered whose misshapen and bent body he inhabited. And, most importantly, he wondered what it was he searched for. What answer did he seek? It was difficult for him to remember, difficult to think things through. He winced, shook his head, tried to snap the loose wires back into place. At once the world shifted, focused, and in that moment of ultra-clarity he realized what he was being beckoned toward, but as swiftly as the thought formed, it dissipated, narrowly escaping his tenuous grasp.

He was not used to walking, to any sort of exercise. He stopped repeatedly, panting for breath until his mouth tasted rust. He looked behind him at where he had come from, and it was unfamiliar. Nothing was as it had been. Not the path taken, not his marriage, not his family or friends, nothing was the same, because everything was gone. His heart raced, his breathing rushed, and all he could smell was the sweat building beneath his clothes. He took off his wedding jacket and discarded it. He loosened his shirt, desperate for more air in his lungs.

When Manifold saw the large rock ahead, rolled to the edge of the path, he wondered if it was the same rock he had been sitting on earlier. But this rock was covered almost entirely by black lichen and bore no evidence of human contact. There was certainly no cell phone left upon its stone tableau, though Manifold could feel a residual ring echoing from below its surface.

His sweat had not abated since discarding the jacket, and his jaw chattered in such a way he worried he might be suffering a stroke. His vision blurred; his legs threatened to give way. He questioned not only his senses, but his slipping sanity. Nothing around him appeared real. Especially not the advancing creatures resolving from the aether. They slithered through the underbrush, fallen leaves sluicing off their shadowy form. Manifold managed to scramble onto the large rock as they passed under foot, and he was panting as he watched them go, fading between the trees.

Manifold slowly climbed down, careful to avoid further scraping his feeble legs. When he stood, he realized his shirt had been stained black by lichen, a map of the rock's surface across his chest. It was ruined. One more cherished symbol of his love for Sandra destroyed.

Manifold unbuttoned his shirt with trembling fingers. He sensed Sandra there, shaking her head, not understanding, but paused when he felt another presence, appearing from nowhere in the wooded depths. He lifted his head to see a tall lean man watching him, standing where the trunks of the trees were their thickest; where, even leafless, the branches blotted out the sun. The dark-skinned stranger wore a thick fur coat that gave him a goatish appearance and smoked a long-stemmed wooden pipe. It was pungent and smelled of musky foreign tobacco. Manifold dropped his shirt and hobbled forward, stumbling over a root snaking from the ground. Cold prickled his naked back and arms.

"Excuse me," he said, straining to be heard over the birds chirping in the branches above. "I don't know where—I need help. I can't remember how I got here."

The man smiled and leaned against a tree. The wide trunk bent beneath his weight.

"Where do you think you are, old man?" The stranger placed the pipe upon his tongue as it puttered bluish grey fumes.

"For the life of me I don't know. I don't know how I got out here."

"Is out here not where you want to be?" An eyebrow raised.

"I don't know. I don't know where I want to be."

The man nodded sharply, then removed the pipe from his mouth and knocked the bowl against the flat of his heel. It made a hollow pop, and the birds in the branches above dispersed, scattered to the sky. The man put the pipe in his fur's pocket.

"Then come with me."

Manifold held his arms tightly, trying to shield himself from the chill. He half-suspected the stranger had made off with his shirt and jacket, just biding the time until he could secure the rest, but Manifold did not yet know why. It was becoming difficult to piece things together. To think. Much easier, then, to follow.

They walked for aeons, the sky shifting colors as though floating on oil. Manifold's feet burned, and he looked down to discover his shoes were missing, his socks in tatters, his crooked yellowed toes exposed and bleeding. He felt mold and dirt and moss underfoot, squeezing between his digits. He looked to the stranger for some explanation, but the man had vanished, leaving Manifold alone. The buzz of insects had increased, and with it the rattling of branches as animals scurried.

It was then Manifold saw the tree.

Had there been ten of him, holding hands, their bodies pressed up against the deep-grooved bark, they could not have encircled its massive trunk. The giant tree was dark grey and old, and it reached up through the canopy woven by the woods' branches—up into the heavy blanket of grey clouds.

Ripples moved along the ridges of the trunk, and it took Manifold a moment to realize it was not his failing watering eyes but hundreds of thousands of insects of all sizes covering the tree. Flies buzzed around it, circled it, lighting for an instant before flying away. Ants scurried along the deep grooves, walking around and over the dull black beetles that remained still. And the branches, full of birds chirping and screeching discomforting songs. Everything in the woods was converging on that one place, at that one moment, and a chill trickled down Manifold's back. He was dreaming yet could not wake.

He wanted to scream, the wave of drowning emotions flooding over him, but he couldn't make a sound. And yet the creatures had no trouble. The birds chirped, the insects buzzed, the woodland animals rustled and chittered and howled as they climbed over exposed roots or hung from hollowed-out tree knots.

Was this what the stranger had been leading him too? The giant tree, incongruous with what surrounded it? Was it what everything lead to?

There was a sound, beneath the buzzing and rustling and chirping. A sound like a voice, one he knew better than any he had ever heard. A sound he longed for so that it tore pieces from his heart. "Manny," it said, the voice from the distance, from somewhere up in the tree. "Manny."

It could not be Sandra's voice, but he knew it was. He gazed up into the thick tangle of gnarled branches and saw the amorphous swell of clouds, swirling among the canopy of twigs and branches. He strained, looking for movement in the mist, but ultimately found nothing. Only shadows of hopes.

He was naked, stripped of all ballast. His clothes, his family, his wife, his job—everything he had known, every place he had belonged, everything he ever had—was gone. What remained was only this: the tree; the birds; the insects; the animals. All he had left was in front of him. The rest receded into darkness.

"What are you going to do?" the stranger said, and Manifold saw him leaning against the wide trunk of the tree, once again smoking his pipe, grey smoky tendrils twisting upward, up around the lowest of the branches.

Manifold paused in thought. He felt insects light on him, crawl over his flesh, buzz every few steps. Then he forgot they were there at all.

"I think—" he tried. "I think I'm going to—" He looked up again at the giant tree endlessly looming above. He looked behind him at the path he had travelled, his footsteps filling with dirt and moss. He looked ahead at the path that quickly faded away into nothing. A dead end. "I think I want to climb."

The man shook his head, blinked twice, then barred his teeth and laughed like some strange animal. His feet clopped like hooves on the rocky ground.

"You found it," the man said. "Allow me to help you on your way."

Mirthfully, he put his pipe in his mouth and meshed his wrinkled hands. They looked familiar, but Manifold stepped into them anyway.

Hand over bloodied hand, foot over bloodied foot, Manifold climbed the tree, leaving everything behind him. He climbed upward, higher and higher, ascending into that beautiful grey fog.

THE SOMNAMBULISTS

The lobby of the Hotel Russo was large enough to get lost in, despite the enormous gold and crystal chandelier that hung at its centre. The decoration hovered so close to the ground that Seymour felt an irresistible urge to duck his pale balding head while passing beneath it. He jotted down a reminder in his pad to ensure it complied with municipal code.

At the front desk, the young woman didn't immediately see him. He had to clear his throat before she looked up, and when she did her confused expression suggested she wasn't certain what to do. She was the only clerk there, dressed in a fine vest and pressed white shirt beneath a burgundy nylon jacket, and eventually it occurred to her to ask if she could be of any help. Seymour looked into her eyes—a pair of dilated pupils surrounded by deep flecked green—and doubted her ability to deliver.

"I'm here for your preliminary inspection," Seymour said, producing a business card with his name and occupation printed squarely upon it. Perhaps the clerk was dressed more like a bellhop, with the sort of round hat he thought only existed in movies. The clerk's eyes grew wide and shifty while her forehead convulsed.

"Do—do you have a badge?"

"No. I have a card."

The bellhop clerk continued to stare at it as small beads of sweat appeared at the edge of her eyebrows. Seymour snatched the card from her hands.

"Just get me the manager," he said, and turned away to make another entry in his notebook.

Nothing about the Hotel Russo appealed to him. It felt impermanent; transient. There had been a gas station on this street corner a few
days earlier. What happened to it, and how did the Russo get built so
quickly? Seymour did not remember seeing permits or builders, and
yet here it was, erected so swiftly it was a blur. Something about the
place made his whole body tense. Some sense of familiarity he couldn't
put into words.

Across the lobby the clerk spoke with a short dark-haired man.
This, presumably, was the manager. The two indiscreetly glanced Seymour's way, but he pretended not to notice. Perhaps his indifference
would make him more intimidating.

The manager waved the nervous clerk away and immediately strode
toward Seymour, hand extended before he arrived.

"There you are," he said. "I'm Goodwin. I was wondering when
you'd appear."

The manager smiled and looked so familiar that Seymour was momentarily shaken. As though he were someone Seymour had forgotten
from a long time ago.

"I'm here from the Ministry to ensure you're properly equipped to
receive guests."

"Of course that's who you are. But this is a dream hotel. Just look
around."

"Yes, it's very nice, but you cannot operate without an inspection."

"I don't think you understand—" Goodwin said, but Seymour cut
him off.

"Let's not start on the wrong foot. The less you fight me, the faster
this will go."

"But I wasn't—"

Seymour held up his hand.

"Take me to the guest rooms. I want to assess the amenities."

Goodwin hesitated, about to say something, then changed his
mind.

"You got it. Follow me."

Goodwin reached behind the front desk and opened a concealed
small door no taller than shoulder height. Before Seymour could react, the manager crouched and passed through without a word. The
clerk appeared oblivious to Goodwin's exit, as though it hadn't actually happened. A small part of Seymour doubted what he'd seen until

Goodwin's voice echoed from beyond, beckoning him through. With hesitation, Seymour crouched and followed.

The two stood in a long, carpeted hallway, wooden doors alternating along the length of both walls.

"Are you going to be sick?" Goodwin asked.

"Pardon?"

"You don't look so well."

Seymour looked back at the door they'd come through and wondered if it had shrunk. How had he and Goodwin fit through? It was barely large enough for a child.

"The door—"

"I told you. This is a dream hotel. You get used to it."

"I don't understand..."

"Here," Goodwin said, opening one of the hallway doors. He was holding a giant key ring, but where had it come from? "Let's go inside and I'll try to explain."

Once past the door, the room did not look like a hotel suite. It looked more like the guest room of a house, with its bland decorations and worn furniture. Seymour had seen this layout, this mix of old and new, time and time again. Even as far back as the spare room in his parents' home. They were all the same. Through the walls he heard the murmurs of an argument he couldn't quite make out. It was no different from anything else there; whatever he tried to focus upon blurred and slid into the periphery of his senses.

"What is this? Is this a suite or some sort of joke?"

"What do you mean? These rooms are fantastic," Goodwin said. He pointed at the notepad. "Make sure you work that into your report somehow."

Seymour was not in the mood. Goodwin's effort at being good-natured slipped briefly, and he sighed.

"Sit down," Goodwin urged him. "You'll need a moment when you hear this."

"Hear what?" Seymour said, taking a seat on the edge of the small bed. The argument through the walls was nominally distracting.

"Where are we? Right now, where are we?"

"In an unusually decorated guest room at the Hotel Russo."

Goodwin looked around, then nodded.

"And how did we get into this guest room?"

Seymour glanced around, then offered: "We walked through a small door."

"But did we?"

Of course they had, Seymour thought, but when he tried to retrieve the chain of events from his memory, he found he couldn't. It was gone. Despite how many times he desperately wished he could forget moments from his past, now that it had happened, he found the sensation disturbing.

"What's going on?" he asked.

Goodwin stepped closer. His face was covered in tiny creases like a crumpled paper bag. His eyes, a pair of small black buttons.

"I told you. You're in a dream hotel."

"What does that mean?"

"It's..." He threw his arms wide into the air. "It's a dream hotel. That's what it means."

Seymour said nothing. He tried to take his notebook out of his pocket, but his hands were shaking. The Ministry would not approve of this.

"Look, it's very simple," Goodwin said, walking to the tall window near the bed. He ran his hand slowly down its pane. "This hotel wasn't built with bricks. It was built with dreams."

Seymour frowned. He was confused and resented being so.

Goodwin continued.

"Okay, listen, I'm not an expert on this. I'm just a regular guy who lucked into doing a job he loves. But here's what I heard from someone at corporate but don't ask me who because I can't tell you. She said this hotel actually started with a guy named Russo. We are inside his dream."

Seymour coughed. It was his body's unconscious reaction—an overwhelming mixture of incredulity and inevitability.

"Some guy named Russo?"

"Yes. At first, at least. There are about a dozen Somnambulists now. With just Russo the hotel persisted for only a few days at a time. I think he had part of the lobby in place. It was nice, pretty ornate, but so small and so short-lived that nobody could do anything with it. He treated it like a curse, which I guess it was. He never spoke about it, at least. But nevertheless, that lobby would materialize at Front and Simcoe whenever he dreamed, and eventually people started going inside and looking around."

Seymour made a note, but the words appeared as gibberish. He rubbed his eyes, but it failed to help.

"Then this Russo guy meets Dressler. I'm sure you know Dressler. Big hotel magnate. He probably owns most of the hotels you've inspected. I have no idea how their paths cross—they shouldn't have; they're from two different worlds—but they do, and someone mentions Russo's lobby and Dressler decides he needs to see it for himself. So, he takes his men and visits Front and Simcoe and finds the gas station there. Figures he's been made a fool. Then, pop, there's a half-lobby. Dressler gets one look at it and dollar signs light up his eyes. His guys round Russo up, bring him to a meeting, and Dressler asks how he can get into the Russo business. Deals are made, hands are shaken, and Russo gives everything up to sleep full time.

"It does not go smoothly. They try different ways to build up the hotel and make it permanent—they feed Russo experimental drugs, they put him in a coma, they move him to different locations and different environments to evoke a reaction. It affects Russo's mind to the point he can barely speak or remember his name, and Dressler doesn't care because it makes Russo's dreams more solid and tangible. But the hotel doesn't get bigger or stay longer, not until—and you'll love this part—Dressler's personal secretary, the one who types up all his letters, sees a story online about a woman in France who dreams up kitchens. Just goes to sleep and, boom, a kitchen appears. A full-sized, restaurant-grade kitchen. The lightbulbs ping in Dressler's head. Before the week's out, his team has found eleven more people with the ability to dream up different hotel rooms and Dressler pays to have them flown here and moved in with Russo. And, wouldn't you know it, it works. Not only do these Somnambulists start dreaming the same dream, adding their pieces to the whole, but the hotel also becomes more stable, and once it is, Dressler decides it's time to recoup his investment. That's where I come in. I get hired to manage the place and make sure it turns a profit. It's pretty damn exciting."

It made no sense. The story was familiar, but felt wrong, as though the events were out of order. Seymour rubbed his bald pate confusedly.

"But who are these Somnambulists?"

"Just a dozen random people Dressler's company found."

"So then where are they?"

Goodwin took a breath, then paused and smiled. The argument from the other room continued.

"They're definitely...somewhere. I'm not really sure where," he said, his smile unsure. "Corporate doesn't tell me everything, but I'm sure they know what they're doing. The hotel has already sold out its first two months."

"And none of the guests are worried about what they're getting into?"

Goodwin looked incredulous.

"Worried? Didn't I just say we're sold out for two whole months?"

He stood up somewhat indignantly and brushed the sheen of his dark blue jacket. Seymour suspected Goodwin was less offended than he let on.

"I suppose you need to write up your report now and let the Ministry know everything is okay. Sorry you had to waste your time coming here, but as you can see nothing needs inspecting. It's a dream, and nothing breaks or wears out in a dream. There are no rats or roaches where people don't see them. Other than a touch of vertigo from time to time, there's nothing to worry about."

"My inspection isn't done, I'm afraid," Seymour said, "I still need to see the lower levels. The mechanical rooms."

Goodwin blanched as he stammered.

"The lower levels? I can take you but there's nothing down there. Wouldn't it be better if I showed you the administration offices? You can get a feel for how we're handling the incoming guests. It's a state-of-the-art system, and it's really pretty exciting. I was just telling my wife last night—"

"Goodwin," Seymour said, snapping shut his notepad. "You'll need to take me through everything. Without a complete report, the Russo won't pass, and the Ministry will shut it down immediately. Or would you rather I go through Mr. Dressler's office?"

Seymour remained quiet and waited. The gas station wasn't important, yet it bothered him it was gone. He didn't like a building that sprang up from nowhere, changing the landscape of the city, and he didn't like how cavalier Dressler and Goodwin were about their guests' safety.

Goodwin was no longer smiling when he spoke.

"No need. We'll go to the mechanical level. Please follow me."

Goodwin led him down a papered hallway, a gold rococo design traced on the sky-blue walls. They passed beneath an archway made of red brick and too much plaster which Seymour avoided lingering on too long. He did not like this place. Even the floor was uneven, as though the hardwood were warped beneath the carpets. It was strange, though no more than the raised voices that continuously pursued them.

Around the corner waited an ornately trimmed set of elevator doors. Seymour watched the floor numbers flash without being able to make them out; the constant frustration of everything just of out sight beginning to wear on him.

"There's something off about this place. Things seem to be functioning on the surface, but everything feels unstable and wrong."

Goodwin shrugged.

"I'm not sure what you mean. It all looks fine to me."

"Everything is familiar, as though I've been here before."

"That's part of its charm. It's a dream hotel. No two people are going to experience it the same way."

"That makes no sense. You said people had constructed this place together."

"True, but that's all they're doing—dreaming it into existence. It's just a framework. This place is as much a part of the staff and the guests as it is of the Somnambulists. It's never the same from moment to moment, because it's specific to whoever is looking at it."

"I don't follow."

"I noticed you lingered on that archway back there. Was it familiar to you?"

Seymour glanced back. He'd known immediately it was the archway that held the door to his childhood home. It didn't simply look the same; it *was* the same, down to the crumbling bricks and excess mortar. It was as unnerving as it was impossible.

"Somewhat familiar."

"It means nothing to me. But it's not for me; it's for you. It's like the window back in the suite—it reminds me of my son. I can't explain all the reasons it's so important because they're so personal they wouldn't make sense to you. There's a nuance that only comes from understanding the full context of every little aspect, and unless you've lived my life you couldn't possibly.

"The rest of the hotel is the same. There are no structures here— only meanings. And the Russo is *built* on meanings, on those of the other guests, on those of the Somnambulists, and Dressler believes that rather than falling asleep so people can transverse their personal meanings, they can come to the Russo and experience those meanings filtered through the heightening prism of other people. Who knows? Maybe all those different meanings will intersect and create something new, some grand overlap where we all might finally decipher one another."

"That all sounds fine," Seymour countered.

"Fine? I think it sounds exciting!"

"But if this is such a utopia, then why do I constantly hear people arguing?"

Goodwin started to reply but was interrupted by the elevator bell and the doors parting.

They didn't reveal an elevator car, but, instead, another room. This one a dim living room with an unfinished wooden floor and a pair of torn couches positioned near a large unwashed window. Seymour knew it immediately; he'd sat invisibly in that room listening to his parents snipe at one another many times as a child. The sight of it evoked a desperate need in Seymour to flee.

"What is it?" Goodwin asked.

"This place... this room..." He couldn't speak, couldn't find the breath. Goodwin peered inside, his brow furrowed quizzically, then looked again at Seymour and put his hand on the inspector's shoulder. Seymour stiffened, but didn't protest.

"Do you still want to go on? We need to pass through here to access the rest of the hotel, but we can always turn back."

Seymour didn't know if Goodwin was being sincere, or if it were a ruse to prevent further inspection. Experience told him it was always better to assume the latter.

"I'll be fine," he said, steeling himself. "Lead on."

Goodwin hesitated.

"I need to come clean first."

Seymour had expected this, but it came at the worst possible time. He was already having trouble holding himself together.

"I told you about Dressler's plan for the Russo. What I didn't mention was the problem with it. Well, maybe not a problem. More of a hiccup, really.

"Remember how Dressler brought in the group of Somnambulists culled from all over the world? Well, it turns out that two of them had already found each other. Don't ask me how. Maybe it was through the classifieds or online. But they did and they started talking. And, as people sometimes do, they hit it off and after a time eventually married. There have been rumors about the sort of places they were dreaming up when they were together. Some people said it was the beginnings of a modest home. Other people said it was actually the makings of a palace. A few of the crazier ones said they were dreaming up a child. No one really knows and the couple couldn't tell because neither ever saw their labors. They were asleep, after all. But that was fine, because they didn't really care about houses or children. They were in love. For a while, anyway. Eventually, things went sideways, or so the story goes. Their compatibility didn't translate to the waking world—their dreams for themselves, for their lives, never meshed—and soon the arguments and the stress became too much. The young couple called it quits.

"Unfortunately for everyone, Dressler knew none of this when he found and individually recruited them to his convoy of Somnambulists, and it wasn't discovered until after they were hooked into the system and started dreaming their pieces of the Russo. By then, it was too late.

"Here's the problem: even though they haven't seen each other since before Dressler took them in, somehow each knows the other is there. Maybe it's instinct, maybe it's something else, but when they get going..." Goodwin paused. Shook his head.

"Well, I don't want to say more than I have to. Let's just go to the mechanical rooms and see how things are. I'm sure they're going to be fine. I just wanted you to be careful."

"What do you mean be careful? What's wrong down there?"

"Probably nothing. But you know how mechanical rooms are. Always a weird buzz or clang coming from someplace."

Goodwin scuttled off before Seymour could ask more questions.

The door at the other end of the room led to a dark set of stairs that Seymour and Goodwin descended. A light shone continuously from an undetected source above, throwing the steps into inky shadow in either direction. Seymour's coat grew heavy and stifling, but there was no railing for support and nowhere to rest, so he was forced to push through his discomfort.

Once they reached the ground, Seymour heard the droning buzz Goodwin had mentioned even though Goodwin, himself, could not.

"I'm probably numb to it," he said. "I've heard it so much it doesn't even register anymore."

But for Seymour the machinery's buzz shook him from inside out, triggering a cascade of sickening ripples along his back. Yet, despite the drone, that incessant arguing remained, except the voices had become more familiar. And more enraged.

"Where are you taking me," he asked. Goodwin didn't stop or slow down.

"Don't you want to see everything?"

"Yes," he said. "But why are you suddenly willing to show me?"

"Because you asked. Because even though Dressler told me to keep any problems quiet until they're resolved there's no way I can do that. Hiding them only makes them seem worse. I'm showing you so maybe you'll understand the Russo better and what we might accomplish if you give us the chance."

They reached a large square door with a giant wheel in the middle. Goodwin turned to Seymour with an uncomfortable look on his face.

"Obviously, guests aren't allowed down here, so this part of the hotel might appear... unfinished. It's not a restful place, but between you and me it's getting better. Dressler's team sent in a variety of specialists to help the Somnambulists find a harmonious balance. I'm not sure how it all works: brain waves, I think, but I'm no scientist. All I know is things are better than they used to be. Today's the first day in a while we've had any issues. I don't know," he laughed nervously. "Maybe it's because you're here."

Seymour was unamused.

"Let's get this over with," he said.

Goodwin nodded and put his hands on the wheel. With each turn, the ground twisted by a nearly imperceptible degree, forcing everything slightly askew. Seymour didn't know if it was real or a figment of the dark. When the metal door swung open, it revealed the small kitchen from Seymour's childhood. Cabinet doors were cracked and hung partially open from their broken hinges, and the stovetop was caked with hardened spill-over around each of the elements. The refrigerator, too, was browned by old fingerprints, and the floor was carved with long grooves from shifted appliances. The memory of the last time he stood there floated just beneath the surface of his psyche—him banging his teenaged fists on the countertop, demanding attention he would never get. Things in the Russo were becoming too personal.

"The machine room is just up here."

Beyond the kitchen lay a dim grey room, sparse and clinical. In its middle, arranged in a circle around a tower of black machines and blinking lights, were nine hospital beds, each occupied by a sleeper connected to an intravenous drip and sensors. No one else was in the room but Seymour and Goodwin, and yet the intense shouting now seemed to surround them.

"These are the Somnambulists," Goodwin said, his voice raised to nearly a yell. "Dressler's team moved them here to try and stabilize the hotel."

"Stabilize it from what?"

As if on cue, a tremor rippled up Seymour's legs. He glanced down for an instant, long enough for his surroundings to transform from his parents' kitchen into their attic. Yet the occupied beds and machinery remained.

"Things shift more the closer we are to the Somnambulists," Goodwin shouted. "Their individual dreams haven't had enough time to synch with one another. It's stranger down here than anywhere else."

"How can you possibly think the Ministry would allow this? What kind of hotel are you running here?"

Goodwin appeared both embarrassed and worried.

"It's—well, like I said, today's been a bad day."

Seymour looked at the beds, at each sleeping face in turn. The Somnambulists appeared untroubled, but what did that mean? He might be able to make sense of it were the disembodied screaming to stop. But it wouldn't. He felt as though he were a child again, lying on the dusty floor of that attic, trying to both hear his parents and yet stifle their sniping voices. Lying in that same musty attic the Somnambulists had occupied now. And as Seymour realized this, the screaming voices became his parents'. He shook his head to dispel the hallucination, then paused.

"Wait. Didn't you say there were twelve Somnambulists?"

"Yeah. We isolated the couple from the group until we know what to do with them. They're here and close by, but like I said they haven't integrated correctly; their dreams aren't fully synched. The seams between them, and between them and the rest, are starting to show. Thankfully, it's only happening here on the lower levels where the guests aren't allowed."

Rumbling returned to Seymour's legs, and the shouting voices so like his parents' filled him with dread. The attic was changing once more, abandoned boxes becoming door frames, dusty lamps becoming framed photographs, different forms melting into one another or swapping with an inaudible pop, and after the shift he found the walls had become those from the old house's hallway, the bedroom doors all ominously closed, but warped enough that light creeped out in thin strips around the frame. He followed them down the hallway toward his parents' bedroom, the door of which appeared to be flickering rapidly out of place. If the final two Somnambulists were anywhere, they would be in there.

As he opened the door, Seymour prepared himself to find the young couple in his parents' bedroom, dreaming their unique aspects of the hotel into existence, because where else would they be but there? Instead, what he found looked nothing like that bedroom, or the attic, or the kitchen, or living room. What he found looked nothing like these things because it looked like *all* things at once, all at tenuous odds with one another. Pushing and pulling with such force that the earth beneath his feet churned violently—asphalt and concrete and hardwood and porcelain ingested and regurgitated, a never-ending collision of rebirth. At the opposite end of the room flickered a dim red light from a glowing exit sign.

"What's going on in here?" he asked.

Goodwin's voice cracked.

"I tried to tell you. Those two Somnambulists are an issue we're trying to resolve. We just can't figure out how yet."

"Do you know who they are? Do you know their names?" Seymour asked, though he already suspected the answer.

"I don't even think Dressler knows their names. They're just Somnambulists, they're all the same. All except Russo. It's his dream they're all building on."

Seymour looked back into the room they'd come from.

"Which one was Russo?"

Goodwin didn't bother looking.

"I have no idea."

It was getting colder and louder, and the red exit light wavered ahead. The walls transformed around Seymour like a kaleidoscope, except instead of colors they were aspects of his life he barely recognized. He pulled his thick coat closer and stepped forward. Underfoot he found a rug from his old home, except soggy and soiled, torn where uneven hardwood surged through. He cursed, and went to take another step, but Goodwin's hand gripped his arm.

"I was wrong. It's not safe."

"Goodwin, you need to help me get to those last two Somnambulists."

"Are you crazy? The dreams here aren't fully meshed. If we go any closer, we might not find our way back."

"I have to see them, Goodwin. I have to know."

"Know what?"

"I have to know who they are. If they're my parents."

"They're too young. And they never had a child. I told you that."

"Are you sure?"

He paused for a moment.

"No," he finally said. "I guess not."

Seymour had trouble returning Goodwin's stare. Everything was too wild, too disconnected, and he couldn't focus on any one point long enough to understand it. Only the flickering exit light was permanent.

"Help me," Seymour said.

So they walked into the inchoate chaos. At times their feet no longer touched anything solid, while around them the world churned and the angry voices grew clearer. With each step Seymour was increasingly convinced his parents' voices rattled across the room's impermanent structures. Bricks slipped away from bricks, mortar dust crumbled, first from one wall, then another. Volley and return, the room shrinking with each word as Seymour dashed toward the red light and into an Escheresque world of upside down stairs and sideways scaffolds in continuous flux. What was once a door became a window became a wall, and more than once Goodwin was the only thing that stopped Seymour from stepping through a collapsing passage. When Seymour's notepad slipped from his pocket it moved straight past his head and spun away as though caught by the wind. But it didn't matter; he no longer needed it.

"Do you know where we're going?" Seymour asked.

"It's just through here," Goodwin said, as if those simple directions weren't disconnected from space.

But in the structureless void Goodwin's hand remained locked on Seymour's arm. There was a tug like a fish on a line and Seymour found himself overwhelmed by a tumultuous current, and then spit out into a small bedroom lit by a corona of sunlight around drawn orange drapes. It was his parents' bedroom. But Seymour was interested only in the two bodies lying beside one another in matching hospital beds, a second tower of black machinery and blinking lights between them.

"Here they are," Goodwin said, but Seymour didn't need to be told. He could feel them. He'd always been able to feel them. Waves emanated outward, lapping against his body like ripples in the sea. He raised his hand, and the waves broke against his palms, slipped between his fingers.

The two bodies were underneath thin grey blankets, chests rising and lowering slowing. They faced away from him, so Seymour saw only the tops of their heads, but the color and style of their hair looked right.

"Is this what you expected?"

Seymour didn't know what he expected. When he tried to remember last seeing his parents together, he couldn't. It was as though it had been witnessed by someone else, some other Seymour with whom he shared only the faintest memories. *That* Seymour must have understood more than this one, because faced with the two sleeping figures he had no idea what he thought would happen. Were they supposed to spring up and hug him, then each other? Were they supposed to remain asleep forever, fading at once from his memory? Was this a moment of hello or goodbye?

"I don't know," he admitted.

Goodwin nodded, put his hand on Seymour's shoulder. "Some of us in the hotel argue about the Somnambulists, about why they'd agree to spend their short lives dreaming for other people. They don't get to experience things like the rest of us, don't get to visit far off places or try new things, fall in or out of love. Sure, they could do these things in a dream, but is it really the same? I spoke to one of Dressler's men once and he told me that according to their research the Somnambulists have always been like this, even in the waking world. Their dreams so consumed them that eventually the only way they could perceive the outside world was through their dreams. Always one step removed from the immediate, from the here and now. I don't know. It doesn't sound like much of a life to me. No wonder they agreed to withdraw into the one place they felt real."

But that's not why his parents withdrew. It wasn't to feel real, because they were real. What they wanted was escape—not from the world, but from him.

His parents abandoned him. They sank into the depths of anger and spite and sneers, slowly wearing away any happiness that lingered, until it was only a memory. Until it was less than a memory. When Seymour tried, he couldn't recall it ever being different. The memories were nothing, burning flash paper floating on air, consumed instantly and utterly.

Seymour approached the beds, taking care not to touch the humming equipment, the wires and lights. He realized his parents' arguing voices, so loud before, were now gone, leaving a still emptiness for the hotel's hum to occupy. Before him were the two sleeping Somnambulists, their faces buried in their pillows. They looked strange, like discarded string puppets waiting for life to be poured into them. The unbearable sadness of seeing them so mortal overtook him; he was witnessing the ineffable transformed into flesh and blood, into the everyday. He reached out to touch his sleeping mother's cheek, to take his father's inanimate hand, and as he did so he realized neither of them had any features. Their faces were blank.

Seymour stood disoriented in a lightless room. It was the size of a shed, walled in by glass and surrounded by counters faced with candy. Pine tree air fresheners hung over his head and gave the enclosure a sickening stench that nevertheless could not disguise the gasoline fumes. He spun around but there was no trace of the hotel, no indication he'd been anywhere else. Even Goodwin was gone, leaving Seymour alone in the shuttered gas station, lit only by the head and taillights moving along Front Street. He felt tired, as though he'd just woken from a fitful sleep; grimy slickness coated his fingers and crept into his bleary eyes. He didn't understand what happened; it made less sense the longer he thought about it.

In his pocket he found his notepad, not lost at all, and was surprised to discover it was filled with scribbles and half-formed scrawls he had no memory of writing. His phone was there, too, but he could not remember the Ministry's number.

Seymour tested the lock on the gas station door, then searched frantically for the key. He found it eventually in a small dish behind the cashier's plexiglass shield, which filled him with relief. He'd escaped whatever insanity he'd been suffering, the terrible dream that had led him unbelievably to a gas station on the other end of the city. Already, the dream was fading, and he was anxious to return home to the warm safety of his own bed. He slid the key into the lock, felt the tumblers click into place, and turned the bolt. The glass door's lock clapped open and swung aside.

And the dark that met him was fathomlessness and unbroken.

"What the hell?" Seymour said, then turned and found the gas station gone as well. The void stretched over everything, leaving nothing but a single red light, flickering in the distance.

"What's going on in here?" he asked.

Goodwin's voice cracked.

"I tried to tell you. Those two Somnambulists are an issue we're trying to resolve. We just can't figure out how yet."

"Do you know who they are? Do you know their names?" Seymour asked, though he already suspected the answer.

"I don't even think Dressler knows their names. They're just Somnambulists, they're all the same. All except Russo. It's his dream they're all building on."

Seymour looked back into the room they'd come from.

"Which one was Russo?"

Goodwin didn't bother looking.

"I have no idea."

But didn't he? Because Seymour had been here before, in this spot, watching the ground beneath him in constant flux, listening to the voices arguing, and he didn't see how it was possible not to know who Russo was. If he was the primary Somnambulist, the one onto whose dream all others adhered, then what sense did it make not to protect him? Why even bring him to the hotel at all, to the centre of his own dream? And how could he exist in a place he was creating? If he woke and the hotel disappeared, where would he go?

"The dreamer inside the dream," Goodwin said from beneath the red light, dressed in a matching black winter coat with grey fur trim around the collar, and when Seymour looked at him, baffled, Goodwin laughed. Everything was so much colder, so much darker and drabber, that Seymour thought nothing of the snow that dusted the upturned ground and uneven bricks. Goodwin flickered in and out of sight under the unstable glow of the red exit sign. It was as though he might not even be there at all.

And then he wasn't.

Seymour stood alone in a crumbling room with a small red light in the far corner, illuminating nothing but a twin pair of hospital beds in the middle, the machinery between them inactive. Seymour made his way across the broken chunks of concrete and rock that buckled and sagged toward the beds, toward the two shapes lying there beneath a pair of thin snow-dusted blankets. Seymour's breath clouded before him, but those two shapes did not stir, and he felt out of scale with the world, as though he'd diminished in their presence. Seymour could see only shadows of their hair in the red light, and when he reached forward to peel back the blankets, he wondered what he would say if they woke. If he would ask them what happened, how they got there. Seymour took a corner of each blanket and drew them back to reveal the Somnambulists' faces, only those faces were blank.

He grew more confused the longer he stood next to Goodwin.

"What's going on in here," he asked.

Goodwin's voice cracked.

"I tried to tell you. Those two Somnambulists are an issue we're trying to resolve. We just can't figure out how yet."

"Do you know who they are? Do you know their names?" Seymour asked, though he already knew the answer.

"I don't even think Dressler knows their names. They're just Somnambulists, they're all the same. All except Russo. It's his dream they're all building on."

Seymour looked back through the long series of rooms they'd come from.

"Which one was Russo?"

Goodwin didn't bother looking.

"How many times do I have to tell you?"

Seymour looked at him, baffled, and Goodwin laughed from beneath the red light, dressed in a matching black winter coat with grey fur trim around the collar. Everything was so frigid that Seymour thought nothing of the inches of snow that blanketed the upturned ground and uneven bricks. Goodwin flickered in and out of sight under the unstable glow of the red exit sign. It was as though he might not even be there at all.

And then he wasn't.

Seymour stood alone in a crumbling snow-filled room with a small red light in the far corner, faintly illuminating nothing but a single occupied bed in the middle, the machinery beside it inactive.

The air held no warmth as Seymour attempted to cross the broken ground. He'd been here before. He'd been here many times before. Over and over again, a nightmare of continuous waking, a dream inside a dream inside a dream, all leading him forward a step at a time toward some inexorable truth, some understanding that he wasn't able to grasp. That he'd never been able to grasp, not when his mother and father refused to see him, not when the Ministry sent him to investigate a hotel he could barely remember. All of it meant something, was a stone in the road leading him here, to this room, in this snow and cold that bit so hard he could no longer feel his hands. At the bottom of the hotel, buried beneath so many dreams, where nothing made sense because a dozen people could not agree on anything. Because even two people could not agree on anything, too distracted by their dreams and their dream's dreams to find that one place where they could mesh together. All they did was fight and bicker and make snide comments until Seymour felt four-foot tall. Until he shrank even further than that. And their faces became as large as moons and as red as dusk, and he shouted and stomped and cried in hopes they'd see him, that they'd listen to his frail little voice, that they'd acknowledge he was there, that he was real. Because he was. He was real. Real as anyone. Made of flesh and blood and bone. He was real and present and demanded to be seen. Demanded to be heard.

But there was no one to listen. There was only the single hospital bed. There was only the tiny red light. And it read "exit" over and over again as he stood beneath it, the only light left. And under its nascent glow he saw the bed and the twisted lump of blankets upon it. He searched for some sign of who it was hidden in the folds, dreaming and dreaming and dreaming, but there was nothing. Just the rise and fall of someone breathing. The machinery around the bed hummed and lit up, little colored lights flickering on and off and Seymour reached forward to take a corner of the blanket—to do what he had done so many, too many, times before—and slowly peeled it back to reveal the bald pale head beneath. Then pulled further until the sleeper's full face was revealed. He stared at it a long time, trying unsuccessfully to remember where he'd seen it before.

INTERIOR DESIGNS

PART I

I

Ha-Yoon watched a solitary wasp crawl across her cracked windshield and tried to stay calm. She'd only agreed to the design job for a chance to work with Katherine Awl—that, and to use Royce Ballast as she'd been used by him. If that required dealing with her former mentor again, so be it. There wasn't much worse he could do to her.

And Ha-Yoon needed the work. Anything she could get as long as it kept her from feeling like a failure. The last thing she wanted was to end up back with her mother—her apartment and independent life forfeited. She couldn't give up, not after suffering and surviving so much. She had to take back control of her life; no more letting things just happen to her, things no one deserved. Things Dr. Scarfke kept telling her to make peace with, no matter how impossible that seemed.

Royce would only call the house "the property" when he laid everything out for her, but Ha-Yoon knew it was more than that. It was a monument to the hell of scrutiny and suspicion Katherine Awl had lived through. Yet it was also a house. A *big* house, but still a house, with a giant gabled roof slanted on both sides that gave way to smaller roofs which, in turn, continued the cascade into a pair of flats. The entire structure was symmetrical, an appeal most likely to the neo-traditionalist architects who had designed it. It was inspiring in size alone.

In every other way, the oatmeal-brown façade was so unremarkable it might well have been invisible. But this was how houses were built today. Without personality. Their problems hidden behind their plain, unappealing exteriors.

But maybe Ha-Yoon was mirroring.

A half-dozen pickup trucks and a large piece of machinery Ha-Yoon didn't recognize were parked out front. Men—large, tanned, or olive-skinned—buzzed around the exterior, digging up bushes or replanting them, carrying long planks of wood in a stream through the front door. Ha-Yoon turned off her engine and watched them with mounting anxiety. She fought the urge to leave and to hate herself for feeling that way.

Despite all she'd suffered to get there, she still wasn't convinced she could do what Royce had hired her for. To calm herself, she removed the folded letter from the inside pocket of her jacket. It was a single sheet of lilac-colored paper, yet its weight was unmeasurable. She skimmed it for the hundredth time. Then skimmed it again, hoping to internalize the words. Hoping to believe them. When she got all she was going to get from it, Ha-Yoon folded the letter once more and placed it back into her jacket, then squeezed her eyes shut. Willed her heart to slow, her breathing to steady. She thought of Dr. Scarfke, and of the past she wanted to leave behind.

When she opened her eyes, she found her hand on the ignition key.

Before she could turn it, a sudden rap on her window made her jump.

2

"Ha-Yoon?"

She flushed, then turned to see who was standing there. Her disappointment was overwhelming. He knocked again, impatiently, so Ha-Yoon begrudgingly rolled down her window an inch. He hooked one arm over the Corolla's roof, then leaned his face into the narrow gap.

"You coming in? Or did you drive all this way just to gawk?"

In the wake of everything between her and Royce, Ha-Yoon had hoped never to see Diego again. Yet there he was, looking more or less the same. A bit older and less polished than before, but the added weather suited him—the dirty boots and collar-length hair curled behind his ears lent him a comfortable ruggedness.

Her envy of him irritated her.

"Come on. Get out of the car," he said.

It wasn't too late to go, she reminded herself.

Instead, she screwed up her remaining courage and shouldered open the car door. Diego retreated a step as she emerged into a world muted by her terror. Instinctively, she cinched her blouse collar tighter before willing herself to stop. Dr. Scarfke would not have approved.

"To be honest," Diego laughed, "when I saw you pull up, I thought you were the new framer we've been expecting. This is a much nicer surprise."

"No one told me you were going to be here," she said.

He smiled. "Would you have come if they had?"

She left the question alone. It didn't need to be answered.

Before either could speak, Diego's phone rang. He quickly withdrew it from his pocket and checked the screen. His face changed immediately.

That's how Ha-Yoon knew who was calling.

He put the phone to his chest. "I'm sorry. I have to take this," he said, then pointed her toward the house. "If you need something, have one of the contractors raise me on the radio."

Ha-Yoon forced a cursory smile for which she hated herself. And the nod she received in return would have been excruciating had it clearly not been meant for her. It was in response to Royce on the other end of the call. She knew because when Diego spoke, he used a different tone than with her—both more direct and aggressive. It was grating, but she didn't have to suffer it long. Almost as soon as he started speaking, Diego was walking away from her without a glance. She grimaced, then pulled the straps of her backpack tighter and strode toward the house.

3

The first thing she saw upon entering were Diego's contractors. They stared through her skin and flesh, likely noticing she was nothing more than a mass of slithering emotions. Then, just as quickly as they looked, they looked away and returned to their tasks. It was so swift and complete that she second-guessed whether they'd noticed her at all.

The large house was full of projects at different stages. Walls were torn down to the studs, sheetrock stacked in tall dusty piles or half-plastered. Wires ran in all directions, some connected to ungrounded steel outlet boxes. Ha-Yoon could tell where the lights were intended to hang by the weighted chains that swung above her. Despite everything being done—the sawing and hammering, the sweating and cursing—Ha-Yoon saw the finished house apparating around her. The unfinished walls and dirty floor were still bones, but beyond them, she saw the specter of muscles and flesh, the haunting of what was to come. It had been the one thing she could do that no one else in her classes could, the thing she once thought Royce valued before she realized how little he valued anything about her. Ha-Yoon *saw*. She saw where the wainscotting would run, where the doorways would arc. She understood how the rooms would be angled to give the illusion of endless space and how the grain of the hardwood floors would direct visitors' eyes to the central staircase that rose in a spiral from the ground like a grand organic helix. It was all there, as clear as morning to her. She didn't even need photographs to record it.

Nevertheless, she fished her camera out of her backpack. It was better to have photographs she didn't need than to not have photographs she did, she thought. But holding the camera to take pictures was also something to busy her hands and keep her from wringing them.

4

Ha-Yoon had been only passingly aware of the Katherine Awl controversy when she accepted the job. Being too young to have lived through it, everything she'd learned she'd gleaned from popular culture. The stories, the late-night monologue jokes, all presented a unified picture of what had happened to Awl and why. It was a picture she believed at the time because why shouldn't she? The world had agreed upon the truth, even if no one came right out and said it: what happened had been her own fault. And yet Awl, until then an unknown actress in a series of television advertisements where she dressed as a bee and hawked car insurance, managed to turn it into a payday. Some people said they were jealous; they'd suffer through the same indignities if it meant being so richly rewarded. Ha-Yoon shuddered at the ignorance of it all. Shuddered and was angered at her own naïve acceptance of the narrative.

5

When Ha-Yoon eventually reached the second floor, the wave of frustration and despair she felt nearly sent her running. It was just as chaotic, just as full of contractors as the first. One dressed in a sleeveless shirt operated a table saw, angling two-by-fours, while another assisted him by stacking the cut pieces in alternating rows. A pair of workers were near another wall, their heavy-gloved hands pulling foot after foot of black and white wiring out of a small square hole. Hammering and electrical whining surrounded her, bowing the strings of her nerves. And the smell? It was as though the entire room, perhaps the entire house, was doused with a rancid musk. Her throat and nose were caked with it. The stench of men.

At least none of them had noticed her yet. But their wolf ears might perk and turn toward her at any moment. She had to decide: did she start taking photographs, taking measurements; or did she leave? Wade in or run? Her stomach clenched. How *dare* those be her only two options? It wasn't right, the things she'd had to endure. So many terrible things cascading. It was infuriating and made her—

Ha-Yoon swung her head around. Looked down the staircase.

Did she just—?

She could have sworn—

No, there was no one there. It just felt as though there were. Like someone closing in, crowding her. Suffocating her.

Enough. Royce may have wanted otherwise, but Ha-Yoon was determined to extract the career he'd stolen from her. She would not let him win. Would not be controlled. Not again. She took a deep breath and held it. Let it trickle out slowly. Then, holding her camera ahead of her as a shield, pushed forward into the breach.

The second floor was no smaller than the first but felt tiny, with so many of Diego's crew filling it, their sweating bodies swallowing up space and oxygen. Stepping from stairwell to hallways, Ha-Yoon felt a wave of sticky humidity slam into her, inducing an unsteadiness that she had to combat. The last thing she wanted was to stand still. Men shoved past as though she weren't there—each a funhouse mirror, more distorted than the one before. Her every cell was on high alert, awaiting that moment they turned on her, eyes watering with hunger, lips engorged with blood. She sensed their coiled muscles, their bodies tensed in silent anticipation of violence. All they needed was opportunity. Ha-Yoon snapped photographs of the rooms as quickly as she could and kept moving deeper into the house.

How she wished she could have confronted those staring men. Dr. Scarfke said it was natural and that her wounds would heal if she didn't worry them. But they didn't feel any less raw. If anything, they felt deeper. Ha-Yoon told her she didn't know if she could work through it, but Dr. Scarfke had something for that as well. She said the work is never easy. That's why it was called work. Ha-Yoon didn't know about that. What she did know was she'd been trapped under the weight of what Royce had done for too long.

Navigating the unlit half of the floor was harder than she expected. It was a large house, and enough walls were erected to block her from where the contractors were working, but she was startled by how easy it was to get lost. Hadn't she taken a simple turn? Why, then, were there walls where there should have been doors? It was upsetting to realize she might be simply traveling in circles and would soon come across the same men she'd hoped to avoid.

As if in response, someone darted past the end of the hallway. At least, she thought they did. It wasn't movement so much as the impression of movement. As though she'd looked up just in time to see the air disturbed by their wake.

"Hello?"

In the dark her voice seemed insufficient. And the hallway remained empty. But something was just around the corner, waiting. Some*one*, she meant. Small lights reflected against the walls, a glittering shimmer. A faint buzzing grew louder as she proceeded down the hall.

Ha-Yoon followed it to a door at the end of the house. It looked out of place, made of old reclaimed wood, its bottom half stained by something dark. Ha-Yoon pressed her hand against it, and the buzzing seemed to dull. The vibrations made her uncomfortable, inducing an unsettling sickness in her gut. What kind of work was Diego's team doing behind the door? Ha-Yoon clenched her hand into a tight fist. Knocked. The buzzing stopped.

"Hello?"

She tested the doorknob. It was locked.

"Is someone in there?"

She waited, but there was no sound.

Then, something farther down the hallway. Another noise. A different noise. Was it a footstep? Something else? It sounded like something sliding along the floor.

She took a step back.

"Whoever you are, you better stop it."

But it didn't stop. She heard the noise again.

Then again.

Ha-Yoon took another step back. Her backpack was suddenly too heavy, too encumbering.

"Leave me alone," she said, searching the shadowed hallway for movement. "Or you're going to wish you did."

The noise was not warned off. It grew louder, harder to locate. But still inched closer.

"You'd better—" she started, but before she could finish, the panic overtook her, and she was running.

The noise chased after her.

6

Ha-Yoon couldn't think. Her fright was too overwhelming—it flooded her thoughts with unwanted images. She skidded around corners, past unmudded walls, desperate for the way out. Where had it gone? Behind her, the sliding noise grew louder. More intense. Almost on top of her. The hairs on her neck rose; the terrible fluttering in her ears intensified. Everything became a series of flashes. Everything falling to pieces.

In an instant, she was again surrounded by contractors. Each as still as a statue, watching her plow through their workspace. Ahead, the staircase, and she aimed for it, narrowly avoiding sparking equipment and fallen beams. A shadow darted in front of her, but there was no time to stop. She shoved the person aside and kept moving. She was on the stairs when she heard them crash behind her. Clung tight to the railing for fear of losing her footing.

She remained upright long enough to reach the ground floor. Once there, she didn't stop. Not until she was through the front door.

Not until the house was yards behind her. Only then did she realize she was near collapse. She stopped, bent over, and gulped down air while her eyes filled with glittering stars. After a moment, they faded, and Ha-Yoon glanced hurriedly back to ensure she wasn't followed. And kept doing so until she was sure.

Or as sure as she could be.

Then Diego's hand landed on her shoulder, and she screamed.

"Hey," he said, startled. "Are you doing okay?"

7

He stood over her, looking worried. For a second she saw herself though his eyes—short, pudgy Ha-Yoon, a ball of anxiety on the run from nothing. She rubbed her hands through her hair, ignoring how flush her face must be.

"I thought I saw something. I got spooked."

"What did you see?"

"I don't know. Nothing. It just felt like someone was watching me."

"One of my guys was watching you?"

"No. I mean, maybe? I don't know."

Diego looked at her queerly. Then, hesitantly shrugged.

"Well, I hope it was nothing. But let me know if it happens again. I won't stand for it."

"Yeah. I'm sure you won't," she said, then adjusted her backpack and straightened her clothes. She sniffled once, then, worried he'd think she'd been crying, refused to do so again. "Anyway, now that I'm out here, I should take photographs of the exterior. For the proposal."

"Maybe I'll come with you," he said.

"No." She shook her head sharply. "No, that's not necessary."

"I know it's not. I'll come anyway."

"I don't need you to."

Diego shrugged again.

8

She held her camera, hands trembling, as Diego followed too close behind her.

"Do you mind?" she said.

"Mind what?"

Why couldn't he leave her alone? Part of her hated him for what he did. Or, rather, what he didn't do but could have. At least Royce never pretended things hadn't fundamentally changed. It was honest in a duplicitous way, even if she didn't yet know it. But Diego? He wasn't honest then, and he wasn't now. Royce was vile, but Diego's inaction had cut her deep.

She sped up her pace to put more distance between them.

Ha-Yoon only stopped to avoid one of the contractors as he walked past, a coil of wire over his shoulder. Once sure he was out of reach, she lifted her camera and snapped a photograph of the house's faux shutters. Through the viewfinder, things looked blurry. She cursed. The job had been nothing but trouble thus far.

"It's quite a property, isn't it?" Diego said. "It's amazing how much gossip pays. It's almost worth the scandal."

Whatever look she gave him was enough to make him falter.

"I didn't mean..." he started, then trailed off.

Ha-Yoon continued to photograph the house's exterior. The arches below the flat roof drew her attention first, the way they seemed to support the smaller structures, dispersing both their real and implied weight. What really struck her, though, was the peak of the house, which stood like a monolith, surveying the wooded grounds around it—the house's one stained glass eye never blinking.

But Ha-Yoon saw a strange dark hemorrhage in that eye. She raised the camera again; took another photograph. Why were things still so fuzzy? What was that sound in her ears?

She turned her head and saw Diego engaged with a pair of contractors, their arms covered to their shoulders in dirt. They were trying to navigate planting a large bush near the side of the house.

"Careful with that one," Diego said.

"Arborvitae don't like to be moved," said the older of the two. His grey mustache was bushy and faintly yellowed. "Too much stress could kill it."

"Makes sense."

Then, the bald younger worker interjected.

"Did the new framer show, boss?"

"Not yet," Diego said.

"Maybe you should try calling Aahvan again."

The older man gave him a quick sharp look but the younger didn't catch it. One corner of Diego's mouth curled. Just a little.

"If you know where to find him, let me know."

"Yeah. Both you and those cops."

"Shut it," the older man said, and his partner immediately turned his concentration toward getting the bush situated.

Diego grinned, then noticed Ha-Yoon watching him. He kept grinning in the afternoon sun. Everything looked gauzy to Ha-Yoon. But she was less interested in what she was seeing and more in what she'd just heard.

"The police?"

Diego brushed off his hands.

"Ah, don't listen to him. Landscapers are the biggest gossips."

"Why were the police looking for your old framer?"

"Don't know. Something about his wife, maybe?"

Maybe. Such an easy word to use. So full of potential meaning.

"Anyway, it's none of my business. Or wouldn't be if he'd shown back up to work. Now I have to replace him. Something else to worry about."

The old landscaper's shout interrupted them. The bush he and his younger assistant were carrying had begun to tip, and the two were juggling to keep it from rolling over. They almost lost control of it but managed to right it at the last moment. When it was securely upright, the older man gave the younger a look that boiled with anger.

"It's a pretty bush," Diego said once it was safely on the ground. "Problem is it attracts wasps. Too many of those, and they'll start looking for a way in."

"Too late for that," Ha-Yoon said, and when he didn't understand what she meant, she pointed up at the hemorrhage in the stained-glass window.

9

Diego put his hands over his eyes and squinted. Wrinkles crawled out from behind his glasses.

"What am I looking at?" he finally asked. Ha-Yoon loaded the digital photographs, zoomed in, and then flipped her camera around. He took it from her reluctant hands.

"See that shadow around the window?" she said. "That's a wasp nest."

He looked up again.

"I think you're right."

Of course, she was right. Wasps. Not that he should worry. It was already getting too cold for them. The wasps they were seeing were drones. Useless male wasps, kicked out of the nest because they were no longer needed. They were just wandering, waiting to die.

Ha-Yoon fell in love with that fact the first time she heard it. It didn't even matter if it wasn't true. She hoped it was, though.

He turned away from the house and handed her back the camera. Then he took a breath, as though about to say something heavy.

Oh no, Ha-Yoon thought.

"You know, I should have said this earlier—well, a lot earlier, really—but I'm sorry about what happened."

"What happened?" she asked, though she knew exactly what he meant. She wanted to give him the chance to steer away. But, really, why should she? Why give him a way to shirk responsibility? She hated that she wasn't stronger.

"With Royce. What happened with Royce."

Just hearing his name made her nausea worsen. She definitely didn't feel right. Not at all.

"Maybe we should focus on the wasps," she said.

Diego ran his hand through his greying hair, visibly relieved to be let off the hook.

"Yeah. The attic window doesn't open, so I'm going to have to send someone up on an extension ladder to take care of that."

"The attic?"

"It's not finished, but yeah, the house has an attic. Royce had us hide the stairs to it behind an old, stained door he had flown in specially from California."

"I know that door," Ha-Yoon said. "Your men were working on the other side of it earlier."

"What? No. Not my men." Diego's expression transformed so quickly that Ha-Yoon didn't see it happen. She unconsciously clenched at her blouse collar.

"I heard them."

"You couldn't have. No one is working up there. I made that clear."

Ha-Yoon didn't know what she was supposed to say. Diego looked angry. She pulled her backpack strap tighter.

"These guys, they never listen. You're lucky if they even show up half the time. We were supposed to be done this job two weeks ago, but it feels like we've barely started."

Ha-Yoon glanced awkwardly around her. No one was close enough to hear, unless you counted the stray wasps above them. But she still didn't feel right. Not at all.

"I don't want to be in your way—" she started to say, but as she did, she made the mistake of looking up at the stained-glass window again as two terrifying things happened simultaneously.

The first was that the world began to violently churn and spiral away from her. As though she were suddenly falling into a whirlpool of darkness. It rushed toward her, so cold that her entire body went numb. In her panic, she shouted but couldn't hear what she said.

The second was that as she fell, she managed to get one last glimpse of the stained-glass window, and of the silhouette on the other side of it, calmly watching her descent into the eye of that spinning dark storm.

10

Terror. Sweat. Fear. Frantically pacing pacing pacing in front of his office door. Through the frosted window, a dark shape. Another set of legs. Another young brunette. Royce had a type. Nothing like Ha-Yoon.

Then she was in the office, her mouth dry. Water. She needed water but couldn't drink any. Not with her stomach flipped inside out. Revolting.

Couldn't think; something was wrong. The edges of her sight were dark, with creeping shadows. The receptionist fluttered her eyelashes and said something garbled, but lithe arms waved Ha-Yoon in. Past the big door. Into Royce's office.

Every nightmare returned. What was she doing here? Why had she come? Royce. Royce had invited her. Why? To apologize? To warn? To intimidate?

Why was she here?

Was the room upside down? Was she on her back, looking up? Images flashed too quickly. The colors of the room. The light was unnatural. A sunset in the morning.

Royce spoke. Ha-Yoon couldn't hear him. Only a whomping. Like a heart, but not hers. Someone else's. Someone giant. Thumping like a full-fisted knock on the door. Blocking everything out.

His voice a trumpet without accompaniment. He smiled with a million teeth. Lips too swollen for such a pale face. An ape, laughing, incisors bared. Maybe it *was* a warning.

Royce shouted, and the world spun around the axis of his face. He furrowed his brow, so she spoke. Was it right? She might know if she knew what she said. It must have been because he was laughing again.

When did he stand up? When did he walk over to her? His hand, on her shoulder, pinched the nape of her neck. Revulsion convulsed up her spine. She screamed. Maybe. If so, he didn't react.

Royce told her something. Was it about a house? Was that right? No, a job. A job at a house. A job? The darkness around her vision fluctuated, pulsed, inching forward and back. Forward and back. Her back hurt. He was moving forward and back. She closed her eyes, but the darkness didn't leave. Royce offered her a job, but she didn't understand what that meant. It didn't make sense. Didn't he get it? Didn't he know? Ha-Yoon wanted to say something, but she couldn't. The room was no longer his office. The world was no longer his grin. She was outside. How did that happen? Ha-Yoon shivered, looked at her aching hands. There was a sheet of paper in the right one. Light blue, crumpled. There was an address written on it. In her other hand, a smaller piece of paper. A check.

It wouldn't shut up, Mother. But it was close.

Ha-Yoon's deal with the devil.

II

Ha-Yoon opened her eyes to a white void. She blinked, then sat up. No, not a void. The primed ceiling of an unfurnished room. She lay on the floor on a plaster-dusted blanket and saw, beyond a workbench and power tools, a staggered line of contractors as they walked past the doorway. None of them would look at her, yet they felt like sentries, there to ensure she couldn't leave. Diego appeared from behind them. His grey curls more pronounced than ever.

"Good. You're awake."

"What happened?"

"I don't know. We were outside, then you shouted some gibberish and fainted."

"I what—?"

Immediately, she checked her clothes. They were on right. And the letter? The letter was in her breast pocket where she kept it. She felt relieved, but it was short-lived. Fragments of what happened returned suddenly. There was shouting, then something else. Something....

She turned cold.

"I have to go," she said.

"You can't. Not until I'm sure you're okay."

Before she could insist, one of Diego's contractors stopped and whispered something to him. Ha-Yoon suspected she knew what it was about. She scanned the room quickly for her backpack. It leaned against the wall near the door.

"I'm leaving," she said, forcing herself to her feet.

But the world flipped before she took her first step, and when it righted, she was in Diego's arms.

"You need to be careful."

Ha-Yoon struggled to free herself and then pushed him away.

"What did you do to me?"

Diego made a face.

"Do? I didn't do anything."

"Then what happened to me?"

"How should I know?" he said, backing away. She bent down and picked up her backpack. Its weight seemed right, but still, she quickly rifled through its contents to be sure.

She mumbled a half-hearted apology as she did so, not looking at him, but she remained irritated. And afraid. He had so causally and thoughtlessly used his size to intimidate her. She wondered if he even knew he was doing it.

She looked up when he sighed.

"Listen," he said, eyes closed, thumb against his temple. "I'm the one who should be sorry. I should have been more considerate considering... considering everything. What you've been through."

"Oh yeah?"

"You know I don't like Royce much, either, right? But what was I supposed to do back then? I needed my job."

Ha-Yoon nodded, but inside, so many emotions roiled and conflicted with one another. Fear and shame and rage. An immense amount of rage. It boiled hot. She stopped going through her bag because she couldn't see through the red.

Dr. Scarfke. She held her breath. She counted from ten.

She only got to six.

"You needed it, did you?" she seethed.

"I still do. I guess you do, too, since you're here."

The fire in her flared. Diego must have seen it; he immediately raised his hands and surrendered. "Look, all I'm trying to say is I understand."

"Well, don't say it. Because you don't. You can't."

She couldn't bear to listen to his response, so she tuned him out, returned to her backpack, and frantically went through its pockets.

"Where are they?" she said, interrupting him. "Where are my car keys?"

Diego looked reluctant. And guilty.

"I told you," he reluctantly said. "I can't let you leave yet. Not until I know you're okay."

"You're keeping me *prisoner*?"

"No, not a prisoner, but... I mean, be reasonable. I'm just asking you to stay with me for a few minutes. Just until we're sure you're okay."

"I'm not going to follow you around like a puppy."

"That's fine. *I'll* be the puppy. It doesn't matter."

Ha-Yoon huffed. She was wary, but he was right: he hadn't caused her dizziness. No one had. It had come from something or somewhere else, and it left her vulnerable. Nothing had happened to her, but she was angry, mostly because she didn't know what she could have done differently to protect herself.

"So then, where are you taking me?"

"That depends. Are you okay to climb some stairs?"

"Why wouldn't I be?"

Diego smiled, but it disappeared quicker than it arrived.

"Good. We need to go to the second floor. I need to know who's working in the attic so I can make sure this is the last time he works on one of my sites."

12

As Ha-Yoon and Diego climbed the staircase he stopped each man descending and asked if they'd been working in the attic or knew who had been. No one admitted to it, but before shaking their heads, they glowered at Ha-Yoon accusatorially. The first few made her shrink, but she grew more indignant, more defiant, as she and Diego traveled further. By the time they reached the second floor, Ha-Yoon was glaring at the contractors before Diego could question them. She'd already survived the worst thing she could imagine and had come for her reparations. There was nothing more any of them could do to her. And if they tried... heaven help them if they tried.

"I'll figure out who it was," Diego said once they reached the second floor. "And it won't go well for them."

"I wasn't looking to get anyone fired."

"I know. But I'm glad you told me. I needed to know."

"It was probably just a weird echo."

Diego looked at her. Arched his eyebrows. "Was it an echo?"

She admitted it wasn't.

They resumed walking.

"Maybe I don't feel better after all," Ha-Yoon admitted. She hadn't realized how she was sweating. How her legs trembled. Diego stopped again to assess her. His expression was overly serious.

"Do you feel lightheaded? Like you might pass out?"

"No," she supposed.

He thought a moment. "All right," he said. "We'll keep going then. The door is just around this corner."

But the door wasn't around that corner. Nor was it around the next.

13

Orange light streamed through the windows as the sun worked its way down, extending the shadows in the hallway. All Ha-Yoon heard was their footsteps hanging in the air, and she feared she was no longer in the same house. That when she passed out, she'd been surreptitiously moved to elsewhere. But that was crazy, and the sort of accusation Dr. Scarfke would frown over—the small wrinkles around her thin lips gluey with oily red lipstick—before writing something in her small hardbound notebook.

For a moment, it felt as though someone was following them. But when she turned. no one was there. Yet the phantom footsteps lingered longer than she would have expected. An echo that didn't know it was no longer welcome.

"It's got to be around here," Diego said. And Ha-Yoon nodded quietly. The further they ventured into the house, the more uneasy she became. She just had to remind herself he hadn't done anything inappropriate. He'd barely even looked at her if she were honest. If she didn't feel safe, it was likely because she would never feel safe again. Safety was just a matter of degrees now.

"There it is," Diego said, his voice amplified by the tight hallway, and Ha-Yoon recognized the strange wood of the attic door. Had the stain soaked deeper and creeped higher? Was it darker, wetter? She couldn't say, but she scowled when Diego pressed his ear against it.

He turned toward her. "I don't hear anything," he whispered. "How about you?"

She didn't.

Diego straightened himself. Put his hand on the knob. Jiggled it.

"It's locked," she said plainly. As though it were her hand on the rustic brass. He gave a short nod, then reached into his pocket and produced a ring of keys. He inserted the first into the lock—or tried to, but it wouldn't go in. He removed it and tried the second. Then the third. And so on around the ring. Each failed to unlock the door, which drew a quiet curse from under Diego's breath. By the eleventh key, he was unhappy.

"Why didn't we label these?" he asked himself. She didn't have an answer. He paused to look at the ring, then up at the door. Barely audible were the voices of contractors elsewhere on the floor. She stepped back and looked down the hallway for them.

A thunderous crack made her jump. She turned and saw the attic door swung open, a hole where the knob used to be. Diego shifted his weight as he set his booted foot down. Then he put the key ring back in his pocket. He must have seen Ha-Yoon's horror because he shrugged and gave her a grin.

"I'll fix it later."

All Ha-Yoon's instincts told her to leave. That no reward she'd have at the end of the job was worth dealing with Diego and, by extension, Royce. But she also knew if she left, she'd only be proving her mother right: that she was a failure. It didn't matter how sane the reasons were, nor how anyone who heard them would understand. If she left, she'd end up with nothing and would have to return to her nothing life. Ha-Yoon touched her breast pocket and girded herself.

"After you," Diego said, his arm extended in a sweeping motion past the open door. She frowned. Shook her head. And one-half of Diego's mouth curled up. "Okay," he said. "After me, then." And stepped through the damaged door. Ha-Yoon followed, squeezing her body against the opposite side of the frame as she passed through.

A set of narrow, unfinished wooden steps led upward. The air was hinted with something floral.

"Do you hear that?" Diego asked. Ha-Yoon nodded. "Is that the sound?"

"It's louder," she said.

Diego stared upward. Ha-Yoon shifted in discomfort.

"Hey," he shouted. "Who's up there?"

He waited, but there wasn't a response.

Ha-Yoon looked past him to the top of the steps. A dim but colored light crested over the last one, and she could see large motes of dust floating in it. They moved slowly, not touching the ground as though caught in a perpetual updraft. Their movements were hypnotizing, and as she watched them veer in different directions, a sense of calm crept over her, disconnecting her mind from her body. It felt so strange. They look like feathers, she thought. Feathers floating down from above.

But they weren't feathers.

Ha-Yoon realized this when she saw Diego swat motes away from his face. That's when the hum she'd been hearing became clear.

"Wasps," he said. "The goddamn wasps must have got into the attic through the window."

"Oh no."

"Yeah, it's not great, but we'll be okay if they haven't gotten into the walls. I need to see how bad it is. Are you okay to go up?"

Ha-Yoon looked to the top step again. Now that she knew what they were, the things flying in the air didn't look like dust or feathers at all. She still felt lightheaded, but the effect had been dampened.

"Are you going to kill them?"

"Not now. Not today. But I need to assess it. Figure out if we need to call someone in."

He motioned for her to follow as he started climbing. Ha-Yoon hesitated, thoughts of insects in her hair or clothes making her itchy, but somehow this was different. Safer. She didn't understand why. Maybe it was because Diego was there. She didn't like thinking that, but maybe it was true.

As she climbed, she watched Diego ahead of her, stepping upward into the colored light. "They don't seem to be too agitated," he said. "We'll probably be okay as long as we don't threaten the nest. It's amazing how loud it is, though."

He was right. She already had trouble hearing him.

"There are more up here," he continued. "We're definitely going to need—"

He stopped at the top step and looked into the attic. Ha-Yoon looked up at him. She still heard the buzzing, though it seemed to have changed pitch. She wasn't sure what that meant.

Then, Diego was gone. He dashed from her sight into the attic. He shouted something, but she couldn't hear what. She had to climb to the top step before his voice carried over the buzzing.

"Don't!" he shouted. Ha-Yoon saw his terrified face, then whatever he was kneeling in front of.

"What is that?"

At first, she thought it might be an old sandy duffle bag, but that was impossible. "I don't understand," she said, as though Diego might offer an explanation.

The attic was as bare and unfinished as Diego had said. The large circular stained-glass window emitted its colored light in a solid beam. Against it, against the wall, was the misshapen thing surrounded by a flurry of wasps. As she stepped closer, the shape changed. Resolved into a pair of splayed arms and crossed legs, and she finally realized what she was seeing. A mannequin. One warped by rain and mold until it was barely recognizable. And the giant protruding mass of wood in its chest was a large paper wasp nest. She knew because she saw wasps streaming into and out of the opening—the simulacrum acting as a passage for the swarm to move between the world in which she was living and the world outside.

Everything was so loud near the nest that when Diego spoke, Ha-Yoon couldn't make out what he said. It was swallowed by frantic buzzing. Only one word made it through, but that word was enough.

"Aahvan!" he yelled.

And Ha-Yoon realized with sickening horror that there was no mannequin.

PART II

14

Nine weeks was a long time. Much longer than Ha-Yoon expected she'd be away from the Awl estate. Once the police were called, the investigation took time to complete—long enough that Diego had to release his contractors to other jobs. When they were eventually free to return to finish their renovations, the snow had just started to fall.

In contrast, when Ha-Yoon was finally given a date to stage the house, nothing delayed her. She'd been stuck in her tiny Spadina Avenue apartment going over her plans and the budget, ensuring everything would be perfect, doing her best not to remember the sight of Aahvan, wasps crawling through his body and across his dead eyes. The only breaks she took were to eat and sleep. And occasionally to stare out the window at the passing streetcars and ask herself what was wrong with her. Sometimes, her mother called, and Ha-Yoon usually knew better than to answer. She already felt as bad as she wanted to feel.

The letter from Katherine Awl kept her going. She had it unfolded on her desk, weights on opposite edges to keep it flat. She drew strength from it every time she saw Awl's thin cursive, the blue ink swirling to form her signature. It was enough to enlighten her whenever things turned dark, help light her way out of her momentary despairs. Had she not had Katherine Awl's story to model, she shuddered to think what would have happened. Where she would have ended up. Perhaps begging to get back into Royce's good graces. Or perhaps dead.

It was Royce's assistant who finally broke the cycle. Ha-Yoon knew why as soon as she heard the young girl's voice on the telephone. She didn't know whether it was the same brunette assistant she'd met when Royce offered her the Awl job six months earlier. Six months. Ha-Yoon was almost certain the girl was new. It was the quaver in her voice, a sign she was nervously stepping into a new role. Or maybe it was someone on her way out, someone who learned the same horrible lesson Ha-Yoon had. Ha-Yoon wanted to warn her as they spoke, but didn't know how. She regretted it as soon as the call ended.

15

There was a stark difference between Ha-Yoon's first trip to the house and her return. The most significant was the cold, but as her almond Corolla slipped out of the city, she noticed other changes as well. The leaves had not only shifted from verdant green to a combination of deep ochre and burnt umber but also most had fallen from the trees, creating soft strips down the middle and along the sides of the road. The rows of skeletal branches left behind clawed and scratched at the muted, grey expanse above.

Ha-Yoon lost herself, dreaming of how things might finally change for her once the house was finished.

The only route there was along Highway 35 through the Township of Crichton, and Crichton was still forty minutes away from the house. Ha-Yoon had expected the town to be small but assumed that the large hospital on its outskirts—the only one for all of Laurier region—indicated it was populous enough to warrant at least one coffee lounge and perhaps even a bakery. But she found neither as she drove through, confronted with barely any shops, and what were there were hardly more than shacks. Had the Corolla's gasoline needle not been dangerous in the red, she might have driven straight through and onto the Awl house without even slowing.

She stopped at the first and only gas pump she found, and as she filled the tank, she noticed across the deserted street a worn-out general store with a sign that offered antiques for sale. She felt drawn to checking it out; every minute she spent in the store delayed her an extra minute from returning to the house and remembering what she saw there. Besides, she excitedly reasoned, so far outside the city, it might not have yet been picked clean by hunters, and she might find something unique that would properly celebrate Katherine Awl.

16

The store was cramped with shelves, but disappointingly, those shelves were stocked with rubbish. Scads of miniature ceramic sculptures of rabbits and elves, sets of chipped overworn plates, and two small chandeliers made of crystal and tarnished brass. There were vases of all shapes and colors, each worse than the one before, and three chairs for a dining room set that lacked its matching table. Ha-Yoon almost accepted her hunt was in vain until she stumbled upon the back room, partially disguised by the sheer blue drape that hung across the entrance. It was filled with more faded bric-a-brac, but at the rear, raised on a plinth to survey all who entered, was a white marble statue of Athens, Goddess of the Hunt, symbol of power and determination. It was perfect. Athena, triumphantly standing above her detractors, spear in hand, perseverant eyes glaring out from beneath her visor. The longer Ha-Yoon examined it, the more right it became.

The woman at the register was tall and silver-haired, face taut like an overstuffed sausage. She beamed when she saw Ha-Yoon lugging the heavy statue in her trembling arms.

"Just put that up here, dear."

Ha-Yoon heaved the statue onto the counter with a heavy thud. She was damp and exhausted and hadn't even reached the house yet.

The woman looked at the tag around the statue's neck, then at Ha-Yoon. Her face was inscrutable. Ha-Yoon swallowed.

"Passing through?" she asked with a soft twisted-upward twang.

"Yes, I'm doing work at a house nearby."

"You mean the one that sex woman bought?" The woman laughed. "Imagine, going on television, making up stories so you can get rich quick. I guess it worked, though, so joke's on us."

"I don't think..." Ha-Yoon started, then swallowed the lump that had formed in her throat. She looked at the Athena statue on the counter. It looked smaller all of a sudden. The woman didn't seem to notice.

"Serves her right to have someone die in her new house. Now she's got to live with a ghost. Getting haunted for ruining a man's life is some sort of justice, don't you think?"

"I—I don't... I mean...."

"You heard what happened, didn't you? Of course, you did. You were working there. I had to read about it in the newspaper. At least it wasn't that Awl woman's fault this time. Everyone says it was drugs."

Chills pulsed up Ha-Yoon's spine, into her face, down her arms, into her hands. She felt sick, clammy. The woman was everything Ha-Yoon feared, a firehouse of judgment that might have just as easily been aimed at her. Her, and Royce. How could she make a woman like this understand? How could she make anybody when their lives were built on *not* understanding?

"I'm in a hurry," Ha-Yoon said, reaching with both hands for the statue. The woman casually slid it aside.

"It's a crazy story. Apparently, this man who'd been working on the house just disappeared one day. No one knew where. A couple weeks later, they found him in the attic, dead from an overdose, covered in bugs."

"I—I know," Ha-Yoon whispered. She didn't want to think. She could barely speak. The woman was undeterred.

"And the worst part was his wife hadn't even reported him missing. She didn't even care." As she related that part, the woman shivered, then quickly lowered her voice. "The papers hinted there was some trouble at home. It's despicable. No one needs to know what goes on between a man and his wife behind doors. But you know how it is nowadays: the news always makes it out to be the man's fault somehow, even when he's the one who's dead."

Every word felt like a blade going into Ha-Yoon, slitting open the black curtain that hid everything she'd gone through. The only way Ha-Yoon could continue functioning each day was not to look behind it, but the woman seemed insistent on drawing it back. Ha-Yoon wanted to do something but didn't know what. It was too hard to think. It was too hard to breathe.

"Please. Please, I need to go."

"They say all the same things," the woman continued, her hands on the statue now. "She didn't know he was missing; he hadn't been home in a few days; she was at the hospital when he disappeared. They always write their stories like the woman is some sort of saint. If you asked me, she probably killed him."

Ha-Yoon squeezed her eyes shut. All she saw were wasps. Buzzing past her head. Crawling out of Aahvan's still body. Then that body turned into Royce's. Pale and sweaty.

"Please...."

"Some women will do anything for attention."

The buzzing. It circled Ha-Yoon's head. She felt sick. Woozy. Her mouth full of cotton. With every word, more memories of Royce returned to her, shrouded in the fog of her disrupted memory. Ha-Yoon said something but wasn't sure what. It was as though someone else were speaking. She heard the woman ask from the other side of the store if she was okay. Or was it from across the street? Everything spun, and she was beginning to worry over its frequency.

"I need..." she said but couldn't continue. It was hard to form words. Her mouth wouldn't obey. Royce, eyes glazed, face twisted. "I need to...."

"What's wrong?"

She couldn't answer.

"I just need to go," Ha-Yoon said and turned toward the door, ready to flee.

"Wait!" the woman said. "Don't you want your statue?"

Ha-Yoon closed her eyes, tried to gather herself, and nodded. The woman was already ringing the item through the register. Ha-Yoon fumbled open her wallet, but images of Royce, of Katherine Awl, of the horror of waking up alone and sluggish, swamped her, and her pocketbook slipped from her hand, and her credit cards spilled out across the floor. She couldn't believe this was happening. Not again. She felt the wisps of her anger trying to slip free from where she struggled to contain them. It would be so easy to relax and let them take over, but she breathed deep instead. Then she knelt and retrieved her cards.

When she stood, the woman handed her the statue, nearly dropping it into Ha-Yoon's unprepared arms.

"Come back any time," she said, but her tone was off. Ha-Yoon didn't care. She was barely listening as she lugged the statue to the door as quickly as possible. The world was already swinging on its axis.

"And be careful," the woman called after her. "Who knows what they get up to at that house when no one's around." But Ha-Yoon wasn't paying attention. She was too focused on remaining upright.

17

She staggered out into the harsh early winter sunlight, blinded to where her car was. Memories of her trauma resurfaced, and with each, her stomach churned and threatened to expel whatever it contained. Why was this happening? Why, at this moment? Everything felt on the precipice of collapse, and she didn't know what to do. Weakness consumed her. For a moment, all her senses went dark.

When they returned, she was on her scuffed knees. In front of her was the statue of Athena, her sword-wielding arm in pieces, her face cracked irreparably..

Ha-Yoon felt herself scream but didn't hear it. She screamed again. And again. And kept screaming, waiting for the sound to reach her ears. And when it didn't, she knew she had no choice.

She stood, unlocked her car door, and started the engine. As she did, her phone rang. She didn't answer.

If she hurried, she'd be at the house before the hour struck.

18

It was almost a relief when she arrived. Ha-Yoon had made the trip from the Township of Crichton as quickly as she could and still remain safely in control of the car, but even as she fled from the memories of what Royce had done, she found herself growing more terrified by what else was coming. So many voices echoed through her head that she worried they'd veer her off the road and into the leafless trees. She forced herself to grip the wheel tighter, narrow her eyes, and hope.

The house looked different under the thin blanket of first snow that clung to the various roofs. Maybe it was the lack of contractors filling the yard. Maybe it was the bushes and landscaping that Diego's team had rushed to complete after the police investigation was over. It was clear what Katherine Awl had seen in the place.

She opened the front door, and what rushed to greet her was an overwhelming feeling of warmth and welcome, as though the house were some sort of respite from her day so far, a sanctuary from everything she'd been made to endure. For as long as she could remember, Ha-Yoon dreamed of escaping. From her mother, from her childhood home, from every class in every school in every city. From every person she'd ever met.

But not from the Awl house. There, she felt as though she might belong.

It was thanks to Diego's team, of course. The marble arches had been intricately carved with a series of vines, the hearth of the ground-floor fireplace still free from soot. Ha-Yoon walked to the kitchen and found sleek steel appliances; traveled through three interconnected bedrooms and discovered that they circled the sitting room as ducklings might their mother.

As she toured the ground floor of the empty house, she marveled at the detail work in the empty rooms, at the moldings and large warm windows, and tried to remain in the moment. Her terrors were still there, waiting as always, but if she didn't look at them directly—if she did as Dr. Scarfke recommended and told herself they weren't real—maybe she could remain at ease a little while longer.

As if by cue, her cell phone rang, disrupting her peace. She felt her serenity flutter away, leaving her alone with only its echoes. She sighed then answered.

Thirty-minutes. The first delivery driver would arrive in fewer than thirty minutes.

It had very nearly slipped Ha-Yoon's mind. The entire reason for her trip back to the house. She'd gotten so lost in how the house made her feel that she'd forgotten it wasn't she who was supposed to feel it. It was Katherine Awl's sanctuary, and Ha-Yoon was the intruder, co-opting Awl's peace.

Thirty minutes would give her enough time to see what had been done to the second floor. Plenty of time. She rationalized it away by telling herself she needed to inspect everything before the deliveries arrived, before furniture left the trucks and was carried up the stairs. What if something that should have fit didn't? What if the color of the walls was wrong? The flooring angled incorrectly? Better to be safe, she told herself and dashed up the stairs.

19

But when she reached the second floor, she was greeted by a different feeling, one she did not like. She felt off, much as she had when she groggily woke in Royce's bedroom. Whatever was disturbing her needed to be solved before Katherine Awl arrived. Ha-Yoon closed her eyes and listened. There was only silence, but she felt an electric tingle at the root of her spine. She opened her eyes. Nothing appeared different, yet she was certain something must have moved. Was there a cloud of dust settling at the end of the hallway? A sheet of paper fluttering to the ground? She saw no signs of it. And somehow that was worse.

Ha-Yoon stopped, looked back toward the stairs, looked forward, wondered what to do. She hated how helpless she felt. But at least it lit her anger because it was that anger that pushed her forward.

She increased her pace, and as she did so, she'd heard a creak echo down the hallway. She snapped her head around, but no one was there. Yet she'd heard it. Like footsteps. Like someone following her.

"Hello?"

She sped up. Told herself to not run, to be foolish. She was the only one in the house. Those footsteps she heard had to be her own echoed back. But that didn't reassure her. Nor did glancing back again. The nothing seemed conspicuously empty. As though a shimmer had blinked away when she turned.

As she approached the end of the hallway, she saw the attic door. Shouldn't it be further into the house? How had she gotten turned around again? Ultimately, it didn't matter: she knew it had been waiting for her, the proverbial pin in the bedding. It was unavoidable. And in that moment, it was clear it was the door's fault. The door, the attic, what had happened to Aahvan up there—that was the reason she felt so off since getting there. Why everything on the second floor seemed so wrong when the first floor hadn't. It was the attic.

Ha-Yoon chuckled with relief and let out a deep sigh filled with her fleeing anxieties. It was going to be okay. There was nothing to worry about.

Then someone stepped into the hallway behind her.

Ha-Yoon shrieked.

20

"**S**orry, I didn't mean to startle you," Diego said.

Ha-Yoon put her hand on her chest, urging her heart to slow.

"Why didn't you tell me you'd be here?"

"Royce said he would."

Maybe that was the phone call she'd refused to answer.

"Well, he didn't."

Diego nodded toward the attic door.

"I thought being here would be easier," he said.

"It's never easier." It felt even truer after she'd said it.

"Did you hear the police think Aahvan was hiding here?"

"From his wife?"

He shrugged. That told her everything.

"I didn't know him well, but he seemed like a good guy."

"Yeah, they all seem like good guys," she laughed. "That's why his wife was in the hospital, and he was sleeping in the attic."

"Still, what happened to him...."

"It wasn't enough."

He looked at her, but she couldn't read his expression. His eyes seemed moist, but his mouth was turned down.

"You know—" he started, then a loud rumbling sound interrupted. Ha-Yoon looked immediately at the attic door. But that's not where it was coming from.

"Sounds like the movers are here," Diego said, his demeanor lifting. Ha-Yoon's was less eager.

"You don't need to be here," she said. "I'd prefer to do this on my own."

"I know you think that's what you want, but it'll be easier with two of us. I don't mind."

No, she thought. *But I do.*

"Let's just start. If you find you really don't need me, I'll go finish the touch-ups I came to do. Deal?"

He held out his calloused hand.

A heavy thud on the ground floor. It didn't sound anywhere near the front door.

Diego pulled his hand back. "Well, I'm going to go see what they brought us."

Before Ha-Yoon could respond, he was returning to the giant staircase. She watched him go, heard his boots echo back toward her, then looked at the attic door and tried to remind herself she chose this.

21

Deliveries arrived throughout the day, each carried in by teams of two or three men. They all looked the same to her, though. Duplicates of one another, with crushed faces and arms big enough to pin a woman down. The similarity of their hands, though, stood out most. She noticed them as couches and chairs and tables were unloaded. Their hands were large and knotted and could easily wrap around her mouth and most of her head. She imagined what it would have been like to have them there without Diego around and shuddered.

Not for the first time, Ha-Yoon asked herself if any of this was worth it. Re-reading the letter she carried in her pocket assured her it was the right thing, but the bargain she had to make sickened her. She tried focusing on what she was getting out of it, both for Katherine Awl and for herself, but she wasn't sure the cost was something she could live with. Dr. Scarfke had urged her to begin taking risks again, yet this felt like something wholly different.

Ha-Yoon closed her eyes. Took a deep breath. Struggled to stay present. Keep her thoughts from spiraling.

The job was almost done. She repeated it to herself like a mantra: the job was almost done. She simply had to stage the house and collect her payment. Two days, maybe, and that would be it. Then it would be Katherine Awl's home, and Ha-Yoon would be free of the burden. Free of Royce. Free of everything and on her way back to the career she deserved. The career that was stolen too soon from her.

She opened her eyes and saw Diego directing the delivery men. Slapping them on the back and speaking that strange language men speak to one another. He'd seen the trouble she was in and wordlessly stepped in to take control. She hated that she needed him, but at least this time he helped. Changed or not, maybe it was enough.

22

After the last delivery van left the property, Ha-Yoon felt good. She would soon see the end result of her hard work, Royce be damned, and no matter what he was or what he'd done, he couldn't take away what she was giving to Katherine Awl.

When she took a good look at the stacks of boxes and wrapped furniture, she became overwhelmed by the knowledge that her job was only beginning. There was too much for her alone. Even if she spent a week working, it wouldn't get done in time.

Diego must have sensed her encroaching despair because he appeared on the second-floor landing and shouted down to her.

"Do you need a hand?"

Ha-Yoon hesitated, then, begrudgingly, accepted his offer.

"You're going to have to tell me where things go," he said after jogging down to meet her. "I can help with rearranging the furniture if nothing else."

"Anything you can do."

Diego smiled at her. It was awkwardly returned.

23

With two, things went quicker. Diego was able to move couches without her help and was faster at assembling furniture than she thought possible. While she unpacked plates and arranged books, he carried lamps to where she wanted them and positioned the antique armoire she'd found against the wall in the alcove behind the central staircase. Beside it, a plinth. She had thought to put the statue of Athena there, but would now have to come up with another idea. Maybe just a vase?

Ha-Yoon shrugged. Not perfect, but close.

24

By the time they started on the second-floor bedrooms, Ha-Yoon's exhaustion had given way to a driving need to complete the project. It provided the strength, along with Diego, to lift the large leather centerpiece couch she'd bought for the landing. Even so, that strength was almost not enough.

"Oof," Diego grunted. "I think we did this backward. We should have built the house *around* the furniture."

Ha-Yoon chuckled.

He smiled. "See?" he said. "I knew I'd break you eventually."

Immediately, she stopped. But she also wondered if he was right. If she was cracking.

As afternoon neared its end, they'd managed to stage the largest couches in the rooms they were earmarked for. The house transformed from an empty shell to the refuge she'd imagined for Katherine Awl. There was more work to be done, but Ha-Yoon could see it approaching her vision. She could really see it.

"Hey, I have to grab something from my truck," Diego said. "Give me a minute?"

Ha-Yoon nodded, then unrolled a Ziegler rug in the alcove and set the reclaimed coffee table on it. As she stood alone in the vast house, she thought she heard the creak again on the floor above. She looked up at the ceiling and waited for it to reoccur.

Instead, she heard the front door open.

Diego appeared in the doorway. It took Ha-Yoon a moment to realize what he held.

"I thought we should celebrate," he said, waving a bottle of whiskey so forcefully she could see its contents sloshing back and forth. His other hand tossed the keys to his truck onto the expensive coffee table. He then produced a pair of clear plastic drinking glasses from the pocket of his coat.

"What are we celebrating?" she asked, taking a glass from him

"The work the team did on this place?" he said as he broke the seal. Ha-Yoon watched closely as he poured an inch into her glass. Then his own. "Or maybe the work you've done and are still doing? Or that you're still here at all?"

Diego lifted the glass and shot the whiskey down his throat. He hooted when he was done and laughed before pouring himself another. Ha-Yoon held her glass up to her eye and considered it with suspicion until she was satisfied.

"I'll drink to that," she finally said, then slung back the whiskey. It poured easily down her throat.

Only afterward did it sting.

25

The whiskey hit Diego much earlier than Ha-Yoon expected. The way his hair instantly mussed, his eyes turned wet and bulging, gave him away. But Ha-Yoon wasn't far behind. She knew because she'd been watching him, making sure to drink slower, but nevertheless, she felt her face warm as it always did, the embarrassing glow she'd inherited from her parents, for some reason, though she didn't mind.. Maybe the whiskey was good enough—it made the world soft and cozy, like a warm slipper on a damp winter day. Or maybe it was the house embracing her, making her feel everything was going to be all right, that the entirety of her troubles were printed on paper, and it was aflame.

She tried to express this to Diego but was having trouble arranging her thoughts. How could she explain it? This strange, disconnected feeling—almost like a suspicion, unfounded and unprovable, and yet also true? The house was a safe space for her, and it would be a safe space for Katherine Awl, too. Nothing bad could happen to her here. Nothing bad would find either of them.

As if to congratulate her on seeing the truth, the house's warmth embraced her tighter. Ha-Yoon might have laughed, but she couldn't be sure through the whiskey buzz.

"Why are you staring like that?" Diego asked.

"I'm just making sure."

"Making sure of what?"

Ha-Yoon didn't have the words to answer him. She could see his thoughts struggling against the effects of the whiskey, trying to figure out what was going on. He looked like a kicked dog; she almost felt sorry for him. Almost.

"Wait," he said. "Does this have something to do with Royce?"

"Don't even say his name," she blurted.

"Christ, Ha-Yoon. Did something happen?"

"Forget about it."

"No," he said, putting his glass down on the table. She noticed the plastic made an unsatisfying sound. "I won't forget about it. Tell me what happened?"

The room around her—around them both—was soft. Unreal, almost. As though if she stuck out her arm too hard, too fast, she might puncture it. She raised her hand slowly, pushed gently. It was like pushing a cloud. A warm cloud. And on the other side something she didn't want to see. So, she closed her eyes. Then, opened them.

"Do you really want to know?"

"Yes," he said. "I do. I need to."

Ha-Yoon thought for a moment. Then decided to stop thinking at all. Instead, she took a sip, took a breath, and told him. Maybe she shouldn't have, but she did.

Or maybe it was the whiskey that did the talking.

26

"**R**oyce Ballast is a monster. There's no other way to put it. No other way to think about it, and god knows I've tried. I've tried as hard as anyone could. Do you remember the party we had after the Newsome house was done? Well, I don't. Not really. I remember you and I were talking, then I remember Royce joining us and me feeling anxious—I was always anxious near him; he was like a god to me. I was just out of school and would have done anything, taken any job, no matter how far away from design, if it meant not having to listen to my mother remind me about all the things I'd done wrong and could be doing better. Finding the internship was pure luck. A case of knocking on his office door at the right time. He told me he loved my portfolio, and I believed him. So, while everyone else from my classes was working as a barista or at a call center, I found myself shot to the front of the line. I was so determined not to fuck it all up that it only made me more anxious.

So, when Royce offered me two pills that he said would help me calm down, I took them without question. The next thing I remember, it was morning, and I was waking up in a strange bed. I didn't know where until I saw the photographs on the wall. Then I pieced together what had happened: I'd gotten drunk, made a fool of myself. Slept with Royce, the famous designer who liked my work enough to bring me on as an intern. The only reason I didn't die right then was because he wasn't home when I finally gathered up the nerve to get out of bed, and when I saw him at the office the next day, he didn't say a word about it, and more importantly, didn't act differently toward me. I thought he was doing me a favor, to be honest, so I did what I always did and filed the moment away as further proof everything my mother said was true.

"That is until Katherine Awl's story became news. Did you see her interviews? Any of them? So many of the small details sounded so familiar: the drowsiness, the loss of control, then feeling at fault for something that, until then, I'd never thought myself capable of doing. Her story got me wondering about the mistakes I'd been living with and whether they really belonged to me. I was relieved to realize that night hadn't been my fault, but that relief was minor because I knew what it implied. A whole new kind of weight started to crush me."

"But you didn't tell anybody?" The quiver in Diego's eyebrow gave away his reluctance. Ha-Yoon chuckled. Took another sip from her plastic glass.

"He was Royce Ballast. Who the hell was I? But it was obvious he knew I figured out what really happened. I guess I didn't hide my horror well enough. So, once I became too much of a risk, I was fired—or as fired as an unpaid intern can be. Suddenly, all my luck was gone. He'd taken everything away from me: my dream job, my innocence, my trust, my hero. And I never once saw him bothered by it. I never saw him remotely care. My eyes now open, I remembered the other interns that had come and gone while I worked with him, sometimes disappearing without warning, and I wondered how many of those women went through the same thing. I wonder how many more went through it after I left. How many have you seen come and go?"

"I'm... I don't know. I've been with him a long time. It's natural for people to leave."

"Sure, but how many? How many young women?"

He hesitated before awkwardly shrugging. She didn't need to know the number. She could guess.

"Here's the worst part of all this. Well, maybe not the *worst* part— the worst part was when Royce drugged me and did what he did—but the almost-worst part was what happened after he fired me. I tried to tell myself it would be okay. That I was better off not having to see him. And the time I spent working there would look good to prospective employers. But that wasn't true at all. Most of the résumés I sent out were ignored, most of my phone calls went unreturned. I only managed to get one interview, but though it went well, suspiciously, I never got a callback. I'm not saying Royce did or said something to torpedo things, but I don't know. If he was capable of drugging and assaulting me, then was it a stretch to imagine he might blackball me to keep me quiet? Eventually, I stopped trying to find a design job and settled for one of those barista jobs everyone else had just to make ends meet. Except they'd all moved on to better things at better places. I was at the bottom and had to start again. I'd been ground down to nothing."

Diego shook his head. He looked like he was trying to speak but had forgotten how.

"Well," she shrugged. "You asked."

27

Diego took a sip of his whiskey, hesitated a moment, then tilted his glass and swallowed the rest. He wiped his mouth when he was done and looked at her. For some reason, his eyes were wet.

"You never told me."

Ha-Yoon laughed.

"Why would I have told you?"

"I could have done something."

"You did plenty."

"What do you mean?" he said. He looked like an animal afraid of being kicked. Ha-Yoon was all too willing to do it.

"I didn't know something even happened for a long time. I have no memory of that night. You, though, were standing right there when he gave me the pills. Right there. And you didn't do shit. Not a single thing to stop it."

"What? No. Ha-Yoon, no. No. I didn't... I didn't.... Hell, even you don't know... I mean, you can't even be certain...."

Ha-Yoon thought she'd feel better after telling him. She thought she'd feel relieved. Unburdened. But she didn't. She just felt sick.

"I know what happened," she said. "But it doesn't matter. It was a long time ago. I'm here now, working for Royce. Taking his money, using his clout to try to restart my career. I don't know why he offered this job to me—I don't know if it's some warped apology or if he just doesn't remember what he did, but I'm going to take advantage of it. I'm going to get my life back. I'm going to get what I deserve. And maybe, one day, so will he."

Diego struggled for something to say, but he couldn't find the words. And Ha-Yoon refused to help. She just let the truth weigh on him like a goddamn stone.

"Are you here for some kind of revenge?" he finally asked.

She chuckled.

"In a way," she said, patting her breast pocket. Then she surprised herself by pulling out the letter and handing it to him. "This is why I'm here. Or who I'm here for."

Diego stood and took the envelope from her. As he removed the sheet of paper, Ha-Yoon felt the worry rise from her whiskey stupor. Behind the warmth, she felt something else, an ache that ran deep, cleaving her in two. She wanted to cry but wouldn't let herself. She'd already done too much crying.

"This is from Katherine Awl?" he said, surprised.

"Yes."

"She says she looks looking forward to working with you."

"That's right."

"But that's all it says." He seemed confused. He didn't understand. Ha-Yoon took the letter back from him. Folded it and put it back in her pocket.

"It's not what it says. It's what it means. It's what it means to me."
She was feeling angrier now. Dr. Scarfke's voice was still there, trying
to keep her focused, but the drink had muted her. Ha-Yoon didn't
mind.

"Well, I'm glad you showed it to me," he said. "And I'm glad you're
here."

She straightened herself. In the light, she felt like an idiot. Nothing she'd just said or done had made a difference. It was all for naught.
These reminders of the past were the last thing she wanted.

"I should go," she said. "I'll come back after you're done and finish
staging."

"You can't," he said.

"Oh, yes, I can," she said, setting the plastic glass down firmly. It
fell over and spun lightly on the table.

"No, I just mean—I just mean you need to wait. You shouldn't
drive home. Neither of us are in any condition to be on the road."

He was right. A tickle of panic rose in her, but the whiskey helped
keep it at arm's length.

Diego scratched his head. "I suppose," he started slowly. "I suppose there's no harm in us sleeping here. Separately, of course," he
rushed to clarify. "In completely different rooms. There are at least
four different beds we set up today that we could use."

Ha-Yoon eyed him coldly.

"Was this your plan?" she asked.

Diego's face changed too quickly for her to track. From shock to
pain to fear and to anger, then some combination of all. A muddle of
reactions she'd need a lifetime to untangle.

"Of course not," he said. "That's ludicrous."

But could she trust him? Staying at the house... it was such a bad
idea, but she didn't know how bad. The whiskey made it hard for her
to think past her disappointment in herself. She felt its weight pushing
on her.

She was quiet for a while, lost in her thoughts.

"I guess I don't have much of a choice," she admitted warily.

28

They stumbled up the staircase, taking each step cautiously to keep from falling. The further they travelled, the harder it was for Ha-Yoon to organize her thoughts amid her rising concern. She looked at Diego through clouded eyes and tried to determine what he was doing, where he was leading her. She slowed to see how he'd respond, and when he didn't hesitate to pass her instead of shunt her forward, she started climbing again. The second floor was closer than it looked but it still took forever to reach. At the top, Ha-Yoon looked down the long hallway driven through the center of the house. Right in front of her was the first bedroom.

"You take this one," Diego said, trying to keep from swaying. "I'm going to go to the other end of the hall and sleep there. It's as much space as I can give you."

"Thank you," she said, and didn't want to say anything else, so she stood there, her hand absently twisting the collar of her blouse tighter. He looked down at her, his eyes rheumy and suddenly she worried he was going to do something she didn't want. She stepped back before he could and closed the door between them. She leaned her head against it and listened.

"Have a good sleep," he said, the sound muffled by the door, then was silent. She could feel him out there though, waiting. Breathing. She kept listening. After a she heard his footsteps. Quieter than before. They faded down the hallway. And once gone Ha-Yoon opened the door and silently dashed into the room across the hall. She turned the lock on the door slowly so it wouldn't make too much noise. And to be safe, she wedged a chair underneath the doorknob so it couldn't be opened from the outside.

Only then was she able to relax enough to lay on the bed to stare at the ceiling. It spun for a long, long time.

29

She woke violently in the dark, not sure where she was. Only that someone was on top of her, holding her down. Or, at least, they had been. She sat up, worriedly scanned the darkness, but saw no one. The door was still closed, the chair was still there. And yet she could still smell him. The ghost of Royce's cologne. She shivered and wiped her face. It was only a dream, but it lingered.

She put her head in her hands. The hum of power tools from somewhere else; it sounded like snoring. But that couldn't be right. Not in the night. Not in the dark.

The room wavered as she rubbed her arms, attempted to make sense of the shadows. Her head throbbed. Whatever Diego had given her she shouldn't have drank. Humiliation cascaded over her in waves. She didn't feel safe, though maybe safer now that she was awake.

She stood on wobbly legs and put on her coat, then removed the chair jammed under the doorknob. She should leave while Diego slept, but the idea of going out to her car in the dark of night worried her. It was better to stay inside. Warmer.

But that hum... She still heard it, as though it was coming from inside her room. But, also, from elsewhere. Echoing toward her down the hallway.

Ha-Yoon opened the door and peered out into the shadows, past where Diego slept and toward where that old wooden door should be. Was someone there in the dark, watching her too? She squinted but saw nothing.

Yet she still felt someone was there.

As she walked in stockinged feet down the hall, led in a stupor toward the source of the hum, the hallway suddenly brightened. It wasn't the moon through the skylights but something glittering as it loped ahead of her, shaped like a person made of coin-sized stars. Ha-Yoon stopped, and it did the same before looking back at her. Ha-Yoon's stomach dropped. The chill that overtook her was different from before. It was the sort from which no coat was thick enough to shield her. By the time Ha-Yoon forced herself to blink the figure was gone, back to the aether with all her other half-sober dreams.

Even in her state she knew what she thought she saw was irrational, but she didn't care. She didn't have to see the attic door to know that. So instead, she put her hand against the recently painted wall and guided herself back to her bedroom, stopping only long enough to confirm no one or thing had followed. Once inside she shut the door. Turned the lock. Jammed the chair back under the knob. Then she lay on the bed and watched to make sure her precautions held.

In the dark, fragmented shadows jittered across the ceiling like ocean waves. Ha-Yoon found it hard to breathe, hard to feel warm again. She reached for her phone on the nightstand and turned on the flashlight. By the time she realized it was a mistake it was too late. The light had already crawled onto the ceiling and illuminated the dozen wasps there, crawling in circles, stirring up lazily eddies of pre-dawn darkness.

30

By morning the wasps were gone. Ha-Yoon wasn't sure when during her vigil she'd fallen asleep, but the sunlight creeping through the newly-curtained window was enough to wake her. She felt damp, uncomfortable in her day-old clothes, and her head itched as though it were packed with straw. Every part of her was uncomfortable, and she wondered again if the whiskey had been worth it.

She removed the chair and opened the door slowly so she could peek out into the hallway. No one was there, and the door across from her—the door behind which Diego had left her—remained firmly shut. It didn't appear as though anyone, invited or otherwise, had crossed its threshold since she'd closed it. That was something, at least.

The noises she'd heard in the night were gone. No matter how much she strained there was no hum, no phantom footsteps. Not even a voice. The quiet brought an unexpected flood of relief, the current so strong it nearly knocked her over. Or perhaps it was the remnants of whiskey in her system, threatening her balance, numbing her tongue.

Ha-Yoon wrapped her hand tightly around the railing as she made her way downstairs, groggily taking care to maintain her balance. Once she reached the ground floor, she discovered Diego sitting on the new Vitton couch in the south alcove. Unbelievably, he looked worse than she felt—with unkept hair and a face carrying bags large enough to fit all his worldly belongings. Stubble peppered his chin in a formless beard. He looked drained and exhausted and when he glanced at her his paleness was startling. Alcohol had made fools of them both.

"Sleep okay?" he asked.

"It was cold."

He nodded. "I guess that whiskey was a bad idea."

"For both of us, I think."

He chuckled. Rubbed his eyes.

"Yeah, I didn't sleep well either. I kept dreaming someone was pacing around my room."

"It wasn't me," she said, then wondered if that was what had woken her a few hours earlier.

"Listen," he said, his expression turned serious. Ha-Yoon grew uneasy. "About last night...."

"What about it?" Her fingers knotted together, turned white.

"I just... what you said. I just want you to know that I believe you. And that I really didn't know. I didn't realize...."

Ha-Yoon couldn't listen to this.

"It's fine."

"No, it's not fine. If I'd known...."

"If you'd known what? What would you have done differently?"

Diego looked at his shoes. Hung his head. Was he ashamed or about to throw up? Ha-Yoon recalled something her mother said once but pushed it out of her head before the memory fully formed.

"Anyway," she said. "Royce got what he wanted out of me. Now I'm going to get what I want out of him."

Diego stood. Looked uncomfortable.

"I guess I better get to work," he said. "I still have a few things left to do. I can't put it off again just because... because I got distracted."

"Yeah. Sure. Well, I have to finish staging the house anyway," she said. Readjusted her backpack.

They both remained in place, though, for an awkward minute, staring elsewhere. Waiting for the other to speak. But Ha-Yoon refused to go first. She refused to give in.

"Okay," Diego finally said. He staggered onto his unsteady feet. "If I get done early, I'll come see if you need another set of hands."

"Sure," she said. "If you're done early."

He looked at her and tried to smile, though it looked more like a grimace. She didn't reciprocate, and eventually he left, disappearing into the house.

And after he was gone Ha-Yoon realized she'd made a mistake.

31

Ha-Yoon put it and him out of her mind. She had to, otherwise she wouldn't have the house ready in time for Katherine Awl's arrival.

In one of the crates the couriers left were framed posters from the films Awl had appeared in. Ha-Yoon had ordered them from a warehouse shop online as a surprise for when the actress arrived. Who wouldn't want to be surrounded by images of their success? But now that Ha-Yoon was looking at the them, she wondered if it was indeed the sort of thing the actress would want. Would they be seen as accomplishments or reminders of an industry that had so mistreated her?

Ha-Yoon wished she could avoid her own reminders, but they came every day regardless. Like a committee of vultures, they perched nearby, always watching and waiting. Dr. Scarfke once told her feeling that way was normal, especially in cases such as hers, where the trauma has been so disassociated from the causal event, and where the victim refuses to report what happened. But what Dr. Scarfke didn't realize was that the only reason Ha-Yoon didn't report Royce was that no one cared enough to believe her. She knew this was true because she made the mistake of first telling her mother.

Her mother had never been the warmest person, but after Ha-Yoon's father passed, she became someone else entirely. Someone who hated Ha-Yoon. Why else would she treat her the way she had? With such a painful mixture of disdain and disappointment? Ha-Yoon was hard-pressed to remember a single time her mother was on her side. Even after Ha-Yoon had gone to her for support when she realized what Royce had done, her mother had instead narrowed her eyes and, through razor-thin lips, told Ha-Yoon why it was impossible.

"You're not pretty enough for someone like him to do that," she said.

Ha-Yoon sat down. Her emotional scar wept painfully. She'd gone to Dr. Scarfke to help make sense of it but was starting to doubt there was a way out of her predicament. A way to put everything behind her and find peace.

Put everything behind her. What kind of advice was that, anyway? What did it even mean? How could she forget what happened? Forget feeling so... so used and disposable? How could she leave what happened in the past and move on? It was a giant chain wrapped around her neck, and no matter how often she adjusted it, it kept getting heavier.

Meanwhile, somewhere in the house and out of her sight was Diego. She heard his hammering echo both needlessly and overtly aggressively, his barely disguised anger like a beacon. Was he any better than the rest of his contractors? All those men who stared at her? Talked about her? Sure, he gave her worried looks and a wrinkled brow as he told her how much he didn't know, but Ha-Yoon wondered how that was possible. No matter what he said, how could anyone work for someone like Royce for that long and not know what Royce was and what he was capable of doing? Diego should have been able to smell it, that foul patina of corruption. And he should have done something about it. He should have protected Ha-Yoon when she needed him. Not now when she doesn't.

Ha-Yoon stopped to breathe. She looked down at her hands gripped tightly around the poster frame's edge, her knuckles white and trembling. The urge to destroy it, to give her anger an outlet, was powerful, but she knew what would happen if she succumbed. And she knew it wouldn't make her feel any better.

Because how could she blame Diego for not noticing what Royce was when she had missed it, too? She'd had such stars in her eyes that she was blinded, and his compliments and support deafened her to his sweetened lies. She'd let herself be tricked, manipulated, and the worst part was afterwards, he made her feel as though *she* had been the one who made a mistake. If anyone was to blame, wasn't it her?

She hated that feeling. Emotionally at fault but logically absolved. Two sides at war inside of her and no matter how many tools Dr. Scarfke gave her, she couldn't ease her gnawing guilt.

Ha-Yoon closed her eyes. Inhaled as deep a breath as she could. And held it. Held it and counted to ten silently. Counted and imagined all her anger gathered in a thick dark cloud, like the smoke from a burning building. She summoned more and more of it inside her chest and, when she reached ten, exhaled it all in a steady stream, forcing every last ounce from her lungs, hoping all her anger went with it.

That's why when she opened her eyes, she wasn't able to scream. Not at first.

32

Diego came rushing in and found Ha-Yoon doubled over, panting. "Are you okay?"

His face was beaded with sweat, and stuck inside the crevices around his eyes were particles of greyish dust. In his hands he held a thin package wrapped in newspaper, the size of a large book. Ha-Yoon only glanced at him as she tried to shake her temporary paralysis.

"It's okay," she said, waving him off. "I thought... I thought I saw someone again. Down there. Just for a second."

But it wasn't true. She hadn't really *seen* anyone. Instead, she'd *felt* them. Felt them in the time it took her eyes to open.

Diego looked behind him, down the hallway, and made a noise. Ha-Yoon straightened, suppressed her discomfort.

"Sorry I took you away from what you were doing."

"I was coming over here anyway. This is for you," he said, thrusting the package into her hands. "I made it. It didn't take long, but I thought you'd like it.

Ha-Yoon nervously unwrapped the paper. Inside the package was a frame with a tanned parchment matte. She looked at him, confused. He pointed to her pocket. "I thought you'd like to frame that letter. Keep it safe."

Ha-Yoon looked at the frame again. She could see the beveling, the scooped cove, and knull. She'd only shown him the letter the night before—he must have put the frame together while she was going through the posters, fuming. It made her feel guilty, and simultaneously resentful she felt that guilt.

"Thank you," she eventually said.

Ha-Yoon felt him watching as she took the letter from her pocket, unfolded it, and slipped it behind the glazing. When the frame was fully assembled, she propped it up on the edge of the reclaimed table and stood back to marvel. It had been so long since anything had made her feel good. She grinned despite herself. Diego grinned, too.

"I'm glad you like it," he said.

"I do like it. But shouldn't you have been working on the house?"

He shrugged. "The only thing left is the attic. Maybe I'm trying to avoid going back."

Ha-Yoon's smile faded.

"You haven't gone yet?"

"Have you?"

She blushed. She did not want to relive the experience. Aahvan had been turned into something grotesque after dying, and as much as Ha-Yoon thought he'd gotten his comeuppance, she wished she hadn't witnessed it. The image of him, half-devoured by wasps, was enough to haunt the rest of her miserable life.

"I'm sorry," he said. "I didn't mean—"

"It's all right," she said. "I probably deserved it."

He shook his head.

"You can't talk like that. Nobody deserves anything. You most of all."

"I appreciate that. I really do. But you don't understand. Not really."

"No, I suppose I don't. But do know letting things fester inside will rot you out."

She nodded, smiled, and hoped that was the end of it. She didn't need more facile advice. She didn't need answers to questions she was trying very hard not to ask. She just wanted him to stop talking.

Then, a sudden crash overhead solved that problem.

33

It happened in slow motion. The sound hit her chest before her head could register it—something too loud to describe, followed by a long trailing vibration that rattled her teeth. The ceiling above them shook under the onslaught, and both Ha-Yoon and Diego ducked in case it collapsed. Along the wall, the poster frames rattled against one another, and the vases threatened to topple. It didn't sound as though something had fallen; more like something had violently exploded.

"What was that?" Ha-Yoon asked once the shock dissipated. Diego's eyes were glazed and distressed.

"Guess I can't put off going up there any longer," he said.

Before he could leave, she reached out and stopped him.

"I'm coming with you," she said.

"Stay. Finish setting up the house."

Ha-Yoon turned her head to look down the hallway. Nothing moved.

"It can wait. I'd rather have company. Even if it's you."

He looked at her and squinted, then glanced down the hallway himself and smiled. It was wide and genuine and lit up his face in a way that made Ha-Yoon feel something though she didn't really understand what.

"Okay," he said. "Let's go."

34

Ha-Yoon felt an overwhelming sense of dread as they climbed the staircase. Perhaps she was still shaken, her thoughts and sense of safety threatened where only a day earlier she'd felt more protected than she'd ever been. Or maybe it was the last remnant of her dream, unwilling to give up the hold on her psyche. Whatever it was, it made her skin prickle as though something were crawling over it.

The two of them stormed through the second floor in silence, listening to the house around them. There was the hum of the furnace forcing air through the vents, the blower rhythmically turning off and on, overwhelming the subtle whine of the LED bulbs that lit their way. But there was another sound that attracted her attention. Or, rather, the lack of sound. Because behind the quiet, normal hum of the house, the nothingness screamed. An oppressive awkwardness that she'd felt only once before when she awoke in a bed not her own and realized she had no idea how she'd gotten there.

Ha-Yoon felt haunted. She wished she hadn't ever taken the job from Royce. It had always been a devil's bargain, but she'd hoped being aware of that meant she could manipulate things in her favor. But things didn't feel so favorable any longer. Instead, they felt like a mistake.

And a foreseeable one. She thought of the Athena statue she'd bought for Katherine Awl, thought of how strong the goddess was, how defiant, and wished for a sliver of that power to get her through everything that was coming. To make her feel complete. Because, at that moment, there was a hole in her and something was slipping out of it. She didn't want to see what.

35

When they reached the wooden attic door Ha-Yoon felt something she knew was irrational. That the door was currently not where they'd left it. The first time that happened she'd chalked it up to the dizzying layout of the house turning her around, but now that she'd been there longer, it had to be the door that was in the wrong place.

No, she had to be remembering it wrong. Dr. Scarfke had warned her these sorts of lapses would happen, after-effects of her trauma.

And it was okay for Ha-Yoon to have those feelings as long as she didn't act on them. But Ha-Yoon didn't want to act on them. Instead, she felt the urge to turn around and run as fast as possible. That feeling was overpowering and took a tremendous amount of effort to defy.

Diego put his hand on the doorknob, and Ha-Yoon held her breath.

He didn't move for a moment. Stared at his hand. Then he turned his face and looked at her with a pained expression.

"He seemed like a good guy, you know."

"Who?"

"Aahvan. Troubled, sure. And I think we all knew he was having problems at home... but no one deserves to die like that, do they? Even if they're not perfect. Even if they make mistakes."

Ha-Yoon looked at him and tried to decide what he wanted to hear. Or, maybe, what he was *willing* to hear.

"Men like that, who treat women like that—as objects that can do what they want with; things without feelings—they aren't men at all. They shouldn't have a place in the world. And yet not only do they, but they have the whole fucking thing."

"Even so... I mean, he was a person. He was complicated, but he was a person."

"It's funny how only men get to be people. I bet what happened to his wife has happened to every woman you've known or loved in your life, but they're too afraid to tell you. Because when they do, this happens: You make apologies and excuses."

"That's not fair."

"What does fair have to do with it? Is it fair Aahvan's wife was in the hospital? Was that her choice, too? Did she deserve it? I don't know her, but I know exactly what her life was like, the kind of fear she lived with every day. I bet she lay in that hospital bed staring at the door the entire time, expecting him to come bursting through. Dreading it. And even though he's gone, I bet she's still staring at her door, waiting for her punishment. One ghost waiting for another."

Ha-Yoon's face was hot. Diego appeared confused. He didn't speak.

"Well," she said, finally straightening the straps of her backpack. "You brought it up."

"I did," he mumbled.

Then he unlocked the door.

Ha-Yoon held her breath as the door opened. A sudden chill of fear rolled over her, as though there were horrible specters waiting for her: the remnants of Aahvan, floating like an apparition; Royce, towering, laughing, drunkenly unfastening his trousers; and blackness—unyielding and never-ending blackness. But behind the door were none of these things. There was, in fact, nothing at all. Just the same set of unfinished wooden steps she'd seen months before, lit by the same pale rainbow of stained glass. The air was still, as though she'd returned to a moment stuck in time.

"Are you up for this?" Diego asked.

"Are you?" she shot back.

He didn't answer, but from the way his body tensed, she already knew. Ha-Yoon waited for him to do something until she couldn't take it any longer.

"Move," she said and pushed past.

36

She took the first step. Then, because there was no railing, she put a hand on the wall. The bare wood was rough and uneven and felt as though it were moving, as though every imperfection was a bristle responding to her touch. The sensation grew stronger when she took another step up and advanced her hand further.

Something flew past. A shadow, small and quick, so fast she barely more than glimpsed it. Behind her was Diego, looking up with wide child eyes, uncomprehending and innocent. Colored light flickered across his face.

Then, the shape again. Just past her eyes.

Something landed on her hand. So softly, so gently, she wasn't sure it hadn't always been there. A wasp. She watched it trace random patterns on her flesh, in time with the vibrations through the wall. The sensation was warm, enervating. She closed her eyes. For a brief moment, in that silent stairwell, she felt a tranquil calm.

Then Diego shattered it.

"Oh, fuck," he yelled, and she whipped around to see him stumble backward, head immersed in an unexpected cloud of wasps. She didn't know where they'd come from, but they had engulfed him. Diego waved his arms ineffectively as he fell, frantically shaking his head to keep the swarm from landing on him. But she saw their tiny yellow bodies collecting on his face, on his neck. They flew into his mouth as he shouted. She had no time to think or react. She was frozen, watching him tumble down the steps. Reaching the bottom, bent and crumpled. By then, he was no longer shouting. By then, he wasn't doing much of anything.

Then the spell broke, and it was Ha-Yoon who was shouting.

37

She heaved him out of the stairwell into the hallway and slammed the door shut. Wasps still clung to his face, so she swatted them away. Then used her hand to wipe off the sweat and blood. He was already swelling.

"Are you okay?" she asked. It was a stupid question, but she didn't know what else to do. His moans were horrifying. But at least he wasn't dead. Ha-Yoon saw his swollen lips part as he tried to speak, but his words were too choked to make out. "You've been stung pretty bad," she said. "Can you... can you sit up?"

He slurred and mumbled but started to move his quivering arms under him. She tried to help, but he was too heavy for her. Once he was sitting, his back pressed against the humming wooden door, he was better able to communicate. At least his words had air in them.

"How... how does it look?" he slurred. Ha-Yoon didn't want to scare him.

"Can you breathe?"

He shook his head. Tried to take a deep breath. Ha-Yoon heard a high-pitched wheeze.

"Are you in pain?"

He nodded. Then nodded more fervently. She needed to get him help.

"Get up," she said.

Diego mumbled. Shook his head. Winced.

"Get up!" she shouted, then grabbed hold of his arm and pulled until he effortfully rose.

She managed to get him to his feet, but he couldn't walk without using her as a crutch. His weight on her shoulder was crushing, but she knew there was no other way to move him, and she didn't know how much time they had. If she could get him down the stairs, she could get him out the front door to her car. She'd drive like mad to get them to the hospital on the outskirts of Crichton. She just hoped he'd last that long. Hope he didn't have an allergy that would cut off his breathing altogether. If he went into anaphylactic shock, the only thing she could do would be watch him die.

They made it to the front door, Ha-Yoon dragging him with each step. Only when she got him to the driveway did she look up and despairingly realize her error. She couldn't drive Diego to the hospital in her tiny Corolla. His truck had penned it in.

"Your keys. Do you have your keys?" she shouted. He shook his head. If he didn't have them, then where were they?

Her legs were beginning to weaken. She didn't have much time. She led him to his truck. Eased him onto the edge of the flatbed.

"I think I know where they are. Hang on."

He groaned something, then folded over.

Under the stare of that round, stained-glass eye, she turned and ran as fast as she could back to the imposing house. She prayed the keys were still where she'd last seen them.

38

She burst through the door, no space in her head to think. Just get the keys—get Diego help. She flew through hallways and around corners, doors slamming behind her until she arrived at the alcove. The reclaimed coffee table was there, and so was her backpack, but the keys she remembered him tossing weren't. They had somehow ended up on the Stark rug beneath. She didn't know how, and there was no time to wonder. She bent down and snatched them, then rose to go.

And stopped.

The shimmering figure from her dream was at the opposite end of the hallway. And it was moving toward her. Hunched over and staggering, waving its broken arms. Ha-Yoon couldn't scream because its incongruity with waking life was petrifying. She couldn't process it, and its slow approach only made it harder to grasp the truth: this was no dream. It was there and getting closer. Lumbering and glittering, its blinding lights as bright as sunshine. Ha-Yoon covered her eyes and shouted.

"Go away!"

And when she uncovered them, it had.

Ha-Yoon hesitated, looked down at her hand, and saw the keyring clutched there. Then she checked the hallway again. She was alone.

So, she ran.

Diego was on the ground next to his truck. Writhing, face like a smudged balloon, streaked with muddy tears. Ha-Yoon unlocked the passenger door, threw her backpack in, then heaved him up and into the truck. Once he was seated, she pushed his legs into the cab and slammed the door.

A few seconds later, she was in the driver's seat, throwing the truck into gear. Then, heading down the drive, racing toward the Township of Crichton and its hospital as fast as she dared. She didn't want to think about what might happen if she didn't get him there in time.

But it was better than thinking about that glittering thing she'd left behind.

Or her mounting terror.

39

Diego's truck was monstrous. She'd never driven something as large nor driven as fast. But she had no choice: Diego's choked groans were getting increasingly worse. The sound tore at her, and she thought there was no sound in the world that could be more terrifying. Until, halfway to Crichton, he stopped making noise altogether. Ha-Yoon cast a terrified glance at the passenger seat to ensure he was still alive and was aghast. His blood had pressed up against the skin, turning it blotchy, discolored. His head took the shape and texture of a rotted pumpkin, and both eyes were so swollen as to be completely shut. Diego jerked, gasping, and took in an enormous gulp of air. His body was desperately trying to stay alive. Ha-Yoon pressed down harder on the accelerator.

"Don't die," she pleaded as they hurtled down the two-lane highway. "Please don't die."

She listened to his struggled breathing as she raced across the cold asphalt, convinced she was not going to make it in time. When, from out of nowhere, the top of the hospital crested the tree canopy, she was shocked and elated. She shouted: "I see it. We're almost there!"

Diego wheezed triumphantly.

She barely slowed as she careened the truck into the Emergency driveway, narrowly threading the space between concrete barriers and loitering patients. Ha-Yoon threw the gear shift into park and leapt out of the truck, screaming for help as she ran around to the passenger door. Inside, the swollen Diego struggled for air. Ha-Yoon reached over and unbuckled his seat belt.

He fell onto her. Luckily, she was strong enough to catch him. She didn't know if she could drag him out of the truck without hurting him, though. Without hurting both of them.

There were voices behind her, and then the weight on her lessened. She stepped free as a pair of EMTs in seafoam green scrubs laid Diego on a gurney. Ha-Yoon was frantic, asking if he'd be okay, but they didn't acknowledge her. For once, she didn't argue. They then started running—one pushing the struggling Diego, the other clearing the path by shoving open glass Emergency doors.

The last things she saw of Diego were his hands, his bluish-purple hands, swollen to twice their size and squeezed into tight fists like the bell of a wasp's nest. Then, as fast as the EMTs appeared, they were gone, disappeared into the heart of the hospital, and Ha-Yoon was left alone on the concrete and asphalt, her worries swarming around her.

PART III

40

Ha-Yoon sat by Diego's bed as he ate breakfast.

The hospital was bleach-clean with fumes that crawled into Ha-Yoon's head and nested in her sinuses. She tried not to think about how sick they made her feel. There was no place for that at the moment.

"I'm glad you stuck around," Diego said, spooning green Jell-O into his mouth. His gown was still crisp, and his face barely looked touched at all. Maybe it was just the sunlight through the window, but he was glowing.

"It's completely fine," she said. "I'm really glad you're feeling better."

"I hope I didn't scare you too much."

"No, not much," she said, and they both laughed because they both knew she was lying.

Outside, in the fluorescence of the hallway, nurses walked by in proper white uniforms, little paper hats pinned to their buns, and Ha-Yoon found herself charmingly surprised. She didn't know nurses still dressed that way. Like extras from a movie.

"Are you going back to the house?" Diego asked. He was sipping on what was left in his juice box. "Still a lot of work to do."

"I know," she said. Sighed. "I guess I should, but it's such a nice day out I don't know if I want to."

Ha-Yoon glanced out the window. The sun was so bright, so blinding. She closed her eyes and felt the light dance across her eyelids, like the shimmering from a pool of water. As she basked in it, she heard the sound of dragging footsteps behind her.

"Just here to check on your progress," the doctor's voice said, but it was hard to tell if the voice belonged to a man or a woman. It was somehow neither and a bit too buzzy. She turned around but must have done so too quickly because her eyes were still full of sunlight, and she couldn't see the doctor. Instead, there was a blur of bright dots where the doctor should have been.

"I'm feeling a lot better, Doc. When will I get to leave?"

"I just have to make sure everything is in place," the lights said. "Do you mind lying down?"

Diego scooted down the bed like a giggling child, then pulled the covers up over his body. The doctor approached and checked his side, his hands. Ha-Yoon had to squint to watch him, though.

"Do you think you could step out of the light?" she said. The bright flickering hurt her eyes.

"What do you mean?" the doctor asked. He hadn't stopped prodding Diego. When his hands reached the stomach, Diego gagged.

"It just... it's so bright," she said and turned to the window. To her surprise, it was already late afternoon. She wondered how long she'd been there. Where had the day gone?

The doctor, though, was still a collection of bright dots, shimmering. Their voice even more androgynous than before. It sounded like a motor humming. Their hands, too, moved as though motorized, pushing into Diego's stomach like pistons, harder and faster. Diego looked suddenly in pain, gasping for breath he couldn't catch.

"Hey," Ha-Yoon said. "Hey, stop that."

"It's to help him," the doctor said, pistons up and down. Diego began convulsing.

"Hey," Ha-Yoon said. "Stop it!"

But the doctor didn't stop. Ha-Yoon looked around but found no one to help. No one to care. So, she leaped at the doctor, wrapped her hands around the lights where thick wrists should be. "Stop it!" she shouted.

Diego moaned, cried in pain. The humming worsened. A buzzing drone that was strengthening as Diego convulsed and seized. His entire body contorted, twisting in on itself.

"You're killing him!" Ha-Yoon shouted, and as if to agree, Diego's mouth fell open in a silent scream, stretched so wide she saw deep into the blackness where his throat should have been. It was a hole. A deep cavernous hole. And from it, somehow, she knew something was approaching.

"No," she said, stepping back. But she couldn't stop staring into that emptiness, staring and waiting. Whatever it was wasn't far away now. It was almost there. Only a moment longer until it arrived. Diego's face was swollen again like a rotted pumpkin, cracking as chunks of purplish-red flesh broke away. Ha-Yoon didn't want to look into that nothingness any longer, but she couldn't stop. Not when it was so close.

And then they emerged. The wasps. And they came in waves of millions. Streamed from his mouth and into the air. A geyser of yellow carapaces.

Ha-Yoon shrieked. Then fell back into her own darkness.

41

And when she opened her eyes, she was in Diego's room, still seated beside his discolored body struggling for breath in the cold morning gloom. No matter how many times or how hard she rubbed her eyes Ha-Yoon couldn't scrub the image of those wasps streaming out of his mouth. The lingering dream kept superimposing itself on reality, making her question which of the two was real. She had a sour taste in her mouth, either from the hour or the antiseptic air being pumped into the room. She felt as sick as Diego looked. Perhaps sicker. Even her ears were ringing from it all.

No, she realized. Not her ears. That was her phone.

She ignored it. Stretched her arms above her. Tried to pull out the kinks and the twists. She'd been sitting in the hard plastic chair all night, watching over Diego, making sure he was okay. She wasn't quite sure why, though. True, she had his truck, and without it she had no way of getting back to the house to retrieve her Corolla. But she also felt some responsibility, too. She'd brought him in; she couldn't just abandon him. What if he woke and found himself alone?

At least his swelling had eased. When they had arrived, Ha-Yoon was worried he might already be dead—he was so swollen, so purple, that he looked close to it—but the ER doctor gave him a shot of something immediately and the nurse hooked him up to a web of tubes. They assured her Diego would recover. That was slight relief. He was still jaundiced, lips still blue, oxygen tube wrapped around his face. And when he breathed it was worryingly uneven.

She stood and paced to the window to get the blood in her legs moving. The morning light was brighter than she expected, and looking out she realized why. More snow had fallen while she was asleep, a blanket of white that muted the cars and people below. The brightness reminded her of something, maybe her dream, but the memory was too slippery to catch.

Maybe she *should* leave. What more could she really do at the hospital, anyway? She barely knew Diego anymore, and she didn't know if she wanted that to change. She didn't know if she'd ever be able to see him as separate from her past.

Her phone jumped to life, startling her. She fumbled it out of her pocket and, not wanting it to wake Diego, unthinkingly answered.

"Hello?"

"Ha-Yoon. Where are you?"

"Mom?"

"I've been calling all morning."

Ha-Yoon rubbed her eyes again.

"You know I'm working in Crichton. I told you about this."

"I thought you gave all that up because you weren't successful."

Ha-Yoon swallowed.

"Mom, what is it? I'm busy."

"Too busy for your umma? Who raised you to be so inconsiderate? It certainly wasn't me."

Diego's machinery beeped faster. Ha-Yoon pressed the phone against her chest, stepped outside the room.

"Mom, I can't be on the phone right now."

"I know when you're lying; I'm your umma. I'm starting to think there's something wrong with you. Call that shrink of yours. Maybe someone else can make sense out of what you're saying."

Ha-Yoon rubbed her forehead.

"It's too early in the morning for this, Mom. You won't even listen to me."

"I'll listen when you start making sense."

Ha-Yoon flushed with anger and sadness. No matter what changes in her life she tried to make she still felt so useless, so unnoticed. All the words she wanted to say on the tip of her tongue, but she couldn't speak. Then, in an instant, as though a switch were thrown, all that anger turned into overwhelming sorrow. It took her by such surprise her knees weakened. She would have fallen backward had the wall not been there for support.

"Really, I have to go now, mom."

"You don't sound well. I'm coming over."

"I told you I'm in Crichton. I'm not at home."

"When will you be?"

"I don't know. Tomorrow, maybe?"

"Okay, I'll come tomorrow."

"No wait—" Ha-Yoon said but it was too late. Her mother had disconnected.

42

Ha-Yoon cursed. Everyone in the hospital hallway stopped to stare at her.

And the nurse approaching was the worst of them. His expression was set in concrete.

"Keep it down," he said. The nurse's voice was graveled, enough that Ha-Yoon could feel its roughness drag across her skin. He was over a foot taller than she was, and as he spoke his aggression made her instinctively retreat. "You're disturbing the patients."

"I'm sorry," Ha-Yoon said. "I didn't realize I was being so loud."

"You were. The entire floor heard you."

Ha-Yoon lowered her head. Her mother had a way of causing problems even when she wasn't there.

The nurse scanned the hallway. Everyone was moving again, but his expression stayed taut.

"And who are you here for, anyway? Visiting hours haven't stared yet."

Ha-Yoon pointed at Diego's room behind her.

"I brought him in last night. He... I thought he might die."

The nurse made a noise like a snort, then picked Diego's chart out of the hanger on the door. He skimmed a few pages then put it back. Ha-Yoon waited for his dour expression to slip.

"Nothing in here suggest he's critical. And you said you're family?"

"No," Ha-Yoon admitted. "I'm a... a friend, I guess."

"Well, friends, and those who *guess* they are, are only allowed during visiting hours."

"The nurse last night said I could stay with him."

It was here his expression finally broke, but only briefly, and not in the way Ha-Yoon had hoped. The way the corners of his mouth curled in an insincere smile sent a shiver down her back. He didn't say anything, though. He just shrugged as though powerless to do anything more.

"Is there at least someone who can tell me when he'll be discharged?"

"I'm sure his family will update you," the nurse said. "You can sit in the waiting room until they arrive, if you'd like."

Ha-Yoon stifled the fantasy of slapping him as hard as she could. It wasn't easy. Especially as he stood in the doorway, watching her collect her things. She said goodbye to the unconscious Diego and had an urge to say more but didn't know what. All her words were trapped inside her. Instead, she laid her hand on his for a moment, then turned as the nurse ushered her into the hallway. He promptly closed the door behind her.

43

The waiting room was through a set of doors and at the end of the hallway. She was too far from Diego to know what was going on, and didn't know what she should do. Taking the truck had been the right call, but she wished she'd had her car instead. At least then she wouldn't feel trapped at the hospital. She'd be able to go back to the house and finish getting it ready for Katherine Awl's arrival. It was so close to being done. Her masterpiece complete. Ha-Yoon reached into her jacket for the letter so she could reread it for the umpteenth time.

But it wasn't there.

There was a moment of numbing panic. She checked all her pockets, then scrambled through her backpack, trying to remember where and how she could have lost it. Then, suddenly, she stopped.

Diego's gift. She saw herself mounting the letter. Propping up the frame on the table. Then that distracting noise that she and Diego went to investigate. Ha-Yoon had not taken the letter with her. It was still there. At the house.

She felt sick. That letter was everything—a talisman of her future, a symbol of her perseverance and escape from everything done to her. It was her defense, her armor, and she'd left it behind.

Ha-Yoon slumped on a hard plastic chair, anxious and empty without the letter's protection. She wanted desperately to go back for it, but she couldn't leave Diego. Not until he woke. She'd have to be patient. But it wouldn't be easy, and her lingering dream only made things worse. There was something about shimmering lights, though she couldn't recall what they were or meant. Nor why they came for her. She closed her eyes and reminded herself it couldn't have been real.

Ha-Yoon scanned the sad worried faces gathering in the waiting room around her. Each wore an expression she knew well. She'd seen it any time she told someone the truth about Royce. A sympathetic tilt of their head, an understanding gathering of their brow—not because they believed her, but because they didn't. Someone as famous and respected as Royce *couldn't* do such a thing, so it had to be Ha-Yoon who was in the wrong. But she'd show them. Once they finally saw the Awl house, they'd understand there was nothing she'd ever need from him.

If they saw the Awl house, she corrected herself. And they wouldn't. Not if it wasn't finished.

She contemplated leaving the truck, finding a cab willing to take her all the way back. As long as she avoided the attic, she could grab the letter, finish all that remained undone, and leave. It would be both a tribute to a woman who had suffered and overcame it, while also severing Ha-Yoon's own tether to the past. She tried to imagine what Dr. Scarfke would advise and realized she already knew. A gust of winter air rolled into the waiting room. It smelled of freedom.

Ha-Yoon stood. Fished her phone out of her pocket. Looked for the number of a taxi service.

Before she found one, a heavy hand pressed on her shoulder. She froze, her resolve instantly evaporating.

"Hello, Ha."

44

"**R**oyce."

His name was sour on her tongue. She let it drop lifelessly to the floor between them.

"Is Diego all right?"

"What are you doing here?"

"One of my Project Managers is in the hospital. Where else would I be?"

"But how did you know?"

"I tried to get hold of either of you two all night. Finally, this morning a nurse answered Diego's phone, so I rushed up here."

"Rushed? We're hours away."

"Maybe I wouldn't have had to if you'd answered your phone."

Ha-Yoon reached for the collar of her blouse.

"Ha," Royce snapped, over-enunciating his words. "Is Diego okay?"

"I don't know," she admitted.

"You didn't ask?"

"I'm not family. They won't tell me."

"Nonsense," he said, then abruptly stormed out of the waiting room, tearing down the hallway toward the nurse's station.

Ha-Yoon, dazed, could suddenly breathe again. Had Royce grown? He seemed to tower over her, dressed in his heavy herringbone overcoat, silk scarf tied around his thick neck. He seemed like an exaggerated version of a person, which only made more obvious the monster hidden beneath his skin. Or, no, maybe it was a virus in there. Something incurable she'd be burdened with for the rest of her days.

Down the length of the hallway, she heard him bellowing at a nurse. She hoped it was the one she'd run into earlier, but doubted she'd be so lucky. She also doubted Royce would treat another man so abhorrently.

A pair of security guards hurried past the waiting room entrance. Ha-Yoon eagerly leaped to her feet to watch them descend on Royce. His scowling face was red and contorted as blotches travelled across it. He grew angrier while the guards remained calm and neutral. Did they not know who he was? Ha-Yoon was impressed. Royce eventually ran out of steam and quieted.

Then he saw her watching. He smiled.

She did not like it.

45

A few minutes later, Royce returned to the waiting room as though nothing had happened. Trailing behind him were the two stone-faced security guards. But Royce was unrushed. When he stopped to address Ha-Yoon, the two guards stopped, too.

"They're going to keep him longer," he said.

Ha-Yoon nodded. Her eyes shifted to his impatient escorts, each with a hand on their belted radio.

"Let's go," he said. "I want to see what the two of you have done at the property. The photos Diego sent weren't sufficient."

Ha-yoon stammered. "Photos?"

Royce reached into his pocket, pulled out a phone much too small for his gargantuan hands. He slid his fingers across the screen, tapped twice, then turned the phone around to present it to her. The screen showed a photograph of the Awl house, and as he flicked it aside another took its place . Then another. All captured the work she'd done at various stages, all cataloguing the time she'd spent designing and perfecting the interior. Learning Royce had been secretly privy to everything she'd done since setting foot there felt worse than she could have imagined. It felt like a betrayal. And it retroactively stained the house before Katherine Awl could lay her eyes on it.

"I think it looks good," he said, reading her thoughts. "Maybe a touch spartan for me, but that's what's popular with these celebrity types. Or perhaps I should say *celebrity-adjacent*, considering her past."

"No," Ha-Yoon said bluntly. "I don't think you should."

Royce smiled. Put his phone away.

"Well, whatever the reason, she needed a house, and we put it together. I just need to give it a once-over. Make sure everything's in place. It's my reputation on the line. Besides, too much time has passed since I last saw your work in person and would like to know how you've matured."

Ha-Yoon's first instinct was to refuse. And she knew it was what she should do for so many reasons. And yet, she couldn't let him go there without her. Not if he might find the letter. That letter was hers. And the possibility he might hold it, or worse, *keep* it... no, that was something she could not allow.

And, as utterly as she detested both the feeling and herself for feeling it, he was still Royce Ballast. Celebrity designer. So much a hero that she'd convinced herself for years she was to blame for waking up drugged in his bed. Even after everything that happened, the suggestion he wanted to see her work made her pulse quicken autonomically.

Before she could speak, one of the guards interrupted by tapping on Royce's shoulder.

"Yes, yes. All right. We're *going*," Royce said, throwing his scarf around his neck. He strode away and toward the bright daylight shining through the hospital's entrance.

Ha-Yoon hesitated, then, with mounting regret, followed after him.

46

It was snowing again, and the flurries were already starting to accumulate. The security guards remained at the door, arms crossed, watching Royce brush off his herringbone overcoat. Ha-Yoon fought the urge to run back inside.

"I was surprised to hear about Diego," Royce said over his shoulder. "And I was especially surprised by the time of year. Seems strange, doesn't it?"

"What do you mean?"

"Just that I've never heard of wasps being a problem in winter, let alone stinging someone enough to send them to the hospital."

"You didn't see Diego's face. If you had you wouldn't think that."

He shrugged. "You obviously have an opinion about what happened, and nothing I say that will change your mind. That's always been clear."

"What are you—?" she started to ask, but he interrupted her.

"I'm parked just over there."

Royce pointed a gloved finger at the dark black Lexus at the curb. A bright yellow ticket peeked out of the snow that covered his window. He turned around and looked at her. "Come on. I can't idly stand in the cold chatting with you. I need to see the property."

Royce led her to his car and opened the passenger door.

Alarms rang for Ha-Yoon. But she needed that letter. Needed her car....

Ha-Yoon unslung her backpack and climbed in. Royce slammed the door shut. As he cleared off the windows with his gloved hand, she squeezed her pack against her chest and shivered like a hare. When Royce finally opened the driver's side door and slid in, she was holding her bag so tight she could hardly breathe. Royce grinned.

"Next stop: the property."

47

They drove in silence, snow lightly crackling against the windshield. The Lexus's heater was set just high enough that Ha-Yoon felt sick. If only she could get out and walk. Or, better, get out and run. She pressed herself against her door to keep as much distance between her and Royce as possible. It didn't make a difference. He swallowed all the space.

Dr. Scarfke would be proud, though. Surely, deciding to ride in the car with the person who assaulted her was some sort of therapeutic victory. Proof that Ha-Yoon was getting better, able to forgive a past she couldn't change. So then, why didn't Ha-Yoon feel proud? Why wasn't she unburdened? It occurred to her—trapped as she was in that over-warm car, an arm's length from the source of her torment—that the reason was that the anger she was supposed to let go of was not something easily released. Dr. Scarfke had failed to realize that Ha-Yoon's anger had become part of her, no less important to who she was than her heart, her lungs, her spine. Were Ha-Yoon to let go of her anger, she might simply cease to exist—fracture into a thousand swirling pieces and scatter across the sky.

All that time with Dr. Scarfke had not only been a waste, Ha-Yoon realized for the first time, but had also been dangerous. She'd made a grave mistake putting her faith in the woman. Dr. Scarfke could not be trusted. No one could. No one but Ha-Yoon herself.

And if no one could be trusted....

She looked at the hulking Royce Ballast. Swallowed.

48

The bleating ring of her cellular phone interrupted the quiet. She let it ring, too afraid to glance away from her captor.

"Not going to answer that?" he finally asked.

"No," she said.

"How do you know it isn't important?"

"If it is, they'll leave a message."

"Maybe," he mumbled dubiously.

Out of spite, she wrestled the phone from her pocket and unlocked it. The ringing had stopped but sure enough, a new voicemail was waiting for her. Royce said something, but she ignored him. Instead, she made a show of putting the phone to her ear so she alone could listen to the recording.

At first, there was no sound. She put her hand over her other ear to quiet the noise of the road, the noise of Royce. There was, at first, a small amount of static before heavy breathing broke in and gave way to a barely recognizable voice. It sounded like Diego, if his mouth were stuffed with cotton.

"I been thinking about it. You were right. I think you were right. It's too dangerous," he said before trailing off. There was another voice in the background. It demanded something. Ha-Yoon felt helpless. Then Diego's voice returned. Fainter. Further away and shouting. "It's too dangerous for—!" was as far as he got before the message ended.

Quietly, Ha-Yoon put her phone away and then looked at Royce. She pressed herself harder against the passenger side door. Pulled her collar so tight that she coughed.

49

They arrived at the house with Ha-Yoon fidgeting in her seat. She needed to get out of the car and out of Royce's reach. And she needed that letter.

The snow was thick, blanketing the multiple roofs, leaving the attic window visible yet dark, a single lidless eye following their treacherous walk to the front door. Royce's attention, however, was on the house's façade and on the landscaping Diego's team had done, all of which was buried in white. Ha-Yoon brushed flakes off her arms in hopes it would alleviate how cold she felt.

Royce stomped his feet at the entrance and tried the handle. The door swung open eagerly. That familiar wave of warmth greeted Ha-Yoon.

Royce turned to her, wearily.

"You couldn't lock up before you left?"

"I was a bit preoccupied."

He shook his head. Then made an exaggerated sweeping motion with his arm to usher her first over the threshold.

Ha-Yoon had almost forgotten how comforting and comfortable the background hum of the house felt. Most of the lights were off, yet even the darkest hallways were empty of threat. Whatever it was she'd seen the night before was no longer there. Maybe it never was.

"Well done," Royce said, scanning the foyer with wide eyes. "Show me around."

Ha-Yoon glanced at the door. Pulled her collar tighter. How could she collect her letter without Royce noticing?

"You should start upstairs without me. I want to finish off a few things down here. Make sure they're perfect."

Royce shook his head. "Ha, I need you with me. How am I supposed to know what you've done if you don't take me through it? I'm not asking for a full inventory, but I expect you to earn your fee."

She briefly considered abandoning Awl's letter. If she made a sudden dash, she could be in her car and driving away before Royce was able to stop her. But even if the Corolla weren't buried in snow, she'd lose more than the letter if she ran. She'd lose all credit for the work she'd done on the house, which meant she'd lose any hope of resurrecting her career. And this time, it would be lost for good. As much as she hated herself, and regardless of how much more she hated Royce, for now, she needed him.

"We have to be quick," she said. "My mother is expecting me back home."

The words tasted horribly sour. Royce's satisfied smile did nothing to make them sweeter.

50

Ha-Yoon led him through the first floor, down the warmly lit hallways, into the open kitchen with its butcher block islands and antique barstools. He ran his fingers along the drapes and across the furniture.

As they approached the alcove beneath the stairs, Ha-Yoon's heart began to race. Ahead of them was the framed letter, still atop the reclaimed wood table, leaning against the wall. Panic threatened to overwhelm her. What if she couldn't distract him long enough to rescue it? But she needn't have worried. Once they reached the alcove, Royce did not register the framed letter. Not before she was able to slip it surreptitiously into her backpack.

"Marvelous," he said, and the conflicting emotions that raised simultaneously embarrassed and sickened her. "You went all out."

"Why shouldn't I?"

"No reason, I suppose. And this is within budget?"

"I got lucky with some deals. Found some items in town." Like the statue of Athena, she thought sadly. "I wanted Katherine Awl to feel safe here."

Royce snorted. "I can't imagine she wouldn't. That said, a little bird told me she may have money issues. Seems one of her previous producers is going to sue her for defamation after that TV interview she did. You know the one. Everything is quiet at the moment, but I expect the news programs will be running with the story soon enough. They can smell blood."

"That's... that's horrible," Ha-Yoon said.

"There's a lot about the whole thing that's horrible. A lot of people have been hurt by what she's been saying. Some careers irrevocably damaged. And for what? We don't know if any of it is true, and we never will. It's impossible to know for certain what really happened."

"But is it?" Ha-Yoon asked. "Because I find it quite easy."

But Royce had stopped listening. He was staring above her head, past her, and up the large, curved staircase to the second floor. He seemed shaken. She turned, expecting the worst, but only found the steps falling into darkness. When she turned back, Royce appeared shaken.

"What did you see?" she asked. He shook his head. Then, as though a switch had been flipped, his eyes lit up, and he became his oily self again.

"What else do you have hiding from me up there?" he asked. Ha-Yoon didn't like his expression. She touched her neck.

51

Enough was enough. Ha-Yoon had her letter. It was time to end the charade.

"I'll leave the rest to you," she said. "I need to get home before the snow gets worse."

He looked at her askance. Did he know she was lying? Did she care?

Royce loosened his scarf. Unbuttoned his overcoat.

"Fine," he said, fluttering his hands. "I release you. But before you go, please show me where you claim Diego got stung."

"He *did* get stung."

"I'm not accusing you of lying, Ha," he said as though he'd never done it before. "But I do need to see this for myself. If Diego is out of commission, I'll have to deal with it, and as I said, it won't be easy finding an exterminator who works in the snow."

Ha-Yoon glanced over her shoulder at the way they'd come. The entrance was back there. Royce looked down at her over the top of his glasses. She gritted her teeth.

"I'll take you," she said. "But only to the door. I'm not going up. I don't want to be stung."

"Who does?" Royce said.

52

With a knot in her stomach, Ha-Yoon hoisted herself up the staircase. Royce followed close behind. As her anger built, she wondered how could he be so blasé. How could he be so comfortable? Had he forgotten what he did? Or had he done it to so many others his assaults blurred together? The idea of that made her shiver with cold fury.

Ha-Yoon stopped when they reached the second-floor landing.

"The door to the attic is just down that hall. You can't miss it. It's wooden with a large stain."

"Well, let's go," Royce said, reaching to take her arm.

She shrank back. There was something in his face, but it was too fleeting to register. Rejected, Royce put his hands up in mock surrender.

"Take it easy," he said. "I'm not dangerous. I just want you to show me the way."

Ha-Yoon started trepidatiously down the hall. Royce followed. With each step, she felt more endangered, stuck alone in the empty house, just her and her mistakes. She'd let ambition blind her, let it convince her that if she put herself at risk this one last time, then she'd be free of it forever. As though the poison was its own cure. It was ridiculous, yet there she was, her mother's idiot daughter, still not thinking things through.

Her pace increased with her anger, growing faster the further down the spiral she travelled.

"Slow down," Royce said. "I can't keep up."

But she didn't obey. She kept moving as fast as she could. Each step echoed from the walls of the hallway as though they were in pursuit.

The attic door was not where it had been the night before. Instead, there was an empty wall. Ha-Yoon stopped, confused. It should have been right where they were standing. It had to be right there.

"You do know where you're going, don't you?"

She frowned.

"I don't know—" she started but was interrupted by a slam. It came from around the corner.

She looked at Royce, who looked at her. Neither spoke. They simply crept to the end of the hallway. Ha-Yoon had an irrational worry that someone would be waiting for them around the corner. Or rather, she worried there wouldn't be.

And, of course, there wasn't. What there was, though, was the attic door. Its stain had finally taken it over despite only a few hours passing. None of it made sense.

"For someone who says they want to leave, Ha, you sure seem to be dragging things out. I presume this is the way to the attic?"

She nodded.

"And you're telling me if I go through this door, I'll get stung by wasps?"

"I'm telling you, Diego did. And Aahvan did. And I'm telling you, I'm not going up there again."

"Suit yourself," Royce said. Then, his massive body descended on her.

53

Ha-Yoon leaped back, drove herself into the wooden door. She raised her arms instinctively to claw at her attacker.

But Royce only reached out his hand and took the knob immediately behind her. Then he opened the attic door.

Ha-Yoon staggered backward, nearly tripping over the attic steps. She pressed her hands against the walls to stop her descent, barely keeping from landing backpack-first and smashing the framed letter stowed there. Royce smirked as she righted herself.

"I knew it," he said, scanning the stairwell. "No wasps."

Ha-Yoon looked up at him.

"What the hell is your problem?"

He frowned. Held out his hand for her. Shrugged when she swatted it away.

"I don't know what really happened to Diego, but it's clear you made the whole thing up. What I don't understand is why. Are you trying to keep Katherine Awl from moving in?"

"Of course not," she said, brushing off her clothes. "And what I told you was true. What else could it have been?"

Royce made a noise. Squinted at the top of the narrow set of steps. "Well, I don't see anything."

"Well, you will," she shot back. "Just go on up."

Only then did Ha-Yoon herself turn to look. The late-morning light had fallen through the stained glass, but the colors were dulled by the time of year. She heard the snow gently crackle against the window, but the buzzing she'd heard before was not present. If there were no wasps, how else could she explain what happened to Diego?

"Let's go upstairs and see for ourselves."

"I have no intention of going up there again."

Royce shook his head. Then he closed the door behind them.

54

"**W**hat are you doing?" Ha-Yoon said. She was unable to hide the quaver in her voice. Royce filled the space between her and the door. There was no room to push past him.

"Enough games, Ha. We're going upstairs, and we're going to get to the bottom of this. You need to start taking this job seriously."

"I do take it seriously."

"Then prove it. The stairs are behind you."

Ha-Yoon fumed. She wanted to jab up and crush his nose into his skull. She wanted to dig her fingers into the flesh of his neck and squeeze. She wanted to call him names and spit in his face. But what good would it do? Even if she managed to kill him first, the world would mourn him as though he deserved their affection, leaving Ha-Yoon to fade further into obscurity. She had to play along.

And that made her angrier still.

Ha-Yoon climbed the narrow staircase quickly, not wanting to be anywhere within arm's reach of Royce. When she reached the top, she had a few moments to get over the disquiet of being where Aahvan had died. Even though it had been months, she could still see his ghost curled by the window. It was unnerving, even if it wasn't real. She remembered his vacant-eyed stare and his buzzing chest as wasps spiraled out of the hole. She saw no wasps now, though. Royce was right. The two of them were alone.

55

Royce stopped too close behind her.

"So, you're telling me Diego got stung down by the door, and the other guy, the framer—What's his name?"

"Aahvan."

"And Aahvan died up here from a drug overdose, and wasps then ate their way through him from the outside or vice versa. And all of this happened in a house soon to be occupied by a failed actress who first became famous for playing a bee. Is that what I'm supposed to believe?"

"That's what happened."

"And, yet, as you can see, no wasps."

Oh, how Ha-Yoon hated him.

"No, I guess not."

Royce struggled to kneel so he could inspect the window frame. He placed his hand flat near the bottom edge.

"There's definitely a hole here. I can feel cold air coming in. How long did the police say the framer was hiding here?"

"A few weeks."

"Not long, considering all the problems he caused."

"He was causing problems long before he got here."

Royce looked up at her with red and unsympathetic eyes.

"Maybe it's time we stop dancing around this."

"Around what?"

He kept his eyes locked on her as he slowly stood. Brushed the dust off his knees.

"You think you're being clever, Ha, but you're not. I've felt your aggression bleeding out since I first offered you this job. Frankly, considering the lies you told my intern, I was surprised you took it. I have to admit, despite your work here, I regret offering you this job. Had it not been for Diego, I probably wouldn't have."

"It was Diego's idea?"

"And yet all you've done is make not-so-sly comments about me, and from what I hear, treat Diego like something you've scraped off your shoe. I don't know how to tell you this, but you aren't owed or entitled to anything. Clearly, you want to blame me, but it's not my fault your career floundered after you left. I took you on, gave you chances, taught you tricks, but now you think you know everything and don't need me. Maybe people were right: maybe it was my fault for believing in you."

Ha-Yoon felt ashamed, then her flaring anger interrupted the spiral. Why was she the one feeling bad? She reached for her collar. Stopped herself. Lowered her hand.

"That might mean more if it weren't for the little matter of you raping me."

That seemed to take him by surprise.

"That didn't happen. You're confused."

"No, I don't think I am. I remember what happened at the Newsome house party."

Royce tugged his scarf off his neck. Gripped it in his clenched fist. His complexion was pink.

"I have no idea what you mean."

"That's what worries me the most. That you really *don't* remember. That you've done this to so many interns, you can't keep them all straight."

"It's clear you've tightly wound yourself up in this accusation, enough that you've convinced yourself it's true. But if it were, wouldn't there be some sort of proof?"

"You gave me pills."

"To calm you down. Because you get—" He fluttered his hands again toward her. "—like how you are."

"I woke up in your bed, naked."

"You passed out. I graciously left you to sleep. Is that all?"

"It's enough, isn't it?"

"Then why didn't the police come knocking at my door if you were so convinced all this happened?"

"I didn't know it had. Not at first...."

"Oh, you found *later*, did you? I'll tell you what I think: I think you had buyer's remorse. Or, worse, maybe you decided you got all you needed out of me, and when you realized afterward you were still nothing, instead of owning up to your failure, you invented a reason that made you the victim. I became the big bad wolf in your fairy tale because the fantasy was easier for you to stomach. The only problem is I'm a real person, and these lies have real consequences. Maybe I was right the first time: maybe I should never have given you a chance to work on the property."

"Listen to you. *The property*. You can't even say her name, can you? Katherine Awl. She was drugged, just like me. She was used and discarded, just like me. And this house is her revenge on all of you. You say you gave me another chance by giving me this job? I say her bravery is the only reason I would ever have agreed to work with you again. I would have gladly rotted away behind the counters of shitty coffee shops if it meant never hearing your name again. But Katherine Awl deserves more than what someone who hates her could give her."

"I don't hate her, Ha. And despite what you think, I don't hate you. I feel sorry for both of you. And if she were here, I'd tell her the same thing I'm going to tell you: It's time you stop playing the victim and face the truth. You've brainwashed yourself into believing your own lies. And in the end, what are your lies going to get you? This?" He swung a long arm wide, gesturing toward the steps and the house to which they led. "This place isn't freedom. It's a cage. A gilded cage meant to make you feel like you accomplished something special. But it's built on sand and on the lives of good people who got vilified in the press and had their lives ruined. People who didn't deserve it."

"And by people, you mean men."

"Well... yes. But only because they're the actual victims in all this. Katherine Awl is vaunted while the people she accused can't work— can't do anything anymore. Their lives are over. Meanwhile, she buys fancy properties to hide in, away from all the damage she's caused."

Royce shook his head. Sighed.

"What happened to you, Ha? What happened to that innocent girl I used to know?"

Ha-Yoon burst into laughter.

"Oh, shit," she said when she finally managed to catch her breath. "Jesus Christ. What happened to the old Ha-Yoon? What happened to her is you killed her, you asshole. You killed her, and you pissed on her grave."

"This is what you call pissing on your grave? Giving you this opportunity?"

"It's working for you—working *with* you—that's the insult. How do you not get that?"

"Oh, I get lots of things, Ha. Lots and lots of things."

Ha-Yoon had been too fired to notice the scarf in his hands until that moment. How he'd wrapped an end around each hand. How he was pulling it taut with firm yanks as though to test its strength. Suddenly, she remembered how empty the house was, how isolated. How no one knew she was there. How even Diego was confined to a bed far away. She swallowed hard. Tried to step back, but there wasn't enough space between her and the wall behind her.

56

"What are you doing?" she asked, wishing she could see the stairs behind him.

He shrugged. Snapped the scarf taut for a moment.

"You want to leave? After you just hurt my feelings?"

"I'm sure your feelings weren't hurt," she said, inching sideways. He mirrored her.

"The one lesson you never seemed to learn," he said as he stepped closer, "was if you want to be successful, you need to be nicer to the people helping you get there."

Royce was close enough that Ha-Yoon could smell him, an odor thick and tangy. She turned her head away as much as she dared.

He snapped the scarf tighter. She winced.

"Royce, you don't have to do this."

"What am I doing?"

"I'll leave. You can keep the money. You can tell everybody you designed the house. Whatever you want. Just let me go."

Royce's hands stopped moving. He looked at her queerly.

"What is it you think I'm going to do?"

Ha-Yoon swallowed. She couldn't look at him but couldn't look away.

"Maybe I should ruin you," he said. "It wouldn't take much. A few phone calls and it would all be over for you. For good this time. No one would ever work with you. If you start spreading lies about me, I might not have much choice. And if you think you're going to blackmail me into giving you work again, you're deluded."

Royce chuckled. "It's funny," he said as he slowly unwrapped the scarf from around his hands. Folded it lengthwise neatly. Hooked it back around his neck. "If it weren't for me, you wouldn't be here right now. Literally."

Ha-Yoon felt the hole in her stomach growing larger, threatening to suck her in. Blood buzzed in her ears. Her fists clenched. She was so terrified she couldn't contain her anger.

"You think I'm here?" she spat. "I'm not here at all, you asshole. I haven't been since you raped me."

"You know what your problem is?" he asked, but he didn't get a chance to answer before Ha-Yoon's fist connected squarely with his nose. He made a surprised whoop, but Ha-Yoon was already sprinting across the attic toward the steps. If she could get there, she might be able to get through the door at the bottom and lock it behind her. It was solid wood; it was strong enough to hold the devil. It would hold him.

But she didn't make it more than a few steps before being yanked back by her backpack and tossed across the room. She slid to a painful stop against the sudden wall.

"You broke my nose, you ungrateful shit!"

The left side of her body was numb from shock. Her thoughts scrambled; she barely knew what was happening when Royce grabbed her by the neck and hoisted her to her feet as though she were a doll. He choked her hard. His face was bright red as he yelled.

But she couldn't hear him. In her airless daze, she was too far away. And where she was, the only sounds were flutters and buzz and the gentle tinkle of glass shards ribboning the letter in her backpack. She felt the loss deep inside.

Ha-Yoon raised a feeble arm to protect herself from Royce's fury, but everything was oddly blurred, as though she were seeing it from underwater. Odder still, even amid the violence, she saw a wasp clung fast to it. Yellow and black, beating its wings while riding her sense-less knuckles. Everything moved so slowly that she saw the tiny insect raise its cocked head toward her. It stared at Ha-Yoon as she mused on what it wanted. What it was trying to tell her. As she fell further away, leaving her body behind, she tried to tell it goodbye. But something crawled into her mouth and down her throat, where it pierced the flesh with a long needle.

Ha-Yoon spasmed violently. It was enough to stun Royce. He stopped. Loosened his grip. And his eyes grew wide with horror as he released her.

Ha-Yoon's wobbly legs crumpled. She fell to the floor, coughing and gasping. Royce stepped back, confused.

But Ha-Yoon couldn't stop coughing. She grabbed at her throat. It wasn't the pain. The pain was gone, replaced by some sensation beyond pain, beyond anything she'd ever imagined. It was as though she'd swallowed lightning, and it was arcing from organ to organ inside her. It was impossible to be still. Her limbs twitched, her digits curled then straightened. Thoughts raced through her, and it took a moment to understand what it was she was feeling. Not pain. Rage. It was rage flowing out of her.

Or something very much like it.

"What the fuck?" Royce said.

57

She looked up and saw him swatting wasps away with his hands, face covered in burning red welts as he shouted nonsense. Royce swung furiously and uselessly. As more wasps appeared, Ha-Yoon realized they were coming from her. She was erupting with them. Each its own angry storm.

When the frantic Royce tripped over his feet and tumbled to the attic's floor, Ha-Yoon did not hesitate. She leaped up and bolted for the steps. She didn't care about Royce. She just cared only about her freedom.

But by the time she reached the steps, she'd stopped caring about that, too.

Instead, she turned around. Watched Royce rolling on the floor, sweating, arms failing as he swatted at the gathering wasps. His eyes locked on her. Fuming.

"Get back here," he screamed.

So that's what she did.

A sudden storm, her anger flared. Burned. Buzzed. Like ashes swirling in a violent tempest, tiny yellow-black bodies darted past, multiplying. Each wasp was a portent of her anger, of the betrayal she felt, the pain and humiliation. They swarmed around her, a spherical cloud, membranous wings tearing the air, ripping the world until reality itself trembled and threatened to unglue.

Through the sheet of buzzing wasps, she saw Royce. Face white, eyes stretched as wide as his screaming mouth. She didn't know what he was saying, and she didn't care. Not any longer. Not ever again.

She raised her arms, spread them wide, and the mass grew denser, angrier. A swarm of violence encompassed her. Royce skittered backward on his hands. Pressed himself up against the stained-glass window as it was pelted by tiny uncontrollable anger. The furies pinned him there as she watched through dazzled, blood-soaked eyes.

More wasps surrounded her. First by hundreds, then thousands. They crawled up and down her arms, fluttering. Crawled through her hair and around her eyes and ears. Ecstatic shivers rippled across her body, a euphoric frisson of transcendental power. The air electrified, churned around her legs and feet. The wasps' wings beat a deafening thunder that drowned out Royce's screams, turned him mute, mouthing nothings.

As if in response to his attempts to reach her, the wasps flew faster and grew more frenzied, in league with her own growing fury over what he'd done, what he'd said, and what he would do again if she did not stop him. So many lives were destroyed by this sniveling creature beneath the window—this thing that cared for nothing but itself—this abomination who lied and manipulated anyone who trusted their life to it.

It overwhelmed Ha-Yoon, too much for her body to contain. It spilled and seethed out of her. From her mouth. From her ears. From the corners of her eyes. Like thick, sugary ichor. And the wasps... they gathered on her, lapped it up, became even more frenzied. The swarm buzzed so loud she felt her ear drums pop and melt away. But she still heard everything. The vibrations were that loud. Louder than Royce could ever scream.

The winds around her were strong. The colored light more intense. Ha-Yoon felt herself growing lighter as everything that tethered her came undone. Fell away into an endless void. She was unburdened and weightless for the first time in a long time.

"Do you understand now?" Ha-Yoon asked Royce, the swollen, bloodied shell of a man that was curled up on the attic floor. That wheezing thing that licked its swollen lips and struggled to speak. "Do you know what you've done?"

Ha-Yoon knew but wanted him to say it. She wanted to hear it from his drooling mouth. Wanted to know that he knew. That everything he'd done had brought him here. That it was his fault. She wanted an admission. She wanted contrition. She wanted the truth to ache inside him forever as it would always ache inside of her.

But instead, he laughed.

"I didn't do anything," he slurred. "I did nothing. You... you.... I did everything I could to help you. And you... you failed and blamed me for it." Royce wiped his sleeve across his face, leaving red streaks up to his elbow. He kept slurring. "You made up stories so you'd feel better about yourself. Poor Ha never caught a break from anyone. If only things had been different. If only this or that hadn't happened. If only if only if only...."

Royce spat blood on the ground. The swarm around Ha-Yoon swelled, then slowly contracted. Then swelled again.

58

After that, things moved quickly. Royce's eyes, once shining and sly, were bloodshot and wide as he screamed a scream no one had heard before. Full of pain, terror, humiliation, and shame. But it wasn't enough. It would never be enough. Ha-Yoon wanted him to know what was coming. She wanted him to be afraid during every moment of what was left of his miserable life. She wanted him to pay.

And the wasps obliged.

By the thousands, the swarm left Ha-Yoon's body and streamed toward him. They crawled over his fleshy face and hands, stinging him again and again. Royce howled, and they crawled into his mouth, down his throat, stinging the wet pink flesh there, too. His eyes... even though he squeezed them shut, the wasps stung his eyes, which immediately swelled, sealing him away behind his own flesh. Royce blindly swung his hands, and they stung his bloated fingers, stung the skin between his fingers, stung him under his nails, and around his wrists. Royce couldn't speak, his throat sealing fast, his tongue too thick and large. But he could moan. He could wail. And he did so as he pulled himself to his feet.

Ha-Yoon watched him ineffectually stagger across the attic and felt nothing. Her anger had gone, metastasized into the furious swarm that sought out Royce and meted out his punishment. It felt good to watch him struggle, good to watch him in pain. And it felt good to see him reach his breaking point and hurl himself, face first, through the circular stained-glass window of Katherine Awl's new home.

59

Ha-Yoon did not see him fall. She was not fast enough for that. But she heard him bounce from roof to roof, and when she reached the window, she saw where he landed. In the snowy bushes Diego and his team had so carefully planted. But Royce was no longer there, either. Ha-Yoon saw his trail of footprints in the snow lead away from the house. Saw him stumbling into the storm, arms failing to disperse the torments that haunted him.

The wasps would never leave. She was sure of that. They would sting him and crawl over his body in a giant quivering mass forever now. They beat their tiny glittering wings so fast that in the moonlight, Royce looked as though he were shimmering.

Lost and wandering and shimmering.

Like stars in the dead black of the cold northern night.

ACKNOWLEDGEMENTS

My thanks to the editors who selected many of these stories for publication: Laird Barron, Sam Cowan, Ellen Datlow, Paula Guran, Stephen Jones, S. T. Joshi, Michael Kelly, Silvia Moreno-Garcia, Mark Morris, C. M. Muller, Erik Secker, and Justin Steele.

Inspiration for this work was drawn in part from the following: Peter Straub, Brian Evenson, Samantha Hunt, Kelly Link, Paul Auster, Kenneth J. Harvey, M. John Harrison, and others.

Thank you to Steve Berman and the team at Lethe Books for all they've done to bring this book to life.

Finally, my sincerest thanks to all the readers who have read my stories over the years and have helped spread the word. I wish upon you the darkest of nightmares for the remainder of your days.

— Simon Strantzas, Toronto, 2025

PUBLICATION CREDITS

"The Beautiful Fog Ascending" first appeared in *Searchers After Horror*, Fedogan & Bremer, 2014

"Everything is White" is original to this volume

"Interior Designs" is original to this volume

"Jason's in the Garden" first appeared in *Nightscript 5*, 2019

"The Needle Song" first appeared in *Northern Nights*, 2024

"The Nineteenth Step" first appeared in *Shadows Edge*, Gray Friar Press, 2013

"Not the Same Place" is original to this volume

"Shepherd Not Sheep" first appeared in *Bourbon Penn 32*, 2024

"Showing" is original to this volume

"The Somnambulists" first appeared in *Shadows & Tall Trees* 8, Undertow Publications, 2020

"Stemming the Tide" first appeared in *Dead North*, Exile Press, 2013

"Still Packed" first appeared in *Looming Low 2*, Dim Shores Publishing, 2022

"That House" first appeared in *Bourbon Penn 25*, 2021

"Witch's Clutch" first appeared in *Darkness Beckons*, Flame Tree Press, 2023

ABOUT THE AUTHOR

Simon Strantzas has written several volumes of short fiction, edited the award-winning *Aickman's Heirs*, and is a columnist for *Weird Horror* magazine. His work has been reprinted in various "best-of" annuals and been a finalist for four Shirley Jackson Awards, two British Fantasy Awards, and the World Fantasy Award. He lives with his wife in Toronto, Canada.

ABOUT THE TYPEFACE

This book is typeset in IM Fell Double Pica, a modern revival font based on The Fell Types which take their name from John Fell, a Bishop of Oxford in the seventeenth-century. The original type-case was cut by Peter de Walpergen in 1684 then digitally reproduced in 2000 by Igino Marini, an Italian civil engineer.

The titles and drop caps in this manuscript are set in **Alderwood**, a hand drawn condensed typeface designed by Jeremy Vessey for his type foundry, Hustle Supply Co.